BLOODY YORK

tales of mayhem, murder, and mystery in Toronto

Dedication

To all those past, present, and future interested in Toronto's local history and caring about its heritage;
and, my wife, Ann, for caring about me.

Acknowledgements

I am indebted to Peter A. Sellers for the title, and to Dr Geo. A. Vanderburgh for drawing my attention to "The tattooed man" by Vincent Starrett and supplying a copy.

tales of mayhem, murder, and mystery in Toronto

A celebration of the romance and excitement of a great city.

Edited with an introduction and notes by

DAVID SKENE-MELVIN

Editor of

Crime in a Cold Climate

Investigating Women

Simon & Pierre
Toronto • Oxford

Editor: David Skene-Melvin
Designer: Sebastian Vasile
Printer: Webcom

Canadian Cataloguing in Publication Data

Bloody York: tales of mayhem, murder and mystery in Toronto

ISBN 1-88924-273-9

1. Detective and mystery stories, Canadian (English). — I. Skene Melvin, David, 1936-

PS8323.D4B56 1996 C813/.087208 C96–990004–X
PR9197.35.D48B56 1996

Publication was assisted by the Canada Council, the Book Publishing Industry Development Program of the Department of Canadian Heritage, and the Ontario Arts Council.

Care has been taken to trace the ownership of copyright material used in this book. The author and the publisher welcome any information enabling them to rectify any references or credit in subsequent editions.

Printed and bound in Canada

Printed on recycled paper. 

Simon & Pierre
2181 Queen Street East
Suite 301
Toronto, Ontario, Canada
M4E 1E5

Simon & Pierre
73 Lime Walk
Headington, Oxford
England
OX3 7AD

Simon & Pierre
250 Sonwil Drive
Buffalo, NY
U.S.A. 14225

CONTENTS

Preface

Originally known as Toronto, the town soon after its founding in 1791 was officially named YORK and during the first quarter of the nineteenth century became known as "MUDDY" York because of the appalling condition of its unpaved streets. In 1834, upon incorporation as a city, it reverted to the original name of Toronto. Hence, for this compilation of tales dealing with death and dishonour within its precincts, the title as a play upon the appellation once ascribed to the struggling frontier town that has become Canada's premier city.

The Queen's Hotel, Front and York, Toronto.
[Unknown artist, "The queen's Hotel", ca 1887. Coloured lithograph by Rolph, Smith & Co., Toronto. National Archives of Canada PAC 119990.]

Introduction

Toronto's streets may never have been as mean as those of New York or Los Angeles, and may they never be, nor does it have the labyrinthine sewers of Paris, but its byways, lanes, and alleys are no less mysterious than those of London, no less places where adventure can happen. Adventure can be found in the city as well as in the fields and wild places of the earth and many authors have set their thrilling tales of crime, detection, espionage, intrigue, mystery, and suspense in Canada's foremost metropolis. The handful of stories presented here in this celebration of the romance and excitement of Toronto are but a meagre gleaning of the rich harvest of mayhem, murder, and mystery that lurks in the asphalt jungle of Canada's Queen City.

The beginnings of Canadian criminous exegesis were the broadsides published in 1783 and 1785 of the dying speeches and confessions of convicted criminals about to be hanged for murder and theft. Alas, only the advertisements of these ephemeral issues survive; the actual documents themselves are part of the dust of history. Had we them to hand, they probably would not differ from the similar publications that were popular in Great Britain at this time.

Canadian criminous literature falls into five periods: from the earliest begetters to 1880; 1880-1920; 1920-1940; 1940-1980; and, 1980 to date. The decade 1970-1980 is one of transition in which the genre as a truly Canadian expression of national consciousness is finding its feet.

There are two kinds of writing about the Past: writing at the time — contemporary; and, writing after the fact — historical. Of the five stories set in Toronto's past that we present here, only one, Barr's, is contemporary, the others by Dent, Batten and Bliss, Starrett, and Jennings are historical in that the authors are writing about and recreating a time gone by.

The first piece of criminous writing in Canadian literature to utilize Toronto as an identifiable setting is John Dent's "The Gerrard Street mystery" that appeared in his collection *The Gerrard Street mystery; and other weird tales* published in 1888. The four stories that comprise this collection were contributed by Dent at considerable intervals to different periodicals, but did not see publication in book form until appearing posthumously in the year of his death, thus they properly belong in the first period of Canadian criminous writing despite their date of imprint.

The story is a valuable snapshot of middle-class commercial life in mid-nineteenth-century Toronto, which comes alive on Dent's pages as a city in which anything can happen — and does. Dent's talents could have made him the fantasist of his age, to rival Robert Louis Stevenson's tales of the fog-shrouded streets of Edinburgh and London, but he chose to devote his labours to Canadian history, for which students of Canadian constitutional development will always give thanks.

Of *The Gerrard Street mystery*, Messrs Barzun and Taylor in their *Catalogue of crime*[1] remark that the eponymous story "is the most interesting, with its blend of the supernatural (a ghostly uncle) and the very natural and absconding forger". It is set in 1861, when Toronto was on the threshold of establishing itself as the business capital of Canada, but still took second place to Montreal as the commercial centre of the soon-to-be new nation, and begins with William Francis Furlong waxing reminiscent about his mysterious adventure twenty-odd years before. "There are also a good many persons of middle age, not in Toronto only, but scattered here and there throughout various parts of Ontario, who will have no difficulty in recalling my name as that of one of their fellow-students at Upper Canada College. The name of my late uncle, Richard Yardlington, is of course well known to all residents of Toronto, where he spent the last thirty-two years of his life. He settled there in the year 1829, when the place was still known as Little York. He opened a small store on Yonge Street, and his commercial career was a reasonably prosperous one. By steady degrees the small store developed into what, in those times, was regarded as a considerable establishment. In the course of years the owner acquired a competency, and in 1854 retired from business altogether. From that time up to the day of his death he lived in his own house on Gerrard Street."

The original name of the settlement on the north shore of Lake Ontario at the mouth of the stream that came to be called the Humber River was "Toronto" — "the meeting-place" in the Iroquoian tongue of the Hurons. In late July 1793, John Graves Simcoe, Lieutenant-Governor of the colony of Upper Canada in British North America, worried about potential American invasion, moved his capital from the then-named Newark, now Niagara-on- the-Lake, to the site of Toronto, which he named York in honour of the Duke of York. When the town of York achieved incorporation as a city in 1834, it reverted in name to the original Toronto.

This brief description is replete with grist for the mill of the social historian. Already in the mid-nineteenth century the foundation was laid for the dominance of the dissenting non-conformist Anglo-Celtic commercial class. "Trade" was never a pejorative term in the Canadas. The country was founded on trade, and all the great fortunes were trading ones, not dependent on land. The nephew attends Upper Canada College, today Canada's equivalent of Eton in the United Kingdom or Groton in the United States of America, the respective havens for the male offspring of the elite establishments of those nations, but in the 1850's simply the best school for the aspiring merchants and tradesmen who wanted a decent education for their heirs. By "College" is meant secondary school, and young Furlong goes no further: "After sending me to school and college for several years, he took me into his store, and gave me my first insight into commercial life." Neither he nor his uncle would have understood if you termed him "a counter-jumper", that is, a clerk with pretensions. All clerks in the gestating Dominion had pretensions to become the merchant princes of the land in their turn; this was the Canadian dream.

Young Furlong is offered a chance to make his fortune in Australia and he embarks. "I pictured myself returning to Canada after an absence of four or five years with a mountain of gold at my command, as the result of my own energy and acuteness. In imagination, I saw myself settled down with Alice in a palatial mansion on Jarvis Street, and living in affluence all the rest of my days."

Although today it is respectable, Jarvis Street has had its vicissitudes and at one time was synonymous in Canada, not just in Toronto, so notorious was it, for any red-light district. In Toronto the Good, it was the plague-spot of sin. But it began life as the fashionable quarter for the upper-crust, and so it was in William Furlong's day. Vestiges of Jarvis Street's glory still remain, the best examples being on the final stretch northward from Carlton to Bloor, of which the Massey family home, now a restaurant, on the east side immediately north of the gas station on the north-east corner of Jarvis and Wellesley Streets is the most outstanding. This was the style of home Furlong wished to emulate. The Masseys were Canada's pre-eminent family in the late nineteenth and early twentieth centuries, of whom the famous Canadian editor and litte'rateur, B(ernard) K(eble) Sandwell, longtime editor of the popular periodical *Saturday Night*, wrote, a la` the Cabots and Lodges, "In Toronto/There are two classes/The Masseys/And the masses". The best known members of the family are the Hon. Vincent, one-time Governor General of Canada, and his brother, Raymond, the famous actor, amongst whose first cousins can be found the noted art historian, Ruth, (Mrs H. M. Tovell), also author of *The crime in the Boulevard Raspail*, (Edinburgh/Toronto: Thos Nelson/NY: Nelson — as: *Death in the wind*; 1932), and Charles Albert "Bert" Massey jnr, whose murder in Toronto by his housemaid, Carrie Davis, on 8 February 1915 is fictionalized in *Master and maid; the Charles Massey murder* by Frank Jones, (Toronto: Irwin; 1985).

After four years, our hero had made a small pile, and being homesick was not adverse to accepting his uncle's invitation to return home. After a long trip via Boston and Albany by way of Liverpool, he arrived in Upper Canada.

"A heavy snow-storm delayed us for several hours, and we reached Hamilton too late for the mid-day express for Toronto. We got there, however, in time for the accomodation leaving at 3:15 p.m., and we would reach Toronto at 5.05. ... We were not more than three minutes behind time, as we glided in front of the Union Station."

His uncle meets him and they proceed to the family home. "We passed from the station, and proceeded up York Street, arm in arm. ... Just then we came to the corner of Front Street, where there was a lamp-post. ... We had walked up York Street to Queen, and then had gone down Queen to Yonge, when we turned up the east side on our way homeward. At the moment when the last words were uttered we had got a few yards north of Crookshank Street, immediately in front of a chemist's shop, which was, I think, the third house from the corner."

Furlong stops to pass the time of day with an acquaintance and when he turns back to his uncle the old gentleman has gone. "I hurried along, making sure of overtaking him before reaching Gould Street, for my interview with Grey had occupied barely a minute. In another minute I was at the corner of Gould Street. No signs of Uncle Richard. I quickened my pace to a run, which soon brought me to Gerrard Street." And from there Furlong proceeds to his uncle's home alone.

One today can still trace the route followed by Willie Furlong and his uncle. York, Front, Queen, Yonge, Gould, and Gerrard Streets are all still there; the only one that has disappeared is Crookshank Street, the south side of which in 1842 marked the northern limit of the city, and which ran east from Yonge Street for four blocks between Shuter and Gould Streets. In those days, Gerrard was also only four blocks long, running east from Yonge. There is a different Union Station, but it is around the corner from its predecessor used by our hero. Of the buildings that would have stood in 1861, only the Bank of Montreal, now housing the Hockey Hall of Fame, at the north-west corner of Yonge and Front Streets still stands. The massive fire of 19 April 1904 that began that evening in a warehouse on the north side of Wellington Street near Bay raged for more than twenty-four hours and obliterated over 14 acres of the downtown. All has since been rebuilt.

The second period — 1880-1920, is the heyday of the "Northern" and the literary exploration of Canada's remote and romantic frontiers. This is the time when Canadian criminous writing began to flourish and Canadian popular culture had its most telling societal impact.

"Most of these books are now out of print, and are no longer read by the reading public. They are not regarded as serious literature by the literary critics of our day; the pictures of Canadian life they present have been overlooked by cultural historians. Yet the Canadian fiction-writers between 1880 and 1920 were read more widely by their contemporaries, inside and outside Canada, than have been the Canadian fiction-writers — collectively — since. Because they wrote in the grain of the dominant feeling of their Anglo-North-American world, their fiction had a significant reciprocal relation with their times. It reflects, through direct representation or through fantasy, many aspects of the pluralistic life in Canada between 1880 and 1920; it also provided images of Canadian life which formed a definition of Canadian identity, at home and abroad.".[2]

These writers were the entertainment of a literate age, the age of reading, not just listening as with radio, (but at least that required an active use of the imagination), or merely watching a flickering screen, as with film and TV. No, these writers were the explorers of that country of the mind that the reader entered at his or her own peril, a country of infinite geography, for each time it was encountered it was individually interpreted. The Greeks said that a person is immortal as long as his/her name is remembered, so by perpetuating a record of their one-time existence we are serving to preserve the immortality of these writers. It is an immortality they deserve. They would have been the last to claim they wrote great literature — they wrote to entertain. They were storytellers, spinning yarns to be printed and read as their predecessors in the minstrelry recited and were listened to. And entertain they did! Through their countless tales of adventure and derring-do they brought romance and colour to the drab hard-scrabble lives of countless millions who could do no more than dream.

From late in the Nineteenth Century well into the Twentieth Canadian crime writing in particular suffered from the serious problem of the slighting of Canadian authors due to economic reasons as did Canadian literature in general. It was too expensive to produce small domestic editions when the country was swamped in American culture and had to compete with imported British culture as well. Yet, some authors made it as Canadians, while others masqueraded as either Americans or British.

Crime writing as a field of endeavour for Canadian authors during the 1980s was not a virgin land waiting for the plough. More than trails had been blazed from the late Nineteenth Century onward through this country of the mind. Clearings had been made in the bush, crops sown, harvests gathered.

One of the most enterprising and popular pioneer agriculturalists sowing his imagination and reaping royalties in this fecund period of Canadian authorship was Robert Barr.

Only two Canadian authors make the honour roll of *The Haycraft-Queen List of Detective-Crime-Mystery Fiction; two centuries of cornerstones*: Robert Barr for *The triumphs of Eugene Valmont* in 1906 and Harvey J. O'Higgins for *Detective Duff unravels it* in 1929, the first psychoanalyst detective.

Robert Barr's short stories were good, fast-moving tales that were immensely popular with mass audiences. Our example here, "A slippery customer", is taken from his collection *The face and the mask* published in 1894. "When John Armstrong stepped off the train at the Union Station, in Toronto, Canada", it was at the Union Station on the west side of York Street south of Front Street.

There have been a number of railway stations on Toronto's waterfront, most situated in the general area where the present architecturally-magnificent Union Station stands.

The first station was at the south-west corner of Front and Bay Streets, opposite the Queen's Hotel, and was erected by the Northern Railway in 1853. It had only a brief life in this location and then the Northern Railway moved its terminus to a spot now run through by Spadina Ave.

The original location, however, had many advantages as the site for a station, and in 1855 the Grand Trunk Railway erected a station on the same corner, which became the first "Union Station" in the same year when the Great Western Railway reached an agreement with the Grand Trunk to share the facilities. In 1858, the building was replaced by a larger structure.

In 1866, the Great Western constructed its own station at the north-east corner of Yonge Street and the Esplanade, which endured until 1952, although it ceased to be a station in 1882 when the Great Western amalgamated with the GTR. The building was demolished to make room for the O'Keefe Centre, today known as the Hummingbird Centre.

By 1871, the Bay and Front Streets station was proving inadequate, and the railroad replaced it with one on the west side of York Street south of Front Street, which officially opened on 1 July 1873. In 1887, the CPR began running into this station.

The reader should be aware that the tracks for these stations ran at grade and the viaduct that now carries them over the streets between York Street on the west and the Don River on the east was not constructed until the building in 1914-1919 of the present Union Station. Prior to that, all the streets running south of Front Street went over level crossings.

In 1895, a new wing was added to the 1873 station, and this terminus served Toronto until 1927 when the present Union Station was officially opened by the then Prince of Wales, the Nazi-phile Edward VIII.

On 19 April 1904, Toronto's "Great Fire" wiped clean most of what had been the city's manufacturing core south of King Street and west of Yonge Street. It is an ill wind, etc., for the railways, armed with the power of expropriation, and now saved the cost of demolition, moved in to pick over the charred carcass. The Grand Trunk Railway took up the frontage along the south side of Front Street between Bay and York Streets and laid plans to shift itself from the west side of York Street. Since title to this particular parcel of land was held by the civic corporation, the GTR cut a deal: the City retained ownership of the land while the railroad got a perpetual lease provided the land was used "only as a passenger station". Eventually, the Grand Trunk and the Canadian Pacific Railway finally quit squabbling long enough to let construction contracts in 1914, but not before the CPR had built its North Toronto Station on the east side of Yonge Street between Roxborough Street East and Summerhill Ave, now used as a Liquor Control Board of Ontario retail outlet. The present Union Station was completed in 1919, but, unbelievably, inter-railway bickering let it sit empty until 1927 when it was finally declared open for business. Those interested in this architectural treasure are referred to *The open gate; Toronto Union Station*, (Toronto: Peter Martin Associates; 1972).

In the Great Fire of April 1904, which began in the E. & S. Currie factory on the north side of Wellington Street west of Bay Street, practically the whole area west of Yonge Street over to York Street and south of King Street to the waterfront was laid waste. Notable exceptions to the wholesale destruction were the Queen's Hotel at the north-east corner of York and Front Streets, where the Royal York Hotel now stands, and the Bank of Montreal and Custom House at the north-west corner of Yonge and Front Streets, now the Hockey Hall of Fame.

It would have been at the Queen's Hotel that William L. Staples, alias "John Armstrong", and Walter Brown, alias "John A. Walker", registered and met in the smoking-room and bar. In its day, the Queen's Hotel was known to every visitor of prominence to the flourishing city of Toronto.

Operated as Sword's Hotel from 1856 to 1862, the Queen's Hotel by the early 1890s had grown into a luxurious inn with accomodation for 400 guests and a staff of 210. East of the hotel, along the north side of Front Street, was the hotel's private garden, with fountains and flower beds set into its carefully kept lawn. Renowned for the quality of its food, the hotel remained fashionable for 60 years, even after the opening of its main rival, the King Edward, on the south side of King Street between Victoria and

Church Streets, in 1899. In 1927, the year the present Union Station finally opened, the CPR purchased the property and demolished the Queen's Hotel, replacing it with the present Royal York Hotel, completed in 1929 and at the time the largest hotel in the British Commonwealth, and since added to.

The Queen's Hotel was at the height of its glory in the late 1880s and early 1890s when Walter Brown tracked down his quarry in its anterooms.

What eventually became the hotel was built in 1838 as a brick terrace of four three-storey houses by Captain Richard Thomas, who became wealthy operating steamboats on Lake Ontario, on the north side of Front Street running eastward from York Street and were occupied by Rev. Michael Willis, D.D., later Principal of Knox College; Mr James Smith, a tutor; and, William Botsford Jarvis, Sheriff of Toronto. In 1844, Knox College was founded and the dwellings were knocked into one as the college's first premises. In 1856, Knox College moved into Elmsley Villa at the corner of Grosvenor and St Vincent Streets, and the building was turned into a hotel by a Mr Sword. In 1859, the Government moved to Quebec and Sword gave up the business, to be succeeded by B. J. B. Riley, who called it the Revere House. On the death of Riley in 1862, the hotel passed into the hands of "Captain Dick", as Captain Thomas was familiarly known, who had built and still owned the building, who took over the management of the hotel, which became known as the Queen's Hotel. He considerably altered and enlarged the premises and refitted the structure with all the requirements of a state-of-the-art hotel of the time. In 1863, Capt Dick added east and west wings, followed by a second west wing in 1865 and a second east wing in 1869. In May of 1869, Mark Irish, an agent of the American Express Company and Mr McGaw took over the hotel in partnership. In 1871, the partnership was dissolved and Irish rented the rival Rossin House. McGaw operated the Queen's Hotel by himself until 1 May 1874, when he entered into partnership with Mr Winnett, and they jointly purchased the concern from Thomas. Messrs McGaw and Winnett operated it right up into the 1890s, continually improving it as they went along. After Mr McGaw died, his widow continued in partnership with Winnett. By the early 1890s, it stood as a white fronted structure with long balconies and verandah and many windows, shaded by noble chestnut trees. From its windows, there was a view of the bay and the Island beyond the immediate foreground of the Esplanade and its network of railway tracks.

As for iceboating, as an early commentator put it, "There is nothing more thrilling than the iceboat in a heavy gale, doing a full sixty miles an hour and turning corners on two runners to make the simple-minded passenger singularly contemplative."[3].

The next offering is a historical pastiche, "Sherlock Holmes' great Canadian adventure" by Jack Batten and Michael Bliss, that extends the immortal Canon of tales of Sherlock Holmes and takes us back to the romantic Toronto of the 1890s. Set in 1891, we find Holmes and Watson residing at the Queen's Hotel, recently frequented by Messrs Staples and Walker.

The Toronto references in the story are more than adequately explained in Trevor Raymond's annotations accompanying it.

Vincent Starrett's "The tattooed man" first appeared in book form during the so-called "Golden Age of Detective Fiction" between the Wars when the puzzle-mystery was predominant and the "cosy", still going strong today, came into its own with the fabrications of Agatha Christie. But its internal dating places it back before the turn of the century.

"I am a physician. My name is Fielding — Charles Fielding. I live in that village of Parkdale, not far from Toronto." So begins the narrator of "The tattooed man". We read no more of Parkdale in the story, which indeed could be set anywhere, but Starrett has chosen to immortalize a suburb of his birth-city in this way.

Parkdale was annexed to the City of Toronto by 1900, so the time of Starrett's tale must be dated to the closing score of years of the nineteenth century.

"The pleasant village, or rather town, of Parkdale, has long been all but identical with the city, from which it is separated by Dufferin Street, immediately west of the Exhibition Grounds. There is no doubt whatever, that Parkdale, like Yorkville and the other suburbs, will soon be absorbed in the municipality of Toronto. Meanwhile it is one of the pleasantest of our suburbs, and furnishes an easily available health resort in summer to those whose business duties do not allow them to remove any great distance from the city. There is a continuous line of houses and stores from the centre of Toronto, at the corner of Queen and Yonge Streets, along Queen Street to the main street of Parkdale. This street is furnished with stores and hotels on a scale equal to that of the best streets in the city. Radiating from this in all directions, north and south, are avenues, which are rapidly being filled up with handsome private residences and villas."[4].

This was Parkdale in 1884. For a long time, it was a chosen suburban district and the short wide avenues leading from Queen Street to the shore-line were lined with charming houses. This is where some of Toronto's most extensive grounds and best kept flower gardens were to be found. Today, alas, it is the most insalubrious part of the city, its onetime mansions cut up into over-crowded rooming houses, populated by former psychiatric patients turned onto the streets, a haven of drug-users and dealers and whores, the port of last call for the homeless and derelict.

Parkdale sprang into existence in the 1870s on the undeveloped lands beyond Dufferin Street, the City's western boundary. By 1878, it was "rapidly growing and will soon become thickly inhabited and covered with charming villas."[5].

It became a village in 1879, was promoted to the status of town in 1886, and was annexed to Toronto in 1889.

In 1893, Mazo de la Roche, the famous Canadian novelist and creator of the "Jalna" saga of the Whiteoaks family, lived there on Dunn Ave, south of King Street, and where there are now railway tracks described it in one of her volumes of autobiography thus: "fields of tall feathery grass and daisies ... There were a few large houses with gardens by the lake ... My grandfather's house was one of five that stood on a tree-shaded street that ended in a kind of wooden terrace with seats, overlooking the lake. It had a deep stone porch ..."[6]. Charles Fielding's abode would have been similar.

By World War I, Parkdale was almost completely built up.

Our last look at crime in Toronto of yore is an historical "Gothic" by Maureen Jennings set at the turn of the century.

"The Furness house was near the corner of Queen and Sumach Streets, the end one of a row of workers' dwellings. Even at night, the smell of hops from the Dominion Brewery across the road was sweet and cloying on the air." This was the heartland of the original Cabbagetown, that working class district of Toronto clustered around St Paul's Roman Catholic Church, with its Italianate campanile, at the south-east corner of Queen Street East and Power Street, stretching from Parliament Street on the west eastward to the Don River and northward from the gasworks down on Front Street, where most of the male residents were employed, to Gerrard Street. Some of the workers' cottages still stand, all now mostly commercial establishments with store fronts. The Dominion Brewery building is still there, now gussied up into offices. It was a good beer in its day.

The Jubilee at which John met Mary Ann was the Diamond Jubilee of Queen Victoria in 1897; the Exhibition grounds were those of the present Canadian National Exhibition at the foot of Strachan Avenue over to Dufferin Street on the west — the area once reserved as the Garrison Common, the military training ground for the troops at Fort York over toward Bathurst Street, and used for several different institutional purposes over the years until the CNE settled in permanently. The forerunner of the CNE was the Toronto Industrial Exhibition, first staged in 1878.

The third period, 1920-1940, coincides with Canada's coming of age. As remarked by Sandra Gwyn in her *Tapestry of war*, "... it is the Great War that marks the real birth of Canada. Thrust for the first time upon the world's stage, we performed at all times creditably and often brilliantly —

holding the line under gas attack at Second Yypres in 1915, capturing Vimy Ridge in 1917 and Passchendaele Ridge later the same year, performing in the vanguard in 1918 during the Hundred Days of the astonishing counter-attack that ended, abruptly, in the Armistice. As has been remarked many times, the effort of mobilizing and equipping a vast army modernized us, and our blood and our accomplishments transformed us from colony into nation. Prime Minister Borden's separate signature on the peace treaty of Versailles put the seal upon our new status; even without that symbolism, Canadians knew they had won it."[7].

With the advent of the third period, we find the contrast and the conflict between the great outdoors versus the inner streets, the frontier versus the city. As society became urbanized, so did crime. Consequently, we move from the Mountie in the wilds to the municipal policeman in the towns and cities. This was the "Golden Age" of detection when private-sector professional and amateur sleuths abounded.

Although "Northerns" continued to be penned, and, in truth, the form is still alive, Canadian writers were moving away from the frontier ethos and a colonial cast of mind. They no longer saw themselves as inhabitants of a frontier, but as the citizens of a nation. Whereas, formerly, despite Confederation, they had still considered themselves as being, firstly, Overseas British, subjects of the greatest Empire in world history, and, secondly, as Maritimers or Lower or Upper Canadians or residents of the North-West Territories or British Columbians, now they saw themselves as Canadians first and were proud of it without either forgetting or neglecting their respective regional heritages. The idea of Empire had faded before national consciousness and national sovereignty. When before writers had written about the Territories as territorials or about the Atlantic Provinces as Maritimers, now they wrote about these regions as Canadians; the parts had coalesced into a greater whole. Sadly for Canada in the long run, there was an exception to prove the rule. The War that had cemented the fledgling country into a true nation-state had also guaranteed that one part of it would turn inward. The Anglo- and Franco-Canadas had hardened into the two solitudes. Until the Quiet Revolution of the '60s, Quebec,ois criminous writing was a sub-set of the roman policier prevalent in Continental France.

In what could be termed "soft-boiled with back bacon on the side", Canadian crime writers explored Canada's mean streets.

The two decades between the World Wars were a rich time for popular culture. The period has been called the "Golden Age" of detective fiction and was dominated by Dorothy L. Sayers, Agatha Christie, and Ngaio Marsh. Competing with this dazzling trio, and holding their own, were a number of Canadians, many of whom wrote about what they knew and set their mysteries in Canada, and were published regardless, even in Great Britain and the U.S.A. These good, solid, Canadian crime writers interpreted their society for their fellow Canadians and for readers abroad.

Other Canadians endeavoured to buck the trend and, eschewing "Mountie/Northern" novels, wrote classic detective/mystery novels and set them in their own land. In 1929, Morley Callaghan, for example, published his first novel, *Strange fugitive*, a criminous tale of racketeering, filled with adventure, power, and incident, set in Toronto. These writers weren't being published by small nationalistic Canadian houses, but by commercial British and American firms, which shews that there was a market abroad for crime fiction set in Canada if all those Canadian crime novelists busily hiding their identity had been prepared to come out of the closet. What was happening was that Canadian writers at home and Canadian writers resident abroad who were writing crime fiction only produced "Mountie/Northern" novels when they chose to portray their homeland.

By the fourth period, 1940-1980, crime had become largely localized as an urban phenomena, at least in popular mythology, and although Mountie novels and "Northerns" continue to be published, they have become marginalized, pushed to the edge of the crowd by the new favourites portraying professional public- and private-sector sleuths and the occasional amateur in a thoroughly urbanized setting. Danger now lurks in the mean streets, adventure can be found in the back-alleys. It is the city that is both the lair of evil and the hiding-place of the treasure. The gold that is sought is no longer raw in the ground, but represented by the paper of currency and stocks and bonds.

However, despite early efforts, particularly in the 1940s by writers such as the Canadians Margaret Millar and Frances Shelley Wees to set crime novels in Canada featuring Canadian detectives, whether amateur or professional, the norm remained for Canadian authors, for the most part, to set their novels outside of Canada.

During the closing years of the 1970s, crime fiction as a distinctive element within Canadian letters burgeoned, so much so that there were sufficient practioners in the genre to warrant the founding of the Crime Writers of Canada in 1981.

With the current period of 1980 to date, we have the efflorescence of Canadian criminous writing that has produced a plethora of authors, some of whom who have deservedly achieved international recognition and status. Increasingly, in reflection of the Canadian popular consciousness, the protagonist is an employee of the state, a civil servant, although perhaps not a bureaucrat, rather than an entrepreneur.

The Canadian crime novel as by Canadians set in Canada and featuring a truly Canadian hero finally made the breakthrough and came into its own with the works of Howard Engel and his Benny Cooperman series beginning in 1980 with *The suicide murders*; Ted Wood and his series about Reid Bennett and his dog, Sam, a worthy successor to all those noble animals who so ably assisted their masters in the Mounted Police, who were introduced in *Dead in the water*, (1983); and, Eric Wright, with his character Inspector Charlie Salter of the Metropolitan Toronto Police Department whose fictional career began in *The night the Gods smiled*, (1983), three quite different, but all fine, novelists. It is true that Ted Wood hedged his bets for the international market by making his central character, Reid Bennett, a Viet Nam vet, (albeit a Canadian volunteer), a situation he redeemed by his creation of Canadian John Locke, a "minder", brought forth under the pseudonym "Jack Barnao" in *HammerLocke*, (1986), although Locke is ex-S.A.S.; and, Eric Wright succumbed to setting his third Charlie Salter adventure, *Death in the Old Country*, (1985), in England where his hero is vacationing, but these are mere missteps in the forward march of a truly Canadian indigenous crime genre.

The roll-call of Canadian crime writers since 1980 is replete with names that will stand the test of time. Howard Engel, Ted Wood, and Eric Wright have assured themselves a place in the pantheon of Canadian novelists alongside the likes of Margaret Atwood, Robertson Davies, Margaret Laurence, and Alice Munro. John Ballem, Chrystine Brouillet, Timothy Findley, Maurice Gagnon, L. R. Wright, Richard B. Wright, (none of these Wrights are related), and Tim Wynne-Jones are only some of their peers who will gather with them in celebration of Canadian letters.

In this anthology we have as representatives of this literary legion telling contemporary stories Eric Wright, James Powell, Rosemary Aubert, and Peter Sellers.

Bethell in Eric Wright's tale could live in Cabbagetown, Rosedale, The Annex, the Republic of Rathnally, Deer Park, Moore Park, Leaside, that amorphous northward finger of the city generically called North Toronto, or even the Beaches in the far east end. Of these desirable residential neighbourhoods in Toronto, I like to think Bethell lives in the Beaches; it is the romantic in me. Please note that it is "the Beaches" — plural — not "the Beach" in the singular, despite the attempts of real-estate agents to pervert history, that part of the city bounded by the Kingston Road on the north, Lake Ontario on the south, Victoria Park Ave, (the eastern boundary of the city between it and Scarborough), on the east, and Lee Avenue on the west, once again despite how some real-estate agent desperate to unload a property will try to convince you otherwise. The traditional Beaches consisted solely of the public school districts of Williamson Road and Balmy Beach Public Schools. There were and are two beaches: Kew Beach at the foot of Lee Avenue eastward to Maclean Ave, where once before World War One there was an amusement park, subsequently eclipsed by Sunnyside at the other side of the city, and Balmy Beach, that encompassed the shoreline between Beech and Silverbirch Avenues, the home of the Balmy Beach Canoe Club, from which during the day hearty argonauts took out their rowing shells, while at night the heady melodies of dance bands made it one of the two most popular, and notorious, dance halls in the province, the other being Dunn's at Bala in Muskoka, which was strictly for the summer trade.

Toronto is shaped like a half-moon, an open fan with its bottom resting on the north shore of Lake Ontario. The St Lawrence Market is situated in the centre of the bottom edge where the handle of the fan would be at the original site of the old Town of York, as Toronto used to be. The St Lawrence Hall sits on the south-west corner of King and Jarvis Streets, facing north. Behind it are two market buildings, the North Market filling in the space southward between the St Lawrence Hall and Front Street, and the South Market across Front Street on filled land reclaimed from the lake. From 5:00 AM to 5:00 PM on Saturdays both Markets are thronged, the North offering primarily produce while the South, on two levels, has more permanent stalls and is the mecca for those who have not yet adopted vegetarianism.

The St Lawrence Market was originally laid out as the Market Square in 1803. A building was erected in 1833, which perished in a fire in 1849, to be replaced by the present St Lawrence Hall, designed by William Thomas, which has been thoroughly and lovingly restored. In its day it served not only as a market, but also as the leading concert and recital hall. Jenny Lind, the Swedish Nightingale, who during my childhood was commemorated by a famous line of chocolates, sang there on 21 October 1851, the year the building was inaugurated.

When Bethell went to the cop shop to ascertain where he might find a den of thieves, at the time the story was written he would have gone to the north-west corner of Charles and Jarvis Streets. Prior to that, he would have attended to the Stewart Building on the south side of College Street between University Avenue and McCaul Street, a monumental institution originally designed and constructed by Edward J. Lennox, who gave Toronto its "Old" City Hall facing down Bay Street from its site on the north-east corner of what is now Bay, but was once Terauley, Street and Queen Street West, as the Toronto Athletic Club, which now houses the subsidiary campus of the Ontario College of Art. Today, he would seek information at the relatively new post-modern building on the north side of College Street that girdles the Kennedy Building on the north-east corner of College and Bay Streets.

The Don Jail, at which Bethell contemplates spending only one night, sits on the east side of the Don River between the river and Broadview Ave, north of Gerrard Street. At one time it was a major penal institution, even a place of execution, but of late it sits all but empty, used only as holding cells, a relict of a more incarcerating past. Yet it is an imposing piece of architecture, and its main door is truly a thing of beauty, one of the more memorable doors in the city.

CJRT, of which the surveyor is a supporter, was the radio broadcasting studio of the Radio and Television Arts programme of the former Ryerson Polytechnical Institute, now elevated to the status of a University, and is currently an independent FM station justifiably renowned for its programming, especially classical music.

When Bethell chooses the name "Royce Dupont" to use on his fake business cards, it is a moniker that would stike a chord in any native Torontonian, for Royce Dupont Poultry is a long-established wholesale supplier in the city and its trucks delivering to restaurants and butchers are a familiar sight.

Thanks to the waves of Italian immigration following World War Two, Toronto can boast many fine Italian restaurants. Although there may be a very few that serve execrable meals, the majority range from good to excellent. It is typical of Sligo that his choice would be wrong.

If Yonge Street is the longest north-south street in Toronto, then Eglinton Avenue can well boast to be the longest east-west thoroughfare. Yonge Street is the spine of the city and all streets are divided as being east or west of it, so Eglinton [Avenue] West, where Bethell rents the station wagon that is to be his get-away-car, is that stretch of the road that runs westward from Yonge Street out through the companion cities of York, for which it is the main drag, and Etobicoke into the suburban wilds of Mississauga, Canada's rival to the urban sprawl of Los Angeles, California.

Toronto is justifiably famous for and proud of its numerous parks and green spaces, one of the most popular, especially for summer picnics, being the Toronto Island(s). Originally, it was a peninsula formed from a sandbar that stretched out from the eastern side of the bay that fronted Toronto and curved toward the west. Eventually, in April of 1858, a storm broke through and turned the peninsula into what is singularly referred to as "The Island", although in truth it encompasses several small islands all linked by bridges. The ferry over to the Island, which Bethell pretends to have taken, (there are actually several all going to different points), leaves from the docks at the foot of Bay Street. During the 1880s and '90s, the island was a popular summer resort whereat there were many fine summer homes, until improved transportation replaced it by Muskoka, and then it was one of the more salubrious suburbs of the city. Today, it is all, save for a few pockets, and the Island Airport at its western edge, a public park.

Harbourfront, where Bethell disposes of the incriminating evidence, is a glaring example of opportunity missed. When in the '60s the process began of revitalizing the grungy industrial belt that ran along Toronto's lakefront, a superb promenade and park that would have been the jewel in the city's crown could have been created. Instead, greed prevailed and what should have belonged to the people became the trendy purlieu of wealthy yuppies accommodated in a seemingly endless row of tasteless condominiums. At least one can walk along the lakefront, and there are some attractions, but it is only a pale reflection of what might have been.

James Powell's chilling tale of surrogate homicide takes place in Allan Gardens, the site of the municipal greenhouses holding a variety of tropical plants. The almost-13-acre park occupies the entire rectangular block of land bounded by Jarvis Street on the west, Carlton Street on the north, Sherbourne Street on the east, and Gerrard Street on the south, save for the frontage on the east side of Jarvis Street occupied from north to south by St Andrew's Lutheran Church on the south-east corner of Jarvis and Carlton; the collegiate institute, (now demolished and the area incorporated into the park); some dwellings, (now replaced by the Baptist Seminary); and, Jarvis Street Baptist Church on the north-east corner of Jarvis and Gerrard.

In 1858, the Toronto Horticultural Society was offered a five acre parcel of land as the site for a garden by the Honourable George Allan, a prominent local politician and cultural leader. On Saturday 8 September 1860, it was inaugurated, in the worst possible weather, as the Horticultural Gardens, by Albert Edward, Prince of Wales, later Edward VII, who planted the inevitable maple sapling in the grounds. In 1864, the City purchased the surrounding land from Mr Allan, which it added to his original gift. That same year, the Horticultural Society erected a rustic pavilion. In 1879, this bosky edifice was replaced by the new `Horticultural Pavilion', an impressive 75' X 120' structure designed by the Toronto firm of Langley, Langley, and Burke built after the style of the Crystal Palace in London, England, three storeys high, mainly consisting of iron and glass, with a wooden substructure. Latterly, a 45' X 48' Conservatory was added to the south side. For many years, the Pavilion Music Hall at the west side of the Horticultural Gardens was the platform of choice for speakers and visiting lecturers and was in constant demand for promenade concerts, gala balls, conventions, and, of course, flower shows. The auditorium stage could easily accomodate a chorus and an orchestra of as many as 200 musicians. The Pavilion was the focal point of the City's fiftieth birthday celebrations in 1884, and Oscar Wilde lectured here during his famous tour of North America. Before the construction of Massey Hall, it was the venue for great concerts, but these were the days when "upper Jarvis Street presented as fashionable an appearance as that of any North American city of its size."[8]. In 1888, under financial strain the Horticultural Society surrendered its interest to the City, which initiated a programme of improvement and expansion, culminating in the modernization of the Conservatory in 1894 and its replacement with a more spacious facility 90' X 61'. Shortly after his death in 1901, the accomplishments of George Allan, whose original gift had set the course for this landmark, were recognized by the name of the Horticultural Gardens being formally changed to Allan Gardens in his memory. Tragically, on 6 June 1902 a disastrous fire destroyed the Horticultural Pavilion and parts of the Conservatory. Its replacement, the classically proportioned domed Palm House that occupies the site today, was designed by the then City Architect, Robert McCallum, and opened in 1909. During the 1920s, two new display greenhouses, in which cyclical displays of plants and flowers continually feed the souls of the citizenry, were added respectively to the north and south ends of the Palm House. Additional greenhouse wings were added in 1957. The grounds of the park serve as an arboretum.

When Allan Gardens were established, handsome residences surrounded the park on the streets forming the boundaries. Alas, the neighbourhood has come down in the world, although it has somewhat recovered from its nadir as an adjunct to Toronto's "tenderloin" district centred around Jarvis Street from the First Great Depression of the Twentieth Century until the wave of "white-painting" and gentrification in the Sixties after the Second World War.

That part of central Toronto lying to the north of College Street that extends from Yonge Street westward over to Queen's Park Crescent and northward to Wellesley Street in which Rosemary Aubert's "Shaving with Occam's razor" is set is almost entirely occupied with offices of the provincial government, although not exclusively. Both the Centre for Forensic Sciences and the Morgue, which are situated where the author says they are, have conducted-tours for groups. If your organization is looking for something new and entirely different to do for its next outing, why not consider visiting one or the other of these institutions? One piece of advice if you do decide to go: plan to eat afterward, not before.

The section of Bloor Street West with its cafes that lies between Spadina Ave and Bathurst Streets where Gregoire and Menard meet

Dumoulin in "Bombed" by Peter A. Sellers is the heartland of Toronto's intellectual bohemianism, (the artistic Bohemia of Toronto's painters, musicians, and sculptors holds its rendezvous in the bars along Queen Street West between University Avenue and Bathurst Street where a little later on you'll meet Tanya Huff's Vicki Nelson). Here on Bloor Street West intense young men and women in tweeds can philosophize over desultory games of chess and discuss, as our heroes do, how their particular brand of politics will cure the ills of the world.

It is a pleasant stroll down Yonge Street from St Clair Ave to Bloor that Hannigan takes. This is the trendy stretch of Yonge Street, which becomes increasingly seedy as it approaches Lake Ontario until at Queen Street it remembers its faded glories and begins to reflect the proper attitude that befits the historical artery of the town and the eastern boundary of the financial district. But between St Clair and Bloor it is lined with chi-chi boutiques, trendy restaurants, up-scale groceterias, and expensive condos. This is a stretch of road with an attitude.

Hannigan's Susan lives in the Beaches. By now you know all about that part of Toronto — that's where we decided Bethell lives. It was then, it is now, and it probably always will be, middle-class-ville. Not the tony, haute couture upper-middle-class of Forest Hill or Rosedale, but the well-educated middle-class of the intelligentsia who populate academe and its associated territories such as broadcasting and publishing.

The West End of Toronto proper, the original city before it exploded into the suburbs after the Second World War, which encompassed generally everything west of the University of Toronto, was traditionally the area settled by new immigrants from the Continent of Europe, particularly the Ukrainians and the Poles. For the Polish community, its main street was and still is Roncesvalles Avenue that runs northward from where King Street West curves up into the western terminus of Queen Street West to where Dundas Street West crosses Bloor Street West, (believe it or not, the two actually do this twice). Roncesvalles is the eastern boundary of the district known as High Park, where Hannigan's Susan used to live, a quiet residential section of older homes that lies between it and the public land known as High Park, the vast tract of woodland presented to the city by John G. Howard in 1873, a gift for which nature-loving Torontonians will always be grateful. Up and down Roncesvalles can be found some of the best delicatessens, bakeries, and patisseries in the city, replete not only with Old World delicacies, but also with Old World charm. Small wonder that once having tasted their delights, Susan returns regularly. Many people who have never lived there faithfully do their shopping in that neighbourhood.

The Toronto of the occult, that other-dimensional Toronto that exists in a parallel world, a Toronto where anything can happen, and does, a science-fictional Toronto where horror is an everyday occurrence and inside the smoke and behind the mirrors the shadows have substance, the Toronto where reality blends into the surreal and the natural becomes the supernatural, is the Toronto of a talented trio of short-story writers.

Tanya Huff's tale of Vicki Nelson's vicissitudes is as contemporary as today's newsflash. Queen Street West is the abode of the chic, the punk, the habitue's of the "Goth" bars named not in memory of the Teutonic tribesman that toppled Rome, but in honour of the Gothick tradition in English literature that gave us Horace Walpole's *The castle of Otranto* and Matthew Gregory Lewis's *The monk* and Bram Stoker's *Dracula*, the wellspring of all vampirism.

The "[Art] deco building on the corner of Queen and John", (it's the south-east corner), renovated by CITY-TV, which really exists, upon the roof of which Vicki crouches as a gargoyle was built as the headquarters for the Ryerson Press, which began as the printing arm of the Methodist Church of Canada, later the bulk of the United Church of Canada, and became one of the major commercial publishing houses in the country until it was sold to American interests and exists now as McGraw-Hill Ryerson. As Vicki checks the bars, one can sense the pulse of Queen Street West. Huff has captured the essence and vibrancy of the Queen Street scene and brought it to the pages of her story. Just as Weiner's "The map" is of Toronto and nowhere else, so too one cannot imagine Vicki's "town" being any other than Toronto. Go pub-crawling along Queen Street West or dine at one of the many excellent eateries offering their fare and as you walk along look up the alleys and side-streets. Yes, that shadow you saw flitting is Vicki. She is *there.*

"Lost in the mail" by Robert J. Sawyer could be set almost anywhere in Canada, but it seems right to assume that Jacob Coin lives in Toronto without it being implicitly stated. After all, that is where Ryerson Polytechnical University and the Royal Ontario Museum are situated, and Jacob doesn't call the latter on long-distance. Toronto *feels* just right as the setting for this story — it has a Toronto tinge to it.

Whereas with Starrett's "The tattooed man" Toronto is only incidental to the story and it could be set anywhere in the English-language civilized world of the late Nineteenth Century, Andrew Weiner's "The map" is integral to Toronto. "The map" **is** Toronto and could not be anywhere else. To understand "The map" requires a considerable knowledge of the historical geography of Toronto. Weiner obviously has both the understanding and the knowledge and a real feel for the city. Church Street from Dundas Street south to Queen Street and beyond houses the main concentration of pawnshops in the city. Would Toronto be as Weiner pessimistically views it had British North America never coalesced into the Dominion? I don't think so, but this is not the place for that debate. The Toronto in which Dennis Stone dies is a real Toronto that once was, a Toronto that lies behind and underneath the Toronto we have around us. There are in a very real sense parallel worlds in the history that surrounds us in the form of our streetscapes and landscapes. We are where we are. "Geography and the seasons govern all military operations", said the Romans. They could as well have said that geography and the seasons govern all history, and all culture for that matter. The foreign policy of a nation is governed by its geography, regardless of the political ideology of the government of the moment. So it is then that citizens of a particular locale are moulded into a set of characteristics, a pattern of behaviour, by their surroundings the streets they walk and the buildings they inhabit. Thus we are Torontonians, not New Yorkers nor Londoners nor yet Parisians nor the urban collectivity of any other metropolis. We are Torontonians because of what Toronto has been and is, and it is because of what it has been. The shadows of York and the echoes of Upper Canada limned in Weiner's tale can be glimpsed out of the corners of our eyes and ring faintly in our ears. Look about you and listen, but be careful that you stay firmly rooted in the here and now, for those who journey to the there and then rarely ever come back.

The mute bricks of Toronto have many stories locked in their hearts. If you listen carefully, you can hear them murmuring to you as you walk by. They tell a rich tale of an exciting city where romance and adventure have gone hand-in-hand, a city where terror has stalked the streets, a city in which mystery has held court while minstrelry echoed through its corridors of power, a city that has endured invasion and recovered from insurrection, that has erupted in riot, and been a haven of good times. A city in which one can be proud to live, a city with a vibrant past, a glorious present, and a bright future. It is a city that has in its repertoire as many stories as there have been residents. Some of these stories have been told here, others are told elsewhere. All are worth listening to. Find them. If we do not know from where we have come and how we got here, we do not know where we are, and cannot figure out where we go from here. Discover Toronto, it's well worth the effort.

NOTES

1 Barzun, Jacques, and Taylor, Wendell Hertig. *Catalogue of crime; [being a reader's guide to the literature of mystery, detection & related genres]*. 2nd imp. corr. NY: Harper & Row; 1971.

2 Roper, Gordon, Beharriell, S. Ross, and Schieder, Rupert. "Writers of fiction 1880-1920" IN Klinck, Carl F., (ed.). *Literary history of Canada; Canadian literature in English.* 2d ed. Toronto: University of Toronto Press; 1976.

3 Middleton, Jesse Edgar. *Toronto's 100 years; [the official centennial book 1834-1934].* Toronto: The Centennial Committee; 1934. p.121.

4 Mulvany, C. Pelham. *Toronto: past and present; a handbook of the City*. Toronto: W. E. Caiger; 1884. p.257.

5 *Illustrated historical atlas of the County of York*, Toronto; 1878.

6 de la Roche, Mazo. *Ringing the changes; an autobiography*, Toronto: 1957.

7 Gwyn, Sandra. *Tapestry of war; a private view of Canadians in the Great War*. Toronto: HarperCollins; 1992. p.xvii.

8 Hale, Katherine. *Toronto; romance of a great city*. Toronto: Cassell; 1956. p. 160.

"We were not more than three minutes behind time, as we glided in front of the Union Station..."
[Toronto Union Station 1858–1871, ca 1859, waterfront, west of York Street. Watercolour, pen and brown ink over pencil by William Armstrong. Metropolitan Toronto Reference Library, J. Ross Robertson Collection T12188.]

John Dent

The Gerrard Street mystery

(*The Gerrard Street mystery; and other weird tales*. Toronto: Rose; 1888/reprinted IN *Crime in a Cold Climate*. Ed. by David Skene-Melvin. Toronto: Simon & Pierre/Dundurn; 1994.)

Biographical information about the author will be found at the back of the book.

As John Burdon Sanderson Haldane put it in his *Possible worlds* in 1927, "Now, my suspicion is that the universe is not only queerer than we suppose, but queerer than we *can* suppose"; or, as someone else said, "In a universe of infinite chance, anything is possible". William Furlong would be inclined to agree with these sentiments as the reader will discover.

The Gerrard Street Mystery

My name is William Francis Furlong. My occupation is that of a commission merchant, and my place of business is on St. Paul Street, in the City of Montreal. I have resided in Montreal ever since shortly after my marriage, in 1862, to my cousin, Alice Playter, of Toronto. My name may not be familiar to the present generation of Torontonians, though I was born in Toronto, and passed the early years of my life there. Since the days of my youth my visits to the Upper Province have been few, and – with one exception – very brief; so that I have doubtless passed out of the remembrance of many persons with whom I was once on terms of intimacy. Still there are several residents of Toronto whom I am happy to number among my warmest personal friends at the present day. There are also a good many persons of middle age, not in Toronto only, but scattered here and there throughout various parts of Ontario, who will have no difficulty in recalling my name as that of one of their fellow-students at Upper Canada College. The name of my late uncle, Richard Yardington, is of course well known to all residents of Toronto, where he spent the last thirty-two years of his life. He settled there in the year 1829, when the place was still known as Little York. He opened a small store on Yonge Street, and his commercial career was a reasonably prosperous one. By steady degrees the small store developed into what, in those times, was regarded as a considerable establishment. In the course of years the owner acquired a competency, and in 1854 retired from business altogether. From that time up to the day of his death he lived in his own house on Gerrard Street.

After mature deliberation, I have resolved to give to the Canadian public an account of some rather singular circumstances connected with my residence in Toronto. Though repeatedly urged to do so, I have hitherto refrained from giving any extended publicity to those circumstances, in consequence of my inability to see any good to be served thereby. The only person, however, whose reputation can be injuriously affected by the details has been dead for some years. He has left behind him no one whose feelings can be shocked by the disclosure, and the story is in itself sufficiently remarkable to be worth the telling. Told, accordingly, it shall be; and the only fictitious element introduced into the narrative shall be the name of one of the persons most immediately concerned in it.

At the time of taking up his abode in Toronto – or rather in Little York

– my uncle Richard was a widower, and childless; his wife having died several months previously. His only relatives on this side of the Atlantic were two maiden sisters, a few years younger than himself. He never contracted a second matrimonial alliance, and for some time after his arrival here his sisters lived in his house, and were dependent upon him for support. After the lapse of a few years both of them married and settled down in homes of their own. The elder of them subsequently became my mother. She was left a widow when I was a mere boy, and survived my father only a few months. I was an only child, and as my parents had been in humble circumstances, the charge of my maintenance devolved upon my uncle, to whose kindness I am indebted for such educational training as I have received. After sending me to school and college for several years, he took me into his store, and gave me my first insight into commercial life. I lived with him, and both then and always received at his hands the kindness of a father, in which light I eventually almost came to regard him. His younger sister, who was married to a watchmaker called Elias Playter, lived at Quebec from the time of her marriage until her death, which took place in 1846. Her husband had been unsuccessful in business, and was moreover of dissipated habits. He was left with one child – a daughter – on his hands; and as my uncle was averse to the idea of his sister's child remaining under the control of one so unfit to provide for her welfare, he proposed to adopt the little girl as his own. To this proposition Mr. Elias Playter readily assented, and little Alice was soon domiciled with her uncle and myself in Toronto.

Brought up, as we were, under the same roof, and seeing each other every day of our lives, a childish attachment sprang up between my cousin Alice and myself. As the years rolled by, this attachment ripened into a tender affection, which eventually resulted in an engagement between us. Our engagement was made with the full and cordial approval of my uncle, who did not share the prejudice entertained by many persons against marriages between cousins. He stipulated, however, that our marriage should be deferred until I had seen somewhat more of the world, and until we had both reached an age when we might reasonably be presumed to know our own minds. He was also, not unnaturally, desirous that before taking upon myself the responsibility of marriage I should give some evidence of my ability to provide for a wife, and for other contingencies usually consequent upon matrimony. He made no secret of his intention to divide his property between Alice and myself at his death; and the fact that no actual division would be necessary in the event of our marriage with each other was doubtless one reason for his ready acquiescence in our engagement. He was, however, of a vigorous constitution, strictly regular and methodical in all his habits, and likely to live to an advanced age. He could hardly be called parsimonious, but, like most men who have successfully fought their own way through life, he was rather fond of authority, and little disposed to divest himself of his wealth until he should have no further occasion for it. He expressed his willingness to establish me in business, either in Toronto or elsewhere, and to give me the benefit of his experience in all mercantile transactions.

When matters had reached this pass I had just completed my twenty-first year, my cousin being three years younger. Since my uncle's retirement I had engaged in one or two little speculations on my own account, which had turned out fairly successful, but I had not devoted myself to any regular or fixed pursuit. Before any definite arrangements had been concluded as to the course of my future life, a circumstance occurred which seemed to open a way for me to turn to good account such mercantile talent as I possessed. An old friend of my uncle's opportunely arrived in Toronto from Melbourne, Australia, where, in the course of a few years, he had risen from the position of a junior clerk to that of senior partner in a prominent commercial house. He painted the land of his adoption in glowing colours, and assured my uncle and myself that it presented an inviting field for a young man of energy and business capacity, more especially if he had a small capital at his command. The matter was carefully debated in our domestic circle. I was naturally averse to a separation from Alice, but my imagination took fire at Mr. Redpath's glowing account of his own splendid success. I pictured myself returning to Canada after an absence of four or five years with a mountain of gold at my command, as the result of my own energy and acuteness. In imagination, I saw myself settled down with Alice in a palatial mansion on Jarvis Street, and living in affluence all the rest of my days. My uncle bade me consult my own judgment in the matter, but rather encouraged the idea than otherwise. He offered to advance me £500, and I had about half that sum as the result of my own speculations. Mr. Redpath, who was just about returning to Melbourne, promised to aid me to the extent of his power with his local knowledge and advice. In less than a fortnight from that time he and I were on our way to the other side of the globe.

We reached our destination early in the month of September, 1857. My life in Australia has no direct bearing upon the course of events to be related, and may be passed over in a very few words. I engaged in various enterprises, and achieved a certain measure of success. If none of my ventures proved eminently prosperous, I at least met with no serious disasters. At the end of four years – that is to say, in September, 1861 – I made up my account with the world, and found I was worth ten thousand dollars. I had, however, become terribly homesick, and longed for the termination of my voluntary exile. I had, of course, kept up a regular correspondence with Alice and Uncle Richard, and of late they had both pressed me to return home. "You have enough," wrote my uncle, "to give you a start in Toronto, and I see no reason why Alice and you should keep apart any longer. You will have no housekeeping expenses, for I intend you to live with me. I am getting old, and shall be glad of your companionship in my declining years. You will have a comfortable home while I live and when I die you will get all I have between you. Write as soon as you receive this, and let us know how soon you can be here – the sooner the better."

The letter containing this pressing invitation found me in a mood very much disposed to accept it. The only enterprise I had on hand which would be likely to delay me was a transaction in wool, which, as I believed, would be closed by the end of January or the beginning of February. By the first of March I should certainly be in a condition to start on my homeward voyage, and I determined that my departure should take place about that time. I wrote both to Alice and my uncle, apprising them of my intention, and announcing my expectation to reach Toronto not later than the middle of May.

The letters so written were posted on the 19th of September, in time for the mail which left on the following day. On the 27th, to my huge surprise and gratification, the wool transaction referred to was unexpectedly concluded, and I was at liberty, if so disposed, to start for home by the next fast mail steamer, the *Southern Cross,* leaving Melbourne on the 11th of October. I *was* so disposed, and made my preparations accordingly. It was useless, I reflected, to write to my uncle or to Alice, acquainting them with the change in my plans, for I should take the shortest route home, and should probably be in Toronto as soon as a letter could get there. I resolved to telegraph from New York, upon my arrival there, so as not to take them altogether by surprise.

The morning of the 11th of October found me on board the *Southern Cross,* where I shook hands with Mr. Redpath and several other friends who accompanied me on board for a last farewell. The particulars of the voyage to England are not pertinent to the story, and may be given very briefly. I took the Red Sea route, and arrived at Marseilles about two o'clock in the afternoon of the 29th of November. From Marseilles I travelled by rail to Calais, and so impatient was I to reach my journey's end without loss of time, that I did not even stay over to behold the glories of Paris. I had a commission to execute in London, which, however, delayed me there only a few hours, and I hurried down to Liverpool, in the hope of catching the Cunard Steamer for New York. I missed it by about two hours, but the *Persia* was detailed to start on a special trip to Boston on the following day. I secured a berth, and at eight o'clock the next morning steamed out of the Mersey on my way homeward.

The voyage from Liverpool to Boston consumed fourteen days. All I need say about it is, that before arriving at the latter port I formed an intimate acquaintance with one of the passengers – Mr. Junius H. Gridley, a Boston merchant, who was returning from a hurried business trip to Europe. He was – and is – a most agreeable companion. We were thrown together a good deal during the voyage, and we then laid the foundation of a friendship which has ever since subsisted between us. Before the dome of the State House loomed in sight he had extracted a promise from me to spend a night with him before pursuing my journey. We landed at the wharf in East Boston on the evening of the 17th of December, and I accompanied him to his house on West Newton Street, where I remained until the following morning. Upon consulting the time-table, we found that the Albany express would leave at 11.30 a.m. This left several hours at my disposal, and we sallied forth immediately after breakfast to visit some of the lions of the American Athens.

In the course of our peregrinations through the streets, we dropped into the post office, which had recently been established in the Merchant's Exchange Building, on State Street. Seeing the countless piles of mail-matter, I jestingly remarked to my friend that there seemed to be letters enough there to go around the whole human family. He replied in the same mood, whereupon I banteringly suggested the probability that among so many letters, surely there ought to be one for me.

"Nothing more reasonable," he replied. "We Bostonians are always bountiful to strangers. Here is the General Delivery, and here is the department where letters addressed to the Furlong family are kept in stock. Pray inquire for yourself."

The joke I confess was not a very brilliant one; but with a grave countenance I stepped up to the wicket and asked the young lady in attendance:

"Anything for W.F. Furlong?"

She took from a pigeon-hole a handful of correspondence, and proceeded to run her eye over the addresses. When about half the pile had been exhausted she stopped, and propounded the usual inquiry in the case of strangers:

"Where do you expect letters from?"

"From Toronto," I replied.

To my no small astonishment she immediately handed me a letter, bearing the Toronto post-mark. The address was in the peculiar and well-known handwriting of my uncle Richard.

Scarcely crediting the evidence of my senses I tore open the envelope, and read as follows: –

> "TORONTO, 9th December, 1861.
> "MY DEAR WILLIAM – I am so glad to know that you are coming home so much sooner than you expected when you wrote last, and that you will eat your Christmas dinner with us. For reasons which you will learn when you arrive, it will not be a very merry Christmas at our house, but your presence will make it much more bearable than it would be without you. I have not told Alice that you are coming. Let

it be a joyful surprise for her, as some compensation for the sorrows she has had to endure lately. You needn't telegraph. I will meet you at the G.W.R. station.

"Your affectionate uncle,

"RICHARD YARDINGTON."

"Why, what's the matter?" asked my friend, seeing the blank look of surprise on my face. "Of course the letter is not for you; why on earth did you open it?"

"It *is* for me," I answered. "See here, Gridley, old man; have you been playing me a trick? If you haven't, this is the strangest thing I ever knew in my life."

Of course he hadn't been playing me a trick. A moment's reflection showed me that such a thing was impossible. Here was the envelope, with the Toronto post-mark of the 9th of December, at which time he had been with me on board the *Persia,* on the Banks of Newfoundland. Besides, he was a gentleman, and would not have played so poor and stupid a joke upon a guest. And, to put the matter beyond all possibility of doubt, I remembered that I had never mentioned my cousin's name in his hearing.

I handed him the letter. He read it carefully through twice over, and was as much mystified at its contents as myself; for during our passage across the Atlantic I had explained to him the circumstance under which I was returning home.

By what conceivable means had my uncle been made aware of my departure from Melbourne? Had Mr. Redpath written to him as soon as I acquainted that gentleman with my intentions? But even if such were the case, the letter could not have left before I did, and could not possibly have reached Toronto by the 9th of December. Had I been seen in England by some one who knew me, and had not one written from there? Most unlikely; and even if such a thing had happened, it was impossible that the letter could have reached Toronto by the 9th. I need hardly inform the reader that there was no telegraphic communication at that time. And how could my uncle know that I would take the Boston route? And if he *had* known, how could he foresee that I would do anything so absurd as to call at the Boston post office and inquire for letters? *"I will meet you at the G.W.R. station."* How was he to know by what train I would reach Toronto, unless I notified him by telegraph? And that he expressly stated to be unnecessary.

We did no more sight-seeing. I obeyed the hint contained in the letter, and sent no telegram. My friend accompanied me down to the Boston and Albany station, where I waited in feverish impatience for the departure of the train. We talked over the matter until 11.30, in the vain hope of finding some clue to the mystery. Then I started on my journey. Mr. Gridley's curiosity was aroused and I promised to send him an explanation immediately upon my arrival at home.

No sooner had the train glided out of the station than I settled myself in my seat, drew the tantalizing letter from my pocket, and proceeded to read and re-read it again and again. A very few perusals sufficed to fix its contents in my memory, so that I could repeat every word with my eyes shut. Still I continued to scrutinize the paper, the penmanship, and even the tint of the ink. For what purpose, do you ask? For no purpose, except that I hoped, in some mysterious manner, to obtain more light on the subject. No light came, however. The more I scrutinized and pondered, the greater was my mystification. The paper was a simple sheet of white letter-paper, of the kind ordinarily used by my uncle in his correspondence. So far as I could see, there was nothing peculiar about the ink. Anyone familiar with my uncle's writing could have sworn that no hand but his had penned the lines. His well-known signature, a masterpiece of involved hieroglyphics, was there in all its indistinctness, written as no one but himself could ever have written it. And yet, for some unaccountable reason, I was half disposed to suspect forgery. Forgery! What nonsense. Anyone clever enough to imitate Richard Yardington's handwriting would have employed his talents more profitably than indulging in a mischievous and purposeless jest. Not a bank in Toronto but would have discounted a note with that signature affixed to it.

Desisting from all attempts to solve these problems, I then tried to fathom the meaning of other points in the letter. What misfortune had happened to mar the Christmas festivities at my uncle's house? And what could the reference to my cousin Alice's sorrows mean? She was not ill. *That,* I thought, might be taken for granted. My uncle would hardly have referred to her illness as "one of the sorrows she had to endure lately." Certainly, illness may be regarded in the light of a sorrow; but "sorrow" was not precisely the word which a straightforward man like Uncle Richard would have applied to it. I could conceive of no other cause of affliction in her case. My uncle was well, as was evinced by his having written the letter, and by his avowed intention to meet me at the station. Her father had died long before I started for Australia. She had no other near relation except myself, and she had no cause for anxiety, much less for "sorrow," on my account. I thought it singular, too, that my uncle, having in some strange manner become acquainted with my movements, had withheld the knowledge from Alice. It did not square with my pre-conceived ideas of him that he would derive any satisfaction from taking his niece by surprise.

All was a muddle together, and as my temples throbbed with the intensity of my thoughts, I was half disposed to believe myself in a troubled dream from which I should presently awake. Meanwhile, on glided the train.

A heavy snow-storm delayed us for several hours, and we reached Hamilton too late for the mid-day express for Toronto. We got there, however, in time for the accommodation leaving at 3.15 p.m., and we would reach Toronto at 5.05. I walked from one end of the train to the other in hopes of finding some one I knew, from whom I could make enquiries about home. Not a soul. I saw several persons whom I knew to be residents of Toronto, but none with whom I had ever been personally acquainted, and none of them would be likely to know anything about my uncle's domestic arrangements. All that remained to be done under these circumstances was to restrain my curiosity as well as I could until reaching Toronto. By the by, would my uncle really meet me at the station, according to his promise? Surely not. By what means could he possibly know that I would arrive by this train? Still, he seemed to have such accurate information respecting my proceedings that there was no saying where his knowledge began or ended. I tried not to think about the matter, but as the train approached Toronto my impatience became positively feverish in its intensity. We were not more than three minutes behind time, as we glided in front of the Union Station, I passed out on to the platform of the car, and peered intently through the darkness. Suddenly my heart gave a great bound. There, sure enough, standing in front of the door of the waiting-room, was my uncle, plainly discernible by the fitful glare of the overhanging lamps. Before the train came to a stand-still, I sprang from the car and advanced towards him. He was looking out for me, but his eyes not being as young as mine, he did not recognize me until I grasped him by the hand. He greeted me warmly, seizing me by the waist, and almost raising me from the ground. I at once noticed several changes in his appearance; changes for which I was wholly unprepared. He had aged very much since I had last seen him, and the lines about his mouth had deepened considerably. The iron-grey hair which I remembered so well had disappeared; its place being supplied with a new and rather dandified-looking wig. The oldfashioned great-coat which he had worn ever since I could remember, had been supplanted by a modern frock of spruce cut, with seal-skin collar and cuffs. All this I noticed in the first hurried greetings that passed between us.

"Never mind your luggage, my boy," he remarked. "Leave it till tomorrow, when we will send down for it. If you are not tired we'll walk home instead of taking a cab. I have a good deal to say to you before we get there."

I had not slept since leaving Boston, but was too much excited to be conscious of fatigue, and as will readily be believed, I was anxious enough to hear what he had to say. We passed from the station, and proceeded up York Street, arm in arm.

"And now, Uncle Richard," I said, as soon as we were well clear of the crowd, "keep me no longer in suspense. First and foremost, is Alice well?"

"Quite well, but for reasons you will soon understand, she is in deep grief. You must know that – "

"But," I interrupted, "tell me, in the name of all that's wonderful, how you knew I was coming by this train; and how did you come to write to me at Boston?"

Just then we came to the corner of Front Street, where was a lamp-post. As we reached the spot where the light of the lamp was most brilliant, he turned half round, looked me full in the face, and smiled a sort of wintry smile. The expression of his countenance was almost ghastly.

"Uncle," I quickly said, "What's the matter? Are you not well?"

"I am not as strong as I used to be, and I have had a good deal to try me of late. Have patience and I will tell you all. Let us walk more slowly, or I shall not finish before we get home. In order that you may clearly understand how matters are, I had better begin at the beginning, and I hope you will not interrupt me with any questions till I have done. How I knew you would call at the Boston post-office, and that you would arrive in Toronto by this train, will come last in order. By the by, have you my letter with you?"

"The one you wrote to me at Boston? Yes, here it is," I replied, taking it from my pocket-book.

"Let me have it."

I handed it to him, and he put it into the breast pocket of his inside coat. I wondered at this proceeding on his part, but made no remark upon it.

We moderated our pace, and he began his narration. Of course I don't pretend to remember his exact words, but they were to this effect. During the winter following my departure to Melbourne, he had formed the acquaintance of a gentleman who had then recently settled in Toronto. The name of this gentleman was Marcus Weatherley, who had commenced business as a wholesale provision merchant immediately upon his arrival, and had been engaged in it ever since. For more than three years the acquaintance between him and my uncle had been very slight, but during the last summer they had had some real estate transactions together, and had become intimate. Weatherley, who was comparatively a young man and unmarried, had been invited to the house on Gerrard Street, where he had more recently become a pretty frequent visitor. More recently still, his visits had become so frequent that my uncle suspected him of a desire to be attentive to my cousin, and had thought proper to enlighten him as to her engagement with me. From that day his visits had been voluntarily discontinued. My uncle had not given much consideration to the subject until a fortnight afterwards, when he had accidently become aware of the fact that Weatherley was in embarrassed circumstances.

Here my uncle paused in his narrative to take breath. He then added, in a low tone, and putting his mouth almost close to my ear:

"And, Willie, my boy, I have at last found out something else. He has forty-two thousand dollars falling due here and in Montreal within the next ten days, and *he has forged my signature to acceptances for thirty-nine thousand seven hundred and sixteen dollars and twenty-four cents.*"

Those, to the best of my belief, were his exact words. We had walked up York Street to Queen, and then had gone down Queen to Yonge, when we turned up the east side on our way homeward. At the moment when the last words were uttered we had got a few yards north of Crookshank Street, immediately in front of a chemist's shop which was, I think, the third house from the corner. The window of this shop was well lighted, and its brightness was reflected on the sidewalk in front. Just then, two gentlemen walking rapidly in the opposite direction to that we were taking brushed by us; but I was too deeply absorbed in my uncle's communication to pay much attention to passers-by. Scarcely had they passed, however, ere one of them stopped and exclaimed:

"Surely that is Willie Furlong!"

I turned, and recognised Johnny Grey, one of my oldest friends. I relinquished my uncle's arm for a moment and shook hands with Grey, who said:

"I am surprised to see you. I heard only a few days ago, that you were not to be here till next spring."

"I am here," I remarked, "somewhat in advance of my own expectation." I then hurriedly enquired after several of our common friends, to which enquiries he briefly replied.

"All well," he said; "but you are in a hurry, and so am I. Don't let me detain you. Be sure and look in on me tomorrow. You will find me at the old place, in the Romain Buildings."

We again shook hands, and he passed on down the street with the gentleman who accompanied him. I then turned to re-possess myself of my uncle's arm. The old gentleman had evidently walked on, for he was not in sight. I hurried along, making sure of overtaking him before reaching Gould Street, for my interview with Grey had occupied barely a minute. In another minute I was at the corner of Gould Street. No signs of Uncle Richard. I quickened my pace to a run, which soon brought me to Gerrard Street. Still no signs of my uncle. I had certainly not passed him on my way, and he could not have got farther on his homeward route than here. He must have called in at one of the stores; a strange thing for him to do under the circumstances. I retraced my steps all the way to the front of the chemist's shop, peering into every window and doorway as I passed along. No one in the least resembling him was to be seen.

I stood still for a moment, and reflected. Even if he had run at full speed – a thing most unseemly for him to do – he could not have reached the corner of Gerrard Street before I had done so. And what should he run for? He certainly did not wish to avoid me, for he had more to tell me before reaching home. Perhaps he had turned down Gould Street. At any rate, there was no use waiting for him. I might as well go home at once. And I did.

Upon reaching the old familiar spot, I opened the gate, passed on up the steps to the front door, and rang the bell. The door was opened by a domestic who had not formed part of the establishment in my time, and who did not know me; but Alice happened to be passing through the hall and heard my voice as I inquired for Uncle Richard. Another moment and she was in my arms. With a strange foreboding at my heart I noticed that she was in deep mourning. We passed into the dining-room, where the table was laid for dinner.

"Has Uncle Richard come in?" I asked, as soon as we were alone. "Why did he run away from me?"

"Who?" exclaimed Alice, with a start; "what do you mean, Willie? Is it possible you have not heard?"

"Heard what?"

"I see you have *not* heard," she replied. "Sit down, Willie, and prepare yourself for painful news. But first tell me what you meant by saying what you did just now, – who was it that ran away from you?"

"Well, perhaps I should hardly call it running away, but he certainly disappeared most mysteriously, down here near the corner of Yonge and Crookshank Streets."

"Of whom are you speaking?"

"Of Uncle Richard, of course."

"Uncle Richard! The corner of Yonge and Crookshank Streets! When did you see him there?"

"When? A quarter of an hour ago. He met me at the station and we walked up together till I met Johnny Grey. I turned to speak to Johnny for a moment, when –"

"Willie, what on earth are you talking about? You are labouring under some strange delusion. *Uncle Richard died of apoplexy more than six weeks ago, and lies buried in St. James's Cemetery."*

II

I don't know how long I sat there, trying to think, with my face buried in my hands. My mind had been kept on a strain during the last thirty hours, and the succession of surprises to which I had been subjected had temporarily paralyzed my faculties. For a few moments after Alice's announcement I must have been in a sort of stupor. My imagination, I remember, ran riot about everything in general, and nothing in particular. My cousin's momentary impression was that I had met with an accident of some kind, which had unhinged my brain. The first distinct remembrance I have after this is, that I suddenly awoke from my stupor to find Alice kneeling at my feet, and holding me by the hand. Then my mental powers came back to me, and I recalled all the incidents of the evening.

"When did uncle's death take place?" I asked.

"On the 3rd of November, about four o'clock in the afternoon. It was quite unexpected, though he had not enjoyed his usual health for some weeks before. He fell down in the hall, just as he was returning from a walk, and died within two hours. He never spoke or recognised any one after his seizure."

"What has become of his old overcoat?" I asked.

"His old overcoat, Willie – what a question," replied Alice, evidently thinking that I was again drifting back into insensibility.

"Did he continue to wear it up to the day of his death?" I asked.

"No. Cold weather set in very early this last fall, and he was compelled to don his winter clothing earlier than usual. He had a new overcoat made within a fortnight before he died. He had it on at the time of his seizure. But why do you ask?"

"Was the new coat cut by a fashionable tailor, and had it a fur collar and cuffs?"

"It was cut at Stovel's, I think. It had a fur collar and cuffs."

"When did he begin to wear a wig?"

"About the same time that he began to wear his new overcoat. I wrote you a letter at the time, making merry over his youthful appearance and hinting – of course only in jest – that he was looking out for a young wife. But you surely did not receive my letter. You must have been on your way home before it was written."

"I left Melbourne on the 11th of October. The wig, I suppose, was buried with him?"

"Yes."

"And where is the overcoat?"

"In the wardrobe upstairs, in uncle's room."

"Come and show it to me."

I led the way upstairs, my cousin following. In the hall on the first floor we encountered my old friend Mrs. Daly, the housekeeper. She threw up her hands in surprise at seeing me. Our greeting was brief; I was too intent on solving the problem which had exercised my mind ever since receiving the letter at Boston, to pay much attention to anything else. Two words, however, explained to her where we were going, and at our request she accompanied us. We passed into my uncle's room. My cousin drew the key of the wardrobe from a drawer where it was kept, and unlocked the door. There hung the overcoat. A single glance was sufficient. It was the same.

The dazed sensation in my head began to make itself felt again. The atmosphere of the room seemed to oppress me, and closing the door of the wardrobe, I led the way down stairs again to the dining-room, followed by my cousin. Mrs. Daly had sense enough to perceive that we were discussing family matters, and retired to her own room.

I took my cousin's hand in mine, and asked:

"Will you tell me what you know of Mr. Marcus Weatherley?"

This was evidently another surprise for her. How could I have heard of Marcus Weatherley? She answered, however, without hesitation:

"I know very little of him. Uncle Richard and he had some dealings a few months since, and in that way he became a visitor here. After a while he began to call pretty often, but his visits suddenly ceased a short time before uncle's death. I need not affect any reserve with you. Uncle Richard thought he came after me, and gave him a hint that you had a prior claim. He never called afterwards. I am rather glad that he didn't, for there is something about him that I don't quite like. I am at a loss to say what the something is; but his manner always impressed me with the idea that he was not exactly what he seemed to be on the surface. Perhaps I misjudged him. Indeed, I think I must have done so, for he stands well with everybody, and is highly respected."

I looked at the clock on the mantel piece. It was ten minutes to seven. I rose from my seat.

"I will ask you to excuse me for an hour or two, Alice. I must find Johnny Grey."

"But you will not leave me, Willie, until you have given me some clue to your unexpected arrival, and to the strange questions you have been asking? Dinner is ready, and can be served at once. Pray don't go out again till you have dined."

She clung to my arm. It was evident that she considered me mad, and thought it probable that I might make away with myself. This I could not bear. As for eating any dinner, that was simply impossible in my then frame of mind, although I had not tasted food since leaving Rochester. I resolved to tell her all. I resumed my seat. She placed herself on a stool at my feet, and listened while I told her all that I have set down as happening to me subsequently to my last letter to her from Melbourne.

"And now, Alice, you know why I wish to see Johnny Grey."

She would have accompanied me, but I thought it better to prosecute my inquiries alone. I promised to return some time during the night, and tell her the result of my interview with Grey. That gentleman had married and become a householder on his own account during my absence in Australia. Alice knew his address, and gave me the number of his house, which was on Church Street. A few minutes' rapid walking brought me to his door. I had no great expectation of finding him at home, as I deemed it probable he had not returned from wherever he had been going when I met him; but I should be able to find out when he was expected, and would either wait or go in search of him. Fortune favored me for once, however; he had returned more than an hour before. I was ushered into the drawing-room, where I found him playing cribbage with his wife.

"Why, Willie," he exclaimed, advancing to welcome me, "this is kinder than I expected. I hardly looked for you before tomorrow. All the better; we have just been speaking of you. Ellen, this is my old friend, Willie Furlong, the returned convict, whose banishment you have so often heard me deplore."

After exchanging brief courtesies with Mrs. Grey, I turned to her husband.

"Johnny, did you notice anything remarkable about the old gentleman who was with me when we met on Yonge Street this evening?"

"Old gentleman? Who? There was no one with you when I met you."

"Think again. He and I were walking arm in arm, and you had passed us before you recognized me, and mentioned my name."

He looked hard in my face for a moment, and then said positively:

"You are wrong, Willie. You were certainly alone when we met. You were walking slowly, and I must have noticed if any one had been with you."

"It is you who are wrong," I retorted, almost sternly. "I was accompanied by an elderly gentleman, who wore a great coat with fur collar and cuffs, and we were conversing earnestly together when you passed us."

He hesitated an instant, and seemed to consider, but there was no shade of doubt on his face.

"Have it your own way, old boy," he said. "All I can say is, that I saw no one but yourself, and neither did Charley Leitch, who was with me. After parting from you we commented upon your evident abstraction, and the sombre expression of your countenance, which we attributed to your having only recently heard of the sudden death of your Uncle Richard. If any old gentleman had been with you we could not possibly have failed to notice him."

Without a single word by way of explanation or apology, I jumped from my seat, passed out into the hall, seized my hat, and left the house.

III

Out into the street I rushed like a madman, banging the door after me. I knew that Johnny would follow me for an explanation so I ran like lightning round the next corner, and thence down to Yonge Street. Then I dropped into a walk, regained my breath, and asked myself what I should do next.

Suddenly I bethought me of Dr. Marsden, an old friend of my uncle's. I hailed a passing cab, and drove to his house. The doctor was in his consultation-room, and alone.

Of course he was surprised to see me, and gave expression to some appropriate words of sympathy at my bereavement. "But how is it that I see you so soon?" he asked – "I understood that you were not expected for some months to come."

Then I began my story, which I related with great circumstantiality of detail, bringing it down to the moment of my arrival at his house. He listened with the closest attention, never interrupting me by a single exclamation until I had finished. Then he began to ask questions, some of which I thought strangely irrelevant.

"Have you enjoyed your usual good health during your residence abroad?"

"Never better in my life. I have not had a moment's illness since you last saw me."

"And how have you prospered in your business enterprises?"

"Reasonably well; but pray doctor, let us confine ourselves to the matter in hand. I have come for friendly, not professional, advice."

"All in good time, my boy," he calmly remarked. This was tantalizing. My strange narrative did not seem to have disturbed his serenity in the least degree.

"Did you have a pleasant passage?" he asked, after a brief pause. "The ocean, I believe, is generally rough at this time of year."

"I felt a little squeamish for a day or two after leaving Melbourne," I replied, "but I soon got over it, and it was not very bad even while it lasted. I am a tolerably good sailor."

"And you have had no special ground of anxiety of late? At least not until you received this wonderful letter" – he added, with a perceptible contraction of his lips, as though trying to repress a smile.

Then I saw what he was driving at.

"Doctor," I exclaimed, with some exasperation in my tone – "pray dismiss from your mind the idea that what I have told you is the result of diseased imagination. I am as sane as you are. The letter itself affords sufficient evidence that I am not quite such a fool as you take me for."

"My dear boy, I don't take you for a fool at all, although you are a little excited just at present. But I thought you said you returned the letter to – ahem – your uncle."

For a moment I had forgotten that important fact. But I was not altogether without evidence that I had not been the victim of a disordered brain. My friend Gridley could corroborate the receipt of the letter and its contents. My cousin could bear witness that I had displayed an acquaintance with facts which I would not have been likely to learn from any one but my uncle. I had referred to his wig and overcoat, and had mentioned to her the name of Mr. Marcus Weatherley – a name which I had never heard before in my life. I called Dr. Marsden's attention to these matters, and asked him to explain them if he could.

"I admit," said the doctor, "that I don't quite see my way to a satisfactory explanation just at present. But let us look the matter squarely in the face. During an acquaintance of nearly thirty years, I always found your uncle a truthful man, who was cautious enough to make no statements about his neighbours that he was not able to prove. Your informant, on the other hand, does not seem to have confined himself to facts. He made a charge of forgery against a gentleman whose moral and commercial integrity are unquestioned by all who know him. I know Marcus Weatherley pretty well, and am not disposed to pronounce him a forger and a scoundrel upon the unsupported evidence of a shadowy old gentleman who appears and disappears in the most mysterious manner, and who cannot be laid hold of and held responsible for his slanders in a court of law. And it is not true, as far as I know and believe, that Marcus Weatherley is embarrassed in his circumstances. Such confidence have I in his solvency and integrity that I would not be afraid to take up all his outstanding paper without asking a question. If you will make inquiry, you will find that my opinion is shared by all the bankers in the city. And I have no hesitation in saying that you will find no acceptances with your uncle's name to them, either in this market or elsewhere."

"That I will try to ascertain tomorrow," I replied. "Meanwhile, Dr. Marsden, will you oblige your old friend's nephew by writing to Mr. Junius Gridley, and asking him to acquaint you with the contents of the letter, and the circumstances under which I received it?"

"It seems an absurd thing to do," he said, "but I will if you like. What shall I say?" and he sat down at his desk to write the letter.

It was written in less than five minutes. It simply asked for the desired information, and requested an immediate reply. Below the doctor's signature I added a short postscript in these words: –

"My story about the letter and its contents is discredited. Pray answer fully, and at once. – W.F.F."

At my request the doctor accompanied me to the post office, on Toronto Street, and dropped the letter into the box with his own hands. I bade him good night, and repaired to the Rossin House. I did not feel like encountering Alice again until I could place myself in a more satisfactory light before her. I dispatched a messenger to her with a short note stating that I had not discovered anything important, and requesting her not to wait up for me. Then I engaged a room and went to bed.

But not to sleep. All night long I tossed about from one side of the bed to the other; and at daylight, feverish and unrefreshed, I strolled out. I returned in time for breakfast, but ate little or nothing. I longed for the arrival of ten o'clock, when the banks would open.

After breakfast I sat down in the reading-room of the hotel, and vainly tried to fix my attention upon the local columns of the morning's paper. I remember reading over several items time after time, without any comprehension of their meaning. After that I remember – nothing.

Nothing? All was blank for more than five weeks. When consciousness came back to me I found myself in bed in my own old room, in the house on Gerrard Street, and Alice and Dr. Marsden were standing by my bedside.

No need to tell how my hair had been removed, nor about the bags of ice that had been applied to my head. No need to linger over any details of the "pitiless fever that burned in my brain." No need, either, to linger over my progress back to convalescence, and thence to complete recovery. In a week from the time I have mentioned, I was permitted to sit up in bed, propped up by a mountain of pillows. My impatience would brook no further delay, and I was allowed to ask questions about what had happened in the interval which had elapsed since my over-wrought nerves gave way under the prolonged strain upon them. First, Junius Gridley's letter in reply to Dr. Marsden was placed in my hands. I have it still in my possession, and I transcribe the following copy from the original now lying before me: –

> BOSTON, Dec. 22nd, 1861.
> DR. MARSDEN:
>
> "In reply to your letter, which has just been received, I have to say that Mr. Furlong and myself became acquainted for the first time during our recent passage from Liverpool to Boston, in the *Persia,* which arrived here Monday last. Mr. Furlong accompanied me home, and remained until Tuesday morning, when I took him to see the Public Library, the State House, the Athenaeum, Faneuil Hall, and other points of interest. We casually dropped into the post-office, and he remarked upon the great number of letters there. At my instigation – made, of course, in jest – he applied at the General Delivery for letters for himself. He received one bearing the Toronto post-mark. He was naturally very much surprised at receiving it, and was not less so at its contents. After reading it he handed it to me, and I also read it carefully. I cannot recollect it word for word, but it professed to come from his affectionate uncle, Richard Yardington. It expressed pleasure at his coming home sooner than had been anticipated, and hinted in rather vague terms at some calamity. He referred to a lady called Alice, and stated that she had not been informed of Mr. Furlong's intended arrival. There was something too, about his presence at home being a recompense to her for recent grief which she had sustained. It also expressed the writer's intention to meet his nephew at the Toronto railway station upon his arrival, and stated that no telegram need be sent. This, as nearly as I can remember, was about all there was in the letter. Mr. Furlong professed to recognise the handwriting as his uncle's. It was a cramped hand, not easy to read, and the signature was so peculiarly formed that I was hardly able to decipher it. The peculiarly consisted of the extreme irregularity in the formation of the letters, no two of which were of equal size; and capitals were interspersed promiscuously, more especially throughout the surname.

"Mr. Furlong was much agitated by the contents of the letter, and was anxious for the arrival of the time of his departure. He left by the B. & A. train at 11.30. This is really all I know about the matter, and I have been anxiously expecting to hear from him ever since he left. I confess that I feel curious, and should be glad to hear from him – that is, of course, unless something is involved which it would be impertinent for a comparative stranger to pry into.

Yours, &c.,
"JUNIUS H. GRIDLEY."

So that my friend has completely corroborated my account, so far as the letter was concerned. My account, however, stood in no need of corroboration, as will presently appear.

When I was stricken down, Alice and Dr. Marsden were the only persons to whom I had communicated what my uncle had said to me during our walk from the station. They both maintained silence in the matter, except to each other. Between themselves, in the early days of my illness, they discussed it with a good deal of feeling on each side. Alice implicitly believed my story from first to last. She was wise enough to see that I had been made acquainted with matters that I could not possibly have learned through any ordinary channels of communication. In short, she was not so enamoured of professional jargon as to have lost her common sense. The doctor, however, with the mole-blindness of many of his tribe, refused to believe. Nothing of this kind had previously come within the range of his own experience, and it was therefore impossible. He accounted for it all upon the hypothesis of my impending fever. He is not the only physician who mistakes cause for effect, and *vice versa.*

During the second week of my prostration, Mr. Marcus Weatherley absconded. This event so totally unlooked for by those who had had dealings with him, at once brought his financial condition to light. It was found that he had been really insolvent for several months past. The day after his departure a number of his acceptances became due. These acceptances proved to be four in number, amounting to exactly forty-two thousand dollars. So that that part of my uncle's story was confirmed. One of the acceptances was payable in Montreal, and was for $2,283.76. The other three were payable at different banks in Toronto. These last had been drawn at sixty days, and each of them bore a signature presumed to be that of Richard Yardington. One of them was for $8,972.11; another was for $10,114.63; and the third and last was for $20,629.50. A short sum in simple addition will show us the aggregate of these three amounts –

$8,972 11
10,114 63

20,629 50
$39,716 24
which was the amount for which my uncle claimed that his name had been forged.

Within a week after these things came to light a letter addressed to the manager of one of the leading banking institutions of Toronto arrived from Mr. Marcus Weatherley. He wrote from New York, but stated that he should leave there within an hour from the time of posting his letter. He voluntarily admitted having forged the name of my uncle to three of the acceptances above referred to and entered into other details about his affairs, which, though interesting enough to his creditors at that time, would have no special interest to the public at the present day. The banks where the acceptances had been discounted were wise after the fact, and detected numerous little details wherein the forged signatures differed from the genuine signatures of my Uncle Richard. In each case they pocketed the loss and held their tongues, and I dare say they will not thank me for calling attention to the matter, even at this distance of time.

There is not much more to tell. Marcus Weatherley, the forger, met his fate within a few days after writing his letter from New York. He took passage at New Bedford, Massachusetts, in a sailing vessel called the *Petrel* bound for Havana. The *Petrel* sailed from port on the 12th of January, 1862, and went down in mid-ocean with all hands on the 23rd of the same month. She sank in full sight of the captain and crew of the *City of Baltimore* (Inman Line), but the hurricane prevailing was such that the latter were unable to render any assistance, or to save one of the ill-fated crew from the fury of the waves.

At an early stage in the story I mentioned that the only fictitious element should be the name of one of the characters introduced. The name is that of Marcus Weatherley himself. The person whom I have so designated really bore a different name – one that is still remembered by scores of people in Toronto. He has paid the penalty of his misdeeds, and I see nothing to be gained by perpetuating them in connection with his own proper name. In all other particulars the foregoing narrative is as true as a tolerably retentive memory has enabled me to record it.

I don't propose to attempt any psychological explanation of the events here recorded, for the very sufficient reason that only one explanation is possible. The weird letter and its contents, as has been seen, do not rest upon my testimony alone. With respect to my walk from the station with Uncle Richard, and the communication made by him to me, all the details are as real to my mind as any other incidents of my life. The only obvious deduction is, that I was made the recipient of a communication of the kind which the world is accustomed to regard as supernatural.

Mr. Owen's publishers have my full permission to appropriate this story in the next edition of his "Debatable Land between this World and the

Next." Should they do so, their readers will doubtless be favoured with an elaborate analysis of the facts, and with a pseudo-philosophic theory about spiritual communion with human beings. My wife, who is an enthusiastic student of electro-biology, is disposed to believe that Weatherley's mind, overweighted by the knowledge of his forgery, was in some occult manner, and unconsciously to himself, constrained to act upon my own senses. I prefer, however, simply to narrate the facts. I may or may not have my own theory about those facts. The reader is at perfect liberty to form one of his own if he so pleases. I may mention that Dr. Marsden professes to believe to the present day that my mind was disordered by the approach of the fever which eventually struck me down, and that all I have described was merely the result of what he, with delightful periphrasis, calls "an abnormal condition of the system, induced by causes too remote for specific diagnosis."

It will be observed that, whether I was under an hallucination or not, the information supposed to be derived from my uncle was strictly accurate in all its details. The fact that the disclosure subsequently became unnecessary through the confession of Weatherley does not seem to me to afford any argument for the hallucination theory. My uncle's communication was important at the time when it was given to me; and we have no reason for believing that "those who are gone before" are universally gifted with a knowledge of the future.

It was open to me to make the facts public as soon as they became known to me, and had I done so, Marcus Weatherley might have been arrested and punished for his crime. Had not my illness supervened, I think I should have made discoveries in the course of the day following my arrival in Toronto which would have led to his arrest.

Such speculations are profitless enough, but they have often formed the topic of discussion between my wife and myself. Gridley, too, whenever he pays us a visit, invariably revives the subject, which he long ago christened "The Gerrard Street Mystery," or, "The Mystery of the Union Station." He has urged me a hundred times over to publish the story; and now, after all these years, I follow his counsel, and adopt his nomenclature in the title.

"He saw Brown's revolver 'covering' him"
[Picture by A. Hencke from *The face and the mask* by Robert Barr. Photograph courtesy of Metropolitan Toronto Library.]

Robert BARR

(1850-1912)

A slippery customer

(*The face and the mask*. London: Hutchinson; 1894/NY: Stokes; 1895.)

Biographical information about the author will be found at the back of the book.

An absconding bank cashier with half a million dollars in embezzled funds, a beautiful heiress, a dashing hero, a distraught father, a thrilling ice-boat ride down Lake Ontario from Toronto to Burlington, all add up to excitement in this typical entertainment from Canada's premier purveyor of short stories.

A Slippery Customer

When John Armstrong stepped off the train at the Union Station, in Toronto, Canada, and walked outside, a small boy accosted him.

"Carry your valise up for you, sir?"

"No, thank you," said Mr Armstrong.

"Carry it up for ten cents, sir?"

"No."

"Take it up for five cents, sir?"

"Get out of my way, will you?"

The boy got out of the way, and John Armstrong carried the valise himself.

There was nearly half a million dollars in it, so Mr Armstrong thought it best to be his own porter.

* * * * *

In the bay window of one of the handsomest residences in Rochester, New York, sat Miss Alma Temple, waiting for her father to come home from the bank. Mr Horace Temple was one of the solid men of Rochester, and was president of the Temple National Bank. Although still early in December, the winter promised to be one of the most severe for many years, and the snow lay crisp and hard on the streets, but not enough for sleighing. It was too cold for snow, the weatherwise said. Suddenly Miss Alma drew back from the window with a quick flush on her face that certainly was not caused by the coming of her father. A dapper young man sprang lightly up the steps, and pressed the electric button at the door. When the young man entered the room a moment later Miss Alma was sitting demurely by the open fire. He advanced quickly toward her, and took both her outstretched hands in his. Then, furtively looking around the room, he greeted her still more affectionately, in a manner that the chronicler of these incidents is not bound to particularize. However, the fact may be mentioned that whatever resistance the young woman thought fit to offer was of the faintest and most futile kind, and so it will be understood, at the beginning, that these two young persons had a very good understanding with each other.

"You seem surprised to see me," he began.

"Well, Walter, I understood that you left last time with some energetically expressed resolutions never to darken our doors again."

"Well, you see, my dear, I am sometimes a little hasty; and, in fact, the weather is so dark nowadays, anyhow, that a little extra darkness does not amount to much, and so I thought I would take the risk of darkening them once more."

"But I also understood that my father made you promise, or that you promised voluntarily, not to see me again without his permission?"

"Not voluntarily. Far from it. Under compulsion, I assure you. But I didn't come to see you at all. That's where you are mistaken. The seeing you is merely an accident, which I have done my best to avoid. Fact! The girl said, `Won't you walk into the drawing-room', and naturally I did so. Never expected to find you here. I thought I saw a young lady at the window as I came up, but I got such a momentary glimpse that I might have been mistaken."

"Then I will leave you and not interrupt —"

"Not at all. Now I beg of you not to leave on my account, Alma. You know I would not put you to any trouble for the world."

"You are very kind, I am sure, Mr Brown."

"I am indeed, Miss Temple. All my friends admit that. But now that you are here — by the way, I came to see Mr Temple. Is he at home?"

"I am expecting him every moment."

"Oh, well, I'm disappointed; but I guess I will bear up for awhile — until he comes, you know."

"I thought your last interview with him was not so pleasant that you would soon seek another."

"The fact is, Alma, we both lost our tempers a bit, and no good ever comes of that. You can't conduct business in a heat, you know."

"Oh, then the asking of his daughter's hand was business — a mere business proposition, was it?"

"Well, I confess he put it that way — very strongly, too. Of course, with me there would have been pleasure mixed with it if he had — but he didn't. See here, Alma — tell me frankly (of course he talked with you about it) what objection he has to me anyhow."

"I suppose you consider yourself such a desirable young man that it astonishes you greatly that any person should have any possible objection to you?"

"Oh, come now, Alma; don't hit a fellow when he's down, you know. I don't suppose I have more conceit than the average young man; but then, on the other hand, I am not such a fool, despite appearances, as not to know that I am considered by some people as quite an eligible individual. I am not a pauper exactly, and your father knows that. I don't think I have many very bad qualities. I don't get drunk; I don't — oh, I could give quite a list of the things I don't do."

"You are certainly frank enough, my eligible young man. Still you must not forget that my papa is considered quite an eligible father-in-law, if it comes to that."

"Why, of course, I admit it. How could it be otherwise when he has such a charming daughter?"

"You know I don't mean that, Walter. You were speaking of wealth and so was I. Perhaps we had better change the subject."

"By the way, that reminds me of what I came to see you about. What do —"

"To see me? I thought you came to see my father."

"Oh, yes — certainly — I did come to see him, of course, but in case I saw you, I thought I would ask you for further particulars in the case. I have asked you the question but you have evaded the answer. You did not tell me why he is so prejudiced against me. Why did he receive me in such a gruff manner when I spoke to him about it? It is not a criminal act to ask a man for his daughter. It is not, I assure you. I looked up the law on the subject, and a young friend of mine, who is a barrister, says there is no statute in the case made and provided. The law of the State of New York does not recognize my action as against the peace and prosperity of the commonwealth. Well, he received me as if I had been caught robbing the bank. Now I propose to know what the objection is. I am going to hear —."

"Hush! Here is papa now."

Miss Alma quickly left the room, and met her father in the hall. Mr Brown stood with his hands in his pockets and his back to the fire. He heard the gruff voice of Mr Temple say, apparently in answer to some information given him by his daughter: "Is he? What does he want?"

There was a moment's pause, and then the same voice said: "Very well, I will see him in the library in a few minutes."

Somehow the courage of young Mr Brown sank as he heard the banker's voice, and the information he had made up his mind to demand with some hauteur, he thought he would ask, perhaps, in a milder manner.

Mr Brown brightened up as the door opened, but it was not Miss Alma who came in. The servant said to him: "Mr Temple is in the library, sir. Will you come this way!"

He followed and found the banker seated at his library table on which he had just placed some legal-looking papers bound together with a thick rubber band. It was evident that his work did not stop when he left the bank.

Young Brown noted that Mr Temple looked careworn and haggard, and that his manner was very different from what it had been on the occasion of the last interview.

"Good evening, Mr Brown. I am glad you called. I was on the point of writing to you, but the subject of our talk the other night was crowded from my mind by more important matters."

Young Mr Brown thought bitterly that there ought not to be matters more important to a father than his daughter's happiness, but he had the good sense not to say so.

"I spoke to you on that occasion with a — in a manner that was well, hardly excusable, and I wish to say that I am sorry I did so. What I had to state might have been stated with more regard for your feelings."

"Then may I hope, Mr Temple, that you have changed your mind with "

"No, sir. What I said then — that is, the substance of what I said, not the manner of saying it — I still adhere to."

"May I ask what objection you have to me?"

"Certainly. I have the same objection that I have to the majority of the society young men of the present day. If I make inquiries about you, what do I find? That you are a noted oarsman that you have no profession — that your honours at college consisted in being captain of the football team, and —"

"No, no, the baseball club."

"Same thing, I suppose."

"Quite different, I assure you, Mr Temple."

"Well, it is the same to me at any rate. Now, in my time young men had a harder row to hoe, and they hoed it. I am what they call a self-made man and probably I have a harsher opinion of the young men of the present day than I should have. But if I had a son I would endeavour to have him know how to do something, and then I would see that he did it."

"I am obliged to you for stating your objection, Mr Temple. I have taken my degree in Harvard law school, but I have never practised, because, as the little boy said, I didn't have to. Perhaps if some one had spoken to me as you have done I would have pitched in and gone to work. It is not too late yet. Will you give me a chance? The position of cashier in your bank, for instance?"

The effect of these apparently innocent words on Mr Temple was startling. He sprang to his feet and brought down his clenched fist on the table with a vehemence that made young Mr Brown jump. "What do you mean, sir?" he cried, sternly. "What do you mean by saying such a thing?"

"Why, I—I—I—mean—" stammered Brown, but he could get no further. He thought the old man had suddenly gone crazy.

He glared across the library table at Brown as if the next instant he would spring at his throat. Then the haggard look came into his face again, he passed his hand across his brow, and sank into his chair with a groan.

"My dear sir," said Brown, approaching him, "what is the matter? Is there anything I can —"

"Sit down, please," answered the banker, melancholy. "You will excuse me I hope, I am very much troubled. I did not intend to speak of it, but some explanation is due to you. A month from now, if you are the kind of man that most of your fellows are, you will not wish to marry my daughter. There is every chance that at that time the doors of my bank will be closed."

"You astonish me, sir. I thought —"

"Yes, and so every one thinks. I have seldom in my life trusted the wrong man, but this time I have done so, and the one mistake seems likely to obliterate all that I have succeeded in doing in a life of hard work."

"If I can be of any financial assistance I will be glad to help you."

"How much?"

"Well, I don't know — 50,000 dollars perhaps or —"

"I must have 250,000 dollars before the end of this month."

"Two hundred and fifty thousand!"

"Yes, sir. William L. Staples, the cashier of our bank is now in Canada with half a million of the bank funds. No one knows it but myself and one or two of the directors. It is generally supposed that he has gone to Washington on a vacation."

"But can't you put detectives on his track?"

"Certainly. Then the theft would be made public at once. The papers would be full of it. There might be a run on the bank, and we would have to close the doors the next day. To put the detectives on his track would merely mean bringing disaster on our own heads. Staples is quite safe, and he knows it. Thanks to an idiotic international arrangement he is as free from danger of arrest in Canada as you are here. It is impossible to extradite him for stealing."

"But I think there is a law against bringing stolen money into Canada."

"Perhaps there is. It would not help us at the present moment. We must compromise with him, if we can find him in time. Of course, even if the bank closed, we would pay everything when there was time to realize. But that is not the point. It would mean trouble and disaster, and would probably result in other failures all through one man's rascality."

"Then it all resolves itself to this. Staples must be found quietly and negotiated with. Mr Temple, let me undertake the finding of him, and the negotiating, also, if you will trust me."

"Do you know him?"

"Never saw him in my life."

"Here is his portrait. He is easily recognized from that. You couldn't mistake him. He is probably living at Montreal under an assumed name. He may have sailed for Europe. You will say nothing of this to anybody?"

"Certainly not. I will leave on to-night's train for Montreal, or on the first train that goes."

Young Mr Brown slipped the photograph into his pocket and shook hands with the banker. Somehow his confident, alert bearing inspired the old man with more hope than he would have cared to admit, for, as a general thing, he despised the average young man.

"How long can you hold out if this does not become public?"

"For a month at least; probably for two or three."

"Well, don't expect to hear from me too soon. I shall not risk writing. If there is anything to communicate, I will come myself."

"It is very good of you to take my trouble on your shoulders like this. I am very much obliged to you."

"I am not a philanthropist, Mr Temple," replied young Brown.

* * * * *

When young Mr Brown stepped off the train at the Union Station in Toronto, a small boy accosted him. "Carry your valise up for you, sir?"

"Certainly," said Brown, handing it over to him.

"How much do I owe you?" he asked at the lobby of the hotel.

"Twenty-five cents," said the boy promptly, and he got it.

Brown registered on the books of the hotel as John A. Walker, of Montreal.

* * * * *

Mr Walter Brown, of Rochester, was never more discouraged in his life than at the moment he wrote on the register the words, `John A. Walker, Montreal'. He had searched Montreal from one end to the other, but had found no trace of the man for whom he was looking. Yet strange to say, when he raised his eyes from the register they met the face of William L. Staples, ex-cashier. It was lucky for Brown that Staples was looking at the words he had written, and not at himself, or he would have noticed Brown's involuntary start of surprise, and flush of pleasure. It was also rather curious that Mr Brown had a dozen schemes in his mind for getting acquainted with Staples when he met him, and yet the first advance should be made by Staples himself.

"You are from Montreal," said Mr Staples, alias John Armstrong.

"That's my town," said Mr Brown.

"What sort of a place is it in winter? Pretty lively?"

"Oh, yes. Good deal of a winter city, Montreal is. How do you mean, business or sport?"

"Well, both. Generally where there's lots of business there's lots of fun."

"Yes, that's so," assented Brown. He did not wish to prolong the conversation. He had some plans to make, so he followed his luggage up to his room. I t was evident that he would have to act quickly. Staples was getting tired of Toronto.

Two days after, Brown had his plans completed. He met Staples one evening in the smoking-room of the hotel.

"Think of going to Montreal?" asked Brown.

"I did think of it. I don't know, though. Are you in business there?"

"Yes. If you go, I could give you some letters of introduction to a lot of fellows who would show you some sport, that is, if you care for snow-shoeing, toboganning, and the like of that."

"I never went in much for athletics," said Staples.

"I don't care much for exertion myself," answered Brown. "I come up here every winter for some ice-yachting. That's my idea of sport. I own one of the fastest ice-boats on the bay. Ever been out?"

"No, I haven't. I've seen them at it a good deal. Pretty cold work such weather as we've been having, isn't it?"

"I don't think so. Better come out with me to-morrow?"

"Well, I don't care if I do."

The next day and the next they spun around the bay on the ice-boat. Even Staples, who seemed to be tired of almost everything, liked the swiftness and exhilaration of the ice-boat.

One afternoon, Brown walked into the bar of the hotel, where he found Staples standing.

"See here, Armstrong," he cried, slapping that gentleman on the shoulder. "Are you in for a bit of sport? It's a nice moonlight night, and I'm going to take a spin down to Hamilton to meet some chaps, and we can come back on the ice-boat, or if you think it too late, you can stay over, and come back on the train."

"Hamilton? That's up the lake, isn't it?"

"Yes, just a nice run from here. Come along. I counted on you."

An hour later they were skimming along the frozen surface of the lake.

"Make yourself warm and snug," said Brown. "That's what the buffalo robes are for. I must steer, so I have to keep in the open. If I were you I'd wrap up in those robes and go to sleep. I'll wake you when we're there."

"All right," answered Staples. "That's not a bad idea."

"General George Washington!" said young Brown to himself. "This is too soft a snap altogether. I'm going to run him across the lake like a lamb. Before he opens his eyes we'll have skimmed across the frozen lake, and he'll find himself in the States again when he wakes up. The only thing now to avoid are the air-holes and ice-hills, and I'm all right."

He had been over the course before and knew pretty well what was ahead of him. The wind was blowing stiffly straight up the lake and the boat silently, and swifter than the fastest express, was flying from Canada and lessening the distance to the American shore.

"How are you getting along, Walker," cried Staples, rousing himself up.

"First rate," answered Brown. "We'll soon be there, Staples."

That unfortunate slip of the tongue almost cost young Mr Brown his life. He had been thinking of the man under his own name, and the name had come out unconsciously. He did not even notice it himself in time to prepare, and the next instant the thief flung himself upon him and jammed his head against the iron rod that guided the rudder, with such a force that the rudder stayed in its place and the boat flew along the ice without a swerve.

"You scoundrel!" roared the bank-robber. "That's your game, is it? By the gods, I'll teach you a lesson in the detective business."

Athlete as young Brown was, the suddenness of the attack, and the fact that Staples clutched both hands round his neck and had his knee on his breast, left him as powerless as an infant. Even then he did not realize what had caused the robber to guess his position.

"For God's sake, let me up!" gasped Brown. "We'll be into an air-hole and drowned in a moment."

"I'll risk it, you dog! till I've choked the breath out of your body."

Brown wriggled his head away from the rudder iron, hoping that the boat would slew around, but it kept its course. He realized that if he was to save his life he would have to act promptly. He seemed to feel his tongue swell in his parched mouth. His strength was gone and his throat was in an iron vice. He struck out wildly with his feet and one fortunate kick sent the rudder almost at right angles.

Instantly the boat flashed around into the wind. Even if a man is prepared for such a thing, it takes all his nerve and strength to keep him on an ice-boat. Staples was not prepared. He launched headfirst into space and slid for a long distance on the rough ice. Brown was also flung on the ice and lay for a moment gasping for breath. Then he gathered himself together, and slipping his hand under his coat, pulled out his revolver. He thought at first that Staples was shamming, but a closer examination of him showed that the fall on the ice had knocked him senseless.

There was only one thing that young Mr Brown was very anxious to know. He wanted to know where the money was. He had played the part of private detective well in Toronto, after the very best French style, and had searched the room of Staples in his absence, but he knew the money was not there nor in his valise. He knew equally well that the funds were in some safe deposit establishment in the city, but where he could not find out. He had intended to work on Staples' fears of imprisonment when once he had him safe on the other side of the line. But now that the man was insensible, he argued that it was a good time to find whether or not he had a record of the place of deposit in his pocket-book. He found no such book in his pockets. In searching, however, he heard the rustling of paper apparently in the lining of his coat. Then he noticed how thickly it was padded. The next moment he had it ripped open, and a glance showed him that it was lined with bonds. Both coat and vest were padded in this way — the vest being filled with Bank of England notes, so the chances were that Staples had meditated a tour in Europe. The robber evidently put no trust in Safe Deposits nor banks. Brown flung the thief over on his face, after having unbuttoned coat and vest, doubled back his arms and pulled off these garments. His own, Brown next discarded, and with some difficulty got them on the fallen man and then put on the clothes of Mammon.

"This is what I call rolling in wealth," said Brown to himself. He admitted that he felt decidely better after the change of clothing, cold as it was.

Buttoning his own garments on the prostrate man, Brown put a flask of liquor to his lips and speedily revived him. Staples sat on the ice in a dazed manner, and passed his hand across his brow. In the cold gleam of the moonlight he saw the shining barrel of Brown's revolver `covering' him.

"It's all up, Mr Staples. Get on board the ice-boat."

"Where are you going to take me to?"

"I'll let you go when we come to the coast if you tell me where the money is."

"You know you are guilty of the crime of kidnapping," said Mr Staples, apparently with the object of gaining time. "So you are in some danger of the law yourself."

"That is a question that can be discussed later on. You came voluntarily, don't forget that fact. Where's the money?"

"It is on deposit in the Bank of Commerce."

"Well, here's paper and a stylographic pen, if the ink isn't frozen — no, it's all right — write a cheque quickly for the amount, payable to bearer. Hurry up, or the ink will freeze."

There was a smile of satisfaction on the face of Staples as he wrote the cheque. "There," he said, with a counterfeited sigh. "That is the amount."

The cheque was for 480,000 dollars.

When they came under the shadow of the American coast, Brown ordered his passenger off. "You can easily reach land from here, and the walk will do you good. I'm going further up the lake."

When Staples was almost at the land he shouted through the clear night air: "Don't spend the money recklessly when you get it, Walker."

"I'll take care of it, Staples," shouted back young Brown.

* * * * *

Young Mr Brown sprang lightly up the steps of the Temple mansion, Rochester, and pressed the electric button.

"Has Mr Temple gone to the bank yet?" he asked the servant.

"No, sir; he is in the library."

"Thank you. Don't trouble. I know the way."

Mr Temple looked around as the young man entered, and, seeing who it was, sprang to his feet with a look of painful expectancy on his face.

"There's a little present for you," said Mr Brown, placing a package on the table. "Four hundred and seventy-eight thousand: Bank of England notes and United States bonds."

The old man grasped his hand, stove to speak, but said nothing.

* * * * *

People wondered why young Mr and Mrs Brown went to Toronto on their wedding tour in the depth of winter. It was so very unusual, don't you know.

"Gentlemen, may I present the prime minister of Canada, Sir John Macdonald."

Jack BATTEN
Michael BLISS

Sherlock Holmes great Canadian adventure

with Annotations and an Epilogue by **Trevor S. Raymond**

(*Weekend Magazine*, 28 May 1977/reprinted — as: "The adventure of the annexationist conspiracy" in *Colombo's book of Canada*, ed. by John Robert Colombo, Edmonton, Alberta: Hurtig; 1978 AND IN *Maddened by mystery; a casebook of Canadian detective fiction*, ed. by Michael Richardson, Toronto: Lester & Orpen Dennys; 1982/ revised and reprinted under original title, with annotations and an epilogue by Trevor Raymond, IN *Canadian Holmes*, vol.16:no.2, (Winter 1992)/this last version reprinted as a separate — Shelburne, Ontario: The Battered Silicon Dispatch Box; 1997).

Biographical information about the authors will be found at the back of the book.

It is 1891 and the dragon of Manifest Destiny threatens the Fair Maiden of the North, the Princess of the Snows. A St George is needed and The Father of His Country calls to the rescue none other than The Master himself, Mr Sherlock Holmes ... and yet another annexationist plot is foiled.

Sherlock Holmes and the adventure of the Annexationist Conspiracy

The story that follows relates the adventure in Canada in the early part of 1891 of the celebrated English detective, Mr. Sherlock Holmes, as it was recorded by his close associate, Dr. John Watson. That fact is remarkable enough, but what is more astounding is that the manuscript was only recently uncovered after almost a century of obscurity, by a young history scholar who was researching a book on the personal life of Sir John A. Macdonald. He happened across the manuscript, mysteriously filed in a sealed envelope marked "Patronage — Essex South" in box 429 of the Macdonald papers, apparently one of so many similar envelopes that previous researchers had not bothered to open it. Accompanying the manuscript was a letter addressed to Macdonald from Dr. Watson, dated April 21, 1891, in which Watson explained, inter alia, *that, "I intend to make no effort to publish this story of Holmes' service to yourself in February of this year inasmuch as I am sensitive to its great and potentially harmful political implications for you and for your country. However, as I have been in the custom of documenting Holmes's many adventures, I have done so in this case even if it is only for your eyes. Perhaps you will wish to preserve it among your papers for the eyes of future generations. After all, you above all others know that I am not putting too high a gloss on the matter to say that this document records the historic occasion when Sherlock Holmes saved Canada from annexation to the United States."*

When Sherlock Holmes invited me by messenger to go round to 221B Baker Street on the morning of January 22, 1891, I confess that I was perhaps not so sympathetic to the obvious agitation in which I found him as I might have been. My own heart and head were filled with my happy marriage, which had taken me from Baker Street almost two years earlier, and with my medical practice, which, if not flourishing was at least serving me well. The connection I had with Holmes and his startling feats of detection had fallen away in the previous year. Indeed, I could account for a mere three cases that I had recorded throughout all of 1890.[1] I experienced some guilt and regret that I was not able to share in more of Holmes's affairs, and yet, at the same time, my own were most deeply satisfying.

"My dear Watson, it's good of you to come," said Holmes as I entered the familiar quarters.

"How could I refuse an opportunity to pass a morning with you, Holmes?"

"It's not about Moriarty, you understand," he said quickly, giving me the sense that he was labouring to hold himself in check.

"Moriarty?" I felt genuine perplexity. I had never heard Holmes mention such a person, but more than puzzlement over the new name, I became chagrined at the look of Holmes, paler and thinner than ever and so obviously caught in some wrenching state of mind.

"There it is!" her cried, walking to and fro. "You have no knowledge of the man, nor has the rest of London, but for all that abysmal ignorance, Moriarty reigns as the perverted genius of crime throughout the city. A cunning, secretive phantom, Watson, a man as intellectually gifted as myself. I mean to have him before I rest my career!"

Holmes spoke these words in an outpouring of passion, and then as swiftly as the storm had risen, he affected a calm air and ceased his pacing.

"Put aside Moriarty, Watson," he said, offering me a smile of comfort. "It's quite another matter for which I wished your company on this fine morning."

"Yes?"

"A Canadian adventure."

"I never knew you to be concerned with the colonies, Holmes."

Nor am I now, except that this particular colony may yield me a respite from the cursed Moriarty business. I was approached only last evening by a letter from Sir Charles Tupper,[2] Her Majesty's High Commissioner from Canada, requesting an urgent appointment at 11 o'clock this morning. He hinted not at his business, but I surmise he supposes that I may be of assistance to the Canadian government in some secret capacity such as I have rendered to foreign governments in the past."

"May it not be a simple criminal matter, Holmes, a murder or lesser crime that their authorities are unable to cope with?"

"I think not, Watson. Canada is singularly backward in the occurrence of interesting crimes. There's but a single recent exception that comes to mind, the Birchall case of last year, about which you may have read.[3] But I think the case, sensationally as it was received in the international press, was the exception in Canada. I'm inclined to think that Tupper's business is governmental, and ... ha, this must be him."

A rap on the door from what I recognized as the hand of Mrs. Hudson, landlady at 221B Baker Street, followed on Holmes's last sentence, and in a moment the door was opened to reveal our visitor. Sir Charles Tupper, if this were he, wore long sideburns and full jowls, and possessed the demeanor of an aging, albeit not unappealing, bulldog.

"Mr. Sherlock Holmes," he barked.

"I am," said Holmes. "And I am now in the presence of Sir Charles Tupper, I presume. May I introduce you to my good friend, Dr. John Watson, with whom, if I am not mistaken, you share a profession."

"What?" said Tupper, taken aback but losing none of his aggressive nature. "It is true that I once practiced medicine, but that occurred a good quarter-century ago, before I abandoned it in favour of a political life. How did you know? I've not bruited my background about London."

"Those ancient scars on your hands, Sir Charles. Young students of medicine often inflict incisions on themselves during their attempts at surgery. Some students, as is the case with yourself, never lose the scars."

"I'd heard of your reputation for sagacity, Mr. Holmes," said Tupper, speaking in a level tone. "May I prevail upon you to put that quality at the service of my country?"

"Pray take a seat, Sir Charles. I shall be most happy to hear you out."

I could tell that Holmes was intrigued by the prospects that Tupper presented. Whether it was as an antidote to his concern over Moriarty or as a problem on its own merits I could not be certain. In any event, Holmes composed himself in his chair, eyes half-closed and fingertips pressed together, and prepared to listen.

"Allow me to read a cable I received yesterday," Tupper began. "It comes from my prime minister, Sir John A. Macdonald, and runs as follows. 'Immediate dissolution almost certain. Your presence during election contest in Maritime provinces essential to encourage our friends. Please come. Answer.' I may say, parenthetically, that I have cabled my intention to return by ship tomorrow.

"Sir John and I, Mr. Holmes, are the leaders of the Conservative party. We as much as created Canada in one Dominion in 1867 and I tell you with pride that we have held power for most years since that event to the people's great benefit. They have rewarded us with their trust at the last three general elections. But in this coming election, I judge, we shall have a more formidable task. There are rumblings of discontent from those who lack faith in Canada's destiny, and the Liberals who compose our opposition are led by a naive but politically attractive young Frenchman from Quebec named Laurier."[4]

"I confess, Sir Charles," Holmes interrupted, "that political affairs have only interested me when a criminal element has intruded, and that is not so often as the general public assumes."

"Is treason not a crime, Mr. Holmes?" Tupper snapped back. "Along with the cable I have just read to you, I received a second message from Sir John. It came through diplomatic channels and my oath of secrecy forbids me from revealing the exact contents, but I can advise you, Mr. Holmes, that your name lies among its contents. The long and the short of it is that Sir John requests your services. This fact, I should say, is in itself most remarkable since my leader is a man of long experience and great independence. However, his word to me is that certain underhanded individuals who mean to see the future of Canada betrayed are masking their intentions beneath the usual activities attendant upon a general election. We thought that the Grits[5] were disloyal and now we find that their machinations threaten the very continuity of the British Empire of which Canada is the fairest of our Queen's Dominions. That cannot be headed off through normal governmental action. Sir John indicates that the task requires someone, Mr. Holmes, of your self-sufficiency from the police and from politics."

"You need say no more," Holmes replied, eyes glinting with new life, singularly transformed from the man who had greeted me that morning. "I shall accompany you to Canada. Sir Charles, and I am certain that I may prevail upon Dr. Watson to join us. The sooner I vanish from London's streets, the better I shall like it. Tomorrow we sail."

Events moved swiftly in the ensuing 24 hours. I packed hurriedly, and joined Holmes and Sir Charles early on the morning of January 23 at Victoria Station for the train to Southampton. After a pleasant trip by rail, we boarded a medium-sized ship, the *Cedric*, which was bound for New York City. Canadian ports, I learned from Sir Charles, were beyond our capabilities since Montreal was isolated by the icing-over of the St. Lawrence River and since the suddenness of our departure rendered it too late to obtain bookings to Halifax.

As to myself, our destination became of little consequence for I was immediately overcome by *mal de mer*. The Atlantic pitched and rolled in ferocious winter upheaval, and I passed most of the voyage of seven days reclining in my cabin under woeful duress. Holmes, all this time, devoted his attentions to a fat bundle of newspapers, magazines and books which Sir Charles had procured for him before our departure, all of them from Canada or dealing with that country's social and political life.

"One question provokes me, Sir Charles," Holmes said on an afternoon near the end of our voyage when he and Tupper came to my cabin for tea. "Is your Sir John A. Macdonald a sober, reliable man?"

"I can assure you that he is a man changed from previous excesses," Tupper replied with his customary intent manner. "His wife, Lady Agnes.[6] keeps a solicitous eye on his imbibing habits. Nothing more than an evening glass of port. You need entertain no qualms on that score."

"You set me at ease, Sir Charles," said Holmes, nodding his satisfaction.

The *Cedric* docked in New York, and I had hardly time to regain my equilibrium when we boarded an American train and proceeded to race at feverish speed toward Canada through a wilderness which my imagination populated with a Red Indian behind every conifer. In less time than it takes to travel from London to Edinburgh, though the distance is far greater, we arrived in Montreal, a city that proved a highly agreeable treat. It combined the civilizing aspects of Europe with the outdoor exuberance which I associated with the new continent. Our hostelry, the Windsor,[7] opposite Dominion Square,[8] was as sumptuous as any that one might find in Mayfair, and the baronial homes along Dorchester Street,[9] though they tended to a certain bleakness in the architecture, matched the grandest homes of England. Montreal's winter recreations, however, struck me as singularly abandoned in a way that would be unique to any visiting Englishman. I witnessed tobogganing down lengthy and treacherous slides carved into the snow in the city's principal park, Mount Royal. I saw very combative curling matches on the ice of the St. Lawrence River. And on the grounds of a university which drew its name from a Scotsman named James McGill,[10] I beheld a sport called ice hockey played on sheets of ice by two teams of players, equipped with skate blades on their boots and curved sticks in their hands. It was a graceful if fierce sport and suggested to me a cold-weather version of football carried on at remarkable velocity.

On the afternoon of February 6, Tupper pressed us on to Ottawa, Canada's capital city, whither we proceeded by train. A carriage waited to hurry us directly to Earnscliffe, Sir John A. Macdonald's residence.[11] It lay about a mile from the city in a secluded district and, glimpsed in the gathering dark, it seemed a rambling Gothic edifice, as heavily gabled as any home I have ever seen. A maid showed us from the front door to a large and pleasant office which Holmes remarked was of more recent construction than the rest of the house. Tupper was confirming this to be true when a gentleman entered at the door behind us.

"Macdonald!" exclaimed Tupper with much warmth. "Old friend, how fine to be with you again." Tupper turned to Holmes and myself.

"Gentlemen, may I present the prime minister of Canada, Sir John Macdonald."

As Holmes and the Canadian leader greeted one another, I assessed Macdonald and was at first shocked by his obvious great age. The straggly white hair down the sides of his head, the bald dome and the bushy eyebrows of a startling paleness all emphasized advancing years, just as the bulbous nose spoke of many past hours at the whiskey bottle. And yet there was another quality about the man that a mere physical catalogue could not convey. In my adventures with Holmes, I have had occasion to enter the presence of many men who are accustomed to power. They are a particular and singularly impressive breed. Sir John was one of them.

"I tender apologies for my wife," Macdonald said as he directed us to chairs. "She has retired with a severe headache and is unable to greet you."

"I understand her weariness, Sir John," said Holmes. "It is no doubt exhausting to care for a daughter whose needs are so acute."

"That's most true, Mr. Holmes," answered Macdonald, fussing slightly. "I wonder that you know of the constant care dear Mary requires. But I expect Tupper told you of our burden."[12]

"Tupper mentioned nothing, Sir John. It is my own surmise from the tracks on your carpeting. They were undoubtedly left by a wheelchair but they are hardly deep enough to have been indented by a patient of substantial weight. A person comparatively young in years, I judge, and a female if the small bracelet dropped beside the track leading out of the door is a true sign."

"Our daughter Mary is 22, Mr. Holmes," said Macdonald, suddenly sagging in his chair, "but her mental and physical condition place her far behind others of her age."

Macdonald regained himself and offered us refreshments. All took port, and we settled again into our chairs.

"Tomorrow, gentlemen, I announce the dissolution of Parliament and send the country to the polls," began the prime minister. "I believe my friend Tupper has previously described to you the political struggle which we Conservatives face to maintain our government against the Liberals. Let me enlighten you, Mr. Holmes, as to another struggle that certain members in high standing of the Liberal party are inflicting upon loyal Canadians of every political stripe. Significant Liberal theorizers have long championed a doctrine called Commercial Union or, as they now disguise it, Unrestricted Reciprocity.

"Whatever the designation, its aim is to eliminate tariffs and other commercial barriers between our own land and the United States until the two countries arrive at a condition of entire free trade. That, Mr. Holmes, is to me and to all my clear-thinking countrymen merely a first step towards political union which would result in nothing less evil than the disappearance of Canada, but a tiny morsel, down the giant maw of the United States of America."

"Most threatening, Sir John", Holmes murmured in an abstracted voice. He was slumped in his chair and his eyes had assumed the half-hooded aspect which indicated to me his process of cerebration.

"Treacherous enough," continued Macdonald, his voice taking on an edge of steel that I hardly suspected a man of his age could retain. "But worse is at hand. I have information from reliable friends in Toronto, that Liberals of that city and Ontario, Sir Richard Cartwright[13] foremost in their number, are seeking to hasten the move to annexation. Young Laurier, I may say, is not a party to the plot. He has been gulled in his inexperience. But other and senior Grits are even now negotiating with agents of the American government to arrange Canada's leaving of the Empire and entering into the United States immediately following a Liberal victory, may God forbid, in the election I am on the verge of announcing."

A silence of profound eeriness followed these words. Tupper stared fixedly at the floor, Macdonald's shrewd eyes were upon Holmes, who was slowly straightening his long body in the chair to an erect posture.

"You were quite right to approach me, Sir John," said Holmes, breaking at last the quiet of the study.

"I require tangible proof of the plot, Mr. Holmes," said Macdonald, his voice almost at a hush. "I require documents or papers or other evidence that I may present to the Canadian people who will in their repugnance to annexation refute the Grits at the polls and vanquish the threat of betrayal that hangs over us. I am nearing the end of my life, Mr. Holmes. I was born a British subject, and I wish to die one."[14]

"And so you shall, Sir John," Holmes answered with that calm intensity I knew so well. "And so you shall, although I trust it will not be for many years to come."

"But Holmes, " I blurted, fearing that my friend had overstepped himself, "this matter is immense and much beyond your accustomed criminal investigation."

"No matter, my dear Watson," Holmes answered, as he rose from his chair and inserted his hands in the side pockets of his jacket. "The problems, whether civil or criminal, demand similar methods. Ratiocination, as ever."

"You offer me hope, Mr. Holmes," Macdonald said.

Holmes turned slowly on his heel. "Farrer, Sir John?" he queried in measured tones. "Am I barking up the right tree if I initiate inquires in his direction?"

"I congratulate you, Mr. Holmes," replied Macdonald, whose features registered surprise and pleasure in equal degree. "You are a quick student of our country's nuances."

"Farrer, Holmes?" I asked.

"Edward Farrer, Watson," Holmes said. "A Toronto journalist — and curiously peripatetic according to my readings of the Canadian papers.[15] His byline caught my eye here and there, from the *Mail* of Toronto in the latter years of the past decade and then, as of last summer, at the *Globe*, which, if I'm not erring, Sir John, is an organ of your political enemies."

"Scurrilously so, Mr. Holmes."

"Farrer's writings are clever," Holmes went on," and he makes few bones about his avowal of annexationism. That alone is not sufficient to arouse suspicion about his involvements, but I am intrigued by Farrer's American connections. In the G*lobe* of January 28, as you no doubt observed yourself, Sir John, he printed a personal interview with James Blaine, who is no less than the American secretary of state.[16] Most intimate associations for a Canadian journalist."

The remainder of the evening went by in discussion of Canadian personalities whose names conveyed no meaning to me but seemed familiar enough to Holmes. I found the talk wearying, especially after so much travel in recent days, and was content when, shortly on midnight, Sir John showed Holmes and me to rooms on the second floor of Earnscliffe with assurances that he would arrange transport for us to Toronto on the next day.

Accordingly we were off by train at an early hour, once more rushing through primitive wildernesses, and reaching Toronto in the evening. I registered a suite at a hotel recommended by Macdonald, the Queen's[17] on Front Street near Yonge. While I did so, Holmes unaccountably hung back on the perimeter of the lobby.

"I'll say *adieu*, Watson," Holmes muttered to me in a low voice.

"What?"

"Only for a necessary few days, my friend," said Holmes, glancing to either side and over his shoulder.

"Holmes, it's not this Moriarty hobgoblin?"

"I've not given Moriarty a thought since we boarded ship at Southampton," Holmes answered, drawing the collar of his cloak high around his ears. "No, if I'm to be of service to Sir John, I must act swiftly and surreptitiously. I'll be back with you in due course. Meantimes, amuse yourself.'

And so I did, a pleasure that was made the easier by the genial hospitality of Torontonians. Entire strangers, apparently glad of English company, hailed me almost hourly in the lobby of the Queen's and insisted on my joining them for meals and drink. Though the food was well prepared and generous in the extreme, a simple tea providing enough provender for a week and every luncheon and supper being followed by a courtesy cigar, I found my new companions, gentlemen of money and quality as they were, to possess uniformly shabby table manners.

Toronto, I concluded, was a city of conundrums. On my rambles about the precisely laid-out streets, the large number of churches convinced me that the citizens must be a pious lot until I noted that the places of worship were rivaled in quantity only by places of drink. And these many saloons appeared to manufacture drunkenness, disgorging inebriated fellows into the streets at all hours.

Then, too, it struck me as paradoxical that the agencies for selling magazines were rife with journals from the very country which Canada, according to Macdonald, was intent on rejecting. I found *Harper's,* the *Atlantic*, *Scribner's Monthly* and others, all of United States origin, but only a few local magazines, the liveliest a journal called *Saturday Night*.[18]

I ignored these puzzles and concentrated on visiting the sights of the city, the cavernous Victoria Skating Rink on Huron Street,[19] the hotel maintained on Toronto Island by a retired champion of sculling and most entertaining host named Ned Hanlan,[20] the munificently stocked bazaar store of Mr. Timothy Eaton[21] and the Grand Opera House on Adelaide Street[22] where I dozed through a performance of the local Philharmonic Society. And one evening I dined at the new home of Mr. George Gooderham, a leading distiller,[23] at the corner of St. George and Bloor Streets on the northern reaches of the city, a handsome and ingenious mansion that included among its equipages, a bathtub mounted on railway tracks that wound through much of the second floor.

It was on the late night of my return from the Gooderham residence that I let myself into our rooms at the Queen's and discovered a strange gentleman dressed in white sitting and languidly smoking a cheroot in the sitting room of the suite.

"Sir!" I roared, "As I have committed no error in entering the correct rooms, I must advise you that you are presently in the wrong ones!"

"Ah beg yah pardon, Doctah John Watson," the stranger replied, making no effort to arise. "Ah intended no offense."

"You have the advantage of me, sir," I said, experiencing resentment that this curious though not disagreeable man had availed himself of my name. He was clearly not a Canadian, an American perhaps, since, quite apart from his foreign accent, his drooping white mustaches, long hair of the same shade, and his clothes reminded me of photographs of United States citizens who are indigenous to states south of the Mason-Dixon

Line. I turned from him, intending to summon the manager of the Queen's.

"My dear Watson," said a familiar voice, "will you not condescend to greet me?"

I whirled around in fresh surprise. The southern gentleman had discarded his cheroot and was peeling the mustaches from his upper lip and lifting a white wig from his head.

"Drastic steps have been called for, Watson," he said, laughing. "Not to the exclusion of disguise."

"I trust this marks the end of it."

"Not quite, Watson. Take up the pen on the desk over there, would you, and jot down a message for cabling as I dictate."

Very well, Holmes," I said, moving to follow his instructions.

"These are the words. 'Document on presses in yellow paper at Hunter Rose printing establishment, this city,[24] of greatest interest.' Signed, 'Holmes.' That's sufficient."

"To whom do I address it, Holmes?"

"Sir John A. Macdonald. Earnscilffe. Ottawa."

"Macdonald!"

Yes, Watson," Holmes said, looking merrier than I had seen him in some weeks. "Arrange for the cable this instant, and I promise you that tomorrow we'll put conspiracy behind us for a few days and enjoy the sights of this estimable colony."

I recognized that Holmes had no intention of divulging his recent whereabouts, and I acquiesced in the plans for tourism. on the next day we journeyed westward to Hamilton, a city of noble dimensions whose most impressive architecture was contained in the asylum for lunatics at the summit of its mountain.[25] Niagara Falls lay several score miles beyond, and, when we attained it, I complained mildly that there was less water than I had been led to expect. Holmes, to the contrary, was deeply moved. "Just as I inferred, Watson," he muttered, "just as I inferred."

Our itinerary included Woodstock, the village in which had taken place the Birchall affair, Canada's single murder of international repute as Holmes had told me. We visited various geographical points throughout the village which were, I gathered, connected with the crime, and it was when we were musing about the swamp where the victim's body had been uncovered that a policeman hailed us.

"Is it truly you, Mr. Sherlock Holmes?" asked the officer in awe.

When Holmes confirmed that he was indeed himself, the officer proffered lavish welcome and particularly extended gratitude for what he termed Holmes's "assistance in the matter of the spurious Lord Somerset."[26]

"Good heavens, Holmes!" I exclaimed. "You played a role in the Birchall case?"

"Only by cable, Watson," he replied enigmatically.

We returned to Toronto on the morning of Tuesday, February 17, and over an early dinner at the Queen's, Holmes announced our arrangements for the evening.

"Watson, I promise you a drama at the Academy of Music building,"[27] he said.

"And the principal performer in this piece of theatre?"

"Sir John A. Macdonald."

We made our way on foot through cold and snowy streets to the nearby academy and discovered outside the auditorium a jostling crush of men eager to gain admittance[28].

The interior of the academy was lit by flaring jets and was filled with an air of buoyant expectancy. A small brass band in the orchestra pit favoured the crowd with rousing anthems and march tunes until a group of distinguished gentlemen, nodding and waving to the audience, slowly filed to a row of chairs on the platform. Just as I recognized Macdonald among their number, the band crashed into "For He's a Jolly Good Fellow" and the full hall joined in chorus after chorus while Macdonald smiled his acknowledgments. When at last some semblance of quiet fell on the crowd, our former companion, Sir Charles Tupper, stepped forward to introduce Sir John with great gusto.

Many of the specifics of the early passages of Macdonald's address were, I'm bound to say, lost on me. But there was no mistaking the gist, nay the core, of his remarks. They concerned loyalty to Canada, a quality that Macdonald proclaimed was peculiar to his Conservatives and alien to the other party, the Liberals.

"There is," Macdonald trumpeted in a most loud and clear voice, "a deliberate conspiracy in which some of the leadesr of the Opposition are more or less compromised. I say there is a deliberate conspiracy by force, by fraud or by both to force Canada into the American union!"

This charge excited fierce rumblings in the crowd. Three or four men, apparently Liberals, grew unruly, and at least two bouts of fisticuffs erupted.

"Politics," Holmes remarked to me *sotto voce*, "is Canada's leading participatory sport."

On the platform, meanwhile, Macdonald had removed a sheaf of yellow papers from the inside pocket of his jacket and was displaying them high above his head. The document, he cried, came into his hands by secret and fortuitous means. It was written by the traitorous journalist of Liberal persuasion, Mr. Edward Farrer, with Sir Richard Cartwright, the Toronto

Grit, behind him, and it constituted a manifesto addressed to certain United States politicians instructing them in the most expeditious strategy by which America might absorb its Canadian neighbour. It outlined a program, Macdonald verily shouted, of betrayal.

He began to read from the yellow papers, the early sections of which were, once again, wholly Greek to me, matters to do with the interfering by the United States with a Canadian railway route to a place called Sault Ste. Marie, the arranging for the withdrawal of Britain's support of Canada and other similar details. All of these, contained in the words of Farrer as Sir John read them to the hushed audience, plainly represented steps in a master plan for the ultimate annexation of Canada by the United States.

"'They would secure the end desired,'" Macdonald read from the yellow sheets with quivered in his hand, "'without leaving the United States open to the charge of being animated by hatred of Canada on which Sir John Macdonald trades. Whatever course the United States may see fit to adopt, it is plain that Sir John's disappearance from the stage is the signal for a move toward annexation!'"

At this, thc floor of the academy broke into such a frenzy as I have never before experienced in a large gathering, the pounding of feet, the hooting of voices, whistling, cries and tumult.

Macdonald read on, his voice rising to a crescendo. "'The enormous debt of the Dominion, the virtual bankruptcy of all the provinces except Ontario, the pressure of the American tariff upon trade and industry, and the incurable issue of race have already prepared the minds of most intelligent Canadians for the destiny that awaits them. And a leader will be forthcoming when that hour arrives!'"

Macdonald put aside the yellow pamphlet, stared into the heart of the crowd and cried, "Who is to be that leader?"

The crowd roared as in a single voice, "Sir Richard Cartwright!"

"Infamy!" Macdonald thundered, and once again the academy veered to the precipices of riot.

"I should think," Holmes said into my ear, "that Sir John is set on the desired path."

"These fellows are united enough, Holmes!" I shouted back. The words were no sooner out when the auditorium, led by the platform party, broke into song, the words of which came to my ears as "We will hang Ned Farrer on a sour apple tree!!"

Holmes and I pushed our way from the stormy mob and made course for the Queen's. En route, we passed close by a building that was surrounded by several dozens of Toronto's constabulary.

"What do you suppose the police are seeking in that place, Holmes?" I asked.

"On the contrary, Watson," Holmes replied in a cool voice. "I rather think their task is the reverse — to prevent outsiders from entering the building."

"What might it house?"

"A newspaper, Watson. The *Globe*."

"By jove, Holmes, isn't that Farrer's journal?"

"Quite so, Watson."[29]

Abruptly on the following morning, Holmes insisted that his work was completed in North America and that, in any event, he could no longer put off his confrontation with the demon Moriarty in London. We packed in a few hours and boarded a train that took us on three days' journey across Canada's eastern limits to the port of Halifax, where we engaged passage on a large, handsome and sturdy ship called the *Lucania*. The ocean, to my not inconsiderable relief, had assumed a placid mood. I passed each afternoon in the ship's lounge with beverage and reading matter, and it was on the third day at sea when, in the lounge, I tossed aside my copy of *The Times*, and fell into a brown study.

"You have a point, Watson," Holmes' voice broke into my musings. "It's time I resolved for you the question of my disappearance in Toronto."

"Quite right!" I exclaimed, suddenly realizing that he had gone straight to the bottom of my inmost thoughts.

He settled himself into the chair opposite mine. "Let me ease your puzzlement now, though I might warn you that, at base, the Canadian case called for little more than some nocturnal excursions on my part.

Holmes busied himself for a moment with filling and lighting his pipe while I waited in some anticipation.

"Well, Watson, "Holmes went on, "I should begin by relating that my destination on leaving you after arrival at the Queen's Hotel was the building of the *Globe* newspaper. Edward Farrer was of course the quarry. You'll recall that I'd early determined on the fellow as my starting point in the affair, and I loitered outside his newspaper until he emerged late in the evening. I recognized Farrer from his photographs in various journals and followed him to his flat off Spadina Avenue. I engaged rooms myself with a window that gave on the entrance to Farrer's residence and took up observation. Tedious work, Watson, but fruitful. His first visitor shortly after noon on the next day was a gentleman whose name you'll recognize as much bandied in the election contest, Sir Richard Cartwright, the senior Liberal. Not long after his departure, two more gentlemen called whom I discerned to be American."

"American, Holmes?" I broke in. "How could you tell?"

"There is a difference, Watson. A pair of sentences from a book by one of our own English journalists, J.E. Ritchie, had struck me, a book recounting the author's travels about North America.[30] 'Directly you pass the border you see the difference. There is an astonishing contrast between the healthy Canadians and the lean and yellow Yankees.' I don't wholly subscribe to Ritchie's interpretation, Watson,. Lean perhaps the Americans are, and possessed of a looseness in their gait and an air of brashness that Canadians, if they have it, are at pains to conceal.

"In any event, the juxtaposition of Cartwright and the Americans at Farrer's flat set me on a course of action. I abandoned my observation post and accompanied the Americans at a discreet distance to their hotel, the Walker House[31], where I used a mild subterfuge to obtain the names of the two men. One was of significance — Mr. Benjamin Butterworth, a member of the American Congress, in Washington and a leading exponent of the annexation cause."[32]

"A wonderful discovery, Holmes!" I exclaimed involuntarily.

"Quite so, Watson. I satisfied myself that Mr. Butterworth and his companion were leaving Toronto directly, and then retired to a clothing shop and another that specialized in wigs and other adornments, after which I spent some hours in my new rooms cloaking myself in the guise of a gentleman of the American south."

"Most effective it was, too, Holmes."

"I waited until Farrer was at home that evening and immediately presented myself at his door as Colonel Cletis Dawkins from North Carolina and an associate of Congressman Butterworth. Farrer confessed that my name was unknown to him, but he received me warmly nevertheless. He's an Irishman, Watson, and roguish, not at all an unappealing man but one deeply in love with intrigue for its own sake. At one period earlier in his journalistic career, I happen to know, he edited a town's two newspapers of opposite politics, thus passing his working days in violent controversy against himself. Given such propensities, it wasn't difficult to persuade him that I, as Colonel Dawkins, required him to enter into a clandestine mission. I was present, I said, under circumstances of secrecy that must not be mentioned beyond Farre"s walls. I told him that I spoke for the highest councils in Washington and that I and they required a reasoned setting-out of the means by which to obtain annexation which would persuade our colleagues in the American capital who were, unlike us, either indifferent to or unaware of the annexation cause. I told him we desired a clear and positive program addressed to an American audience and I flattered him that he was uniquely qualified to prepare such a delicate document."

"Holmes," I broke in, "am I being offensive if I protest that you were adopting the unaccustomed role of *agent provocateur* in this matter?"

"Drastic steps, Watson. I suspected from the beginning, as you may have noted, that they might be necessary in the present case as they have been in the past. In any event, Farrer fell in with the notion of the pamphlet. I hinted that I myself held extensive tobacco interests in my home state and looked forward to expanding into profitable Canadian markets on the successful conclusion of annexation. That information deepened for Farrer his conception of me as a fellow conspirator. He promised that several score pamphlets would be in readiness by February 16, that Hunter Rose was a reliable and close-mouthed printer and that, rather as a personal quirk, he would have the job done upon sheets of paper coloured yellow. I swore him once again to secrecy, bade Farrer farewell, and the remainder of the tale you, Watson, were a witness to."

"But Holmes, won't Farrer now come forward and reveal that the pamphlet was written by him as a result of misrepresentation?"

"Hardly, Watson, since in so doing he would also reveal that he had been in communication with an American, or someone he willingly took to be an American. He would thereby play further into Macdonald's hands."[33]

"Quite."

I was satisfied, and the rest of the voyage passed for me in blithe contentment. Such was not the case for Holmes who paced the decks incessantly and devoted long hours to sitting in deep contemplation. When our boat train reached Victoria Station, he vanished with scarcely a word, on his way, I felt certain, to confront Moriarty, an adventure I would no doubt be made cognizant of in due course.

As for myself, I became immersed once again in home and practice. Not long after my return, however, the Canadian affair returned to my attention when I chanced upon a report in *The Times* of the election in the Dominion on March 5. Sir John's Conservatives had held power, winning 123 seats to 92 for Laurier's liberals, the same margin of victory as that attained in the previous election of 1887.

Ontario, according to the account, had ensured the victory, since its voters had almost unanimously subscribed to Sir John's warnings against the Liberal annexationist conspiracy. The correspondent for *The Times* in Canada opined that the Farrer pamphlet had played the key role in persuading the voters to turn back the Liberals. "But," he reported, "the means by which this mysterious document fell so conveniently into the prime minister's hands are not known."

EPILOGUE

There can be no doubt of the import of the contribution made by Sherlock Holmes in the vital election campaign of 1891. Macdonald himself later wrote that the Farrer pamphlet, "enabled us to raise the loyalty cry, which had considerable effect." Macdonald won his Kingston seat with the highest majority of his career and had the pleasure of seeing his son, Hugh John, elected to Parliament as well. Queen Victoria expressed her "great gratification" at the results. But the old Chieftain's triumph was short-lived. He had collapsed from exhaustion while campaigning in Napanee, Ontario, shortly before the election. Too ill to be moved, he lay for days in his private railway car, "The Jamaica", before being taken to Earnscliffe on 4 March, the day before voters went to the polls. Here, he rested for several weeks. When Parliament met on 29 April, he seemed his cheerful old self, but he suffered a stroke a month later. And then another, which took his power of speech. The Queen was informed by cable. The front pages of newspapers carried the simple headline, "He is dying". Donald Swainson writes:

> *For many days he lingered between life and death. Canadians knew that the end was near, and the country seemed to hold its breath while the government almost ceased to function. Political battle was postponed. Street cars near Earnscliffe stopped ringing their bells, and on the Ottawa River steamers slowed their engines in order to give Sir John the quiet he needed.*

John A. Macdonald died at 10:15 on the evening of Saturday, 6 June. By 10:30, citizens of Toronto were in the streets talking about him. Perhaps Meyers, Toronto, the bootmaker from whom Henry Baskerville bought a pair of boots before returning to England three years earlier[34],was among them, but even if Meyers had stayed indoors he would have heard the bells. At 10:45, the bells of St. Lawrence Hall and all the fire halls began to toll, and they tolled for a solid hour. On Monday, the Globe, which had vilified Macdonald so often, published one of the most glowing tributes in a week of eulogies; it was written by John Willison.

In Ottawa, Sir John's body lay in state in the Senate, and was taken after the funeral service by rail to Kingston, where 10,000 people were waiting late at night for the black-draped train. John A. Macdonald had written, "I desire that I shall be buried in the Kingston cemetery near the grave of my mother, as I promised her that I should be there buried." He was.

Notes

1 Watson is likely referring to "Wisteria Lodge", which took place according to William S. Baring-Gould, in March, 1890, to "Silver Blaze" (Sept. 1890), and to ""The Beryl Coronet" (Dec. 1890).

2 Charles Tupper (1821-1915) was born in Nova Scotia, where he began practicing medicine at the age of 22, having earned his degree in medicine from the University of Edinburgh, where Conan Doyle would later earn his. Tupper entered politics in 1855, eventually became premier of Nova Scotia and an advocate of Maritime union before becoming a tireless campaigner for the larger Canadian confederation. He served in a variety of cabinet positions under Macdonald, was knighted in 1879, and from 1883 until 1896 was High Commissioner of Canada in London, except for a period 1887-1888 when he returned to serve as Macdonald's minister of finance. In May, 1896, he returned to Canada to become Canada's sixth Prime Minister, but held that office for less than three months. On 11 July, 1896, Wilfrid Laurier's Liberals ended 18 years of Conservative government.

3 Reginald J. Birchall (1866-1890) was a confidence man who came to Canada in 1889 under the assumed name Lord Somerset, after cashing a number of bad cheques in London. He lured two Englishmen (unknown to each other) into a partnership with him to buy a farm near Woodstock, Ontario. Each of the men brought £500 for the venture; Birhchall's plan was to kill them and take their money. On 17 February, he shot one to death in a swamp; local authorities cabled Toronto for help when the unidentified body was found, and the provincial Detective John Wilson Murray was sent to investigate. Birchall was subsequently arrested, and, as Holmes notes, his murder trial attracted considerable attention in Europe and the United States, because of his background as an Oxford-educated English gentleman and the son of a clergyman. Reporters from every major newspaper in North America covered his trial and the Toronto *Globe* devoted its entire front page to it for eight consecutive days in September, 1990. This is but one of the cases investigated and solved by Murray, who is known as "The Great Canadian Detective"; his autobiography, published in Britain in 1904 were not published in Canada until 1977, following a popular television series very loosely based upon it. (*Memoirs of a Great Canadian Detective*. Toronto: Collins, 1977) A short biography for young readers, *John Wilson Murray*, by Bruce McDougall, was published in 1980.

4 Wilfrid Laurier (1841-1919) was chosen leader of the Liberal party in 1887 and remained Liberal leader for thirty-two years. In 1896, he became the first French-Canadian to be elected Prime Minister of Canada, and served as Prime Minister until his party's defeat in 1911. In 1897, at Queen Victoria's Jubilee celebrations, he was knighted.

5 Grits are members of the Liberal Party. The term was coined in 1849 by Toronto politician David Christie: "We want only men who are Clear Grit," he wrote. John Robert Colombo explains, "The noun 'grit' implies something firm, the adjective 'clear' something positive and unspotted." George Brown used the expression in a *Globe* editorial in December, 1849. Although the term has never become as widely used as *Tories* for Conservatives, it still appears from time to time. Christina McCall Newman's portrait of the Liberal Party, published in 1982, was titled simply *Grits;* eleven months before the 1957 Diefenbaker landslide, Blair Fraser described the declining Liberal fortunes as a *Grittererdämmerung*.

6 Susan Agnes Bernard married John A. Macdonald in London, in 1867, when she was 32. Raised in Jamaica, where her father was a member of the Privy Council, she emigrated to Canada West in the mid 1850s; her brother was a senior official in the Attorney-

General's office and for a time shared bachelors quarters with John A. Despite this, Macdonald saw little of Susan Agnes, and it was a chance encounter on Bond Street in London in 1866 that led to their courtship and marriage. In 1891 she was made Baroness Macdonald of Earnscliffe by Queen Victoria, but she later regretted accepting this title because the standard of dress and entertainment expected of a peer strained her limited budget. She died in England in 1920 at the age of 84.

7 The Windsor, which a 1987 Montreal *Gazette* headline called "the palace of Canada" was opened on St. Andrew's night, 1878, by Her Royal Highness the Princess Louise, a daughter of Queen Victoria. When it was built on Dorchester Street West, that part of the city was remote from the business and social centre of Montreal, a situation that changed a decade later with the construction by the CPR of Windsor Station. Over the years, presidents and monarchs stayed at the Windsor, and it was in a speech there that Mark Twain made his oft-quoted statement: "This is the first time I was ever in a city where you couldn't throw a brick without breaking a church window ." The Windsor was closed in 1981, and its treasured possessions were sold off a year later. Most of the old hotel was demolished, and the 45 story Dorchester Commerce Building has been built on the site. The grand old hotel is not completely gone, however. The ballrooms and a promenade known as Peacock Alley were saved and have been restored.

8 Dominion Square, home to the Boer War Memorial, and to statues of Robbie Burns and Wilfrid Laurier, was renamed Dorchester Square on 1 January, 1988. It can be no mere coincidence that, shortly after the discovery revealed here that Holmes was a guest at the Windsor in 1891, Sherlock's, a new restaurant honouring him, opened on the north side of the square in 1992.

9 After the death of René Lévesque, the eastern section of Dorchester was renamed in his honour; that part which goes through Westmount retains the Dorchester name, honouring Guy Carleton, 1st Baron Dorchester, who was twice governor of Quebec: 1768-78 and 1785-95.

10 James McGill (1744-1813) began his fortune in the fur trade, and later turned to land speculation. When he died, reputedly Montreal's richest citizen, he bequeathed 46 acres of land in downtown Montreal and £10 000 to establish the university which bears his name.

11 Earnscliffe, Old English for 'eagle's cliff', was built in 1855-1857 on a great cliff overlooking the Ottawa River and the panorama of the Laurentians. Macdonald rented this residence 1870-1871, and in 1883 he purchased it for $10 040. (The extra $40. was for a small piece of land at the waterfront, to better ensure privacy.) He lived there for the rest of his life. After his death, Lady Macdonald abandoned her claim under Sir John's will to be a tenant at Earnscliffe for life, and the house was rented to various militia officers before being sold by Sir John's executors for $15 000. The house was up for sale again in 1930, and was purchased by the British government for $90 000. Since then it has been the residence of the British High Commissioner to Canada. British High Commissioner Sir Alan Urwick was quoted in the Ottawa *Citizen* in 1989: "There is no chance whatsoever that the National Capital Commission can get this property. We have occupied this place for 60 years and have no intention of moving now. The Canadian government should be thanking us for having bought this place years ago. For if we had not done so, this would now be the site of a large condominium project." Although it was declared a National Historic Site in 1961, the security fences and guards today make what should be one of Canada's most important museums a virtually inaccessible foreign-owned property.

12 Surely no document in the National Archives is more poignant that Lady Macdonald's diary entry for May 1, 1869, the day she learned that their daughter Mary had been born

with hydrocephalus. The Macdonalds resisted pressure to put her in an institution, and raised her themselves. Mary Macdonald achieved a surprising level of competence and even learned to type (although she could never write), but lived her life in a wheelchair. Sir John spent time with her every day before dinner, shopped personally for her toys and books, and when he was away he wrote to her regularly. Mary Macdonald died in England in February, 1933, in her sixty-fourth year.

13 Sir Richard John Cartwright (1835-1912) was a member of Parliament from 1863 - 1904, after which he became a Senator. He began as a Conservative, but broke with Macdonald in 1869, and sat as an Independent until he joined the Liberals in 1873. At the time of Sherlock Holmes's visit to Toronto, Cartwright was the effective leader of the Ontario wing of the Liberal Party, and led the faction within the party that wanted free trade with the United States. In his memoirs, published in 1912, he said of Sir John: "Had he been a much worse man he would have done Canada much less harm."

14 Macdonald used variations of this line many times. The Montreal *Gazette* quoted him expressing this sentiment in 1875, and a similar line appears in the *House of Commons Debates* in 1882. It became associated with him and was used often in the election of 1891. On February 7, 1891, the day after his interview with Sherlock Holmes and Dr. Watson at Earnscliffe, Macdonald said in the House of Commons in his last spech before he dissolved Parliament: "As for myself, my course is clear. A British subject I was born—a British subject I will die." Certainly this would have been popular in Toronto; more than 90% of the city's 180,000 people were of British ancestry.

15 Edward Farrer (c. 1850-1916) had a long journalistic career in Canada and the United States. John A's son, Hugh John, wrote to his father shortly after moving to Winnipeg in 1883, and told him how unpopular the Winnipeg *Times*, then edited by Farrer, was with Manitoba Tories: "some of our strongest friends are thinking of giving it up and taking the Free Press," he wrote. Farrer later edited the Toronto *Daily Mail*, and under his editorship, the paper attacked Macdonald and prompted an outbreak of anti-French, anti-Catholic feeling following the Northwest Rebellion. In 1890, Farrer became editor of the Liberal *Globe,* and was using this paper to promote union with the United States when Macdonald invited Sherlock Holmes to Canada. The following year, Farrer left the *Globe* to work for the annexationist movement; for the rest of his life, he promoted anti-imperial policies.

16 James G. Blaine (1830-1893) served as Secretary of State during the very brief Garfield administration in 1880, then very narrowly failed to win the Presidency in 1884, winning 48.2% of the popular vote to 48.5% won by Grover Cleveland. Later, under President Benjamin Harrison, Blaine was again Secretary of State, an appointment which, Macdonald observed, "means continual discomfort for Canada." (Blaine once said, "Canada is like an apple on a tree just beyond reach …let it alone, and in due time it will fall into our hands.") On 28 January, Edward Farrer met in Washington with Secretary Blaine and the chairman of the House Committee on Foreign Affairs. Blaine had refused to see an official Canadian delegation, and his interview with Farrer, the editor of a leading opposition newspaper, received wide publicity.

17 The Queen's Hotel operated as Sword's Hotel from 1856 to 1862, and by 1891 it had grown into a luxurious inn with accommodation for 400 guests and a staff of 210. East of the building, along Front Street, was the hotel's private garden, with fountains and flowers set into its carefully kept lawn. Macdonald recommended this inn to Holmes and Watson because he himself always stayed there when he came to Toronto, and always requested the same room. He held court with Tory politicians, planning strategy and charming visitors in the hotel's Red Parlour. Renowned for its meals, the hotel remained fashionable for more than sixty years, even when its main rival, the King Edward

opened in 1899. Among its guests were Grand Duke Alexis of Russia, Jefferson Davis, President of the Confederacy, and the Union's General Sherman. In 1927, the CPR bought the site, on the north side of Front Street across from Union Station and demolished the hotel, replacing it in 1929 with the Royal York.

18 *Saturday Night* had been founded four years earlier in 1877. Until 1962 it was fortnightly; since then it has been monthly, and remains an important Canadian publication. In June, 1891, as Macdonald lay on his deathbed, *Saturday Night* wrote: "Men, busy, apparently unfeeling, rough of speech and often careless of the feelings of others, spoke gently when asking, 'What news of Sir John?' and went upon their way sorrowful when told he was dying. Such a general tribute, such genuine recognition of patriotism, such a downfall of tears make memorable the departure of one whose death will be a national calamity."

19 The Victoria Rink, at 277 Huron Street, was only four years old when Watson visited it and it was indeed cavernous. It had a span of 85 feet, and rose at its vault to 55 feet. It was demolished in 1962.

20 The Hotel Hanlan was opened in 1874 by John Hanlan on what came to be known as Hanlan's Point, on Toronto Island, and provided a relief from the city's summer heat and humidity only a short steamer ride away. John's son, Ned (1855-1908), Canada's first internationally famed athlete, later operated the hotel, and it was he whom Watson met. Ned Hanlan won the Canadian sculling championship in 1877, and in 1878 he won the U.S. title on the Allegheny River. In 1879 he beat the English champion in England by an astonishing 11 lengths, and in 1880 became world champion. He successfully defended his world title six times before losing it in 1884. He continued rowing into the 1890s, winning more than 300 races. In recognition of his achievements the city granted him the lease on his hotel site free of charge. *Toronto: Past and Present - A Handbook of the City,* published in 1884, described the island as the "Coney Island of Canada", for around the hotel was a full-scale amusement park, including the Hanlan's Point Baseball Stadium, where Babe Ruth hit his first professional home run, playing for the Providence Grays against the Toronto Maple Leafs. (Just seven years prior to Watson's visit, a Canadian named Arthur Irwin, playing for the same Providence Grays, invented the padded baseball glove.) The Hotel Hanlan was destroyed by fire, along with most of the amusement park, in 1909.

21 Irish immigrant Timothy Eaton (1834-1907) opened his first store at the southwest corner of Yonge and Queen Streets in 1869, but by 1883 he had outgrown the original 24 by 60 foot shop and had moved to much larger quarters between Queen and Albert Streets. This is the "bazaar store" that Dr. Watson visited.

22 The Grand Opera House (9-15 Adelaide Street West) opened in February 1880, replacing an earlier Grand (built in 1874) that had been destroyed by fire. It seated 1,750 and was the centre of Toronto theatre, presenting international stars such as Sarah Bernhardt, Lilly Langtree and Henry Irving. Competition from the Princess and the Royal Alexandra, which were linked to major British and American touring circuits sent the Grand into a decline, and it was demolished in the 1920's shortly after its owner, Ambrose Small, mysteriously vanished. Small's disappearance remains one of Canada's greatest unsolved mysteries.

23 George Gooderham (1820-1905) was the son of William Gooderham (1790-1881), who, first with his brother-in-law and then with his nephew, built Canada's largest distillery. By 1875, they produced one-third of all proof spirits distilled in Canada and their empire included not only distilling, but railways, lake transportation, retailing, livestock, woolen mills and banking. George, with whom Dr. Watson dined, was president of the Bank of Toronto, as well as overseeing the Gooderham commercial empire, and was

also president of the Toronto College of Music, affiliated with the University of Toronto. At the time of the visit of Holmes and Watson to Toronto, construction was underway for what became officially known as the Gooderham Building, but which is better known to Torontonians today as the Flatiron Building, on Wellington Street. This unique edifice was the only survivor of a lamentable 1964-65 decision by the City of Toronto to demolish all the buildings on the Wellington-Front blocks between Church and Yonge Streets.

24 Scottish immigrant George Maclean Rose, along with Robert Hunter, founded Hunter Rose and Co. in Quebec City in 1861, moving to Ottawa in 1865 when the government moved to its new capital, because they had the federal government printing contract, and then to Toronto in 1871 when they lost it. In Toronto, they were given the Ontario government's printing contract. In 1960, a Conservative successor to John A., Prime Minister John Diefenbaker, congratulated Hunter-Rose on achieving a century of business in Canada; Hunter Rose remains one of the country's major printing companies.

25 The Hamilton Psychiatric Hospital was opened in 1876, isolated upon the Mountain away from the centre of population. Today, of course, the Mountain has been engulfed in suburban expansion.

26 See note no. 3 above.

27 The Academy of Music had been built two years before at 167 King Street West (where today University Avenue crosses King.) It was the first public building in Toronto to be lighted by electricity, and the first Toronto theatre to open its drop curtain from the centre. Four years after the historic evening that Holmes and Watson witnessed, during the interval between theatre seasons, the hall was completely renovated and the name was changed to the Princess Theatre. An 1895 article about it in the *Mail & Empire* tells of its "smoking room" and a "retiring room for ladies". A major venue for opera and Shakespeare in Toronto, it was expropriated by the city in 1930 and destroyed to make way for the University Avenue extension. In January 1993, when David and Ed Mirvish held a press conference to announce the name of their new theatre, it was announced that it would be called The Princess of Wales, "in part, in memory of that other Princess that once stood less than three blocks away."

28 The Montreal *Gazette* of February 17, 1891, reported: "Thousands in Toronto were unable to gain admission to the Academy of Music tonight to hear Sir John Macdonald and Sir Charles Tupper. ... Long before six o'clock the building was crowded ... men were actually fighting to get in."

29 There was, indeed, need for the constabulary. The Montreal Gazette reported on 17 February: "...after the meeting was over a great crowd surrounded the *Globe* building, hooting and yelling at it..."

30 J. E. Ritchie (1820-1898) was the author of *To Canada with Emigrants: A Record of Actual Experience*, published in London by T. Fisher Unwin in 1885, and it is likely this volume to which Holmes refers.

31 The Walker House, one of Toronto's chief hotels, stood on York Street near Union Station.

32 Benjamin Butterworth (1837-1898) was a Republican Congressman from Ohio, who had, in fact, not been re-elected the previous November. He served from 1879-1883 and from 1885-1890.

33 Holmes misjudged Farrer's audacity. Farrer did, in fact, say that he had written his pamphlet (which Donald Creighton tells us, "had been printed under strict conditions of secrecy") at the request of an American. (Or someone he took for an American, as we now know.) The tract, as Creighton describes it, "suggested several methods of

economic retaliation by which the United States could bring the citizens of the Dominion to a realization of the stupidity of their trade and fisheries policy."

34 The distinctive label, "Meyers, Toronto" , had enabled Sherlock Holmes to identify one of the boots when he retrieved it from the Grimpen Mire, in Dartmoor, Devon. The boot is of considerable significance in the adventure Dr. Watson called, *The Hound of The Baskervilles*.

"I live in that village of Parkdale..."

[Jefferys, C.W., "New houses, Parkdale, 1909". Watercolour on paper. Art Gallery of Ontario, Toronto. Gift of Mrs. K.W. Helm, daughter of C.W. Jefferys, Kneedale, California, U.S.A., 1980.]

Vincent STARRETT

The tattooed man

(*Coffins for two*. NY: Covici; 1924.)

Biographical information about the author will be found at the bacj of the book.

In every Eden there is a serpent. Godfrey Ruthven thought he'd found an Eden, but instead of Eve there was her sister Lilith and when he fled he carried the snake with him.

The Tattooed Man

I am a physician. My name is Fielding – Charles Fielding. I live in that village of Parkdale, not far from Toronto. Despite my profession, I am a quiet man, known as a recluse. My journeys to the metropolis are infrequent; I am content to "dodder" in my library and let the world roar past.

I care little for matters of topical interest, exclusive of modern pathological research. My practice is insignificant, and I would not have it otherwise, for I confess I am inclined to regard time passed beyond my book-lined frontiers as time irretrievably wasted.

One or two patients, however, I would not willingly give up. I have as fine a case of elephantiasis as Gregory records; a curious, incurable malady susceptible of long and important study. In the present instance it is confined to the right leg of the victim, a woman of middle age, known for her piety and the excellent grade of her bacon ... And Tomlinson's queerly mottled soles are a matter of surpassing interest which I have not yet brought to the attention of the profession.

But it is not of the Widow Colcord, nor of Tomlinson, that I purpose now to write. They will in due time, and without detriment to my ethical standing, find place in the proper records.

It is my intention to tell, as plainly as may be, what I know of the tattooed man who came secretly to my door, late in the fall of 1904, and for sen,en weeks thereafter dwelt with me in a condition of the most abject terror it has ever been my lot (and, I must add, my professional good fortune) to witness.

There was nothing unusual in his appearance as he came up the walk, through the elms and maples, save that his eyes were sidelong and furtive, and his clothes shabby. I put him down for a vagabond, hardly a professional tramp.

I was prepared to send him smartly about his business, when he caught sight of me at the open window. It seemed that his eyes lost some of their uneasiness.

He came across the grass and stood beneath the window.

"Don't be angry, Doctor," he said, reading the words on my lips. "I'm not a beggar, although appearances are against me. I want to consult you ... professionally."

His voice was that of a gentleman, and there was a whimsical twist to his mouth, as he introduced his business, that I liked. His appearance at close rance was less unfortunate than I had thought.

I let him in, moved by some instinct, I suppose, for I care nothing for transient patients.

No sooner had the door closed behind him than down he dropped onto my hall carpet, in as pretty an impersonation of a dead man as ever I saw. ... I was a bit shocked by his behavior, but in a moment I knew he was not dead. Neither, however, was he shamming.

So I lugged him into my private office and laid him on a couch.

As I tore away his shirt at the throat I had my first glimpse of his strangely illuminated skin; but there was no time then to examine *that*. I suppressed my curiosity and pried his teeth open enough to insert the nozzle of a brandy flask.

He sputtered and gulped and, at length, sat up, looking around him in groggy fashion, evidently trying to establish his whereabouts.

I let him look, and meanwhile I studied *him*.

I might as well have studied the Sphinx, although my first impression made him a sailor, a guess that seemed justified by the tattooing around his neck – a red and yellow necklace of a sort, pricked in with a fidelity that was surprising. His age could not have exceeded thirty-five years, although there was an abundance of gray in his black hair. His eyes were a remarkably deep blue, and he wore a scrubby growth of blue-black brush on his jowl, perhaps a week long. His garments were ordinary and seedy.

When he began to look back at me with a gleam of intelligence, I smiled at him.

"Toppled over, eh?" he grinned. "No wonder at that!" he added, and his smile vanished. "Wonder I didn't go down in the street. If I had ... !"

He shuddered, and reached for my brandy flask. His capacity in this connection was extraordinary; yet he did not seem a common drunkard.

It occurred to me that the time had come to make certain inquiries concerning my strange guest.

One thing I knew: his trouble was *fear!*

Whatever might have occasioned it, he had heard the footsteps of fear. I had seen it in his eyes as he came across the lawn to my window, and I had heard it beneath his ribs as he lay in my hall.

I addressed him cheerfully.

"Well, what is it all about?"

He looked at me soberly for an instant. "I'm scared stiff," he frankly confessed. "That's all! Nothing else that I know of. You haven't examined me?"

"I haven't had time."

"Look here!"

He stood upright, on wavering legs, and began to remove his clothing in fumbling haste.

When he got down to his undergarments I remonstrated.

"Is this necessary? Perhaps I can – "

"You can't," he interrupted. "Pardon me, but I know things about myself that even a doctor wouldn't guess."

He was right. As his legs came into view I realized it; and when he removed his shirt and stood naked before me, I fancy my eyes were popping from my head.

The man was tattooed from neck to heel with the most grotesque and horrible pattern.

At first I could not make out what it was; then it began to dawn on me. Involuntarily, I felt my flesh crawl, as at a loathsome reptile.

The outstanding horror was the head of a snake, raised to strike. The fangs were poised directly over the heart, and by beginning at this end and following the design backwards, as it were, it became apparent that most of the hideous decoration was made up of the serpent's coils. The head came down over the left shoulder, from the back, and the rest was wrapped round and round him so many times – about his legs, and around his waist, and across his breast – that my head swam endeavoring to trace it.

My patient watched me with an odd smile.

"Quite a walking picture book, eh?" he commented, with grim amusement. "Illustrated with colored plates!"

"Good heavens!" I managed to observe, at length. "What a horrible thing!"

"It isn't pretty," he admitted. "I'd give a thousand dollars to have it off. ... That's why I'm here," he added suddenly.

I was startled.

"My dear man!" I cried.

He interrupted quickly.

"Don't say it, Doctor! Don't say you won't. My God, I'm trying to be cool, so I won't go off my head again – but don't think it isn't important. It's got to come off! If it doesn't ... I'm gone!"

He turned a haggard face to me.

"If there were anything I could do," I said, kindly, "I would do it. This is beyond me. I have understood that there is no cure, so to call it, for tattooing. ... A small symbol, a set of initials, some trifle, might be partially removed by an electric needle ... but no such pattern as yours. In heaven's name," I concluded, "what possessed you?"

His head had dropped. Now he seated himself heavily in a chair and buried his face in his hands.

"Yes," he muttered, "I was possessed if ever man was."

"Where did it happen?"

He raised his face, looking at me strangely for a moment. "Did you ever hear of Roraima?" he asked.

He seemed relieved to find I had not.

"It is a mountain in Venezuela," said my patient, "seven thousand feet above the level of the sea."

Then, with a sudden rush of eloquence: "Its summit is a tableland that has been isolated from the world for untold ages; a fertile and beautiful country, only a few degrees north of the equator. A forest crowns it, from the midst of which tumbles the most wonderful waterfall in the world. ... Yet no explorer has ever reached its top, and very few its base. It is supposed to be inaccessible."

That sounded like a geography lesson. I looked my surprise.

"Pardon me," he grimaced, catching my expression. "I should have said no exilorer is ever known to have scaled the mountain ... but that's where I got *this!*"

He was a most surprising person.

"You visited this ... this unexplored country?"

"To my sorrow."

"Hm-m!" I said. "Then this mountain must be – "

"Inhabited? It is ... by a race of beautiful fiends!"

"Ah!" said I.

It was all I could say. The whole episode was amazing.

It occurred to me that my patient might be mad, a not unjustified conjecture. But he had been frightened certainly enough; was frightened *now*, and holding himself together only by an effort of will ... aided, of course, by nearly a pint of my best brandy.

He laughed, suddenly and sharply.

"It sounds melodramatic and silly, doesn't it? I know it ... I hardly expect you to believe it. But it's true! It's a long story, and in time you shall hear it all. The chief point is that they've lithographed me according to their infernal custom ... as you see."

"I judge you are in some danger," I observed, slowly, "and that your danger is from the direction of ... Roraima. Yet I know nothing of tattooing. if you could only surgest – "

Suddenly he was beating his fist on his temple.

"Fool!" he shouted – an epithet intended for himself – "of course, I can suggest a way. I should have said so. But it takes time, Doctor ... and patience ... and I must remain safely hidden during the process. ..."

He studied my face appraisingly, apprehensively.

"I know nothing about you," I remarked. "Not even your name."

"My name is Godfrey Ruthven."

That *did* give me a turn.

"Godfrey Ruthven," I said sharply, "disappeared ten years ago.

"Quite true," he remarked simply. "Yet I am Godfrey Ruthven. You will recall that it was in South America he vanished."

It was true, and, when other and satisfying proofs of his identity were forthcoming, I became almost eager to take his case.

I ordered him into a warm bath, to calm his nerves, and then outfitting him from my surplus stock of clothing. When he had shaved and felt the warming influence of a hearty meal inside him, he recovered much of his assurance.

Toward evening Ruthen continued his extraordinary narrative. We sat smoking in the library, my guest having declined an invitation to smoke on the verandah. I caught the old fear in his eyes at the suggestion, and did not press it. He was anxious to get something off his mind, and I gave him the encouragement of silence.

After a few soothing puffs he began again.

"It wouldn't be fair not to tell you that there will be danger, Doctor ... from the outside. There are ... persons ... who are eager to accomplish my permanent disappearance, and who will not scruple to invade your home in that interest.

"You mustn't think I'm an ordinary coward. I've been through some things in the last ten years that have tried me pretty severely, and when I say I'm `scared', I mean it. That's just about all the nerve I have left – enough to admit that I'm frightened."

"Your attitude as you came up the walk was that of a man who believed himself followed," I put in.

"I did believe so," he replied gravely. "I believe so now. It is just possible that I have thrown them off, but I dare not run the risk of believing it. ... "

Dimly I began to realize what I might expect with this man in my home.

"Listen!" said Godfrey Ruthven. "I disappeared, in the language of the world, in 1894. Some time, if I live, a volume will tell of the ten years that followed. If I die ... my notes will allow some hint of what I saw and heard. I shall place them in your hands. It is enough now to say that I disappeared on Roraima.

"Scientists, Fielding, have suggested that the summit of Roraima may hold traces of a former civilization. I am able to tell them that it does, and that ..." he lowered his voice almost to a whisper ... "that it is a civilization that flourishes today! An incredible, monstrous civilization, Fielding, that deifies the lowest and vilest of creatures; that mocks at love, as we know and reverence it; that spits upon all in life that is good and pure and holy!"

Something thudded on the verandah, outside, and scurried across its length with a snarl.

Ruthven came upright with an expression in his face that stopped my heart.

I had to grip myself rigidly to control my voice but I assured him it was a cat, and offered to go outside and look.

He fairly screamed at me to stay where I was. It took the rest of the contents of my flask to reassure him.

"Never open the door, Fielding, unless you know who is outside," he warned me, still shaking.

I thought he had finished for the evening, but after a few minutes he resumed:

"They forced me to take part in their horrible rites, and I fell in with their notions the more readily because I had fallen in love with one of their women ... the most beautiful creature, Fielding, created by God ... and the cruelest. I married her ... or was married to her ... with sacrilegious ceremonies that would have shamed the Witches' Sabbath.

"Then I woke up to what I had done. I had cut myself off from my race as effectually as if I had taken my life; but it was too late to draw back. At the moment, indeed, I was happy enough, or fancied I was. But vaguely a suspicion began to filter through my brain ... a dreadful suspicion ... and in time it became more than suspicion. I shall never forget the day it became a certainty.

"I found my wife with a playmate. ... God! ... Of so loath-some a character, Fielding, that. ..."

"I think I understand you," I said; and flesh revolted ... thinking of the serpent on his breast.

"That was the turning point. I haven't begun to tell the whole of what I saw and heard; that is all in my notes. But you have an idea.

"I see you have Athelney's `Ancient Races' up there. Glance over Volume R casually some day and you'll run onto some mention of Roraima; and when you've read about their practices in those *ancient* days, when the race was known to mankind, remember that for ages now they have been separated from the rest of so-called civilization, and that their own vile civilization has increased and flourished along the evil lines early laid down."

"I begin to imagine the terror and disgust of your situation."

"Do you?" asked Ruthven, queerly. "I wonder if you do! Well, I endured ten years of abject servility, of nameless fear; an unspeakable existence. ... My changed condition was noted, and I was quickly taken to task. I was told plainly enough that unless I accepted things as they were, and joined in them without objections, I would be marked for doom.

"I think I was on the verge of madness during the latter years of my captivity. ... Then I broke away. My epidermic decorations date back five years. They were bestowed on me at a time when their distrust of me was fanatical. My escape was made by the same means employed in reaching Roraimi's summit. It is all in my notes."

"Why are you followed?" I asked. "Because," he said, simply, "I am crammed with their evil knowledge. My revelations would shock the world, if made public, and Roraima would be leveled by the united armies of Christendom. Too, there is the slight matter of private revenge. I am quite cordially hated, Fielding. I will die a terrible death if I am – if I am even seen!"

"I don't understand."

"Ah ... you will! You saw the snake about my body. By their devilish arts they can cause it to come to life ... and, as you saw, the head is ready to strike!"

"Ruthven!" I shouted. "That is madness!"

"Quite so," he responded, with a tired smile. "I said so myself once; but I know better now. The whole design must come off, Fielding, or I'm done."

Clearly, Ruthven's sufferings – somewhere – probably Roraima – had driven him out of his mind, or his mind out of him. His suggestion was incredible – past all belief.

Yet the only possibility of a cure lay in my humoring his madness. ... I gave him a sleeping draught that checked his weird mental activity until almost noon of the following day.

He woke vastly refreshed, and his nerves were noticeably steadier; but there was no lessening of his outlandish obsession.

I attacked the problem of the tattooing, although my own notion was that nothing short of flaying alive could be successful. The abominable pattern seemed brighter than ever.

Ruthven paralyzed me, however, with his own plan of removal. I was stunned by the simplicity of it ... yet for years it had baffled medical and surgical science!

We began at once, working in my laboratory at stated hours, morning, afternoon and evening.

At the end of six weeks of uneventful experience, I am bound to say Ruthven was distinctly whiter. While far from wiped out, the obnoxious design was definitely dimmer; our progress was encouraging. Ruthven's own idea was that it would take six months to remove it entirely.

We talked much of Roraima, and at one time he said:

"You will wonder at my being able to communicate so readily with these creatures. Can you guess, Fielding, the language in which we conversed?"

"A sort of bastard Spanish, I should say," was my reply.

He shook his head.

"An intelligent hazard," he commented, "but actually we talked pure Egyptian!"

"Amazing!"

"Yes, amazing. I have no doubt I am at this moment the only white man, so to speak, with anything like a fluent knowledge of that tongue."

His mental condition during this period remained unchanged. At times he appeared perfectly rational, and seemed to be regaining his grip; again I would find him cringing fearfully in the shadows of his room, like a hunted beast.

Indeed, I think his terror increased as time went on, and often I looked upon him with contempt, so abject was he.

He was always ashamed of himself after a spell of the kind; but the only occasions on which he appeared really at ease were during the process of removing the colored snake from his body. He fancied himself whiter on occasions when, to save me, I could find no difference.

Once, when we were seated in the library of an evening, he rose softly to his feet and crossed the room in two swift strides, suddenly flinging open the door into the corridor.

After which he came back to his chair with a ready apology on his lips.

"The devils!" he said. "I can't be sure of them."

For the most part, however, such displays of heroism – for it was quite magnificent courage for Ruthven – were beyond him. Commonly he sat stooped over in his chair, with his right hand fumbling nervously at his left breast. ...

The account of the seventh and last week of Ruthven's stay in my home I began with profound reluctance.

In spite of everything, Ruthven was a likeable fellow, and he was better than a course of study to me. The information he imparted on a score of obscure points rounded out many unfinished theories and materially added to my education in occult phenomena.

The week opened badly with a scare that even I could not discountenance.

Early Monday morning the maid brought me word that a gentleman was awaiting me in my office. She seemed not to know how he had gained admittance.

He was a queer-looking *gentleman*, too; dark – skinned and darkeyed, and with an almost Chinese cheekbone. He might indeed, have possessed Chinese blood, or Indian, on the authority of his countenance.

He asked me civilly enough, in perfect English, if I could accompany him to the bedside of his wife, a few squares away.

I refused. Politely, but firmly, I told him that pressure of other work made it impossible, explaining that I was not a practicing physician in the ordinary sense.

I directed him to Bentley, in the next block, and he bowed courteously and went away.

He looked back at the house rather curiously as he went down the walk, or so I fancied.

The maid received a severe wigging and a promise of immediate discharge if any more unannounced visitors were allowed to enter into the house.

When I went back to Ruthven, I found him collapsed across the couch in the back room, which he occupied. He had torn away his shirt and exposed his breast, and with a thrill of horror that I cannot describe I saw that the fading colors of the serpent were brighter.

"There's no use," he told me, when I had brought him around. "If we could have had six months we might have beaten them. As it is, our only hope is that this one man is alone on my trail and that we may be able to kill him. It is almost too much to hope. Have you a revolver about the house?"

I had, and very much against my best judgment I let him have it. He promised solemnly not to use it save as a last resort, in the event of a personal attack.

I don't know how I felt after the visit of the pseudo patient, so to call him; certainly he lent color to Ruthven's "madness." That he was an imposter seemed certain, too, for I called Bentley on the telephone and was informed that the man had not been there. There were other doctors near at hand; but ...!

Nothing further occurred until Friday night.

While Ruthven and I worked diligently in the laboratory, I think we both realized that it was a futile task. Even then I did not thoroughly credit

Ruthven's statement about the snake; but I did realize that he was in some frightful danger, and I resolved to follow his directions implicitly.

We retired early on Friday, and I slept soundly until the early hours of the morning. At two o'clock something wakened me. I sat up in bed and, with the aid of a flashlight, looked at my watch.

A moment later the house rang with a scream of maniacal laughter, which seemed to strip the backbone out of me and left me sick and trembling.

Then I leapt from the bed and instinctively ran for Ruthven's chamber.

As I tung open his door something hissed sharply in the darkness, and there was a quick rustle of the window curtains. ...

I half saw, half felt something long and sinuous glide over the sill. ... An offensive odor seemed to hang in the air, like that which nauseates one near the reptile cage at the zoo. ...

My fumbling fingers found the electric switch, and the room was flooded with light.

Ruthven was stretched upon the floor, on his back, his features set in an expression of fear and loathing that I shall carry with me to the grave. My revolver was beside him, and I picked it up and jumped for the window. ...

A leering, horrible human face was looking at me from the outside darkness.

Without hesitation, I fired straight into it.

No shriek followed the shot, but something heavy dropped from the porch roof to the steps beneath, and lay still.

I ripped away the nightrobe from Ruthven's body and fell back with a scream that was strangled in my throat. ...

The serpent was gone!

My friend's skin was as clear and white as my own; but as I stooped over him, feafully, I saw two tiny spots ... mere pinpricks ... over the heart that had ceased to beat. ...

All that was found in the yard, when the police hurried to the scene, was a strange red and yellow snake, its hideous head blown to pieces by the shot from my revolver.

"The Furness house was near the corner of Queen and Sumach streets..." [Photograph Copyright © William Alexander McCoy. Used with the permission of the photographer.]

Maureen JENNINGS

Sharper than a serpent's tooth

(original story)

Biographical information about the author will be found at the back of the book.

King Lear's lament is echoed in fin de sie`cle Toronto, but yet again, perhaps what we hear is actually the cry of the oppressed overburdened by possessive parenting. The reader can listen, but who is to judge ... ?

SHARPER THAN A SERPENT'S TOOTH

The old man groaned pulling his knees to his chest as a spasm of pain gripped him. A candle stub flickered on the oaken table beside his narrow bed and deep shadows darkened his face. His red-rimmed eyes rested on the woman who was seated at the end of the bed.

"I'm thirsty," he whispered.

She stood and picked up a pitcher from the table.

"No, not that, - water," he said.

"This is better."

She poured some pale liquid into a cup and bent towards him. The man pushed her hand away and some of the drink spilled on his quilt. The woman flinched.

"Father-in-law, please drink. It will do you good."

At that moment the front door opened below, heavy footsteps started up the stairs and a man's voice called.

"Mary Ann, Dr Moffat's here."

Quickly, the woman replaced the cup and went immediately over to the fireplace where a dull fire glowed in the hearth. She stirred at the red coals with the poker and when the two men entered she had her back to them.

Both were still dressed in outdoor clothes and the snow had frosted their shoulders and formed little icicles on their eyebrows and moustaches. They brought a waft of cold fresh air into the room thick with the stench of the man's sickness. John Furness, the occupant of the house, was a big-boned man whose normally ruddy face had been whipped to an even brighter colour by the bitter February night. He indicated the woman and the sick man.

"My wife, sir and that there is Alfred Furness, my Pa."

In his haste to fetch help, John hadn't dressed completely and underneath his seal-skin coat he was still wearing his red flannel nightshirt. Quickly he hung his coat on the door hook and hovered at the end of the bed, rubbing his cold knuckles vigorously, a gesture nervous as well as practical. He had the strong sinewy forearms of a teamster.

"Can I take your hat and coat, sir?" the woman said. Her voice was low.

Moffat removed his long coat and fur fedora hat and unwound the cashmere scarf that he had wrapped high about his face. As he handed them to her, Mary Ann gave a little curtesy, like a common servant and stood with the apparel draped over her arm, her face averted. Unlike her husband, she was fully dressed in a plain brown waist and serge skirt. Decent clothes but lacking any style or richness. The doctor's quick appraisal didn't miss the little bow of white silk fastened on her bosom and he frowned. He was very fond of his evening sherry and had a strong aversion to the ardour of the women of the Temperance Union.

"I need more light. How do you expect me to examine the man in the dark." His voice was sharp with irritation.

"I'll fetch a lamp," said Mary Ann, placing the coat and hat on the Morris chair by the fire.

Moffat stepped closer to the bed.

"Feeling poorly then, are we?"

For answer the old man lifted his head off the pillow and retched violently into the bowl placed by his shoulder. John Furness had stationed himself on the other side of the bed and he took the cloth that was on the washstand and tenderly wiped his father's mouth, cleaning the bile off the wispy beard. Alfred Furness lay back in the crook of his son's arm and gazed up at him.

"I'm heading for the grand secret this time, John."

"Oh Pa. Don't say such things."

The doctor pulled his watch from his waistcoat pocket, took up the man's thin wrist and counted the pulse. It was thready and irregular.

"When did the illness come on?" he asked John who was still bent awkwardly over the bed.

"He started to complain of pains right after we'd had our tea. Then he was sick but he said he'd just go up to bed and sleep it off. Mary Ann and me went up a bit later and he seemed better but it was past mid-night when I heard him a-calling. He asked me to fetch a doctor and begging your pardon sir, that alarmed me most of all because Pa never has had much faith with doctors."

Dr Moffat shrugged. He was used to that attitude from people of their class. He himself hadn't been happy to be roused from his bed in the middle of the night but like many physicians these days he didn't like to turn down a fee. John Furness had assured him he could pay the requisite two dollars and so Moffat had got dressed and accompanied him along the silent, snow covered streets. The Furness house was near the corner of Queen and Sumach street, the end one of a row of worker's dwellers. Even at night, the smell of hops from the Dominion Brewery across the road was sweet and cloying on the air.

Mary Ann returned carrying an oil lamp which she put on the mantlepiece. For the first time Moffat got a good look at her. She would have been considered an ordinary woman of middle age, not unpleasing in appearance, except that the entire right side of her cheek and neck was covered by a livid birthmark. Noticing the doctor's gaze, she immediately put her hand, fingers spread, to her cheek. The gesture gave a curious effect of thoughtfulness and surprise as if she were perpetually considering the implications of what was said to her.

Moffat indicated a slop bucket beside the bed.

"Is that what he voided?"

"Yes, sir." answered John.

The matter was liquid and bloody.

Alfred stared up at the doctor.

"Who're you? " he asked.

"This is Doctor Moffat, Pa. You had a bad turn and asked to fetch him."

"He's not going to bleed me is he?"

"Tush! We don't do much of that these days, Mr er, Furness. I'm just here to find out what's wrong with you."

"Poison." Alfred nodded in the direction of his daughter-in-law. "that mort's poisoned me."

"Pa!" exclaimed John, his face flushing with distress. Mary Ann's hand flew immediately to her face and her skin darkened to the colour of the birthmark.

"Why'd you say that, sir?"

"Cos it's the truth." He pointed a shaky withered hand at his daughter-in-law. "I've been ill ever since she come to my house. She wants me out of the way."

"Case of the pot calling the kettle black if you ask me," responded Mary Ann with unexpected spirit.

"Now, now." interjected Moffat. "This is not the time for squabbling." The doctor rather fancied himself as a peacemaker and he said patronisingly to the sick man. "Tell me, Mr Furness, what reason would your daughter-in-law possibly have to get you out of the way as you put it?"

"So she can have my son all to herself. And me money."

Moffat's disbelief was obvious and Alfred spat out. "Don't let her bamboozle you, doctor. She's a fly one."

John hovered between his father and his wife, his broad face full of distress.

"Fact is, doctor, Pa and Mary Ann don't get along too well as of yet. You see before we was married there was just Pa and me. Bachelors together you might say-"

"He was four when his mother died and I brought him up good as any woman could've. And look what thanks I get for it."

John sighed. "I'm grateful, Pa. You know that." He addressed the doctor again, his soft blue eyes pleading. "Mary Ann and me have only been man and wife for three months. As of yesterday as a matter of fact." He cast a glance at the woman that was as sweet and adoring as if he were more fourteen than forty. "I'd never have thought to be a married man," he continued. "But Fate said otherwise."

"How so?" asked Moffat, barely polite.

"July last, I went down to the Exhibition grounds to watch the Jubilee celebrations. There she was, Mary Ann that is, watching the fireworks. I don't know exactly how to say what happened except that at that very same moment, Cupid pierced my heart."

His father snorted. "Cupid! The man's gone batchy. Who'd want to dip his beak in that cabbage-faced dishclout?"

"Come now, Mr Furness, that language is uncalled for I am sure."

"You don't know, doctor. It's not decent at their age neither. I can hear them. Most every night, grunting like rutting pigs."

"Please, Pa."

Crimson with embarassement, John moved closer to his wife and touched her arm. She didn't respond, just stood stiffly with her head averted.

It was a long time since Moffat had grunted like any kind of animal and although he would never have admitted to it, a pang of envy shot through his body.

"I didn't come here in the middle of the night to be adjudicator to some silly, vulgar squabble. Mr Furness let me see your tongue."

Alfred obediently stuck out his tongue which was white-coated and foul. "My throat is burning," he said.

"Has he had an attack like this before?" Moffat asked John.

"I suppose so, sir. Off and on he's had purges since Christmas but none as bad as this."

"What did you eat for your tea?"

"Pork chops and potatoes with cabbage."

"Did you all have the same thing?"

"Yes, sir. We did."

"Any tinned meat or fish?"

"No sir. Mary Ann wouldn't abide that. She buys everything fresh at the market."

"And you say it began at Christmas time. Did he over-indulge?"

"I did not," answered Alfred indignantly. "I hardly ate a thing. She cooked us up a duck that was so fat it'd have choked a sewer. I didn't want none of it. John and me always had a good roast of beef. Why we had to change to some fancy muck is beyond me."

"He's a drunkard," said Mary Ann to the doctor, not looking at her father-in-law.

"I am not, you Jezebel. Taking a spot of porter for your health is not anywhere to be thought a drunkard. Me and John used to enjoy a glass of ale in the evening till she came along-"

"John has taken the Pledge," she said.

"- He was healthier for it," said Alfred.

Still addressing Moffat, the woman said. "John hurt his back two months ago. It had nothing to do with abstaining from liquor. The horses balked."

"All right. All right. Now on these occasions when Mr Furness has been taken poorly, has anyone else been ill?"

"No, sir." answered John. "And the Revered Latimer and his wife ate with us that afternoon and they were in fine health. They considered it to be an excellent meal." he added a touch defiantly.

Moffat sat back. "Well let's say no ale for a week, light broths only until the purging has stopped. If you're no better by Saturday come to my surgery and I'll take another look at you."

Suddenly, the old man let out a bloodcurdling moan and writhed on the bed, clutching at his stomach.

"I'm dying," he moaned. "Johnny I'm dying. She's poisoned me."

He reached out and grasped the doctor's sleeve, pulling him down with unexpected strength. The stench of his breath was fierce and Moffat shrank away.

"You've got to believe me. Look in the wardrobe. That's where my money is. She's after it. She's been stealing I know."

Moffat sighed. He was beginning to long for his warm bed and the man was utterly tiresome. For virtually no fee as well.

"Forty years I've saved," Alfred gasped out. "All silver coins. You see. It's in the sock. There's two thousand dollars."

"He doesn't have close to that much."

Mary Ann gulped, the words out before she could stop them.

"We had trouble with mice, " she added hastily. "I was cleaning out his wardrobe, that's how I know-"

"Ha! And when you find money missing she'll tell you the mice ate it."

"Pa, Mary Ann isn't that way-"

"If I did take money it was only what was our due-"

She was appealing to the doctor now as if he were a magistrate. "John had hurt his back and he couldn't work for almost a fortnight. Father is a tight as paper on the wall. He refused to help. - I took just enough to get us by."

Moffat waved his hand at her impatiently. "That's none of my business."

Alfred Furness pushed himself up into a sitting position in the bed. His eyes glittered. "Begging your pardon sir but it is. Cos I keep trying to tell you. She wants to get rid of me. She knows about me money. She's been poisoning me. Every time she gives me something I get ill as the devil."

Moffat sighed. "What else has she given you then? And why is nobody else sick?"

"First it was beef tea with a simpering smile that would have curdled milk. `Here father try this for your stomach.' Then it was the arrowroot pudding. And I got worse after. Terrible pains like to rip my stomach out."

"Can you describe the pains."

"Like there's somethin inside biting me, as if I've swallowed a serpent. She keeps forcing me to drink that stuff in the pitcher. She's messed with it, I'll wager."

Frowning, Moffat picked up the pitcher from the table. "What's in here?"

"Barley water," answered Mary Ann.

"Did you make it?"

"Yes sir."

Moffat could see small pieces of white sediment in the bottom of the jug. He replaced it and shifted the candle closer so he could better study his patient. The old man's hair was skimpy from age but there were two large dollar sized bald spots on the top of his head and when the doctor touched them the skin flaked away, brown and scaly. The lids of his eyes were red and inflamed.

"Let me see your nails."

Alfred held up his bony hand. The nails were shrunken and standing away from the finger tips.

"Would you say your father has lost weight over the past two months?" he asked John.

"I suppose he has now that you mention it," said the man reluctantly.

""Course I have. My trousers fall right off me."

The doctor tugged nervously on his luxuriant moustache. The other three people watched him intently.

"I regret to say, Mr Furness your father is showing some strange symptoms...it is not impossible he has been poisoned."

"See! Now do you believe me you greenhead. We've been gammoned from the beginning."

John put his hands to his head and squeezed as if he could push out the truth. "I cannot believe this. There must be some other explanation."

"Will you wait til she's throwing dirt on my eternity box? Look at her. Guilty as Delilah herself. You can see it on her cabbage face."

Mary Ann was quite pale, the birthmark a livid splash across her cheek. She was trembling violently and suddenly, she sat down as if her legs could no longer support her.

"Ma'am is it true what your father-in-law says?"

She gazed up in anguish at her husband. "John, my dearest husband. Please forgive me."

"Mary Ann!"

"Ma'am, am I to take that statement as an admission of your guilt?"

She hardly seemed to hear him but with lowered head she said.

"From the beginning, he has wanted to destroy the love between John and me... I could bear it no longer."

Moffat put his hand on her shoulder.

"Ma'am come downstairs with me. We will wait together in the kitchen. There will have to be a police investigation. Mr Furness I'll thank you to fetch the constable at once."

Without another word, Mary Ann rose and walked out of the room, the doctor behind her.

They went down into the chilly kitchen and she took her seat at the pine table. The doctor stood in front of her, regarding her with great severity.

"How a member of the gentler sex can act in such a manner is beyond my comprehension. To systematically administer your poor father-in-law arsenic under the guise of sustenance is an act of the grossest wickedness."

She stared at him in bewilderment and shook her head. "Sir, I never did that."

"Don't dissemble now, ma'am. I heard you admit to such a thing with my own ears."

"Not that. You see, doctor, from the moment I came to live here he was accusing me of poisoning him. Yesterday, I could bear it no longer. John and I wanted to rejoice at our good fortune in finding each other but Father started up his dreadful rants and spoiled our joy. I thought how much happier we would be if we could be alone. I said to myself, `if that is what you think me guilty of, so be it." She moaned, indicating the pine cupboard along the wall. "It wasn't arsenic. I had some tincture. Dog button. For a tonic. I put it in his ale." she smiled bitterly. "It was a fitting place."

Moffat took the bottle of *nux vomica* from the shelf. It was almost empty.

Upstairs, John had made a motion to leave but his father caught him fast by the hand.

"No, son. Stay with me."

He obeyed and like a marionette collapsed into the chair beside the bed. Then he buried his head in his hands and began to moan. He father stroked his hair, kissing his temples tenderly.

"There now, my laddie, don't take on so. It'll be better when she's gone, I promise you. Just like it was before, just you and me."

Lost in his tears, John could not see the smile of triumph on his father's face and he didn't hear when the old man said softly.

"It was all worth it. I'd do it again."

He stopped his caress and swung his thin legs out of bed, reaching down to the washstand cupboard. He took out a bottle of ale.

"I'm thirsty and this is cause to celebrate."

He took a long, deep swallow and offered the bottle to his son.

"Have some."

John hesitated."I made a promise, Pa. I can't go back on it."

"Tush. Things can be different now."

John shook his head and Alfred shrugged. He gulped down some more ale then paused. Below the kitchen door slammed and someone came hurrying up the stairs.

At that moment, Alfred cried out, dropped the bottle, tried to stand but fell to the floor. His body arched so violently, his head and heels were drawn together until they were almost touching. He called out again and his lips pulled back from his teeth.

He looked as if he were smiling a hideous sardonic smile.

"He opened the door and stepped inside — the first absolutely criminal offence."

Eric WRIGHT

The Cure

(*Fingerprints; a collection of mystery stories by the Crime Writers of Canada*. Edited by Beverley Beetham-Endersby. Toronto: Irwin; 1984)

Biographical information about the author will be found at the back of the book.

"Revenge", the Spanish say, "is a dish best eaten cold". Bethell's has well-nigh congealed on the plate, but is none the less sweet for all the time he waited.

The Cure

When Bethell decided to rob his old friend, Sligo, his motive was to teach Sligo a lesson, unsettle him a bit. He had suffered from Sligo for twenty years, seventeen of them as his next-door neighbour. When Sligo moved away, Bethell thought, peace at last, but their wives were friends and Bethell's wife found Sligo a good sort, so he continued to see nearly as much of Sligo as ever. (Sometimes, though, when Bethell raged about him in the bedroom after the two couples had spent an evening together, his wife would say, "For God's sake. Don't see him if he bothers you so much.")

Just why Sligo bothered Bethell was hard for Bethell to explain, because it had its roots in a relationship between the two men that was apparent only to Bethell. It was an attitude that Sligo took to Bethell, an assumption of a mentorial relationship on Sligo's part that Bethell found irritating from the very early days when he otherwise welcomed Sligo's friendship. When Bethell first moved into his house and began repairing the little stone wall that edged his front yard, Sligo appeared from next door and took over. "You haven't had too much experience of this kind of thing, have you?" he said with a chuckle. It was true; Bethell had no experience at all of dry-stone-walling, but he had borrowed a book from the library and he was looking forward to finding out if he could do it. That incident set the pattern. When Sligo saw how incompetent Bethell was, he never let him alone. Whenever Bethell appeared in his backyard with a two-by-four and a hammer, Sligo was over the fence in a moment, ready to straighten him out.

Sligo's protection and advice spread from house repairs into every corner of Bethell's life. Bethell had no garage, so Sligo cleaned out the rubbish in his own two-car garage and told Bethell to park there in the future. He visited the St Lawrence Market and brought back food on Bethell's behalf, specials he knew Bethell should have at those prices. When there was a sale of wine at the local L.C.B.O. he bought extra for Bethell, and Bethell ground his teeth and thanked him. Sligo tasted the soup on Bethell's stove and added salt, talked man-to-man with Bethell's children, re-arranged the logs on Bethell's fire, and dispensed advice like a relative by marriage.

The quality of Sligo's advice and help was as mixed as the next man's. He was far from infallible, but he rarely admitted doubt in the first place or error when something went wrong, finding, when pressed, some fault in the way Bethell had executed the advice. Like Odysseus, he was never at a loss, so that when some question or problem cropped up concerning an area outside his experience he would, (or so it seemed to Bethell), bluff and fake an answer, or claim to know the expert in the field whom he would consult next day. Perhaps the worst of it was that Bethell's wife would often forget how much he resented Sligo. When Bethell has a problem, as often as not she would say, "Why don't you ask Sligo? He might know."

And Bethell *knew* that Sligo lied to preserve his role. For example, he told Bethell how much he had paid to get his house painted, a real bargain, but the painter, whom Bethell hired also, told him the true figure was twice as much, and when Bethell faced Sligo with this in front of their wives, Sligo said that the painter had exaggerated so that he could overcharge Bethell. Bethell looked hard at Sligo's wife during this exchange, but she didn't blink an eyelash, so she was in on it, too.

On another occasion, Bethell was in the market for an old icebox for his cottage, an item he had remembered seeing in rural dumps all over Ontario in the last twenty years and which he expected to pick up for the cost of removing it. When he started to look around he was appalled to discover that he had come too late to the market and iceboxes were now antiques going for around three hundred dollars. Sligo had refused to let Bethell buy one at this price and told Bethell to leave it to him. Bethell got a lot of satisfaction during the next few weeks out of asking Sligo how the search was going, and Sligo had had to agree that iceboxes weren't as easy to find as he had thought. Nevertheless he insisted that he would come up with one, and then, one Saturday afternoon, he came home with a beauty in excellent condition which he picked up "at a farm auction near Belleville" for fifty dollars. Bethell didn't believe him, but would Sligo have paid money out of his own pocket just to keep his reputation intact? Bethell thought so.

It was no comfort to Bethell that his own wife reported back to him that Sligo thought Bethell was a dear, sweet guy, all the more so for being so unworldly. Bethell was a civil servant, and Sligo was a jobber of some kind; he lived in the real world, as he told Bethell, unlike Bethell who never had to worry about his cash flow.

Bethell was aware, mainly from concerned remarks of his wife, that he was taking Sligo too much to heart and he took the chance to talk about Sligo to a psychological counsellor whom he was consulting for advice on some sexual difficulties he was having. Sligo's name cropped up and Bethell let himself go.

The counsellor listened until it was nearly time for their appointment to end, then said, "You have a poor opinion of yourself, Mr Bethell. It shows up in every area. Your friend knows this — subconsciously, of course — and he sees your uncertainty and translates it into a call for help. He wants to look after you."

"But what about when he's wrong and lies about it?" Bethell cried.

"Are you sure he's wrong? If so, perhaps he has his own needs. You never tell people who depend on you that you are fallible. That would seem to be letting them down."

"So what do I do? Avoid him?"

"I don't think so. That would be a defeat. Besides I take it the initiative in this relationship comes from him?"

"Entirely."

"Obviously he loves you. He must be made to respect you as well as love you."

"How? How do I do that?"

"Perhaps by finding some area where *you* are the mentor, the elder, so to speak. And insisting firmly on your role." The counsellor gave a little peek at the clock on the wall.

"I've found a dozen: gardening, fly-fishing, good hotels in Paris you name it, I've taught *him*."

"And what happens?"

"A month or a year later, he explains them back to me. He never gives me credit for having told him about them in the first place."

Now the counsellor openly consulted his watch. "Mr Bethell, I have to speak bluntly," he said. "You sound what we would call paranoid."

"I know *that*, for Christ's sake. That's why I'm talking to *you*."

"Well, we've got you to recognize your problem at least. Let's have another go at it next week."

But Bethell never went back. He continued to suffer and dream of an absolute facer that Sligo would not be able to dodge.

When the opportunity finally came, Bethell did not recognize it at first. At the time he was considering simply finding an excuse to pick a quarrel with Sligo (after twenty years!) so that he could cut him off, even though that would be an acknowledged defeat. But when he tried, the result was only a wretched evening and a mystified wife who wondered what had got into him, and made immediate arrangements to get together with the Sligos again (with apologies) to get their relationship back on its old footing. Then one evening Bethell went into a fit of rage on a matter as small as whether one should lock one's doors.

Like most people, Bethell kept his house locked when he was out of it and had even installed a small alarm system to alert the neighbours if anybody broke in. Sligo never locked his house up, or his car, never had, never would. "If they are going to break in," he said, "they come ready. Then not only do they steal your goods, but they break your door down with it. Same with a car. Any good car thief can open a car easy as pie, but if you leave everything unlocked, he might think you are coming back right away."

"How about amateurs?" Bethell asked, getting sucked in again.

"Amateurs won't touch an unlocked house, either," Sligo said, authoritatively. "If you lock it, they just use axes instead of a crowbar. As for cars, amateurs only steal cars with keys in. They just take them for joy-riding. You always get them back."

Bethell knew this was wrong, and he began to reply, but Sligo had already gone on to something else. "What's the humidity in here?" he was saying when Bethell had got his thoughts together. "You need a gauge. I'll bring over our old one."

Shortly after that Bethell was robbed. The thieves cut the power supply to bypass the alarm, got the door open with a bit of plastic which they left behind, took his television set, his camera, and his trombone, and finding the spare car keys on a hook in the kitchen, drove off in his Rabbit. They were never caught.

"See," Sligo said.

Bethell saw, all right, and began to plan. Sligo was going to have to be robbed, and in such a way that there could be no doubt that the failure to lock his doors was crucial. Bethell set aside, for the moment, the question of whether the robbery would be a joke, to make a point, or whether the robbery would be real. Either way the heist would have to be fairly big and take place in daytime, committed by thieves who evidently acted in the knowledge that they would be able to enter and leave easily. Bethell day-dreamed for a month before the perfect idea fell into his lap. A colleague of his came to the office one morning with the news that his neighbour had been robbed the day before. Thieves using a regular furniture truck had backed up to the man's front door and simply removed the contents of the house in about three hours. No one had questioned them, and when the police went around banging on doors, none of the neighbours could remember what the men looked like — "Kind of guys who move furniture," one neighbour said — or what the name of the company was, or even the colour of the truck.

Now Bethell just had to wait for the next occasion when Sligo was away with his wife, for Sligo left his house unlocked when he went on holiday, too. In the meantime he had to find a furniture-removal truck and four thieves. (He had decided on a real robbery, because he realized that if he made the thing the basis of a practical joke, he would not be making his point; Sligo could afterward claim that just because Bethell was able to walk in and out of his house in no way invalidated his position. The point was that an outsider would not know it was unlocked.)

The first problem was to get in touch with some thieves. He had heard the phrase "consorting with known criminals" as something thieves on probation must not do, and he reasoned that here must be places where criminals consort — pubs, probably, that they favoured, where they planned the next job. Bethell's scheme to find out about these haunts was to ask for an interview with the public relations department of the Metropolitan Toronto Police. The inspector was polite, but wary. "A writer, eh, Mr Bissell," he said. "Not one of those expose' type guys, eh?"

Bethell assured him that the hero of his novel would be a clever policeman, and the inspector listened to his problem. Where did thieves gather in Toronto? He called a sergeant in. "Mr Bissell here is looking for local colour," he explained. "He wants to know where our clients hang out when they are not working. Are there any particular pubs, like?"

The sergeant considered. "Not that I know of, Mr Bissell," he said. "We wouldn't allow it. If you find any, let us know, would you?"

The inspector smiled and showed Bethell the door.

Next Bethell asked a number of taxi-drivers to take him to the sleaziest pubs they knew of, where he spent several evenings drinking beer and watching naked women jousting in imaginary combat. Nowhere did he find what he was seeking. He considered spending a night in the Don Jail. Surely there he would find what he wanted? But the only offence he could think of that would get him a night in jail, but not the possibility of three months, was a refusal to pay parking tickets and it would probably take six months or more to build up to that.

Ruminating on the difficulty of getting into bad company, he was presented one day with an alternative solution. There was a knock on his door and a smiling young man introduced himself as a surveyor commissioned to mark out the property next door for Bethell's neighbour who was selling his house. It would be necessary, the youth said, to enter Bethell's garden, and he was introducing himself so that Bethell wouldn't get alarmed and call the police.

Bethell took the surveyor's card and went out to the street and examined the man's car, which had no identifying sign except a CJRT sticker in the window. Bethell switched his plan.

He designed a card, "Royce Dunlop — Surveyor", ordered a hundred from a cheap printer, threw away ninety-eight, and put the remaining two in his wallet. The rest of the plan required the absence of Sligo.

In the three months that Bethell waited for Sligo to go on holiday, the two couples dined together twice and each time afterward Bethell's wife commented on how well the evening had gone. Sligo chose the restaurant the first time, and the food was horrible. The second time Bethell chose, consulting widely beforehand, even to knowing the name of the restaurant's house wine; they had a splendid meal, and he never felt a thing when Sligo explained why. "This is a Florentine restaurant," Sligo said. "Much better than Milanese."

Then Sligo announced they were going to Bermuda for a week, and Bethell made his move. He chose the Wednesday to avoid any garbage collections on Sligo's street, wanting to eliminate even that much extra activity that might bring the neighbours to their doors. Early in the morning he drove out to a car-rental agency on Eglinton West and picked up the station wagon he had ordered the night before, using his own name. It was the one risk he could not avoid, for he was unable, short of stealing someone's wallet, to think of a way of getting a false driver's licence.

He parked outside Sligo's house at ten o'clock, tucked one of his cards under the windshield wiper, and walked boldly up to the door. Sligo's front door was at the side of the house, obscured from the street, and there was little chance that Bethell would be seen as he opened the door and stepped inside — the first absolutely criminal offence. So far so good. Sweating slightly, he sat down in the kitchen and took off his coat, leaving his gloves on, and ran over his mental list: an antique coffee-pot, a Krieghoff painting, some silver tableware. There was also a gold watch on Sligo's desk. On reflection he decided against the painting and prepared to assemble the loot. As soon as it was piled on the kitchen table he was done for if anyone should walk in. Bethell walked the house like an insomniac, peering out of all the windows at the quiet street, leaping up in the air when the phone rang, then, finally, in a single sweep, he locked the front door, collected the goods together, and looked around for something to carry them in. Here his nerve cracked. A knock at the door had him lying on the floor, then, as he heard faint departing footsteps, peeking through the front window to see the meter-reader from Consumers' Gas leave and move to the next house. He was incapable, he knew now, of walking to the car with a bag full of silver, and he tried to tell himself that perhaps he had gone far enough to make his point. The place had clearly been robbed, and the thief disturbed before he could get away with the loot. Wasn't that enough? But Bethell didn't trust Sligo not to say nothing, to lie silently, and then Bethell would have wasted his time. The solution when it came to him was simple and nearly risk-free. It took him fifteen minutes to set up, and when he was finished he unlocked the front door, drove back to the agency, and returned home in his own car.

His wife said, "Where were you? I phoned the office and they said you'd phoned in sick."

Bethell chuckled. "Caught me, did you? I spent the day in the arms of my mistress, dear."

"No, where *were* you?"

"I took the day off," Bethell said. "I was driving to work and I said to myself, `I need a mental-health day', so I kept on driving and took the ferry over to the Island."

"That's not like you," she said. "Male menopause?"

"Could be," he said. "You'd better keep your eye on me."

When Sligo came back he had a tale to tell and he came over to Bethell's house on the first evening to tell it. "They emptied out all the drawers, the closets, all over the floor," he said. "They got Doris's silver, the coffee pot, and my gold watch. Every thing worth taking except the Krieghoff. They probably thought that was cut out from a magazine."

"That's terrible," Bethell's wife said. "Losing all that."

"No sweat," Sligo said. "It's all insured. I'll probably make money on it."

"But if the insurance company knows the house wasn't locked, surely they won't pay up?" Bethell said. It was an integral part of his new plan. He intended to let Sligo suffer for a few weeks and then arrange for the loot to reappear.

"I'm not that dumb," Sligo laughed. "Before I called the cops I locked the whole house up and kicked in the back door."

"I see," Bethell said, the room dancing in front of his eyes.

"Oh, sure," Sligo said. "I wasn't born yesterday."

Bethell raged silently. Then a lovely thought occurred to him, the realization that Sligo had delivered himself into his hands. For now, whenever he chose, he could pick up the phone and, anonymously, of course, tell the police and the insurance company that they had been defrauded, that in the basement of Sligo's house they would find a wood-box, and under the layer of scrap wood left over from Sligo's last remodelling, they would find some silver, a coffee pot, and a gold watch. There was no rush. It was only June, and Sligo was unlikely to need kindling before October. At some point during the summer Sligo would become intolerable, and then Bethell would phone.

***

It was a glorious summer. Bethell's wife remarked on how much more relaxed the two men were with each other. No longer did Bethell grind his teeth at Sligo's patronage — he seemed not to notice it. Often, when Sligo started to give Bethell advice, Bethell just laughed and told Sligo he was full of it. Sometimes he cut through Sligo's monologues, changing the subject as more important or more interesting subjects occurred to him.

As the summer wore on, Bethell realized that calling the insurance company would accomplish nothing. They *might* assume that Sligo had defrauded them and Sligo might go to prison, which, now that Bethell's sharp need for revenge had faded, was more than he wanted. And, too, they might believe in Sligo's innocence and search for an insider who knew Sligo's domestic habits and where he kept his wood. Bethell knew that if Sligo or the police failed to guess the culprit, his own wife would.

But if he did *not* phone what would happen? Sligo would find the loot, with two possible results. He might keep his mouth shut and try to sell it later, but the coffee pot and the silver were listed with the Robbery Squad, so it would be very risky. He was more likely to announce the find, which would bring the police in asking the same questions and pointing the same finger at him as if Bethell had made his anonymous call. And Bethell had heard that the forensic laboratory could identify him from a single speck of dandruff, never mind fingerprints.

Now October approached with a rush as Bethell grew more and more frightened. In the end he was obliged to improvise, and one dark and rainy night, when his wife was at a movie and he knew that the Sligos were out, he drove over to their house. He tried the door and found it locked, but he had no time to savour his little triumph. He moved round to the back of the house and waited for the noise of a passing car, then kicked the door in. Down in the basement he packed the stuff into a green garbage bag and made a run for it, looking like a cartoon burglar making off with the swag. He drove down to Harbourfront, parked by the yacht basin, dropped the stuff unto the harbour, and drove home, beside himself with fear.

When Sligo came home that night, he phoned Bethell after he had finished with the police. "They didn't take anything," he said, "but the police think those guys have got me staked out. Now I'll really have to lock up tight. I was wondering if I could come by tomorrow night and find out about locks and alarms and stuff. You know all about that, don't you?"

"Sure," Bethell said comfortingly. "sure. I've got information, brochures, on all that kind of thing. Come round and we'll go over what you need."

"Who was that?" Bethell's wife asked as he crept into bed.

"Sligo," Bethell said. "He wants some advice." He kissed his wife and arranged himself for sleep. "I think I can help him," he said.

Allen Gardens, Toronto.
[Picture Copyright © Tom McNeely Ltd. Used with the permission of the artist.]

James POWELL

The Greenhouse Dogs

(*Ellery Queen's Mystery Magazine*, 1989/reprinted, *Criminal shorts; mysteries by Canadian crime writers*. Ed. by Eric Wright and Howard Engel. Toronto: Macmillan Canada; 1992).

Biographical information about the author will be found at the back of the book.

Your Mother always told you never to talk to strangers. Wilfrid Pond should have paid more heed to the maternal advice he received. The next time you're visiting the hothouses at Allan Gardens, stay away from uniformed men, or you might find yourself sharing Wilfrid's dilemma.

The Greenhouse Dogs

Within the park were, among other things, a tree planted by a Prince of Wales, a statue of the poet Robert Burns and a greenhouse with a central dome tall enough to accommodate palm trees. Since his retirement Wilfrid Pond had come to the park every morning to read on a bench which he had chosen for his own dark purpose near the statue of the poet. Pond was a small, quiet-looking man with a tall forehead and a head of immaculately white hair worn parted down the middle and carefully arranged on top. This head of hair was what most people of him saw for Pond was nearsighted. When he raised his face from his book it was to use the pistol of his cocked thumb and index finger to push his glasses back up on his nose. Before lowering his head again he would invariably look around and smile. The park was an old friend. As a boy Pond had often played in the greenhouse with his sister Cecily. In the depths of the Toronto winter strange plants flourished beneath that glass dome and carp lurked like carrots in trickling pools. In one of their games they pretended they were lost in the jungle while Pond, who had been briefly interested in exotic fauna then, would describe the giant lemon-eyed cats that might be crouching in the humid darkness or the lurid snakes hanging in fat coils ready to drop from the overhead branches or the beetles as hard, big and bright as a Sunday shoe hiding under every fern. Cecily had loved to play that game. It was several years later before she started to wake up screaming. Pond still felt a responsibility for that. On this particular spring day something set him wondering if the greenhouse was still the same. It had been forty-five years since he'd been inside. He remembered a plant there called Mother-in-law's Tongue with long glossy green and black leaves as mottled as a fish and a thorn at the very tip. Pond could not say if the name was accurate for he had never married.

The people in the park were all familiar to him. Some he knew by type like the urgent striders who used the main path as a short cut between Carlton and Gerrard. Others he knew by name like old Mrs. Beattie who once taught piano and now had intense conversations with Frederic Chopin or Mr. Fisk way over there by the Gerrard Street gate who would return in mid-afternoon

—as Pond sometimes did to escape the monotony of his fearful sister— and wait until the granddaughter he doted on got off the streetcar in her school plaid skirt and beret. And there were those whom Pond had given nicknames to like the old man he called Knobby because he always sat with his pant-leg pulled up to bare an arthritic knee to the thin wash of spring sunshine.

A policeman came down the path where Pond sat, his pace idle and his thoughts elsewhere. He looked crisp and comfortable in his blue shirt and Sam Brown belt. Pond watched him pass. When he'd been a boy the uniform had been bobby helmets and heavy cloth and high collars at that time of the year and tall black Persian lamb hats for winter. It had been hard for Pond to accept the change. They'd changed the street signs from black on white to white on black not long thereafter. That took getting used to, too.

Pond returned to his book of the moment, Tolstoy's *War and Peace* in the Constance Garnett translation. He had been trying for several days to get through the first fifty pages. But he could never get the patronymics straight or understand the gossip from court. He persisted because it passed the time and, he suspected, because he liked the name Constance Garnett, the garnet being the gem stone of constancy. In the beginning he'd thought how clever of Mr. Garnett to name his daughter Constance. So he'd been a bit taken aback to learn from the jacket blurb that Mr. Garnett had been her husband. After some consideration Pond decided it was even more amazing that a woman named Constance and a man named Garnett would meet and marry.

As Pond sat reading he felt someone sit down on the other end of the bench. He smiled to himself without turning or making any sign he had noticed the new arrival. A conversation was about to be initiated, Pond was sure of that. He hoped it wouldn't be a dullard with some remark about the weather. Pond had learned from experience to close his book and flee such people. The best conversationalists generally slapped at their newspaper or muttered at a slouching teenaged passerby or made a general statement about the world going to hell in a hand-basket. No matter how qualified your agreement the speaker would embrace you as a brother philosopher and the conversation would be off to the races. Pond enjoyed these discussions and liked to think he brought a kind of cheerful wisdom to them. As Pond waited for the man to speak a breeze with winter still in it scattered the fragile spring air. "They don't make springs the way they used to," said a man's voice.

Impressed by this excellent straddle of weather and hand-baskets Pond turned to peer at the new arrival from over the top of his glasses. Then his eyebrows rose in surprise for the speaker, a man in early middle age with a round, unmilitary face, was wearing the full dress uniform of an officer in the Royal Canadian Regiment, complete with white pith helmet with spike and red tunic.

"You're quite right, sir. They don't," Pond agreed.

"You don't have to call me 'sir,'" said the man regretfully. "I'm not a major. The uniform's rented. I wore it last night to a dance." He held out a hand to be shaken. "Gordon Harner."

Pond introduced himself, adding, "I didn't know you could do that. Rent army uniforms, I mean."

Harner nodded. "They probably wouldn't have rented me a Toronto regiment. Like the Royal Canadian Dragoons, eh? But who'd want to?" Here the man crossed his legs and then, as if deciding it made him look unmilitary, uncrossed them. "Have you heard the one about the RCD's regimental colors: 'Blue for the seas they never crossed. Red for the blood they never shed. And yellow the reason why'?"

Pond gave a sudden short laugh. "That's a new one on me," he admitted.

"Now the Royal Canadian Regiment, there's a uniform any man would be proud to wear. The rental contract said I didn't have to bring it back until noon. So I'm keeping it on until then. I'll change at the store." Harner nodded at the overnight bag sitting between his ankles. "It's Moss Park Costumes down on Queen. Do you know the neighborhood? You live around here, Wilfrid?"

"Just around the corner," said Pond, nodding northward. "My sister and I've lived in the same house all our lives."

"You're luckier than you know. Today it's all move here, move there, move some place else."

Pond nodded for the thin pleasure of agreeing. In fact he didn't feel lucky. The neighborhood had changed so much that remembering how it was when he'd been a boy was like news from a very distant land indeed. But Harner's remark gave him an opening to nudge the conversation the way he wanted it to go. "My sister doesn't think so, about our being lucky, I mean. The world's a bit too much for Cecily. She hasn't left the house in thirty years. Says it's too dangerous out here. She finds life overwhelming, I'm afraid." Pond smiled at Harner. "For some people it is, you know. So my coming to the park like this is therapeutic for her or so I like to think. I tell her about the people" —he bowed in Harner's direction— "I see or what we say. She admits it's almost as good as television."

Harner gave him a long, owlish look. "I can see you love your sister very much, Wilfrid," he said.

Pond nodded modestly. Then he said, "With Cecily it's as if years ago she saw some great disaster coming far down the road and's been waiting for it to get here ever since. Do you believe there are people who can see into the future like that, Gordon?" he asked.

"I can't say I do," said Harner.

"Some say your poets are great predictors of the future," said Pond with a backward toss of his head in the direction of the statue. "Some say Burns here predicted the use of local anesthetics in surgery."

"I didn't know that," said Harner with solemn interest.

Pond smiled and sprang his little joke. "Didn't Burns write:

'Would that God the gift would give us,
To see ourselves as others saw us.'?"

Harner winced and looked away. He stared across at the greenhouse for several moments. Then he shook his head. "I sat down here because you looked like a thoughtful man, an ethical man," he said in a disappointed voice. "I told myself I'll bet here's somebody who'll appreciate this little dilemma of mine. I hope to god I wasn't mistaken, Wilfrid. You see, it's a question of life or death. Unless you can talk me out of it, I'm going to have to kill Charles Cornish" —Harner looked at his wrist watch— "in an hour and forty-five minutes."

As convincingly as these words were delivered Pond decided to pretend Harner was joking. He managed to keep an amused expression while his eyes searched the park for the policeman. But the paths and benches were almost empty. The cool breeze had brought clouds and turned the dome of the greenhouse from silver to gray.

As if to explain his time reference Harner said, "Oh, I could kill him now. But I wouldn't want to disgrace the uniform. As I said, I get to wear it until noon."

"But why do you want to kill this person?"

"I don't want to. I must. Because of what happened last night."

"At the fancy-dress ball?"

Harner's face turned livid. "It wasn't a fancy-dress ball!" he hissed furiously through clenched teeth and spittle. Then he caught himself. Taking a deep breath he started to fan himself with the pith helmet, thought better of it and tucked the helmet under his arm military fashion. "Oh, after the company dance last year some big muckety-muck did say, 'Hey, let's make the next one fancy dress.' I thought that was a great idea. You see, I'd always wanted an excuse to rent this uniform. Well, I spent the next six months marching around in it in my imagination. If anybody ever told me that Mr. Mulcaster himself finally put the kibosh on the fancy-dress idea I wasn't listening. That's how bad I was looking forward to wearing the uniform. My big fear was that somebody else might try the Royal Canadian Regiment bit. If anybody did I figured it'd be Cornish. Looking back on it I can see that was crazy. If he'd gone for a dress uniform it would've been Royal Canadian Dragoons. Cornish is a flashy silver-helmet kind of guy if ever there was one. But anyway, a couple of months ago I asked him, you know, just in passing, what costume he was going to wear. He looked at me for a second. Then he said, 'Gordon, you're the third person who's asked me that this week. I didn't tell the others because, frankly, I'm out to win the prize for the best costume. But since you're a man of honor and wouldn't steal my idea I will tell you. I'm going to go as .'"

"For god sake!" said Harner, scornfully. "That was Cornish for you. He couldn't take anything seriously, not even a fancy dress ball. I'd told him as much when he worked for me on 'Our Mutual Friend,' the mutual fund newsletter I edit for Mulcaster Publications. He was the kind of guy who'd walk the halls of our nation's financial capital whistling 'Mexicali Rose.' He never cared much for me either. Claimed I held him back. He wanted to start this business magazine for entrepreneurs who don't take themselves too seriously. When I pooh-pooled the idea he went over my head to Mr. Mulcaster himself who liked the concept. And so *Beeswax Week* was born."

"Oh, dear," said Pond with a little smile.

Harner looked back at him with sad eyes. "Wilfrid," he said, "the damn thing's selling like hotcakes." Harner shook his head ruefully. "Cornish is Mulcaster's white haired boy." He cast a critical eye heavenward before continuing. "But let's get back to our little story. So there I was last night striding into Case Lama all togged out like this. And of course no one else was in costume. Cornish had positioned himself near the entrance to enjoy the show. I could see him biting his cheeks to keep from laughing. But while a lot of people were giving me the fish-eye, I could see through my embarrassment that others were figuring maybe I'd served in the regiment or something and had the right to wear the uniform instead of evening dress. So I decided to brazen it out. And I think I did."

"Then I'd say no harm done," said Pond.

Harner raised a finger against interruptions before continuing. "The trouble is at the dance I met Doreen, this new assistant editor at *Beeswax Week*. I could see she was attracted to me. Oh, sure, the uniform played a large part in that. It's a fashionable regiment, after all. Well, to make a long story short, Doreen and I had a wonderful evening. Mind you, I knew that the next day Cornish would set her straight about my thinking it was fancy dress and my uniform being rented. Even as we danced cheek-to-cheek I could hear her terrible laughter."

"Perhaps she wouldn't laugh," insisted Pond.

"I know whereof I speak," said Harner with authority. "She'll laugh. Oh, what a fool she'll take me for. Still, knowing all that, I resolved to enjoy the evening. I took her home afterward and stood with her outside her door for an hour, talking, hoping to prolong the moment. Stammering like a damn schoolboy I even asked her out again and was overjoyed when she said yes. Isn't that crazy? I mean I knew it'd be all over between us as soon as she saw

Cornish. That'll be this afternoon. You see, today's the day the Mulcaster editors meet over lunch to discuss future market trends. Afterwards they return to their various offices to assign the assistant editors their new projects. Right after lunch, that's when Cornish will let l her in on his little joke." Harner put his hands over his ears and shook his head to ward off Doreen's laughter. "I walked the streets all night, pondering my alternatives. By dawn I knew there was only one way. I had to kill Cornish."

"But it's wrong to kill someone," said Pond.

"Isn't that a simple answer to a complex problem, Wilfrid?" asked Harner. "Can't a man defend himself?"

"But you're not being attacked."

"That man might as well put a bullet in my head," said Harner earnestly. He reached over and tapped Pond's knee. "Okay, call me Mr. Sober-sides. I'm not the kind of guy who plays around with the ladies. Doreen's a once-in-a-lifetime chance for me. If I don't kill him Cornish can destroy it all" —he snapped his fingers— "just like that."

Pond gave him a compassionate look and shook his head. "But suppose you did kill Cornish and got away with it and married Doreen, what kind of a life are we talking about? Suppose the RCR gets called back to the colors for some police action of other?" Pond mimicked the plumy tones of a well-known television anchorman. "'Once again Canada's brave boys answer the United Nations' call. Seen here is a contingent of the Royal Canadian Regiment boarding the transport planes that will take them to Cyprus, that hotbed of Greek and Turkish rivalry.' How would you explain your not going to Doreen?"

"It was a long night. I've thought it all out and I'm away ahead of you," said Harner. "I'd build this secret room in the attic and stock it with food and water. I'd always keep enough money in the bank account to tide her over while I was gone. After Doreen and I had exchanged our tearful goodbyes and I'd kissed little Gordie and Doug in their beds I'd sneak back in the house and upstairs to the secret room. When the regiment returned I'd whip down to Moss Park Costumes and out to the airport and mingle with the welcoming crowd." Switching into a plumier imitation of the television anchorman, he intoned, "'As our brave boys of the Royal Canadian Regiment return home from their stay in Cyprus a great world says "Well done, Canada. Well done!" while one jubilant officer raises a triumphant finger skyward. Yes, we are indeed number one.'"

"But you'd lose your job," insisted Pond.

"And find another," said Harner quickly. "And have many a talk with my wife about immoral companies that wont hold a man's job for him when he's off fighting for peace in our time."

Pond shrugged helplessly. Harner seemed to have an answer for everything.

"Cornish must die," said Harner, "unless, as I said, you can give me some reason why he shouldn't. Yes, by daybreak this morning I'd figured out the why and the where. I just hadn't decided the how. So when I stopped by my apartment to call in sick I picked up a few things." He unzipped the overnight bag and pulled out a hunting knife in a sheath, a pair of leather gloves, a length of picture wire and a pistol equipped with a silencer.

Pond's eyes grew wide at the last item. "How'd you get your hands on something like that in Toronto?"

"Ever heard of Merchants of Death mutual funds?" asked Harner. "Baskets of stock in armament companies, defense contractors and the like —safe, high yield funds we recommend to the conservative investor."

"Like widows and orphans?" asked Pond.

Harner shot him a sharp glance. "This is a serious business, Wilfrid. This isn't something out of *Beeswax Week*. Human life is on the line." He forced his voice to be calm. "Anyway one of these mutuals, the Urban Gunplay Fund which focuses on the stocks of companies manufacturing weapons for everyday self-defence, gave them out as party favors at a recent get-together for the financial press including yours truly."

"Silencers and all?"

"They call them anti-noise pollution devices," said Harner. "But I guess that's neither here nor there since I decided shooting Cornish would be much too fast. Ditto the knife." As he spoke the man began pulling on the leather gloves. "Did I tell you we Mulcaster editors have our weekly lunch at Chez Simon?" (Pond knew the place, a pretentious operation which had started out years before as a King Street lunch counter under the name "Simon the Shepherd's Pie Man.")

"Cornish likes to linger over his food," said Harner. "He's always the last to leave. And he's a tooth-proud man. Maybe that's because he grins so much. Anyway he carries a pocket toothbrush and uses it after every meal. Now there's a janitor's closet in the corridor leading to the men's room. That's where I'll wait." Harner took up the picture wire in his gloved hand and snapped it until he made it hum. He glared at Pond defiantly. "Unless you give me a reason why I shouldn't."

"You can't," shouted Pond, "because if you do I'll go to the police!" He lowered his voice and added firmly, "It's as simple as that, Gordon."

Harner made an exasperated noise, looked away and put his pith helmet back on. Then he turned back to Pond and said angrily, "Good god, man, is that the best you can do? How are you going to go to the police? Didn't you understand that I'd have to kill you, too, if you couldn't give me a reason not to kill Cornish?"

Pond hadn't seen Harner pick up the pistol. Suddenly it was there, pointed at his chest.

"You know," said Harner, "making up your mind to kill your first man takes a hell of a lot of thought. I must have walked for blocks last night stewing over that one. But deciding to kill number two's a real snap." Harner lowered the pistol barrel. "I'll tell you what," he said magnanimously. "I'll give you another chance. Think now. Why can't I kill Cornish?"

Pond's mind raced. He stared past Harner to the main path. There were more people walking there now. But every head was turned away from him and in the direction of the greenhouse. He blurted out, "Because you haven't an alibi. The police will check with the Mulcaster people to see if Cornish had any enemies at work. When they hear that you called in sick you'll be their prime suspect. And you won't have any alibi."

"But I will," said Harner. "Oh yes, after I kill you I'll take your house key and pay your sister Cecily a visit. I suspect I can make myself very unpleasant if I have to. When we're done she'll be glad to say we were together. Your sister will provide me with the alibi I need for Cornish's murder and for yours, too."

Pond was trembling. He knew Harner could feel the bench shake. In his mind's eye he could see the man turning the key in the lock and entering the house that Cecily always insisted they keep so dark. Half fearfully his sister would call out "Wilfrid?" as she always did. But this time Pond's voice would not come to reassure her and there would be a different footstep in the hall. "But that would kill her," insisted Pond hoarsely. "She'd die of fright."

"I doubt that, I do indeed," said Harner. "She's a strong woman and a smart one, too, your sister. She had the sense to know it's dog-eat-dog, tooth-and-nail out here. She had the sense to hide and the strength to stay hidden all these years until you led me to her. You're the foolhardy one, Wilfrid, walking around like no harm could ever come your way." Harner smiled contemptuously. "You're one of Cornish's breed, that's what you are. You don't take life seriously."

"All right," said Pond sharply. Then he repeated "All right" in a humbler voice and stared down at the path. "Leave my sister out of it. I won't go to the police. I'll be your alibi. I'll swear you were here with me."

Harner's smile turned sad and grew in size. "A while back you were telling me it was wrong to kill another person, he said. "Now you'll stand idly by while I take Cornish's life and on top of that you'll supply me with an alibi. How is it I don't believe you?" Harner shook his head. "No, I'm afraid I can't depend on you, Wilfrid. Sight unseen I'd say your sister's my best shot. She sounds smart enough to see the consequences of betraying me and strong enough to stick to our story no matter what. I'm afraid she's got you beaten hands down in those departments, Wilfrid." Harner raised the pistol again. Their eyes met. Pond felt the weapon against his chest. He stiffened and waited.

Then Harner said quietly, "Of course there is a way out of our little dilemma, one that would solve things rather neatly." Harner nodded to direct Pond's eyes to the weapon. Pond found it was the pistol butt against his chest.

Harner nodded. "Here's our way out," he said. "You kill Cornish for me. That way you wont be able to go to the police. And I could provide my own alibi. I wouldn't have to kill you. And we could leave your sister out of the whole business."

Pond's eyes looked close to filling up with tears. "But I don't even know your damned Cornish," he insisted.

"*Our* damned Cornish," corrected Harner. "Look, it'd be easy as pie. You wouldn't have to linger over it the way I would with the picture wire. You hide in the janitor's closet until somebody comes along whistling 'Mexicali Rose.' You step out. You shoot him several times in the heart and pop out the door to the parking lot."

Harner dropped the pistol into Pond's lap. "But believe me, Wilfrid, it's dog-eat-dog. If it turns out I have to kill Cornish myself I'll come after you and your sister. I'll get her first just to give you something to think about. Then I'll kill you, too." While Harner's hands mimed the slow strangulation of someone with invisible picture wire, his head did a twitching imitation of the victim, complete with dry noises and lolling tongue.

In the midst of this Pond scooped up the pistol and, with trembling hands, pointed it at Harner. "You bastard!" he said.

"Be careful," said Harner. "It's not on the safety-catch."

"You be careful," ordered Pond, in a reedy voice. "Just — just put your hands on your head."

"You're not very trustworthy, Wilfrid," observed Harner. "But, no, I'm not going to play along, at least not until you get an ammunition clip for the gun."

Pond lowered the weapon without bothering to look to see if there was a clip in it. He sagged on the bench.

"Buck up, Wilfrid," said Harner. "The clip's taped to the side of the sink next to the wall in the janitor's closet at Chez Simon." Thrusting the knife and the picture wire and gloves back inside the overnight bag Harner got to his feet. "So I'm counting on you, okay? Don't make me come looking for you and Cecily. You won't like it if I do." Without another word Harner picked up the bag and marched off down the path.

Pond followed him with his eyes as he walked out of the park and continued along Gerrard in the direction of Sherbourne, the black iron fence making his figure stutter like those animated corners in big-little books

Pond remembered as a boy. Then Harner turned the corner onto Sherbourne and was gone.

Pond hung his head for a moment, concentrating all his powers on bringing his racing heart and churning stomach under control. He knew he mustn't panic. He needed to think things out calmly. What could he do? What *could* he do? Go to the police. All right. But they wouldn't believe his story, not until Harner killed Cornish himself. Then it would be too late. By then Pond and his sister would be dead, too, killed by a sadistic madman who believed Pond had let him down and helped destroy his life. Pond and his sister couldn't even run away. Cecily wouldn't leave the house. In his mind's eye he saw her face. Suddenly, as though she knew someone was thinking about her, Cecily's expression turned to fear and her lips moved. "Wilfrid?" he knew she was saying.

Pond gave a trembling sigh. But when he raised his head again he had determined what he was going to do. The park was bright now, the main path busy. A streetcar clanged on Carlton. The same policeman was strolling toward him. He stopped when he reached the bench. For an instant Pond thought the man had seen him slip the pistol under his jacket. Then the policeman reached down and picked up the copy of *War and Peace* which had fallen to the ground beside the bench. He read the book's spine as he handed it back and gave Pond a suspicious look. When the policeman had moved on Pond got to his feet and started off in the direction of the restaurant so many blocks away. Yes, it was dog-eat-dog. It was tooth-and-claw. Perhaps, as he crouched in the darkness of the janitor's closet with the clip in the pistol his ears straining for "Mexicali Rose" he would come up with a way out. Perhaps. But for the moment Pond's greatest fear was that when it came right down to it he wouldn't have the courage to kill Cornish, just as back then he hadn't been able to pull the trigger on Harner.

Suddenly a voice said, "Well, good morning, Mr. Pond. Are you all right? You look like you just lost your best friend."

Pond turned to discover a smiling Mr. Fisk sitting on a bench near the Gerrard Street gate. "Oh, hello, Mr. Fisk," he said, adding automatically, "How's your lovely granddaughter?"

"Still head of her class, nice of you to ask," answered the proud grandfather.

Pond had started to walk on. But now he stopped. Suddenly the whole thing was clear to him. Telling himself it was the law of the jungle, that it was dog-eat-dog he went back and sat down on the bench. "Lucky my running in to you, Mr. Fisk," he said, looking at his wristwatch. "I really need your advice on a matter of life and death. You see, unless you can talk me out of it, in forty-five minutes I'm going to have to kill a man named Charles Cornish."

“I zipped back to Yonge Street, shot down a block and skidded to a halt in front of the Coroner’s building on Grenville.”

[Photograph Copyright © William Alexander McCoy. Used with the permission of the photographer.]

Rosemary AUBERT

Shaving with Occam's Razor

(original story)

Biographical information about the author will be found at the back of the book.

There is a town in which every man is clean-shaven, but no one shaves himself, all are shaved by a barber. Who shaves the barber?

The answer to this riddle can be found by shaving the barber with Occam's Razor, the theory of the economy of hypotheses propounded by the mediaeval English philosopher, William of Ockham.

In "Shaving with Occam's Razor", Rosemary Aubert presents a tantalizing little mystery, so strop the blade and see if your wits are as sharp as the narrator's.

Shaving with Occam's Razor

On the way to the morque I nearly got hit at Wellesley. I was late for forensics class for the third time in five weeks. Not my fault. A heavy day at the office, three parolees facing suspension for suspected drug dealing—I was thinking about work when I ran up out of the subway and almost collided with an incoming eastbound bus.

I tore along Yonge, hung a right at Grosvenor, remembered we weren't meeting at the Centre for Forensics like we usually did. Field trip. I zipped back to Yonge, shot down a block and skidded to a halt in front of the Coroner's building on Grenville.

And then I had to wait in the front office while a frantic receptionist tried to find the phone number of somebody's next of kin.

So I was in no mood for sarcasm when I was finally buzzed through, managed to locate the lecture hall, opened the door, walked in and found myself standing beside the instructor at the front of a room full of my fellow classmates, all of whom were staring at me as if I were some sort of specimen.

"We're waiting for you, madam. You're late," the instructor announced, dramatically eyeing his watch. I'd never seen the guy before in my life, but already I knew he was a retired cop. The attitude. The Metropolitan Toronto Police seal emblazoned on the face of the watch.

"Not as late as most of the people in this building," I answered.

The class sniggered. The ex-cop looked shocked. Good.

Of course the only seat left was in the first row, right smack in front of him.

"How many times has this man been shot?" he asked me, before my bottom even touched the chair. I suppose he thought he was tricking me. Silly man. I haven't spent the last ten years as a parole officer for nothing. Manipulative people like crooks and cops always ask quick questions hoping to throw people off guard.

I glanced up at the screen behind him. Projected there, in x-ray, was the outline of what appeared to be an adult male. The poor guy was a piece of Swiss cheese—a couple dozen holes in him, fanned across his torso.

"Once. He's been shot only once," I said, settling into the chair and shrugging off my jacket.

"Why, you're right—" The ex-cop's eyes locked into mine for a second. Nice gray eyes. Wary. Wise. The kind that have seen just about everything—or think they have. Right now they were registering surprise again. I smiled. He addressed the rest of the class, "Here we see the typical pattern produced by the impact of shot from a single shotgun shell...."

There was a click from somewhere behind me and a new image flicked onto the screen. It was another adult male body, this time a schematic outline. Beside each part of the body was a tidy list of the types of evidence the forensic scientist looked for: strands of hair, the characteristic indentations produced by a person's teeth, fingerprints...

Beside me and behind me, I heard the frantic scratching of people taking notes. I was the only corrections person in the forensics class. The rest was divided just about fifty-fifty. Half were cops trying to improve their chances for promotion. The other half were mystery writers trying to improve their chances for publication.

I didn't bother taking notes. It was obvious to me what sort of evidence would be looked for—plus we'd been studying it all term. "Forget your pen?" the instructor asked sweetly.

"No sir," I replied, and I winked.

He blushed. Cops blush all the time. Cry, too. No wonder, considering.

I felt like crying myself when I caught the next slide. It showed the body of a man who couldn't be older than about twenty. He was spread out on a white table. His arms and legs were thin, but still muscular. His thick long auburn hair formed a pool under his head. There was a Y-shaped cut on his chest, one of the beginning steps of an autopsy. In death, his face didn't have any real expression on it, but I couldn't help but see sorrow there. Inset into the slide was another picture. It showed a small square, sewed together with crooked stitches from two dirty pieces of cloth and attached to what looked like an old shoelace.

"Anybody want to venture a guess as to what this might be?" the instructor asked, using a pointer to lightly tap the square on the screen.

I had an idea, but I kept my mouth shut. I'd had about all the attention I cared to have for one night, thank you.

"Valuables—" I heard one of the cops in the class whisper.

"Yes," the instructor replied. "This is the body of a homeless street person. Tied to his underwear, we found—as we often find—a small satchel containing the sum total of his remaining worldly goods."

There was another click, another slide—showing the little squares of cloth separated to reveal the contents—two shining wedding rings, a woman's and a man's.

Seeing this, the writers scribbled faster. The cops didn't bother. There's a million stories in a city morque, and enough people already who think they can tell them.

"Now class," the instructor said, "It's your turn. I need a volunteer." Onto the screen came a strange picture. It showed the slender body of what appeared to be an elderly male seated in an easychair. Over his head was a plastic bag from a well-known supermarket, its logo accidentally looking like a screwed-up human face. The bag was tightened around the man's neck with a rope. One of his arms was bound with the same sort of rope; the other hung limp and free, dangling over the arm of the chair.
"I want a volunteer to analyze this scene for me—tell me what happened here—"

Behind me I heard the embarrassed scrunching down into seats of people who didn't want to be called on. I didn't scrunch down. I didn't think the instructor had the nerve to call on me again. Anyway, I didn't care one way or the other. I knew what the slide showed.

He waited. Nobody volunteered. I looked up. Those gray eyes were on me. When I didn't look away, he handed me his pointer. "Tell us—" he said. I thought he seemed pretty sure I wouldn't be able to.

I stood, took the pointer from his hand, turned to face the class. In my best case-presentation voice I said, "Though this is an apparent homicide, what we're looking at here is not really a murder scene—"

I shot the instructor a glance. For the first time, I saw traces of a genuine smile on his mouth. "Please continue," he said.

I nodded. "First and foremost, there's no sign of struggle—no clothing in disarray, no furniture displaced—" I used the pointer to show a table beside the chair in which the victim sat. It was covered with little knick-knacks—all in a row. "No scratches on the body, no blood...."

"But the man has a rope around his neck—" the instructor interrupted. His voice was challenging, like that of a coach.

"Yes. But it's the same rope that's around his arm. Not just the same kind—the same piece." I slid the pointer along the picture. The rope wrapped around the neck, then seemed to disappear behind the chair, but if you traced carefully, it wasn't hard to figure out that it must loop behind the chair then back around the front—around the man's right wrist. "What this person did," I concluded, "was rig up this rope in such a way that when he yanked his arm, it tightened around his neck...."

The instructor was actually looking pleased now. But I wasn't finished. "There are other reasons to believe this is a suicide," I went on.

"For starters, homicide is a much rarer occurence than suicide. So, statistically, the chances of any questionable death being suicide are much higher than its being murder. Also, the victim is an elderly male. Traditionally, males handle being alone much more poorly than females. And though they don't always turn to suicide, of course, they are far more likely to do so than some other segments of society...."

"Thank you, that's enough," he said, taking the pointer from my hand. I couldn't tell whether he was pleased or whether I'd gone too far. Maybe I embarrassed him. At least now he'd get off my back.

"This is an elderly widower who had just learned he had cancer. He killed himself when he got the news. In this case—and in all cases," he said, "it's best to apply a principle referred to as Occam's razor. Occam was a medieval philosopher dedicated to teaching that truth results from the observation of the physical world. He said that the simplest explanation of any phenomenon is almost invariably the truest. When I myself was studying, I was told, 'When you hear hoofbeats, think of horses, not zebras.' I can offer no better advice."

With that, he adjourned the lecture. I knew what had to be coming next. He led us down a winding corridor and into a brightly lit room that sparkled with white enamel, spotless tile, stainless steel. There were drains in the floor.

"The morque is part of the ministry of the Solicitor General of Ontario," he told us, "and like all government offices, we work business hours. 8:30 to 4:30. No autopsies at night...."

A sigh went around the group that was now huddled around the instructor. Relief from the cops. Disappointment from the writers.

"But here in the autopsy room you see the atmosphere in which we work—and some of the tools of our trade."

Saws, scalpels, knives, picks, hoses. Microphones and tape recorders. He showed us the video room, where bodies were displayed for next of kin too sqeamish to look directly at their loved ones. Scales for weighing dead livers and hearts, jars of organs ready for analysis when "office hours" resumed. A room for isolating bodies infested with insects—whose lifespan, he helpfully pointed out—gave a good clue as to time of death.

"There is a cycle of death that follows the seasons year after year," he told us. "At New Year's we see cases of people who've died accidentally because of alcohol—choking while asleep for example. Late winter-early spring, we get people who've gone through the ice on their snowmobiles. Summer brings drownings. Autumn-early winter, carbon monoxide poisoning from furnaces and chimneys poorly maintained..."

As he talked, he led us toward two tall steel doors. There could only be one thing behind them, but when he pulled on the handle and slowly opened them, I have to admit I was shocked.

Because of the smell, which was not of putrefication, which I would not have expected, or of preservative, which I would have expected. No. The huge refrigerator that held the bodies that were awaiting further action let loose a smell exactly like fresh meat.

I gasped and stepped back. He noticed. A look almost of disappointment seemed to cross his face. I took a breath and stepped back up toward where he stood near the door.

At that moment, he reached down, grasped a steel handle and yanked. Out slid a shelf, not inches from my waist.

And on lay it the corpse of a woman my own age. She was tall and thin. Pretty. Her fair skin was just beginning to be wrinkled. Her blond hair was just a tiny bit tinged with gray. She was naked but her body was modestly covered with a sheet. "What happened?" I found myself asking, even though I knew it was a dumb question.

This was the instructor's opportunity for a smart answer. He could have easily got even with me for my own smartness.

Instead, with the greatest gravity, he said, "That's for my people to find out. And we will not fail her by neglecting to do so—"

A few of the students filed by and studied the body. Most, however, headed for the door. I was the last to leave, the instructor at my heels as we twisted along the corridors that led back to the reception area. Everybody was gone by the time I got there.

I turned to thank the instructor, to apologize for my rudeness. But before I could speak, there was a commotion at the receptionist's desk. I heard a distraught woman yell, "Where is she. Tell me where she is!"

I turned. And what I saw nearly made me faint.

It was the woman on the slab returned to life, tall, slender, pretty. Her fair skin was just beginning to show wrinkles. Her blonde hair just beginning to turn to gray.

I thought it was some sort of sick joke. Some effort to scare or confuse me.

But when I looked at the instructor's face, I saw an expression of such pity that I realized this was no joke.

And besides, he had completely forgotten I was there. He was stepping toward the woman. He reached out his hand and gently touched her shoulder, like it was something he'd done a thousand times before. Cop. Coroner. Bearer of bad tidings.

I stepped aside. But I still didn't know what was happening.

Then, as if he remembered I was still around, he turned. All he said was "Occam's razor."

I was out in the street and back at the subway, narrowly missing get hit by the westbound Wellesley bus before I finally figured it out.

***

Who shaves the barber? No one, because the barber doesn't shave. Every man is clean-shaven and no one shaves himself, so applying the proposition that when you are faced with a variety of solutions to a problem, the simplest is most likely to be the truth, the person who does the shaving, i.e., the barber, is beardless because the barber is a woman.

“One day he was sitting in a Bloor Street West cafe next to the table Gregoire and Menard were using.”
[Picture Copyright © Douglas Purdon. Used with the permission of the artist.]

Peter A. SELLERS

Bombed

(*Ellery Queen's Mystery Magazine*, June 1994; revised, 1996).

Biographical information about the author will be found at the back of the book.

Gre'goire is doubly hoist with his own petard, but at least he goes out with a bang and not a whimper. Ain't science wonderful?

Bombed

Nobody objected at first when Gregoire said they were going to blow up Hannigan.

Nobody objected at all when Gregoire said he would make the bomb and plant it. After all, Gregoire had made and planted bombs all over Montreal and Ottawa back in 1970, during the heady days of the *Front de Liberation du Quebec*.

True, most of those bombs had never exploded. And two that did had gone off prematurely; one of them blowing the left hand and right arm off the high school student who'd unwittingly been paid five dollars to deliver an unmarked package to the British Consulate. But that was over twenty years ago when Gregoire had been very young. Since then, he'd done time and everyone figured he knew a little more now.

They were sitting in a damp cellar in Toronto sipping cheap French wine from plastic cups. They had come to Toronto because that was where Hannigan lived. It was where Gregoire intended Hannigan should also die. It was late afternoon and a thin shaft of sunlight slanted in from the one small, high western facing window. It was the only light. Gregoire insisted on that, and he also insisted on the uncomfortable meeting place. They would all, he said, have to get used to life on the run.

Gregoire knew all about that, too, of course. After the 1970 bombings, he had spent eight months scurrying around Quebec trying to elude the police he thought were chasing him. They, on the other hand, had assumed he was in Morocco with others of his terrorist cell, and would never have caught him if he hadn't started a violent argument with an Anglo shopkeeper in the Eastern Townships who refused to speak to him in French. Gregoire got so angry at the *maudit Anglais* that he punched him in the nose. The local Quebec Provincial Police officer arrested him and a routine check showed Gregoire to be one of the ten most wanted of the FLQ terrorists.

But those were the glory days. None of Gregoire's former compatriots would have anything to do with him now. His ideas were too radical. The politicians seemed only interested in beating the rest of the country into submission with a numbing series of referendums. Even at the universities, once hotbeds of unrest, the students were more interested in business careers and job security than in bombing and manifestos and ransom demands.

So they were three. Menard was still there from the old days, his battered beret at a sloppy angle on the right side of his head while a smoking Gauloise balanced it off by dangling perpetually from the left side of his mouth. He was short and wide and plump and his eyes were moist and unhappy.

Dumoulin, an Anglo from Manitoba who didn't speak French despite his name, was involved by a stroke of chance. One day he was sitting in a Bloor Street West cafe next to the table Gregoire and Menard were using. Their conversation was heated and in French so Dumoulin could not follow it, but he heard the word "plastique" mentioned several times and that was enough.

At first, when Dumoulin spoke to them softly and in English, they ignored him. But when he persisted, and told them if they wanted plastique he could help, they began to listen, Menard translating for Gregoire, who refused to speak, and pretended not to understand, any English at all.

Dumoulin had been dishonourably discharged from the Canadian armed forces the year before. He had taken with him a lingering hatred for the Canadian government and two pounds of plastic explosive, smuggled out in marble sized balls over a period of ten months. He had simply been waiting for an opportunity to use it in a meaningful way.

He kept one of the small lumps of explosive with him at all times, just in case. To show he was serious, Dumoulin took the explosive out of his pocket and dropped it on the table between the Quebecois conspirators. Menard drew back in shock, hands raised as if to ward off the blast. Even Gregoire was startled. Most of his early bombs had been of dynamite, and he had once blown up a telephone booth with nitroglycerine. But he had never seen plastique before, although he understood the theory.

Dumoulin laughed as he picked up the formless blob. "Cool it, boys," he said. "This stuff's stable as dirt. You could play handball with it and nothing'd happen. But detonate it..." he smiled and made a soft "kaboom" with his lips. "...and it's good night, nurse."

Gregoire wasn't sure what nurses had to do with anything. After he was through, even doctors wouldn't help, but he let it go. He knew as well as anyone that all Anglos were crazy.

"You can get more?" Gregoire asked through Menard.

Dumoulin spoke the only French he knew. "*Oui*," he said with a smile. So Dumoulin became a terrorist and Gregoire became armed and dangerous.

"We'll put the bomb in his car," Gregoire said with a smile. He had put bombs in mailboxes and checked them at bus terminals and placed them outside private homes alongside the morning milk delivery. But he had never put a bomb in a car, and the prospect excited him very much.

"Timer?" Dumoulin asked.

Gregoire shook his head. "Too risky," he said, more cautious now than when he was a young man. "He might not be in the car when it goes off. I'm going to hook it up to his cellular phone. Then when he takes the car out, we make a business call."

When Dumoulin left to retrieve his cache of explosive, Menard stayed behind. There was, after all, still the heel of the bottle. He poured the last of it into his glass too aggressively, and some splashed onto his hand. He licked it off, then expressed his concern to Gregoire, "Do you think this is a good idea?"

"*Quoi*? What?"

"Blowing up this 'annigan? He's very well known."

"That's exactly the idea," Gregoire bellowed, slamming his fist on the rickety card table so that Menard had to dive forward to keep his wine glass from toppling.

"But won't it bring the authorities after us too seriously? Perhaps we should start small. With a security guard or the nanny of a government official."

"*Tabernac*!"

"A politician, then," Menard offered meekly.

"We've killed politicians before. Nobody cares about politicians. But 'annigan, the man so many have adopted as the voice of English Canada, his death will cause a stir." He fixed Menard with a reptilian glare. "Who else, other than 'annigan, has denounced us in a book on the New York Times bestseller list and in American magazines, making all separatists out as buffoons, villains and cowards?"

"*Personne*," Menard answered sadly. "Nobody."

"Who else has attacked us, like a coward himself, from the protective bosom of Toronto?"

"*Personne*."

"So, who would be a better first strike for us? Whose death would send up a larger cheer all across *la belle province*?"

"*Personne*."

"Ask me no more stupid questions. It is 'annigan. And it is soon. Is there any more wine?"

Hannigan walked to meet his publisher. It wasn't far, about a mile and a half due south from Hannigan's condo near Yonge and St. Clair to Bulivant's office near Yonge and Bloor. It was one of those perfect autumn days Toronto enjoys. The air was clean and crisp, the sky was blue and clear, the leaves were a wonderful collage of red and yellow and orange. After the meeting, he'd walk back to get his car and drive to Susan's apartment in the Beach area along the lake at the eastern end of the city.

Days like this, Hannigan didn't miss Montreal. He had left initially because he wanted to write about Quebec from a distance; to have a sense of what people outside the province felt about what was going on there. Now he didn't think he could ever return there to live. He kept his summer place in the Eastern Townships, and sometimes he missed the sensual excitement of Montreal at night, but it had changed too much to be his home anymore.

Besides, he had Susan here now. He whistled aloud and shuffled his feet through the fallen leaves as he walked.

Getting into Hannigan's car was a piece of cake. Gregoire had learned about more than just bombs during his time inside.

Gregoire sat on a bench across the road from Hannigan's condominium, the material for the bomb in a brown paper lunch bag at his side. He sat there patiently for slightly over two hours and, finally, he saw the front door of the building open and Hannigan emerge and stroll briskly along the street without so much as a glance in Gregoire's direction. Gregoire sat ten minutes longer before standing, picking up his lunch bag, and walking casually across the road. He walked along the driveway towards the entrance to the underground garage and after two minutes he heard the automatic door begin to rumble open. Ducking behind a garbage dumpster, Gregoire watched a blue mini van emerge and, as soon as it had passed him, he broke from cover and sprinted towards the closing door. He raced down the steep ramp and hurled himself under the door moments before it shut.

Rising, he dusted himself off and began looking for Hannigan's license number. It wasn't hard to find, the garage being almost empty. After a quick check to make sure he was unobserved, Gregoire was inside the car in a matter of seconds. He crouched down below the dashboard and went to work. The plastique he packed under the driver's seat, pushing it securely into the springs. Menard had cautioned him that he had enough of the stuff to demolish a ten storey building, but Gregoire didn't want to take any chances.

"That's a hell of a whooppee cushion," Dumoulin had said. Menard had tried to translate, but Gregoire still wasn't sure what the *maudit Anglais* was talking about.

The rest of the installation was simple enough. Gregoire's home-made detonator was packed into the plastique and attached to two fine black wires that led out to the phone where it was positioned over top of the drive shaft. Gregoire tucked the wire as discreetly as possible into the seams in the carpeting, then wired it into the phone, hooking it up so that the electronic impulse of the phone starting to ring would send a signal snaking down the wire to the detonator, and Hannigan would be annihilated before he even had time to wonder who was calling.

With the bomb in place, Gregoire now had to find the phone number. It wasn't hard. Hannigan, like so many fools, had it written in a small telephone directory in the glove compartment. Gregoire copied the number down on a slip of paper, checked it, then checked it again. Satisfied, he eased himself out of the car and locked the door. He arched his back once to stretch out the kinks, walked briskly through the garage, jumped vigorously on the cable to open the automatic door, and sauntered out into the sunlight, throwing the empty lunch bag into the garbage dumpster as he passed.

"Why don't we just go back to Montreal, now?" Menard asked. "After all, the bomb is planted. Sooner or later someone will call him and blow him to hell, and we'll be three hundred miles away."

Gregoire shook his head. "No," he said. "Someone will not call. I will call. And I will be close at hand when I do." It was a matter of pride with Gregoire. He had declared war, and he wanted to be the one to push the buttons.

"There was another death threat," Bulivant said, tossing a sheet of paper onto his desk in front of Hannigan.

Hannigan looked at it casually. The content was the same as many of the others, barely comprehensible, but this time it had been done on a personal computer, enlivened with a variety of type faces and fonts, to give it more instant visual impact. "It's the prettiest so far," Hannigan said with a smile.

"You can laugh. The police don't think it's funny."

"They've seen this, have they?"

Bulivant nodded. "They have the original. This is a photocopy."

"We've never got one done on a Mac before, have we?"

"No." Bulivant shook his head. "Look, I'm starting to get nervous," he said. "I got into publishing because I thought it would be quiet and safe. Now death threats are arriving at the office every other day, some of them aimed at me. God knows how long before they start sending bombs in padded envelopes marked "Manuscript". I don't know why you find this so amusing, and why you're egging them on."

"I'm not egging them on. But every time something like this arrives it boosts sales. What's the next printing?"

"We just increased it to seventy-five thousand."

"That makes four printings and two hundred and fifty thousand books in just over six months. At that rate, I say, keep those cards and letters comin' in, folks. Besides, these guys won't do a damn thing. Trust me. Assassination is like sex. You don't talk about it, you do it. The guys to worry about are the ones you never hear from."

Bulivant shook his head and sighed. "All I need now is to get Salman Rushdie under contract."

"I think the Ayatollah beat you to it," Hannigan said. "Now let's talk about that last royalty statement."

Gregoire never let his small cadre communicate with the media in any way. He certainly wouldn't have permitted direct contact with Hannigan. Let the fools who wrote to Hannigan draw the attention before the fact. After he was dead, then Gregoire would let them know who was really prepared to take action. Who was really to be listened to. Who was really to be feared. So, no. No threats in the mail. No contact with the quarry. The only time they'd even come close to that would be that one fatal phone call.

Gregoire placed that call for the first time later that afternoon. From their vantage point outside Hannigan's apartment, they watched him drive away and then they walked as casually as the circumstances allowed to a nearby public telephone. Gregoire fished in his pockets for a quarter, but found none. "Have you a quarter?" he asked Menard.

Menard frowned and fumbled through his pockets, eventually digging out a coin. Gregoire slipped it into the phone and carefully dialled the number he'd copied down on his sheet of paper. After dialling he waited in eager expectation for the phone to start to ring. He wondered what would happen when the explosion came. Would he be cut off in mid ring? Would he feel some trembling vibration down the line? Or, and this would be the best of all, would a clinical computer-generated voice come on the line and announce, "We're sorry, the number you have dialled is no longer in service."

Gregoire was so engrossed in these thoughts that he didn't immediately notice that the first ring was not cut off. Nor was the second. Nor the third. And the voice that answered the phone in the middle of the fourth ring wasn't generated by computer, but by a cheerful woman who said, "Hello?"

Gregoire was stunned. He couldn't figure out what was happening. He couldn't think of anything to say.

"Hello?" the voice said again. "Is anyone there?"

Gregoire held the phone as far away from his face as the phone booth would allow and stared at it in a mixture of confusion and irritation. From a distance, he heard the woman's voice repeat, "Hello? Hello?" Then she hung up and the phone in Gregoire's hand began to buzz. After a few more seconds, he slammed down the receiver and left the phone booth.

"What happened?" Menard asked.

Gregoire stared at Menard as if he didn't know who he was. Then he said, "*Je ne c'est pas*. I don't know."

"There was something wrong with the bomb?"

"No, *trou d'cul*, there's nothing wrong with the bomb. There's something wrong with that phone. It misdialled on me. Or there's something wrong with the phone company. They misdirected my call. But the bomb is perfect."

"Perhaps you copied the number down wrong," Menard suggested gently.

"*Tabernac*!" Gregoire exploded, and Menard spat the butt of his Gauloise to the sidewalk and fumbled for a fresh one. "We will try again from another phone."

Two blocks along the street Gregoire and Menard found another phone booth. Gregoire took the slip of paper with Hannigan's phone number on it from his pocket and stared hard at it, frowning. Menard patted his pockets again in search of another quarter but found nothing.

"*Rien*," he said to Gregoire.

"Well let's go and get some," he said, walking briskly away. Menard stuffed his hands into his pockets and shuffled along the street. They stopped in a donut shop and Menard bought them each a day old cruller. He paid with a five dollar bill, giving Gregoire a quarter from the change and Gregoire went to the phone on the wall beside the exit.

Gregoire studied the number one last time before dialling. He punched the numbers slowly and carefully.

This time he didn't think about what might happen on the other end of the line. He restrained himself from visions of twisted metal and severed limbs and focused instead on what he could hear. The musical tone of the number dialling, the crackling pause while he waited for the connection, and then the ringing. Once. Twice. Three times. And the same woman's voice abruptly on the end of the line, "Hello?"

Gregoire was stunned, but this time he knew he had to say something, but what. He hadn't spoken English in such a long time. Suddenly, without being able to stop himself, he blurted out, "Are the pants ready?"

This time the silence was on the other end of the line. Then the woman's voice came back, bemused, "Pants? I'm afraid you have the wrong number."

"*Moi aussi*," Gregoire said. "Me, too. *Pardonez-moi*." And he slammed down the phone, cursing. He knew he hadn't misdialled. This time he knew the phone company had made a mistake. Maybe he should blow them up next. He left the donut shop hurriedly and Menard darted after him, brushing crumbs from his shirt.

"No luck?" Menard asked sadly.

"It's not a question of luck," Gregoire snapped. "Something is not right."

"Are you going to try again?"

"Later. Now I need a glass of wine and time to think."

Menard's expression brightened noticeably.

The third time the phone rang in Susan Bellamy's apartment, she picked it up hesitantly. The last two calls had been odd, and curiously unsettling. True, there'd been no heavy breathing or guttural obscenities, unless you considered a bizarre request about pants obscene. But there was still something not quite right. Susan picked up the receiver on the third ring. "Hello?" she said after a moment's pause.

Then she did hear breathing, what sounded like a sigh of disappointment, and the same thick French accent from before asked, "Is Guillaume there?"

"No," she said. "There's no one here by that name."

The voice sighed again and rattled off a telephone number, interspersing English and French digits intermittently, asking if that was the number he had called. Susan wasn't exactly sure what number he'd quoted, but she recognized enough to know it wasn't hers. "No," she said. "I'm afraid you've got the wrong number." Then she hung up, very puzzled indeed.

"I've had a couple of phone calls," Susan said after she'd shut the door behind Hannigan and kissed him for a very long time.

"Who from?"

"I don't know. There were three, actually. It was very peculiar."

"What was it, a heavy breather?"

"No, it was some guy with a French accent. The third time he called he asked for Guillaume. That's French for William."

"I thought it was French for bean."

"That's legume," she said.

"Ah, so he asked for Guillaume, did he?"

"Yes, but then he gave me the number he had dialled, to check, you know? And usually when people do that, they're off by one digit or they transposed a couple of numbers, or something. But the number he gave me wasn't even close. It didn't make sense at first, but the number seemed familiar. After I hung up, I realized it was your car phone number." She frowned. "You might have told me you were forwarding your calls here. I could have taken a message or helped the fellow out."

"It's just as well you didn't," Hannigan said. "There was another death threat."

"Oh, no," she gave him a worried look.

"Don't worry. It's no big deal. Just another crank who wants to shoot off his mouth. The ones who are serious about it don't want to talk about it."

"But your car phone number isn't listed. How did they get it?"

Hannigan shrugged. "Bribe somebody. Blackmail somebody. Sleep with somebody. Find some ten-year-old whiz kid computer hacker to break into the data base. There are more ways than you could imagine to find out just about anything you want to know."

"So what are you going to do about it?"

"Nothing. Go out for dinner. Have a nice bottle of wine."

"I don't know how you can be so casual about this." She held out her hand. "Look, I'm shaking."

"Glass of wine'll fix you right up. Calm you right down."

"French?"

"Naw. A nice Ontario riesling."

Gregoire's newest weapon was a cellular phone of his own. It hadn't been his idea. Dumoulin had simply shown up with it soon after the first failed attempt on Hannigan's life. It was very small, and it folded almost in half. Gregoire took it from Dumoulin and slipped it into his pocket."

"*Pour vous*," Dumoulin said in his ever expanding French. "I decided to do some research," he continued in English which Menard translated slowly, "to find out what the hell was going on. He's probably having his calls forwarded."

Gregoire and Menard looked blank.

"It's technology, man," Dumoulin continued. "Hannigan has something programmed into the phone so that when you call his number, the call is intercepted and it rings somewhere else. It doesn't ring in the car. So the bomb won't go off."

Gregoire and Menard still said nothing. "That's why I got the phone," Dumoulin told them. He went on to explain that now someone could watch Hannigan and as soon as he was in the car, the watcher could call Gregoire and Gregoire could try to detonate the bomb wherever he was. Eventually, Hannigan would switch the call forwarding off and they'd have him.

Gregoire took the small phone out and unfolded it and turned it over lovingly in his hands. He appreciated the potential, and also the fact that it was registered in Dumoulin's name and he would get the bills. Here was power. Small and lethal. The ability to communicate instantly with anyone from anywhere. He decided to put it to the test. He would call his mother in Trois Rivieres. He hoped he could remember the number.

Susan was puttering in the kitchen when Hannigan woke up. After dinner they'd walked back to her place and Hannigan hadn't gone home. He brushed past her and poured a cup of coffee.

"Do you need your car this morning?" Susan asked.

"No. Why?"

"I have a few errands to run. Mind if I borrow it?"

"Sure. I've got this article that's due in two days and I haven't started writing yet. If I'm here and you're out I can get some work done."

"Not another scathing blast at separatist policies, I hope."

"You know me better than that," he said with a smile.

She took his keys and left.

She liked Hannigan's car. It handled very well and offered steady, even acceleration. It had FM and a tape player, while she was restricted to noisy AM stations. She eased back in the plush seat, adjusted the rearview mirror, altered the tilt of the steering wheel slightly, and started the engine smoothly and easily. Then she switched the radio from jazz to classical. Susan enjoyed the phone, too. She liked the convenience of it and the fact that if she broke down on the highway she could get help right away. She also liked the fact that Hannigan had it set up so that you didn't have to pick the phone up to talk. It always horrified her to see people barrelling along at great speeds, one hand on the wheel and the other clamping a phone to the side of their heads. Before she backed out of the parking spot at the side of her building, she switched on Hannigan's phone and dialled the number of her apartment.

"Yeah?" Hannigan said, with the gruff abruptness he always had when he was disturbed at work.

"It's only me, Tolstoy," she said. "I just wondered if you wanted me to pick anything up for you?"

"Don't think so, thanks. Oh, and listen, turn off the call forwarding for me, will you? I don't want the phone ringing here while I'm trying to work. Calls that I know are for you I can ignore. But if I think they're for me, I'll have to answer and I'll never get this thing done."

"Should I take messages for you?" she asked.

"You can. Or you can just let it ring. You can even switch it off if you want to. Whatever. Now let me get back to work."

"I'll leave it on," she said. "You may want to call me for inspiration. Or I may just phone up all my relatives in Australia."

It was warm in the mid-morning sunshine and Menard had drunk most of a litre of red wine at breakfast. He sat half dozing on the bench in the expanse of park that ran for several kilometres along the lakefront, across the street from Susan Bellamy's apartment building. It wasn't a building really. Not tall and gleaming like Hannigan's. It was a house, renovated into three flats. Menard had no idea who lived here, but Dumoulin had followed Hannigan the night before, and this was where he ended up. He was still in there, according to Dumoulin, wide awake despite being on watch most of the night.

Keeping watch was easy here because there was no underground parking. Hannigan's car stood in plain sight, gleaming in the bright sun, on the paved parking pad at the side of the house. Menard had watched the car steadily for hours and his eyes were beginning to ache. He rubbed them strenuously and yawned. There had been no sign of Hannigan. No activity of any kind. And he was feeling so contented with the wine and the gentle breeze from the lake and the spikes of sunshine through the leaves. He needed to rest his eyes. He'd shut them for just a second.

The dog woke Menard up. It bounced up and down at his feet and yapped angrily. Menard started and opened his eyes wide, looking around wildly, imagining himself surrounded by police with gas masks, riot guns and dogs. But all he saw was one small mottled mongrel and Menard sent it yelping away with a sharp kick. Then he took a deep breath to stop his heart pounding, rubbed the sleep from his eyes, and resumed his watch. He knew right away that something was different. It just took him a few minutes to figure out what exactly. When he did, it drove the air from his stomach in a gasp. Hannigan's car was gone.

Frantically, he looked up the street, then down, praying he would see it just rounding the corner or waiting at a stop sign. But there were no cars in sight at all.

How long had the car been gone, he wondered desperately? How long had he slept? Had it been a minute or a hour? He looked up at the sun as if he could read the time, but he had no idea which way was east and even if he did he realized it would have been useless. He knew all he needed to know. The car was gone. The hare was out. And the hounds had been caught napping.

Gregoire had trained Menard long ago not to run. People notice a running man, Gregoire said. Walk quickly and with purpose. For twenty years, that's what Menard had done. But now panic overtook everything he'd learned and, clamping a hand on top of his beret, he ran.

Menard leaned panting against the phone booth as he fished for a quarter, drew the coin from his pocket and dropped it in the slot. He punched the numbers too quickly in his excitement, hanging up, redialling the number of Gregoire's portable phone. "*Vite, vite*," Menard muttered to himself as he waited for the connection. "Hurry, hurry." He was bouncing up and down in his excitement. He didn't realize at first that the line was busy. Finally the buzzing made itself understood and Menard slammed down the phone.

"*Mon hosti de putaine*," he muttered and lit another Gauloise with anxious fingers.

By eleven o'clock, Hannigan was fed up. The article wasn't going well. He'd written a dozen different openings, none of which was right. He was having trouble focusing and decided he needed a break. And he knew exactly what to do. The kind of shopping excursion Susan was on today followed a predictable pattern. He was willing to bet that he knew exactly where she was at that very minute. He'd surprise her, perhaps be waiting in the car for her, and they'd have lunch together. He'd finish the article in the afternoon.

Shutting off the portable computer, Hannigan stood and stretched, grabbed his keys and his wallet, and went outside to hail a cab. As he settled back on the stiff, cracked upholstery, he looked out and saw a short, fat man in a beret stagger up to a phone booth and lean against it heavily. For a brief second, Hannigan wondered what his hurry was, then he turned his thoughts to Susan and the panting man was forgotten.

Susan drove slowly past the row of parked cars looking for a space. She had cruised west from the Beach, along Lakeshore Boulevard, all the way to High Park where she had lived for ten years before moving to the Beach the summer before. But there were things about the western part of the city she missed, and some stores she returned to religiously despite the drive. Often there were spaces to be had at curbside along these blocks of shops and restaurants. But today everything was taken. As she searched, Susan realized Hannigan was right and she shouldn't worry about the death threats. But these phone calls were different. They were very direct and very personal and there was something unsettling about them. Whoever had called obviously knew Hannigan's cellular number, but not his unlisted home number. What did they want? Absently, she took her right hand off the wheel, reached out and tapped her fingers on Hannigan's phone.

Menard tried again. He fumbled the quarter into the slot and hesitated. He could dial Hannigan's number himself. He was sure he remembered it, having watched Gregoire punch out the numbers so many times. Then he could claim that someone else must have called and the resulting explosion, and Hannigan's death, were serendipity. But no. Menard knew himself. He knew that killing someone was not in him. He hadn't the stomach for it. The same failing that had kept him from climbing higher up the ranks of the FLQ. He dialled Gregoire.

Susan drove past the store she wanted, turned at the next corner and began slowly circling back around the long series of blocks.

"'Allo," Gregoire's voice crackled over the phone on the second ring. Menard could here music and conversation in the background. Gregoire was obviously at that little bistro he liked so well.

"He's out," Menard blurted. "He's gone. He's in the car."

"*Bon*," Gregoire said, and the phone clicked and hummed in Menard's ear. Thank Christ the responsibility was now out of his hands. He walked away from the phone booth and began looking for a place where he could sit quietly and have a glass of wine. Then he remembered it was Toronto and the bars did not begin serving until 11:30 and he cursed Hannigan at length.

Hannigan rolled down the back window of the cab and the freshness of the autumn air poured in. He loved the climate in Canada. True, the winters in Toronto weren't as dramatic as in Montreal, but the feeling he got from the changing seasons was exhilarating. Let other Canadians head for Florida or California. This was his country and he loved it.

Susan wasn't having any luck at all. There were still no parking spots on her side of the street on her second pass. Once, she saw one on the other side but it was taken before she could make a U-turn. So she drove along to the next street and continued her slow circling.

Gregoire picked up his change and went outside the bistro. The sun was shining and the cloudless sky was as blue as the *fleur-de-lys* on the flag of Quebec. It was a perfect day, and it was about to get better. As he strolled along the sidewalk, past convenience stores and grocers and gift shops, he reached into his pocket and took out the piece of paper on which he'd written Hannigan's number. He knew it by heart, but he wanted to make sure. There had been enough mistakes already. He checked the number, put the paper back in his pocket and, standing on the sidewalk as the traffic hummed in his ears, he began to dial slowly. He muttered "*Maudit pelote*, 'annigan," and laughed, causing a woman to walk by him with an uncomfortable look.

Passing in front of the store for a third time, Susan experienced the miracle that sometimes happens to city drivers. Someone was just pulling out of a metered space directly across the street from the front door of the store she was heading to. She pulled up behind the spot, signalled her intention, and waited while the other driver pulled slowly away.

The cab dropped Hannigan off near the shop he knew Susan would be visiting last. He looked up and down the street, on both sides, scanning the people on the street for Susan's familiar face. Not finding it, he turned his attention to the cars parked at the curb and those crawling past them looking hopefully for a place to park. At first, he missed it, obscured by a garbage truck. But then a traffic light changed and the truck chugged ahead and Hannigan saw the car across the road and down the block and he stepped onto the street and started towards it quickly.

Gregoire knew something hadn't gone right. The pause between dialling and ringing was too long. He hoped that didn't mean that somebody else had already called through and robbed him of the pleasure of killing Hannigan himself. Of course, he'd still take credit since the bomb was his and he'd taken the risk of planting it, but there'd always be an empty place inside him that knew he hadn't seen the job through. Angrily, he terminated the call and redialled, pushing each number slowly and aggressively.

Hannigan was almost halfway across the street when the explosion came. His eyes had been darting back and forth from his car, to the traffic around him, to the sidewalk to see if Susan was anywhere in sight. He had just fixed his gaze back on the car when it erupted in flame and a shower of debris. There was a noise that battered against his ears like the right hands from two heavyweights and a concussion that hammered on his chest like a gong. The next thing he knew he was sitting on the road surrounded by honking cars and screaming people. His own car, just moments before parked peacefully at the curb, was now a blackened hulk. Its charred body was blown half onto the sidewalk, while the roof lay on top of the crushed hood of a passing Chevrolet. It smouldered and smoked and occasional tongues of flame licked skyward. "Oh my God," he screamed aloud, "Susan." He stood and found that something was wrong with his right leg, for it nearly collapsed under him. Adjusting for the injury, he limped forward as fast as he could, panic rising with every step.

"Susan," he called out over and over, his voice mingling with the screams and cries of dozens of others in an aria of fear. Then he saw her. She came out of the food store and stood in front of the shattered window. He lurched towards her, still calling her name. She saw him then, too, and dropped her bag of groceries and ran forward. He wrapped his arms around her and squeezed her in relief. He pressed his face into her hair, shut his eyes and for a brief second wondered what had happened to the man who'd been standing beside the car when it exploded. The man who'd been making a call on his cellular phone.

"A few years back, CITY-TV, a local Toronto station, had renovated a deco building on the corner of Queen and John."
[Photograph Copyright © A. Fred Heather. Used with the permission of the photographer.]

Tanya HUFF

This Town Ain't Big Enough

(*Vampire detectives*. Ed. by Martin Greenberg. NY: DAW; 1995/ reprinted, *Investigating Women; female detectives by Canadian writers: an eclectic sampler*. Ed. by David Skene-Melvin. Toronto: Simon & Pierre/Dundurn; 1995).

Biographical information about the author will be found at the back of the book.

Be careful whom you pick up in one of the "Goth" bars along Queen Street West. He or she might want something stronger to drink than alcohol and you may find yourself giving your all. But the next time you pass the old Ryerson Press building that now houses CITY-TV on the south-east corner of John Street and Queen Street West of an evening look again closely at the gargoyles lining the roof, for Victory Nelson Otherworldly Crimes a Specialty, may be watching out over you — you can only hope.

This Town Ain't Big Enough

"Ow! Vicki, be careful!"

"Sorry. sometimes I forget how sharp they are."

"Terrific." He wove his fingers through her hair and pulled just hard enough to make his point. "Don't."

"Don't what?" She grinned up at him, teeth gleaming ivory in the moonlight spilling across the bed. "Don't forget or don't …"

The sudden demand of the telephone for attention buried the last of her question.

Detective-Sergeant Michael Celluci sighed. "Hold that thought," he said, rolled over, and reached for the phone. "Celluci."

"Fifty-two division just called. They've found a body down at Richmond and Peter they think we might want to have a look at."

"Dave, it's …" he squinted at the clock, "… one twenty-nine in the am and I'm off duty."

On the other end of the line, his partner, theoretically off duty as well, refused to take the hint. "Ask me who the stiff is?"

Celluci sighed again. "Who's the stiff?"

"Mac Eisler."

"Shit."

"Funny, that's exactly what I said." Nothing in Dave Graham's voice indicated he appreciated the joke. "I'll be there in ten."

"Make it fifteen."

"You in the middle of something?"

Celluci watched as Vicki sat up and glared at him. "I was."

"Welcome to the wonderful world of law enforcement."

Vicki's hand shot out and caught Celluci's wrist before he could heave the phone across the room. "Who's Mac Eisler?" she asked as, scowling, he dropped the receiver back in its cradle and swung his legs off the bed.

"You heard that?"

"I can hear the beating of your heart, the movement of your blood, the song of your life." She scratched the back of her leg with one bare foot. "I should think I can overhear a lousy phone conversation."

"Eisler's a pimp." Celluci reached for the light switch, changed his mind, and began pulling on his clothes. Given the full moon riding just outside the window, it wasn't exactly dark and given Vicki's sensitivity to bright light, not to mention her temper, he figured it was safer to cope. "We're pretty sure he offed one of his girls a couple weeks ago."

Vicki scooped her shirt up off the floor. "Irene Macdonald?"

"What? You overheard that too?"

"I get around. How sure's pretty sure?"

"Personally positive. But we had nothing solid to hold him on."

"And now he's dead." Skimming her jeans up over her hips, she dipped her brows in a parody of deep thought. "Golly, I wonder if there's a connection."

"Golly yourself," Celluci snarled. "You're not coming with me."

"Did I ask?"

"I recognized the tone of voice. I know you, Vicki. I knew you when you were a cop, I knew you when you were a P.I. and I don't care how much you've changed physically, I know you now you're a … a …"

"Vampire." Her pale eyes seemed more silver than grey. "You can say it, Mike. It won't hurt my feelings. Bloodsucker. Nightwalker. Creature of Darkness."

"Pain in the butt." Carefully avoiding her gaze, he shrugged into his shoulder holster and slipped a jacket on over it. "This is police business, Vicki, stay out of it. Please." He didn't wait for a response, but crossed the shadows to the bedroom door. Then he paused, one foot over the threshold. "I doubt I'll be back by dawn. Don't wait up."

Vicki Nelson, ex of the Metropolitan Toronto Police Force, ex private investigator, recent vampire, decided to let him go. If you could joke about the change, he accepted it. And besides, it was always more fun to make him pay for smart-ass remarks when he least expected it.

She watched from the darkness as Celluci climbed into Dave Graham's care, then, with the tail-lights disappearing in the distance, she dug out his spare set of car keys and proceeded to leave tangled entrails of the Highway Traffic Act strewn from Downsview to the heart of Toronto.

It took no supernatural ability to find the scene of the crime. What with the police, the press, and the morbidly curious, the area seethed with people. Vicki slipped past the constable stationed at the far end of the alley and followed the paths of shadow until she stood just outside the circle of police around the body.

Mac Eisler had been a somewhat attractive, not very tall, white male Caucasian. Eschewing the traditional clothing excesses of his profession, he was dressed simply in designer jeans and an olive-green raw silk jacket. At the moment, he wasn't looking his best. A pair of rusty nails had been shoved through each manicured hand, securing his body upright across the back entrance of a trendy restaurant. Although the pointed toes of his tooled leather cowboy boots indented the wood of the door, Eisler's head had been turned completely around so that he stared, in apparent astonishment, out into the alley.

The smell of death fought with the stink of urine and garbage. Vicki frowned. There was another scent, a pungent predator scent that raised the hair on the back of her neck and drew her lips up off her teeth. Surprised at the strength of her reaction, she stepped silently into a deeper patch of night lest she give herself away.

"Why the hell would I have a comment?"

Preoccupied with an inexplicable rage, she hadn't heard Celluci arrive until he greeted the press. Shifting position slightly, she watched as he and his partner moved in off the street and got their first look at the body.

"Jesus H. Christ."

"On crutches," agreed the younger of the two detectives already on the scene.

"Who found him?"

"Dishwasher, coming out with the trash. He was obviously meant to be found; they nailed the bastard right across the door."

"The kitchen's on the other side and no one heard hammering?"

"I'll go you one better than that. Look at the rust on the head of those nails – they haven't *been* hammered."

"What? Someone just pushed the nails through Eisler's hands and into solid wood?"

"Looks like."

Celluci snorted. "You trying to tell me that Superman's gone bad?"

Under the cover of their laughter, Vicki bent and picked up a piece of planking. There were four holes in the unbroken end and two remaining three-inch spikes. She pulled a spike out of the wood and pressed it into the wall of the building by her side. A smut of rust marked the ball of her thumb but the nail looked no different.

She remembered the scent.

Vampire.

"… unable to come to the phone. Please leave a message after the long beep."

"Henry? It's Vicki. If you're there, pick up." She stared across the dark kitchen, twisting the phone cord between her fingers. "Come on, Fitzroy, I don't care what you're doing, this is important." Why wasn't he home writing? Or chewing on Tony. Or something. "Look, Henry, I need some information. There's another one of, of us, hunting my territory and I don't know what I should do. I know what I want to do …" The rage remained, interlaced with the knowledge of *another.* "… but I'm new at this bloodsucking undead stuff, maybe I'm over-reacting. Call me. I'm still at Mike's."

She hung up and sighed. Vampires didn't share territory. Which was why Henry had stayed in Vancouver and she'd come back to Toronto.

Well, all right, it's not the only reason I came back. She tossed Celluci's spare car keys into the drawer in the phone table and wondered if she should write him a note to explain the mysterious emptying of his gas tank. "Nah. He's a detective, let him figure it out."

Sunrise was at five-twelve. Vicki didn't need a clock to tell her that it was almost time. She could feel the sun stroking the edges of her awareness.

"It's like that final instant, just before someone hits you from behind, when you know it's going to happen but you can't do a damn thing about it." She crossed her arms on Celluci's chest and pillowed her head on them, adding, "Only it lasts longer."

"And this happens every morning?"

"Just before dawn."

"And you're going to live forever?"

"That's what they tell me."

Celluci snorted. "You can have it."

Although Celluci had offered to light-proof one of the two unused bedrooms, Vicki had been uneasy about the concept. At four and a half centuries, maybe Henry Fitzroy could afford to be blasé about immolation but Vicki still found the whole idea terrifying and had no intention of being both helpless and exposed. Anyone could walk into a bedroom.

No one would accidentally walk into an enclosed plywood box, covered in a blackout curtain, at the far end of a five foot high crawl space – but just to be on the safe side, Vicki dropped two-by-fours into iron brackets over the entrance. Folded nearly in half, she hurried to her sanctuary, feeling the sun drawing closer, closer. Somehow she resisted the urge to turn.

"There's nothing behind me," she muttered, awkwardly stripping off her clothes. Her heart slamming against her ribs, she crawled under the front flap of the box, latched it behind her, and squirmed into her sleeping bag, stretched out ready for the dawn.

"Jesus H. Christ, Vicki," Celluci had said, squatting at one end while she'd wrestled the twin bed mattress inside.

"At least a coffin would have a bit of historical dignity."

"You know where I can get one?"

"I'm not having a coffin in my basement."

"Then quit flapping your mouth."

She wondered, as she lay there waiting for oblivion, where the *other* was. Did the *other* feel the same near-panic, knowing that they had no control over the hours from dawn to dusk? Or had they, like Henry, come to accept the daily death that governed an immortal life? There should, she supposed, be a sense of kinship between them but all she could feel was a possessive fury. No one hunted in *her* territory.

"Pleasant dreams," she said as the sun teetered on the edge of the horizon. "And when I find you, you're toast."

Celluci had been and gone by the time the darkness returned. The note he'd left about the car was profane and to the point. Vicki added a couple of words he'd missed and stuck it under a refrigerator magnet in case he got home before she did.

She'd pick up the scent and follow it, the hunter becoming the hunted and, by dawn, the streets would be hers again.

The yellow police tape still stretched across the mouth of the alley. Vicki ignored it. Wrapping the night around her like a cloak, she stood outside the restaurant door and sniffed the air.

Apparently, a pimp crucified over the fire exit hadn't been enough to close the place and Tex Mex had nearly obliterated the scent of death not yet twenty-four hours old. Instead of the predator, all she could smell was frajitas.

"God damn it," she muttered, stepping closer and sniffing the wood. "How the hell am I supposed to find …"

She sensed his life the moment before he spoke.

"What are you doing?"

Vicki sighed and turned. I'm sniffing the door frame. What's it look like I'm doing?"

"Let me be more specific," Celluci snarled. "What are you doing *here?"*

"I'm looking for the person who offed Mac Eisler," Vicki began. She wasn't sure how much more explanation she was willing to offer.

"No, you're not. You are not a cop. You aren't even a P.I. anymore. And how the hell am I going to explain you if Dave sees you?"

Her eyes narrowed. "You don't have to explain me, Mike."

"Yeah? He thinks you're in Vancouver."

"Tell him I came back."

"And do I tell him that you spend your days in a box in my basement? And that you combust in sunlight? And what do I tell him about your eyes?"

Vicki's hand rose to push at the bridge of her glasses, but her fingers touched only air. The retinitis pigmentosa that had forced her from the Metro Police and denied her the night had been reversed when Henry'd changed her. The darkness held no secrets from her now. "Tell him they got better."

"RP doesn't get better."

"Mine did."

"Vicki, I know what you're doing." He dragged both hands up through his hair. "You've done it before. You had to quit the force. You were half blind. So what? Your life may have changed but you were still going to prove that you were 'Victory' Nelson. And it wasn't enough to be a private investigator. You threw yourself in stupidly dangerous situations just to prove you were still who you wanted to be. And now your life has changed again and you're playing the same game."

She could hear his heart pounding, see a vein pulsing framed in the white vee of his open collar, feel the blood surging just below the surface in reach of her teeth. The Hunger rose and she had to use every bit of control Henry had taught her to force it back down. This wasn't about that.

Since she'd returned to Toronto, she'd been drifting; feeding, hunting, relearning the night, relearning her relationship with Michael Celluci. The early morning phone call had crystallized a subconscious discontent and, as Celluci pointed out, there was really only one thing she knew how to do.

Part of his diatribe was based on concern. After all their years together playing cops and lovers she knew how he thought; if something as basic as sunlight could kill her, what else waited to strike her down. It was only human nature for him to want to protect the people he loved – for him to want to protect her.

But that was only the basis for *part* of the diatribe.

"You can't have been happy with me lazing around your house. I can't cook and I don't do windows." She stepped towards him. "I should think you'd be thrilled that I'm finding my feet again."

"Vicki."

"I wonder," she mused, holding tight to the Hunger, "how you'd feel about me being involved in this if it wasn't your case. I am, after all, better equipped to hunt the night than, oh, detective-sergeants."

"Vicki …" Her name had become a nearly inarticulate growl.

She leaned forward until her lips brushed his ear. "Bet you I solve this one first." Then she was gone, moving into shadow too quickly for mortal eyes to track.

"Who you talking to, Mike? Dave Graham glanced around the empty alley. "I thought I heard …" Then he caught sight of the expression on his partner's face. "Never mind."

Vicki couldn't remember the last time she felt so alive. *Which, as I'm now a card carrying member of the bloodsucking undead, makes for an interesting feeling.* She strode down Queen Street West, almost intoxicated by the lives surrounding her, fully aware of crowds parting to let her through and the admiring glances that traced her path. A connection had been made between her old life and her new one.

"You must surrender the day," Henry had told her, *"but you need not surrender anything else."*

"So what you're trying to tell me," she'd snarled, *"is that we're just normal people who drink blood?"*

Henry had smiled. *"How many* normal *people do you know?"*

She hated it when he answered a question with a question, but now she recognized his point. Honesty forced her to admit that Celluci had a point as well. She did need to prove to herself that she was still herself. She always had. The more things changed, the more they stayed the same.

"Well, now we've got that settled …" She looked around for a place to sit and think. In her old life, that would have meant a donut shop or the window seat in a cheap restaurant and as many cups of coffee as it took. In this new life, being enclosed with humanity did not encourage contemplation.

Besides, coffee, a major component of the old equation, made her violently ill – a fact she deeply resented.

A few years back, CITY-TV, a local Toronto station, had renovated a deco building on the corner of Queen and John. They'd done a beautiful job and the six storey white building with its ornately moulded modern windows, had become a focal point of the neighbourhood. Vicki slid into the narrow walk-way that separated it from its more down-at-the-heels neighbour and swarmed up what effectively amounted to a staircase for one of her kind.

When she reached the roof a few seconds later she perched on one crenallated corner and looked out over the downtown core. These were her streets; not Celluci's and not some out of town bloodsucker's. It was time she took them back. She grinned and fought the urge to strike a dramatic pose.

All things considered, it wasn't likely that the Metropolitan Toronto Police Department – in the person of Detective-Sergeant Michael Celluci – would be willing to share information. Briefly she regretted issuing the challenge, then she shrugged it off. As Henry said, the night was too long for regrets.

She sat and watched the crowds jostling about on the sidewalks below, clumps of colour indicating tourists amongst the Queen Street regulars. On a Friday night in August, this was the place to be as the Toronto artistic community rubbed elbows with wanna-bes and never-woulds.

Vicki frowned. Mac Eisler had been killed before midnight on a Thursday night in an area that never completely slept. Someone had to have seen or heard something. Something they probably didn't believe and were busy denying. Murder was one thing, creatures of the night were something else again.

"Now then," she murmured, "where would a person like that – and considering the time and day we're assuming a regular, not a tourist – where would that person be tonight?"

She found him in the third bar she checked, tucked back in a corner, trying desperately to get drunk and failing. His eyes darted from side to side, both hands were locked around his glass, and his body language screamed *I'm dealing with some bad shit here, leave me alone.*

Vicki sat down beside him and for an instant let the Hunter show. His reaction was everything she could have hoped for.

He stared at her, frozen in terror, his mouth working but no sound coming out.

"Breathe," she suggested.

The ragged intake of air did little to calm him, but it did break the paralysis. He shoved his chair back from the table and started to stand.

Vicki closed her fingers around his wrist. "Stay."

He swallowed and sat down again.

His skin was so hot it nearly burned and she could feel his pulse beating against it like a small wild creature struggling to be free. The Hunger clawed at her and her own breathing became a little ragged. "What's your name?"

"Ph … Phil."

She caught his gaze with hers and held it. "You saw something last night."

"Yes." Stretched almost to the breaking point, he began to tremble.

"Do you live around here?"

"Yes."

Vicki stood and pulled him to his feet, her tone half command, half caress. "Take me there. We have to talk."

Phil stared at her. "Talk?"

She could barely hear the question over the call of his blood. "Well, talk first."

"It was a woman. Dressed all in black. hair like a thousand strands of shadow, skin like snow, eyes like black ice. She chuckled deep in her throat when she saw me and licked her lips. They were painfully red. Then she vanished, so quickly that she left an image on the night."

"Did you see what she was doing?"

"No. But then, she didn't have to be doing *anything to be terrifying. I've spent the last twenty-four hours feeling like I met my death."*

Phil had turned out to be a bit of a poet. *And* a bit of an athlete. All in all, Vicki considered their time together well spent. Working carefully after he fell asleep, she took away his memory of her and muted the meeting in the alley. It was the least she could do for him.

Description sounds like someone escaped from a Hammer film; The Bride of Dracula Kills a Pimp.

She paused, key in the lock, and cocked her head. Celluci was home, she could feel his life and if she listened very hard, she could hear the regular rhythm of breathing that told her he was asleep. Hardly surprising as it was only three hours to dawn.

There was no reason to wake him as she had no intention of sharing what she'd discovered and no need to feed, but after a long, hot shower she found herself standing at the door of his room. And then at the side of his bed.

Mike Celluci was thirty-seven. There were strands of grey in his hair and although sleep had smoothed out many of the lines, the deeper creases around his eyes remained. He would grow older. In time, he would die. What would she do then?

She lifted the sheet and tucked herself up close to his side. He sighed and without completely waking scooped her closer still.

"Hair's wet," he muttered.

Vicki twisted, reached up, and brushed the long curl off his forehead. "I had a shower."

"Where'd you leave the towel?"

"In a sopping pile on the floor."

Celluci grunted inarticulately and surrendered to sleep again.

Vicki smiled and kissed his eyelids. "I love you too."

She stayed beside him until the threat of sunrise drove her away.

"Irene Macdonald."

Vicki lay in the darkness and stared unseeing up at the plywood. The sun was down and she was free to leave her sanctuary but she remained a moment longer, turning over the name that had been on her tongue when she woke. She remembered facetiously wondering if the deaths of Irene Macdonald and her pimp were connected.

Irene had been found beaten nearly to death in the bathroom of her apartment. She'd died two hours later in the hospital.

Celluci said that he was personally certain Mac Eisler was responsible. That was good enough for Vicki.

Eisler could've been unlucky enough to run into a vampire who fed on terror as well as blood – Vicki had tasted terror once or twice during her first year when the Hunger occasionally slipped from her control and she knew how addictive it could be – or he could've been killed in revenge for Irene.

Vicki could think of one sure way to find out.

"Brandon? It's Vicki Nelson."

"Victoria?" Surprise lifted most of the Oxford accent off Dr. Brandon Singh's voice. "I thought you'd relocated to British Columbia."

"Yeah, well, I came back."

"I suppose that might account for the improvement over the last month or so in a certain detective we both know."

She couldn't resist asking. "Was he really bad while I was gone?"

Brandon laughed. "He was unbearable, and, as you know, I am able to bear a great deal. So, are you still in the same line of work?"

"Yes, I am." Yes, she was. God, it felt good. "Are you still the Assistant Coroner?"

"Yes, I am. As I think I can safely assume you didn't call me at home, long after office hours, just to inform me that you're back on the job, what do you want?"

Vicki winced. "I was wondering if you'd had a look at Mac Eisler."

"Yes, Victoria, I have. And I'm wondering why you can't call me during regular business hours. You must know how much I enjoy discussing autopsies in front of my children."

"Oh God, I'm sorry Brandon, but it's important."

"Yes. It always is." His tone was so dry it crumbled. "But since you've already interrupted my evening, try to keep my part of the conversation to a simple yes or no."

"Did you do a blood volume check on Eisler?"

"Yes."

"Was there any missing?"

"No. Fortunately, in spite of the trauma to the neck the integrity of the blood vessels had not been breached."

So much for yes or no; she knew he couldn't keep to it. "You've been a big help, Brandon, thanks."

"I'd say *any time,* but you'd likely hold me to it." He hung up abruptly.

Vicki replaced the receiver and frowned. She – the *other* – hadn't fed. The odds moved in favour of Eisler killed because he murdered Irene.

"Well, if it isn't Andrew P." Vicki leaned back against the black trans am and adjusted the pair of non-prescription glasses she'd picked up just after sunset. With her hair brushed off her face and the window-glass lenses in front of her eyes, she didn't look much different than she had a year ago. Until she smiled.

The pimp stopped dead in his tracks, bluster fading before he could get the first obscenity out. He swallowed, audibly. "Nelson. I heard you were gone."

Listening to his heart race, Vicki's smile broadened. "I came back. I need some information. I need the name of one of Eisler's other girls."

"I don't know." Unable to look away, he started to shake. "I didn't have anything to do with him. I don't remember."

Vicki straightened and took a slow step towards him. "Try, Andrew."

There was a sudden smell of urine and a darkening stain down the front of the pimp's cotton drawstring pants. "Uh, D … D … Debbie Ho. That's all I can remember. Really."

"And she works?"

"Middle of the track." His tongue tripped over the words in the rush to spit them at her. "Jarvis and Carlton."

"Thank you." Sweeping a hand towards his car, Vicki stepped aside.

He dove past her and into the driver's seat, jabbing the key into the ignition. The powerful engine roared to life and with one last panicked look into the shadows he screamed out of the driveway, ground his way through three gear changes, and hit eighty before he reached the corner.

The two cops quietly sitting in the parking lot of the donut shop on that same corner hit their siren and took off after him.

Vicki slipped the glasses into the inner pocket of the tweed jacket she'd borrowed from Celluci's closet and grinned. "To paraphrase a certain adolescent crime-fighting amphibian, I *love* being a vampire."

"I need to talk to you, Debbie."

The young woman started and whirled around, glaring suspiciously at Vicki. "You a cop?"

Vicki sighed. "Not any more." Apparently it was easier to hide the vampire than the detective. "I'm a private investigator and I want to ask you some questions about Irene Macdonald."

"If you're looking for the shithead who killed her, you're too late. Someone already found him."

"And that's who I'm looking for."

"Why?" Debbie shifted her weight to one hip.

"Maybe I want to give them a medal."

The hooker's laugh held little humour. "You got that right. Mac got everything he deserved."

"Did Irene ever do women?"

Debbie snorted. "Not for free," she said pointedly.

Vicki handed her a twenty.

"Yeah, sometimes. It's safer, medically, you know?"

Editing out Phil's more ornate phrases, Vicki repeated his description of the woman in the alley.

Debbie snorted again. "Who the hell looks at their faces?"

"You'd remember this one if you saw her. She's ..." Vicki weighed and discarded several possibilities and finally settled on "... powerful."

"Powerful." Debbie hesitated, frowned, and continued in a rush. "There was this person Irene was seeing a lot but she wasn't charging. That's one of the things that set Mac off, not that the shithead needed much encouragement. We knew it was gonna happen, I mean we've all felt Mac's temper, but Irene wouldn't stop. She said that just being with this person was a high better than drugs. I guess it could've been a woman. And since she was sort of the reason Irene died, well, I know they used to meet in this bar on Queen West. Why are you hissing?"

"Hissing?" Vicki quickly yanked a mask of composure down over her rage. The other hadn't come into her territory only to kill Eisler – she was definitely hunting it. "I'm not hissing. I'm just having a little trouble breathing."

"Yeah, tell me about it." Debbie waved a hand ending in three-inch scarlet nails at the traffic on Jarvis. "You should try standing here sucking carbon monoxide all night."

In another mood, Vicki might have re-applied the verb to a different object, but she was still too angry. "Do you know which bar?"

"What, now I'm her social director? No, I don't know which bar." Apparently they'd come to the end of the information twenty dollars could buy as Debbie turned her attention to a prospective client in a grey sedan. The interview was clearly over.

Vicki sucked the humid air past her teeth. There weren't that many bars on Queen West. Last night she'd found Phil in one. Tonight – who knew?

Now that she knew enough to search for it, minute traces of the other predator hung in the air – diffused and scattered by the paths of prey. With so many lives masking the trail, it would be impossible to track her. Vicki snarled. A pair of teenagers, noses pierced, heads shaved, and doc marten's laced to the knee, decided against asking for change and hastily crossed the street.

It was Saturday night, minutes to Sunday. The bars would be closing soon. If the *other* was hunting, she would have already chosen her prey.

I wish Henry had called back. Maybe over the centuries they've – we've – evolved ways to deal with this. Maybe we're supposed to talk first. Maybe it's considered bad manners to rip her face off and feed it to her if she doesn't agree to leave.

Standing in the shadow of a recessed storefront, just beyond the edge of the artificial safety the street-light offered to the children of the sun, she extended her senses the way she'd been taught and touched death within the maelstrom of life.

She found Phil, moments later, lying in yet another of the alleys that serviced the business of the day and provided a safe haven for the darker business of the night. His body was still warm but his heart had stopped beating and his blood no longer sang. Vicki touched the tiny, nearly closed wound she'd made in his wrist the night before and then the fresh wound in the bend of his elbow. She didn't know how he had died but she knew who had done it. He stank of the *other.*

Vicki no longer cared what was traditionally "done" in these instances. There would be no talking. No negotiating. It had gone one life beyond that.

"I rather thought that if I killed him you'd come and save me the trouble of tracking you down. And here you are, charging in without taking the slightest of precautions." Her voice was low, not so much threatening as in itself a threat. "You're hunting in my territory, child."

Still kneeling by Phil's side, Vicki lifted her head. Ten feet away, only her face and hands clearly visible, the other vampire stood. Without thinking – unable to think clearly through the red rage that shrieked for release – Vicki launched herself at the snow-white column of throat, finger hooked to talons, teeth bare.

The Beast Henry had spent a year teaching her to control was loose. She felt herself lost in its raw power and she revelled in it.

The *other* made no move until the last possible second, then she lithely twisted and slammed Vicki to one side.

Pain eventually brought reason back. Vicki lay panting in the fetid damp at the base of a dumpster, one eye swollen shut, a gash across her forehead still sluggishly bleeding. Her right arm was broken.

"You're strong," the other told her, a contemptuous gaze pinning her to the ground. "In another hundred years you might have stood a chance. But you're an infant. A child. You haven't the experience to control what you are. This will be your only warning. Get out of my territory. If we meet again, I *will* kill you."

Vicki sagged against the inside of the door and tried to lift her arm. During the two and a half hours it had taken her to get back to Celluci's house, the bone had begun to set. By tomorrow night, provided she fed in the hours remaining until dawn, she should be able to use it.

"Vicki?"

She started. Although she'd known he was home, she'd assumed – without checking – that because of the hour he'd be asleep. She squinted as the hall light came on and wondered, listening to him pad down the stairs in bare feet, whether she had the energy to make it into the basement bathroom before he saw her.

He came into the kitchen, tying his bathrobe belt around him, and flicked on the overhead light. "We need to talk," he said grimly as the shadows that might have hidden her fled. "Jesus H. Christ. What the hell happened to you?"

"Nothing much." Eyes squinted nearly shut, Vicki gingerly probed the swelling on her forehead. "You should see the other guy."

Without speaking Celluci reached over and hit the play button on the telephone answering machine.

"Vicki? Henry. If someone's hunting your territory, whatever you do, don't challenge. Do you hear me? *Don't* challenge. You can't win. They're going to be older, able to overcome the instinctive rage and remain in full command of their power. If you won't surrender the territory ..." The sigh the tape played back gave a clear opinion of how likely he thought that was to occur. "... you're going to have to negotiate. If you can agree on boundaries there's no reason why you can't share the city." His voice suddenly belonged again to the lover she'd lost with the change. "Call me, please, before you do anything."

It was the only message on the tape.

"Why," Celluci asked as it rewound, his gaze taking in the cuts and the bruising and the filth, "do I get the impression that it's 'the other guy' Fitzroy's talking about?"

Vicki tried to shrug. Her shoulders refused to co-operate. "It's my city, Mike. It always has been. I'm going to take it back."

He stared at her for a long moment, then he shook his head. "You heard what Henry said. You can't win. You haven't been ... what you are, long enough. It's only been fourteen months."

"I know." The rich scent of his life prodded the Hunter and she moved to put a little distance between them.

He closed it up again. "Come on." Laying his hand in the centre of her back, he steered her towards the stairs. *Put it aside for now,* his tone told her. *We'll argue about it later.* "You need a bath."

"I need ..."

"I know. But you need a bath first. I just changed the sheets."

The darkness wakes us all in different ways, Henry had told her. *We were all human once and we carried our differences through the change.*

For Vicki, it was like the flicking of a switch; one moment she wasn't, the next she was. This time, when she returned from the little death of the day, an idea returned with her.

Four hundred and fifty odd years a vampire, Henry had been seventeen when he changed. The *other* had walked the night for perhaps as long – her gaze had carried the weight of several lifetimes – but her physical appearance suggested that her mortal life had lasted even less time than Henry's had. Vicki allowed that it made sense. Disaster may have precipitated *her* change, but passion was the usual cause.

And no one does that kind of never-say-die passion like a teenager.

It would be difficult for either Henry or the other to imagine a response that came out of a mortal not a vampiric experience. They'd both had centuries of the latter and not enough of the former to count.

Vicki had been only fourteen months a vampire but she'd been human thirty-two years when Henry'd saved her by drawing her to his blood to feed. During those thirty-two years, she'd been nine years a cop – two accelerated promotions, three citations, and the best arrest record on the force.

There was no chance of negotiation.

She couldn't win if she fought.

She'd be damned if she'd flee.

"Besides ..." For all she realized where her strength had to lie, Vicki's expression held no humanity. "... She owes me for Phil."

Celluci had left her a note on the fridge.

Does this have anything to do with Mac Eisler?

Vicki stared at it for a moment, then scribbled her answer underneath.

Not any more.

It took three weeks to find where the *other* spent her days. Vicki used old contacts where she could and made new ones where she had to. Any modern Van Helsing could have done the same.

For the next three weeks Vicki hired someone to watch the *other* come and go, giving reinforced instructions to stay in the car with the windows closed and the air conditioning running. Life had an infinite number of variations but one piece of machinery smelled pretty much like any other. It irritated her that she couldn't sit stakeout herself, but the information she needed would've kept her out after sunrise.

"How the hell did you burn your hand?"

Vicki continued to smear ointment over the blister. Unlike the injuries she'd taken in the alley, this would heal slowly and painfully. "Accident in a tanning salon."

"That's not funny."

She picked the roll of gauze up off the counter. "You're losing your sense of humour, Mike."

Celluci snorted and handed her the scissors. "I never had one."

"Mike, I wanted to warn you, I won't be back by sunrise."

Celluci turned slowly, the TV dinner he'd just taken from the microwave held in both hands. "What do you mean?"

She read the fear in his voice and lifted the edge of the tray so that the gravy didn't pour out and over his shoes. "I mean I'll be spending the day somewhere else."

"Where?"

"I can't tell you."

"Why? Never mind." He raised a hand as her eyes narrowed. "Don't tell me. I don't want to know. You're going after that other vampire, aren't you? The one Fitzroy told you to leave alone."

"I thought you didn't want to know."

"I already know," he grunted. "I can read you like a book. With large type. And pictures."

Vicki pulled the tray from his grip and set it on the counter. "She's killed two people. Eisler was a scumbag who may have deserved it, but the other …"

"Other?" Celluci exploded. "Jesus H. Christ, Vicki, in case you've forgotten, murder's against the law! Who the hell painted a big vee on your long-johns and made you the vampire vigilante?"

"Don't you remember?" Vicki snapped. "You were there. I didn't make this decision, Mike. You and Henry made it for me. You'd just better learn to live with it." She fought her way back to calm. "Look, you can't stop her but I can. I know that galls, but that's the way it is."

They glared at each other, toe to toe. Finally Celluci looked away.

"I can't stop you, can I?" he asked bitterly. "I'm only human, after all."

"Don't sell yourself short," Vicki snarled. "You're quintessentially human. If you want to stop me, you face me and ask me not to go and *then* you remember it every time *you* go into a situation that could get your ass shot off."

After a long moment he swallowed, lifted his head, and met her eyes. "Don't die. I thought I lost you once and I'm not strong enough to go through that again."

"Are you asking me not to go?"

He snorted. "I'm asking you to be careful. Not that you ever listen."

She took a step forward and rested her head against his shoulder, wrapping herself in the beating of his heart. "This time I'm listening."

The studios in the converted warehouse on King Street were not supposed to be live-in. A good seventy-five percent of the tenants ignored that. The studio

Vicki wanted was at the back on the third floor. The heavy steel door – an obvious upgrade by the occupant – had been secured by the best lock money could buy.

New senses and old skills got through it in record time.

Vicki pushed open the door with her foot and began carrying boxes inside. She had a lot to do before dawn.

"She goes out every night between ten and eleven, then she comes home every morning between four and five. You could set your watch by her."
Vicki handed him an envelope.

He looked inside, thumbed through the money, then grinned up at her. "Pleasure doing business for you. Any time you need my services, you know where to call."

"Forget it," she told him.

And he did.

Because she expected her, Vicki knew the moment the *other* entered the building. The Beast stirred and she tightened her grip on it. To lose control now would be disaster.

She heard the elevator, then footsteps in the hall.

"You know I'm in here," she said silently, *"and you know you can take me. Be overconfident, believe I'm a fool and walk right in."*

"I thought you were smarter than this." The *other* stepped into the apartment, then casually turned to lock the door. "I told you when I saw you again I'd kill you."

Vicki shrugged, the motion masking her fight to remain calm. "Don't you even want to know why I'm here?"

"I assume you've come to negotiate." She raised ivory hands and released thick black hair from its bindings. "We went past that when you attacked me." Crossing the room, she preened before a large ornate mirror that dominated one wall of the studio.

"I attacked you because you murdered Phil."

"Was that his name?" The other laughed. The sound had razored edges. "I didn't bother to ask it."

"Before you murdered him."

"Murdered? You *are* a child. They are prey, we are predators – their deaths are ours if we desire them. You'd have learned that in time." She turned, the patina of civilization stripped away. "Too bad you haven't any time left."

Vicki snarled but somehow managed to stop herself from attacking. Years of training whispered, *Not yet.* She had to stay exactly where she was.

"Oh yes." The sibilants flayed the air between them. "I almost forgot. You wanted me to ask you why you came. Very well. Why?"

Given the address and the reason, Celluci could've come to the studio during the day and slammed a stake through the *other's* heart. The vampire's strongest protection would be of no use against him. Mike Celluci believed in vampires.

"I came," Vicki told her, "because some things you have to do yourself."

The wire ran up the wall, tucked beside the surface-mounted cable of a cheap renovation, and disappeared into the shadows that clung to a ceiling sixteen feet from the floor. The switch had been stapled down beside her foot. A tiny motion, too small to evoke attack, flipped it.

Vicki had realized from the beginning that there were a number of problems with her plan The first involved placement. Every living space included an area where the occupant felt secure – a favourite chair, a window … a mirror. The second problem was how to mask what she'd done. While the *other* would not be able to sense the various bits of wiring and equipment, she'd be fully aware of Vicki's scent *on* the wiring and equipment. Only if Vicki remained in the studio could that smaller trace be lost in the larger.

The third problem was directly connected with the second. Given that Vicki had to remain, how was she to survive?

Attached to the ceiling by sheer brute strength, positioned so that they shone directly down into the space in front of the mirror, were a double bank of lights cannibalized from a tanning bed. The sun held a double menace for the vampire – its return to the sky brought complete vulnerability and its rays burned.

Henry had a round scar on the back of one hand from too close an encounter with the sun. When her burn healed, Vicki would have a matching one from a deliberate encounter with an imitation.

The *other* screamed as the lights came on, the sound pure rage and so inhuman that those who heard it would have to deny it for sanity's sake.

Vicki dove forward, ripped the heavy brocade off the back of the couch, and burrowed frantically into its depths. Even that instant of light had bathed her skin in flame and she moaned as for a moment the searing pain became all she was. After a time, when it grew no worse, she managed to open her eyes.

The light couldn't reach her, but neither could she reach the switch to turn it off. She could see it, three feet away, just beyond the shadow of the couch. She shifted her weight and a line of blister rose across one leg. Biting back a shriek, she curled into a fetal position, realizing her refuge was not entirely secure.

Okay genius, now what?

Moving very, very carefully, Vicki wrapped her hand around the one-by-two that braced the lower edge of the couch. From the tension running along it, she suspected that breaking it off would result in at least a partial collapse of the piece of furniture.

And if it goes, I may very well go with it.

And then she heard the sound of something dragging itself across the floor.

Oh shit! She's not dead!

The wood broke, the couch began to fall in on itself, and Vicki, realizing that luck would have a large part to play in her survival, smacked the switch and rolled clear in the same motion.

The room plunged into darkness.

Vicki froze as her eyes slowly readjusted to the night. Which was when she finally became conscious of the smell. It had been there all along but her senses had refused to acknowledge it until they had to.

Sunlight burned.

Vicki gagged.

The dragging sound continued.

The hell with this! She didn't have time to wait for her eyes to repair the damage they'd obviously taken. She needed to see *now.* Fortunately, although it hadn't seemed fortunate at the time, she'd learned to maneuver without sight.

She threw herself across the room.

The light switch was where they always were, to the right of the door.

The thing on the floor pushed itself up on fingerless hands and glared at her out of the blackened ruin of a face. Laboriously it turned, hate radiating off it in palpable waves, and began to pull itself towards her again.

Vicki stepped forward to meet it.

While the part of her that remembered being human writhed in revulsion, she wrapped her hands around its skull and twisted it in a full circle. The spine snapped. Another full twist and what was left of the head came off in her hands.

She'd been human for thirty-two years but she'd been fourteen months a vampire.

"No one hunts in *my* territory," she snarled as the *other* crumbled to dust.

She limped over to the wall and pulled the plug supplying power to the lights. Later, she'd remove them completely – the whole concept of sunlamps gave her the creeps.

When she turned, she was facing the mirror.

The woman who stared out at her through bloodshot eyes, exposed skin blistered and red, was a hunter. Always had been, really. The question became, who was she to hunt?

Vicki smiled. Before the sun drove her to use her inherited sanctuary, she had a few quick phone calls to make. The first to Celluci; she owed him the knowledge that she'd survived the night. The second to Henry, for much the same reason.

The third call would be to the eight hundred line that covered the classifieds of Toronto's largest alternative newspaper. This ad was going to be a little different than the one she'd placed upon leaving the force. Back then, she'd been incredibly depressed about leaving a job she loved for a life she saw as only marginally useful. This time she had no regrets.

Victory Nelson, Investigator: Otherworldly Crimes a Specialty.

"He'd waited patiently for his own letter carrier to bring him some exotic mail..."

[Photograph of montage stamps courtesy of Canada Post Corporation. Used with the permission of Canada Post Corporation.]

Robert J. SAWYER

Lost in the Mail

(Victoria, B.C.: *Transversions*, Summer 1995).

Biographical information about the author will be found at the back of the book.

The next time you receive what you think is someone else's mail, check the address again, very carefully. There are those who persist in believing in Free Will and Choice, but I tell you, Destiny will get you every time. Who ever said you could escape Fate.

Lost in the Mail

The intercom buzzer sounded like a cardiac defibrillator giving a jump-start to a dying man. I sprang from my chair, not even pausing to save the article I was working on, threw back the dead-bolt, and hurried into the corridor. My apartment was next to the stairwell, so I swung through the fire door and bounded down the three flights to the lobby, through the inner glass door, and into the building's entry chamber.

The Pope was digging through his bag. Of course, he wasn't really the Pope — he probably wasn't even Catholic — but he bore a definite resemblance to John Paul II. The underarms of his pale blue Canada Post shirt were soaked and he was wearing those dark uniform shorts that made him look like an English schoolboy. We exchanged greetings; he spoke in an obscure European accent.

A hole in the panel above the mailboxes puckered like an infected wound. John Paul inserted a brass key into it. The panel flopped forward the way a pull-down bed does, giving him access to a row of little cubicles. He began stuffing the day's round of junk mail into these — a bed of fertilizer for the first-class goodies. He left my mailbox empty, though, and instead dealt out a full set of leaflets and sale flyers onto the counter that jutted from the wall.

For most people the real mail amounted to one or two pieces, but I got a lot more than that — including a copy of the *Ryerson Rambler*, the alumni magazine from Ryerson Polytechnic University. When he was finished, the Pope scooped up my pile and handed it to me. As usual, it was too much to fit comfortably into the box. "Thanks," I said, and headed back into the lobby.

I'd promised myself that I'd always take the stairs up to the third floor — one of these days I'd lose that spare tire — but, well, the elevator was right there, its door invitingly open ...

Back in my apartment I sat in the angle of my L-shaped couch with my feet, as always, swung up on the right-hand section. The mail contained the usual round of press releases, several bills, and the *Ryerson Rambler*. The cover showed an alumnus dressed in African tribal gear. According to the caption on the contents page, some relative of his had abdicated as chief of a tribe in Ghana and he was off to take his place. Amazing how people's lives can change completely overnight.

I was surprised to find a second magazine stuck to the back of the *Rambler*. *University of Toronto Alumni Magazine*, it said. Down in the lower-right corner of its blue-and-white cover were three strips of adhesive partially covered with a frayed paper
residue. Its address label must have torn off and the glue had stuck onto the back of my magazine.

Intriguing: I'd been accepted by U of T after high school, but had decided to go to Ryerson instead. If I'd stayed with U of T, I'd be a paleontologist today, sifting through the remains of ancient life. Instead, I'm a freelance journalist specializing in the petrochemical industry, a contributing editor of *Canadian Plastics*, an entirely competent writer, and the only life I sift through is my own.

I began thumbing through the magazine. Here, in thirty-two glossy pages, was my past that could have been but wasn't: graduation ceremonies at Convocation Hall, an article about the 115th year of the campus paper, *The Varsity*; a calendar of events at Hart House ...

If I'd gone to U of T instead of Ryerson, the photos might have stirred nostalgic laughter and tears within me. Instead they lay there, halftone shadows, emotionless. Fossils of somebody else's life.

I continued leafing through the magazine until I came to the final pages. There, under the heading "Alumni Reports," were photos of graduates and blurbs on their careers and personal triumphs. I was surprised to find a paleo grad — it was such a small program — but at the bottom of page 30 there was an entry about a man named Zalmon Bernstein. The picture was hokey: Bernstein, a toothy grin splitting his features, holding up a geologist's pick. He'd finished his Ph.D. in 1983, it said, the same year I would have likely finished mine had I gone there. Doubtless we would have known each other; we might even have been friends.

I read his blurb two or three times. Married. Now living in Drumheller, Alberta. Research Associate with the Royal Tyrrell Museum of Paleontology. Working summers on the continuing excavations in Dinosaur Provincial Park.

He'd done all right for himself. I felt a tinge of sadness, and put the magazine aside. The other mail was nothing urgent, so I ambled back to my computer and continued poking at my article on polystyrene purification.

The next day, John Paul greeted me with his usual "'Morning, Mr. Coin." As always, I felt at a disadvantage since I didn't know his name. When he'd begun this route two years ago, I'd wanted to ask what it was. I fancied it would be a mysterious, foreign-sounding thing ending in a vowel. But I'd missed my opportunity and now it was much too late. Anyway, he knows far more about me than I could ever hope to know about him. Because my bank insists on spelling out my name in full, he knows that my middle initial — which I use in my byline — stands for Horton (yuck). He knows what credit cards I have. He knows I'm a journalist, assuming he'd recognize a press kit when he saw one. He knows I read *Playboy* and *Canadian Geographic* and *Ellery Queen's Mystery Magazine*. He even knows who my doctor is. He could write my biography, all based on the things of mine he carries around in his heavy blue sack.

As usual, he was placing my mail in a separate pile. He topped it off with a thin white-and-orange book sealed in a polyethylene bag. I gathered my booty, wished him good day, and headed back. The elevator was only on two, so I called it down. I did that occasionally. If it was on three, I hardly ever waited for it and if it was on the top floor, well, once in a blue moon I might use it.

Someday I'm going to lose that spare tire.

As I rode up, I glanced at the white-and-orange book. It was a scholarly journal. My step-uncle, a university professor, had hundreds of such publications making neat rows of identical spines on the shelves of his musty den. This one looked interesting, though, at least to me: *The Journal of Vertebrate Paleontology*.

For some reason I swung my feet up to the left instead of the right on my L-couch. The *Journal*'s table of contents was printed on its cover. I recognized some of the words in the titles from my old interest in dinosaurs. *Ornithischian. Hadrosaurs. Cretaceous.*

I glanced at the piece of tractor-feed paper that had been slipped into the mailing bag: my name and address, all right. Who would have sent me such a thing? My birthday was rolling around — the big four-oh — so maybe somebody had got me a subscription as a semi-gag gift. The poly bag stretched as I yanked at it. Having written 750,000 words about plastics in my career, you'd think I'd be able to open those things easily.

Subscription rates were printed inside the journal's front cover. Eighty-five American dollars a year! I didn't have many friends and none of them would shell out that much on a gift for me, even if it was meant as a joke.

I closed the book and looked at the table of contents again. Dry stuff. Say, there's an article by that U of T guy, Zalmon Bernstein: *A New Specimen of* Lambeosaurus lambei *from the Badlands of Alberta, Canada.* I continued down the list of titles. *Correlations Between Crest Size and Shape of the Pre-Orbital Fenestra in Hadrosaurs*. "Pre-orbital fenestra." What a great-sounding phrase. All those lovely Latin and Greek polysyllables. Here's another one —

I stopped dead. *Scrobiculated Fontanelle Margins in Pachyrhinosaurs and Other Centrosaurinae from the Chihuahuan Desert of Mexico*, by J. H. Coin.

By me.

My head swam for a moment. I was used to seeing my byline in print. It's just that I usually remembered writing whatever it was attached to, that's all.

It must be somebody with the same name, of course. Hell, Coin wasn't that unusual. Besides, this guy was down in Mexico. I turned to the indicated page. There was the article, the writer's name, and his institutional affiliation: Research Associate, Department of Vertebrate Paleontology, Royal Ontario Museum, Toronto, Canada.

It came back in a deluge of memory. The ROM had undertaken a dig in Mexico a few summers ago. A local newspaper, *The Toronto Sun*, had sponsored it. I remembered it as much because of my dormant interest in dinosaurs as because it seemed so out-of-character for the tabloid *Sun* — best known for its bikini-clad Sunshine Girls — to foot the bill for a scientific expedition.

I was disoriented for several seconds. What was going on? Why did I even have a copy of this publication? Then it hit me. Of course. All so simple, really. There must be someone at the ROM with the same initials and last name as me. He (or she, maybe) had written this article. The *Journal* had somehow lost his address, so they'd looked him up in the phone book to send a contributor's copy. They'd gotten the wrong J. H. Coin, that's all.

I decided I'd better return the guy's *Journal* to him. Besides, this other Coin would probably get a kick out of the story of how his copy had ended up with me. I know I would.

I phoned the Royal Ontario Museum and spoke to a receptionist who had a pleasant Jamaican accent. "Hello," I said. "J. H. Coin, please."

"Can you tell me which department?" she asked.

He can't have made a big name for himself if the receptionist didn't know where he worked. "Paleontology."

"Vert or invert?"

For a second I didn't understand the question. "Oh — vertebrate."

"I'll put you through to the departmental assistant." I often had to contact presidents of petrochemical firms for quotes, so I knew that how difficult it was to get hold of someone could be a sign of how important he or she was. But this shunting struck me as different. It wasn't that J. H. Coin had to be shielded from annoying calls. Rather, it was more like he was a fossil, lost in layers of sediment.

"Vert paleo," said a woman's voice.

"Hello. J. H. Coin, please."

There was a pause, as though the departmental assistant was momentarily confused. "Ah, just a second."

At first I thought that she, too, hadn't heard of J. H. Coin, but when the next person came on I knew that wasn't it. The voice seemed slightly alien to me: deeper, less resonant, more nasal than my own — at least than my own sounds to me. "Hello," he said, politely, but sounding somewhat surprised at being called at work. "Jacob Coin speaking."

Jacob and Coin. Sure, some names go together automatically, like John and Smith, or Tom and Sawyer or, if you believe the Colombian Coffee Growers' commercials, Juan and Valdez. But Jacob and Coin weren't a natural pair. I was named after my mother's father. Not some literary allusion, not some easy assonance, just a random line of circumstances.

I wanted to ask this Jacob Coin what his "H" stood for. I wanted to ask him what his mother's maiden name was. I wanted to know his birth date, his social insurance number, whether his left leg gave him trouble when it was about to rain, whether he was allergic to cheese, if he had managed to keep his weight under control. But I didn't have to. I already knew the answers.

I hung up the phone. I hated doing it only because I know how much I hate it when that happens to me — how much he must hate it, too.

I heeded John Paul's buzz again on Friday. This time, though, I didn't wait for him to assemble my pile of mail. Instead, I snapped up each envelope as he placed it on the counter. The first three really were for me: a check from one of my publishers, a birthday card from my insurance agent, and my cable-TV bill. But the fourth was bogus: a gray envelope addressed to J. H. Coin, Ph.D. The return address was *Royal Ontario Museum Staff Association*.

"Wait a minute," I said.

The Pontiff was busy dealing out lives into the little mailboxes. "Hmm?"

"This one isn't for me."

"Oh, sorry." He reached out to take it. For a moment I thought about keeping it, holding on to that piece of what might have been, but, no, I let him have it.

He looked at it, then frowned. "You're J. H. Coin, ain't you?"

"Well, yes."

"Then it is for you." He proffered the envelope, but now that I'd let it go I couldn't bring myself to take it back.

"No. I mean, I'm not *that* J. H. Coin." The Pope said nothing. He just stood there holding the letter out towards me. I shook my head. "I don't have a Ph.D."

"Take that up with whoever wrote you," he said. "I worry about apartment numbers and postal codes, not diplomas."

"But I don't want it. It's not mine. I don't work at the Museum."

John Paul let out a heavy sigh. "Mr. Coin, it's addressed correctly. It's got sufficient postage. I have to deliver it to you."

"Can't you send it back?"

"I've been doing you a big favour all this time, calling you down instead of stuffing your things into that little box. Don't make me sorry that I've been nice to you." He looked me straight in the eye. "Take the letter."

"But yesterday you brought me *The Journal of Vertebrate Paleontology*. And the day before, the *University of Toronto Alumni Magazine*. None of those things were meant for me."

"Who's to say what's meant for any of us, Mr. Coin? All I know is I've got to deliver the mail. It's my job."

He went back to his bag. The next thing he pulled out happened to be for me, too. Sort of. Instead of placing it on the counter, he tried to hand it to me directly. It was a letter hand-addressed to Mr. and Mrs. Jake Coin.

I shook my head again, more in wonder than negation this time. "There is no Mrs. Coin."

"You have to take it," he said.

It was tempting, in a way. But no, she wasn't *my* wife. She wasn't part of my world. I didn't move.

He shrugged and put the envelope in the empty cubicle that had my apartment number on it.

I didn't want this other Coin's life forced upon me. "Take that out of there," I said.

John Paul continued distributing mail, ignoring me the way he might ignore a stranger who tried to strike up a conversation on the subway. I grabbed his arms and attempted to swing him around. The old guy was a lot stronger than he looked — thanks, I guess, to hauling that great sack of letters around. He pushed me away easily and I fell backward against the vestibule's inner glass door. For a horrible instant I thought the pane was going to break and come tumbling down on me, but it held solid. The Pontiff had wheeled around and was now aiming a tiny aerosol can of Mace at me.

"Don't ever try that again," he said in his mysterious European voice, not shouting, really, but with a firmness that made the words sound loud.

"Just tell me what's going on," I said. "Please."

We held our eye contact for a moment. His expression wasn't the indignation of a man who has suffered an unprovoked attack. Rather, it was more like the quiet turmoil of a father who's had to spank his child. "I'm sorry," he said.

Damn the man's infinite patience. I was angry and I wanted him to be angry, too. "Look," I said at last, "you keep bringing me the wrong mail." I hated the quaver my voice had taken on. "I — I don't want to have to report you to your supervisor."

The threat seemed stupid and my words hung in the air between us. John Paul stared at me, his face waxing reflective. Finally, he laughed and shook his head. He hefted his bag, as if to gauge how much mail he had left to deliver. Then he glanced at his watch. "All right," he said at last. "After all, I don't want to get in trouble with the boss." He laughed again — not hard, really, but there were tears at the corners of his eyes.

I slowly brought myself to my feet, wiping dirt off the bum of my cutoffs. "Well?"

"You're out of place, Mr. Coin," he said, slowly. "You don't belong here."

That's the story of my life, I thought. But I said, "What do you mean?"

"You think you can just up and say you're going to be a journalist?" He put the can of mace back in his bag.

"I didn't just up and say it. I worked hard to get my degree."

"That's not what I meant. You were supposed to be a —" he paused, then pronounced his next word carefully — "paleontologist."

"What do you mean, `supposed to be'?"

"You can't just do whatever you want in this life. You've got to play the hand that's dealt to you. You think I wanted to be a letter carrier? It's just the way it worked out for me. You don't get any choice." His voice sounded far away and sad. "Still, it ain't so bad for me. I get to do this extra stuff as a sideline — putting people like you back on the right course."

"The right course?" The old guy was insane. I should run, get away, hide.

"When did you decide to become a journalist instead of a ... paleontologist?"

"I don't remember for sure," I said. "Sometime during my last year in high school. I got bored; didn't want to spend the rest of my life being a student."

"That was a big decision," he said. "I'd think you'd remember it more clearly." The Pope smiled. "It was April 22nd, 1973, at 10:27 in the evening. That's when the universe split. You ripped up your acceptance letter from U of T —"

"The universe did what?"

"It split, became two universes. That happens once in a while. See, they used to think that every time somebody made a decision, instead of things going one way or the other, they went *both* ways. The universe splitting a million times a second, each one going on forever along its separate path."

I didn't understand what he was talking about. "Parallel universes?" I said, the phrase coming to me out of dimly remembered *Star Trek* reruns. "I guess that's possible ..."

"It's hogwash, man. Couldn't happen that way. Ain't enough matter to constantly be spinning off new universes at that rate. Any fool can see that. No, most of the times the decisions iron themselves out within a few minutes or days — everything is exactly the same as if the decision had never been taken. The two universes join up, matter is conserved, the structure is sound, and I get to knock off early."

Although he sounded cavalier, he didn't look it. Of course, maybe he was always like this. After all, in the twenty-odd months that I'd known the Pope we'd never exchanged more than a dozen words at a time. "So?" I said at last.

"So, every now and then there's a kind of cosmic hiccup. The universes get so out of joint that they just keep moving farther apart. Can't have that. It weakens the fabric of existence, so they tell me. We've got to get things back on course."

"What are you talking about?"

"You ever hear of Ronald Reagan?"

"No. Wait — you mean the actor? Guy who did a bunch of pictures with a chimp?"

"That's him. There was a hiccup almost forty years ago. He got it into his head to be a politician, don't you know. I won't even tell you how high up he made it in the American government — you'd never believe me. It took an army of posties to get the world back on track after that one."

"So you're saying I'm supposed to be a paleontologist, not a plastics writer."

"Uh huh."

"Why?"

"That's just the way it was meant to be, that's all."

My head was spinning. None of this made sense. "But I don't want to be a paleontologist. I'm happy as a journalist." That wasn't really true, and I had a feeling John Paul knew it wasn't, but he let it pass.

"I'm sorry," he said for the second time.

This was craziness. But he sounded so serious, so much like he really believed it himself, that it made me nervous. "But other people get to choose their lives," I said at last.

"No," he said, looking very old. "No, they don't. They think they choose them, but they don't."

"So — so I'm supposed to do some great thing as a paleontologist? Something that makes a difference in the scheme of things?" That wouldn't be so bad, I thought. To make a difference, to count, maybe to be remembered after I'm dead.

"Perhaps," said the Pope, but I knew in an instant that he was lying.

"Well, it's too late for me to go back to school now, anyway," I said, folding my arms across my chest. "I mean, I'd practically be ready to retire by the time I could get a Ph.D. in paleontology."

"You've got a Ph.D. Don't ask me what your thesis was on, though. I can't pronounce most of the words in its title."

"No. I've got a Bachelor of Applied Arts from the School of Journalism, Ryerson Polytechnic University." I hadn't said that with such pride in years.

"Yes. That, too." He glanced at his watch again. "For the time being."

I didn't believe a word of it but I decided to humour the old man. "Well, how's this change supposed to take place?"

"The two universes are mingling even now. We're just suturing up the rift between them. When the posties have everything in place, they'll automatically rejoin into one universe."

"How long until that happens?"

"Soon. Today, maybe, if I finish my route on time."

"And I don't get a say in any of this?"

"No. I'm sorry." He sounded like he really meant it. "None of us gets a say. Now, excuse me, but I really must get on with my work." And with that, the Bishop of Rome scurried out the glass door.

Lubomir Dudek, member of the Toronto Local of the Canadian Union of Postal Workers, came to the last house on his route, a large side-split with a two-car garage. He didn't want to finish, didn't want to drop off a copy of the Jesuit journal *Compass* for a man who was now, because of that fateful day in 1973, one of Toronto's better-known podiatrists instead of a Father in the Society of Jesus. Lubo envied the foot doctor, just as he envied Jacob

Coin, writer-about-to-turn-fossil-hunter. They went on from this point, with new vistas ahead of them. Their alternative lives beat the hell out of his own.

Lubo had known that the two realities would have to be reconciled. He, too, had made a fateful decision two decades ago, back when he was a press operator in a printing plant, a time when his own hiccups had drowned out those of the universe. He'd been pissed to the gills, celebrating — for the life of him he couldn't remember what. Wisely, or so it had seemed at the time, he had decided to call a cab instead of driving home from the Jolly Miller. It should have been the right choice, he thought sadly, but we play the hand that we're dealt.

For a long time he had wondered why he had been selected to be one of those helping to set things right. He'd tried to convince himself that it was because he was an honest man (which he was), a good man (which was also true), a man with a sense of duty (that, too). He'd waited patiently for his own letter carrier to bring him some exotic mail: a copy of a trade magazine from some new profession, maybe, or a dues notice from some union he didn't belong to, or even a dividend check from a stock he didn't own. But nothing of the kind came and finally Lubo was forced to consciously face what he supposed he had really known all along. His one brief moment of free will had let him live when he should have not. In the reunited universe, Jacob Coin would have his thunder lizards, the podiatrist would have his brethren, but Lubo would have only rest.

He came to the end of the driveway and lifted the lid of the foot doctor's mailbox, its black metal painfully hot in the summer sun. Slowly, sadly, he dropped in the sale flyers, bills, and letters. He hesitated for a moment before depositing the copy of *Compass*, then, with a concern not usually lavished on the mails, he gingerly inserted the slim magazine, taking care not to dog-ear its glossy white pages.

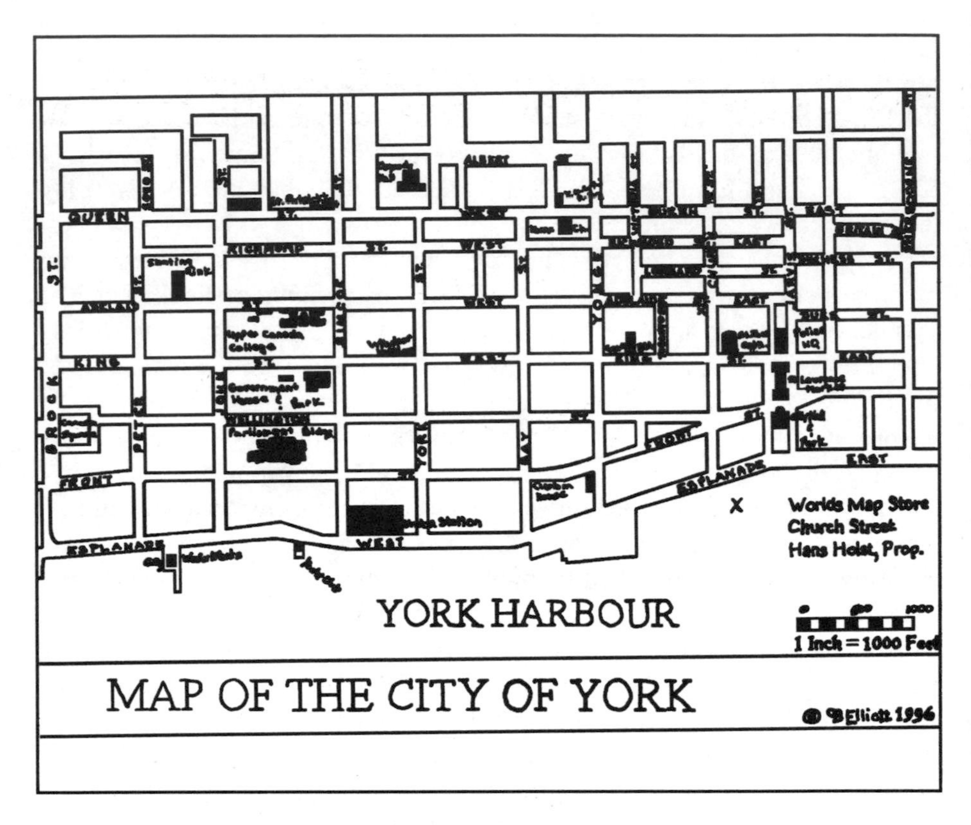

Map of the City of York

[Map Copyright © Philip B. Elliott. Used with the permission of the cartographer.]

Andrew WEINER

The Map

(*Northern Frights*. Ed. by Don Hutchinson. Oakville, Ont.: Mosaic; 1992).

Biographical information about the author will be found at the back of the book.

Walk down the east side of Church Street from Dundas to Queen — the pawnshops sit side-by-side. If you have been pinched by the Second Great Depression of the twentieth century to the extent that you need their services or are merely bargain hunting, who knows, perhaps you may find an old curiosity shop tucked in between them. But remember, curiosity killed the cat. Be careful if you are offered a map and beware. You might discover that you can't get there from here. Or like Dennis Stone, you may find the Point of No Return.

The Map

1.

The body was lying beside the couch on the off-white broadloom, face upwards, arms sprawled at an awkward angle, eyes open and staring blankly. The body was casually dressed: slacks, sweater, sports jacket.

"What have we got?" Walker asked the uniformed officers.

"Dennis Stone," said one of the officers. "Financial controller for an oil company. Didn't show up for work this morning, didn't call in, missed a bunch of appointments. Not like him at all. Didn't answer his phone. They got worried, so they called us. The super let us in. And here we are."

"Here we are," Walker agreed.

He glanced around the living room. It was sparsely furnished: leather couch, chrome and glass coffee table, standing brass lamp, white vertical blinds on the high wide windows that looked down on Lake Ontario, twenty floors below. The walls were decorated with framed maps, possibly antique. Lonely guy modern, he thought.

"He lived alone?"

The second officer nodded. "Daughter in Calgary, according to his office. No other close family."

Both the uniformed officers had dark hair and neatly trimmed moustaches. Both were about the same height and build. Looking at them gave Walker an uncomfortable sensation that he was seeing double.

He looked down again at the body. There was a damp patch around it on the carpet, not dark enough to be blood. He stooped to touch it. It felt damp. So did the man's clothes.

"Was the window open when you came in?" he asked.

The first officer shook his head. "Windows don't open. Central air."

"He's wet," Walker said. "Why is he wet?"

"Maybe he got caught in the rain."

"It hasn't rained all week."

"Maybe he fell in the lake."

"Then came home and died before he could change his clothes? I guess it's a theory."

He wandered through into the bathroom. Everything was in its proper place. Towels on the rods, soap in the dish, tub and shower stall clean and dry.

The bedroom was equally orderly. Bed made, clothes hung up in the closet. More maps were displayed on the walls. Walker returned to the living room and stared down at the body.

"Could be his heart," he said. "Or something like that. But somehow I don't think it is."

"What else could it be?" one of the officers asked.

"I don't know. I really don't know."

2.

Walker pushed aside the medical examiner's report in disgust. He leaned back in his chair.

"Terrific," he said.

"What's terrific?" asked Lomax, his partner, from across the room.

"Report on Dennis Stone. The guy in the lakeshore condo."

"And?"

"He drowned."

"I thought you found him in the living room."

"We did."

"Someone drowned him in the bathtub?"

Walker shook his head. "In the lake. He drowned in the lake. They can track it from the pollutants. Died late Saturday evening, as near as they can place it."

"So it's murder?"

"We don't know that. All we know is that he drowned in the lake, and that someone brought him back to his apartment."

"Strange."

"It is, isn't it? Why drown someone in the lake and then drag them back to their own apartment? Then again, maybe it wasn't murder. There were no marks on the body, no signs of struggle. It could have been an accident. Suicide, even. But whatever it was, you come back to the same question: Who moved him back? And why?"

"What do we know about this guy?" Lomax asked.

"Not a lot. Public accountant, age fifty one. Old Toronto family. Lived alone. No close friends. No family to speak of: parents dead, wife long gone, daughter in Calgary, older brother in Florida. Reasonably well-off, but nothing spectacular."

"Signs of forced entry?"

"No signs. And nothing missing, far as we can tell."

"Neighbours?"

Walker signed. "Saw nothing, heard nothing. You'd think that someone would have seen them carting him up. Must have been real late at night."

"You know these buildings," Lomax said. "People live in them because they don't *want* to know their neighbours. They're just not interested. You could carry a corpse up in the elevator in broad daylight and no one would blink."

"Building security should have noticed. But they didn't. Asleep at the monitors, probably."

"Tape back-up?"

"No tapes."

"So what have we got?"

"A drowned accountant. Who collected maps."

"Maps?" "Old ones. All over his apartment. Also, there was this." He handed over a plastic evidence bag with a business card inside. "We found this in his jacket."

Lomax squinted at the card.

WORLDS MAP STORE
Hans Holst, Proprietor
Fine Maps Of All Territories

There was an address on Church Street, and a telephone number.

"You call him?" Lomax asked.

"Yeah, but the number was out of service. And there was no new listing. Gone out of business, I guess."

"I never saw a map store on Church Street. And that used to be part of my beat."

"These stores," Walker said. "Always opening and closing, you can't keep track of them. But maybe I'll run down and take a look, anyway."

"Why?" Lomax asked. "I mean, what could a map store have to do with his death?"

"I don't know. I thought maybe, if I could find this Holst, he could explain *this*."

He opened a larger evidence bag and took out the map, the infuriating map. "Careful with this one," he said, as he passed it to Lomax. "It's still a little damp."

"You found it on the body?"

"Underneath it, actually."

"You think it's important?"

"I don't know what I think."

Lomax stared at the map. "Looks like an ordinary Toronto street map to me."

"But it isn't."

"Isn't what?"

"Isn't ordinary. Isn't Toronto either. Not any Toronto you or I know."

"Well here's Yonge Street," Lomax said. "And King and Queen and Dundas . . . "

"Take a look at Bloor."

Lomax squinted at the map. Parts of it were unreadable, where the water had soaked through. But much of it was clearly legible. "It's called MacKenzie," he said. "Is that a typo?"

"Take a look at Bayview."

Lomax puzzled over the map. "I can't find it."

"Because it isn't there. And that's not the only street that's gone missing. The whole thing is like that. Some of the streets are the same, but some have different names, and some don't seem to exist at all."

"Must be an antique," Lomax said. "A map of how the city used to be. You said he collected old maps."

"But it isn't old. The lab dates it at no more than a couple of years."

"A reproduction, then."

Lomax jabbed his finer at the blurry title on the bottom of the map. CITY OF YOThe rest was unreadable.

"See," he said. "City of York. Isn't that what they used to call Toronto?"

"The old British settlers did, yeah. And some called it Little York. Which was partly why they changed the name."

"Well there you are," Lomax said. "A reproduction."

Walker shook his head. "They changed the name back in the 1830s. York was a real small town then. On this map, there's development way north of Eglinton. That would have been farmland back then."

"Right," Lomax agreed. "Except it doesn't seem to be called Eglinton. It's called . . . " He strained to read the blurred print.

"Queen Victoria Way."

"Must be a joke map. Some sort of gag."

"Must be," Walker agreed.

3.

He drove around the block twice and saw no sign of a map store at the address on the card. He parked on the next street and walked around the block. He found the store immediately, squeezed in between two pawnshops.

The store was small and gloomy and remarkably cluttered. Maps were everywhere, covering available centimetre of the walls, stacked up in racks, piled haphazardly on tables.

"Can I help you?" asked the man behind the counter. He was short, plump, graying. He had a cherubic face and thick eyeglasses and a faint European accent.

"Mr. Holst?" Walker asked.

"Yes."

"I've been trying to reach you. There seems to be some problem with your phone."

"Phones are often a problem. What can I do for you?"

Walker showed his identification.

"I'm investigating the death of man called Dennis Stone. He was a map collector. I believe he may have been one of your customers."

Holst shrugged. "I don't recall the name. I doubt he was a regular customer."

"He was carrying your business card."

"Many people have my card."

Walker showed him a photograph of the dead man. Holst studied it.

"Yes," he said, finally. "I do believe I have seen this man. He came into my store only last Saturday afternoon, as a matter of fact. And now you say that he's dead? But that's shocking."

"Yes it is," Walker agreed. "It is shocking."

"I'm not really sure how I can be of help. I'd never met the man before. All I can tell you is that he was a serious collector, and a fairly knowledgeable one."

"Did he buy anything from you?"

"He was interested in a number of items, but reached no final decision. I rather expected him to return. He was especially drawn to this one, but found the price rather steep."

Holst indicated a map on the wall behind him. It was an old map of the world, brightly colored, the continents eccentrically drawn, the oceans dotted with mermaids and seahorses and other whimsical creatures.

"Nice," Walker said.

"Yes it is. Quite historic, too, late 17th Century. And for a collector of Canadiana like Mr. Stone, truly fascinating. Look." Holst pointed at North America. "Canada, you see, has no west coast here, nor any northern limits. At the time these territories were still unmapped, unknown, undiscovered. A map like this would itself stimulate further exploration. That was part of the whole exploratory impulse, you see: To fill out the maps. To chart the unknown."

"How much would a map like this cost?"

"This one is $15,000 dollars."

Walker eyebrows arched up in surprise.

"A small price for the serious collector," Holst said.

"Because of the investment value, you mean?"

"There are good prospects for appreciation, if you buy carefully. But that would be a secondary consideration. For the true collector, the main motivation is history. Getting in touch with our past. And understanding our present, our place in the broader scheme of things."

"Still," Walker joked, "it seems a lot to pay for a map that isn't even accurate."

"But what map *is* accurate? Is the world flat? A map is a always a fabrication, a distortion of physical space. And it will always be distorted further by the world view of its creator. This map for example . . . " Holst pointed to another map on the wall. "The British Empire, circa 1950. Observe the great swathes of territory still shaded in imperial red. Rather poignant, actually. But what meaning could such a map have had at the time for a native of, say, the British Gold Coast? For that matter, where *is* the British Gold Coast now? It exists only on these old maps. In a sense, it never really existed in the first place, except on maps. And in the minds of mind."

"Interesting," Walker said, his eyes visibly glazing over.

"Forgive me," the old man said. "You started me on one of my favourite subjects. Was there something else you wanted to ask me?"

"Yes," Walker said. "Yes there was." He pulled the map from his pocket. "We found this map in Stone's possession. I'd like to know what you make of it."

Holst studied the map. "Toronto but not Toronto. Not historical, not contemporary. Possibly an imaginary map, of the kind that might accompany a work of fantasy, such as a map of Tolkien's Middle Earth. Some collectors are interested in these maps. Then again, it could be just a prank."

"A fictitious map?"

"All maps are fictitious. The difference is one of degree. Have you read Alfred Korzybski?"

Walker shook his head.

"Interesting man. General Semantics, and so on. It was Korzybski who said, 'The map is not the territory'. But he was wrong, you see. For most of us, the map *is* the territory. We perceive only that part of the territory defined for us by our maps, both physical and mental."

"I see," Walker said.

"I don't think you do," the old man said. "But perhaps you will."

"This map — have you ever seen it before?"

"Never. I'm sorry. Is it important? Is it what you might call a clue?"

"Yes," Walker said. "It's what you might call a clue."

4.

He's lying, Walker thought, as he left the store. His every instinct told him that Holst *had* seen the map before, and that, almost certainly, he had sold it to Dennis Stone.

Possibly he could prove that, if he could get a warrant to seize the sales records, and if the transaction had been recorded. But that would only tell him what he knew already, that the old man was lying.

Why was he lying?

Deep in thought, Walker walked back to his car.

His car was gone.

Surely not towed, he thought. Not with a police ID clearly visible. Stolen, then.

Christ, he thought. The nerve.

He would never live this down back at headquarters.

He crossed the street to the pay phone and called his office. The dial tone sounded a little odd, but he didn't pay it much attention. There was a screeching noise, followed by a recorded announcement: *The number you have not called is not in service. Please consult the directory listings and try your number again.*

Irritated, he hung up and called again. *The number you have called . . .*

He called the operator and asked her to dial the number. Same result. The operator suggested that he try directory inquiries.

"I work there," he told her, furious. "You think I don't know the number?" He slammed down the phone.

Phones are often a problem, he thought.

He felt, then, the first dim flickers of panic.

He strode back to Church Street, looking for a cab. There were no cabs in sight. He passed the map store. There was a "CLOSED" sign on the door and the lights were out.

He decided to call a cab. There was a bar on the next block, he remembered, one of those glitzy singles bars. He could use the phone there.

He came to the door of the bar and faltered. The place had changed. There was a solid brick facade instead of the big glass windows with the colored neon tubes. There were two doors: one was marked "Men", the other "Ladies and Escorts".

A tavern. An old-style Toronto tavern.

It was almost as if the bar had reverted back to some earlier form. Except that there had never been a tavern here, not as long as he could remember.

He looked wildly up and down the street. Was this Church Street or not? Had there really been a bar here? How could he have made a mistake like that? And why couldn't he get through to the office?

He saw a cab approaching, although it took him a few moments to recognize it. It was one of those big old-fashioned British-style taxis, with the driver in a separate compartment in the front. The sign said "For Hire". Walker flagged it down.

"I didn't know there were any of these things around," he told the driver. The driver stared at him blankly.

"Where to?" he asked.

"Police headquarters."

The driver clicked down the flag and did a U-turn. He headed south, towards the lake, in the completely opposite direction to police headquarters.

"Hey," Walker said. "Where are you going?"

"Police headquarters."

"Police headquarters is the other way."

The driver made a hair-raising turn at Front Street.

"Police headquarters," he said, "is right here."

The driver pulled up opposite the old St. Lawrence Market, at the curb in front of where the new market building should have been. Should have been, but wasn't. In its place was a low-rise red-brick building, clearly labeled "Police Headquarters".

There was a flag flying on the pole in front of the building. Not the Canadian flag, the Maple Leaf, but the old British Union Jack.

Walker closed his eyes, opened them again. Nothing changed.

"Pound fifty," the cabbie said.

"Pound?"

"Pound fifty," the cabbie said again.

Walker found the unfamiliar currency in his wallet. He passed over two of the notes.

"Keep the change," he said.

5.

Instead of entering the police building, Walker crossed the street and sat down on a bench in front of the old market. He pulled the map out of his pocket.

The map, he thought, is the territory.

Somehow he was not surprised to find police headquarters located on Front Street on Dennis Stone's map.

He continued to study the map. As he remembered, there had been something odd about the waterfront.

He got up and walked south, past the old market to the next cross street, Esplanade.

Once, long ago, Esplanade had been the southerly boundary of his own Toronto. It was where the waterfront had begun. Later had come the landfill for the railway lands, leaving the old waterfront high and dry.

In this city, though, that had not happened. This city ended at Esplanade. Where the south side of the street should have been was the lake. No parking lots, no buildings, no railway lines. And looking west, no lakeshore condominium developments, no soaring modern office buildings, no CN Tower, no SkyDome. Just water.

Where am I? he wondered. *Where the hell am I?*

He stared helplessly up and down the street. He saw a newspaper box. It was blue, like the boxes that held the *Toronto Star*. But when he got closer he saw that this box was labeled *Upper Canada Gazette*.

He put a coin in and took out a newspaper. The date on the front page was right. Everything else was wrong.

The lead story was about a debate in parliament. Not the Canadian parliament or the Ontario provincial parliament, but the parliament of Upper Canada.

The governing party appeared to be the Conservatives. The Labour Party formed the Opposition. There was also a small group of Liberals.

The Prime Minister of Upper Canada had proposed a customs union with the Republic of Quebec. The Labour Party were fiercely opposed.

In other news, the U.S. Senator for Alberta had announced his candidacy for the Republican presidential nomination.

The Queen was visiting the Maritime Dominions. She would be in York the following week to open the new Royal Opera House.

London, England was paralyzed by a transit strike. Leeds had leaped to the top of the English football league. There had been heavy snowstorms in the north of England . . . There seemed to be an inordinate amount of news about Britain.

Canada broke up, he thought. No. More likely it never got to be unified. In this world, Upper Canada never became the province of Ontario. It just stayed Upper Canada, an independent dominion, one of a number of weak and squabbling dominions under the British thumb. And the U.S. grabbed the West.

Result: underdevelopment. No national railways, no railways lands. No condo buildings or glitzy singles bars either.

As he walked slowly back up Church Street, the differences became clearer. His own Toronto was part renovated and part modern, increasingly ethnic, moderately dynamic. But this city was gray, grimy, rundown. It was like some British provincial town: Belfast, maybe, or Manchester. The people on the streets were shabbily dressed, almost uniformly Anglo-Saxon.

Little York, he thought.

6.

He found himself, again, at the Worlds Map Store. It was still closed. He rang the bell.

Holst opened the door. He, at least, looked exactly the same.

"What's happening to me?" Walker asked, with no preliminaries.

Holst stood aside to let him in.

"Why don't you tell me what you think is happening?"

"I think somehow you pushed me through into . . . I don't know, some other world. Some different world. The same way you pushed Dennis Stone."

Holst smiled. "I am not a magician," he said. "At most, a tour guide. I pushed no one. You found you own way through. So did the unfortunate Mr. Stone."

"You know how Stone died?"

"He drowned, did he not? In the living room of his condominium. I read about it the paper."

"The *Upper Canada Gazette?*"

"The *Star*, Mr. Walker."

"He bought the map here." It was a statement, not a question.

"Yes."

"And then?"

"I can only speculate. But I believe that he must have gone home and studied the map, and studied it more. And at some point he began to believe it. And in doing so he broke through, so to speak, to the other side."

"Except that his condominium doesn't exist in this world," Walker said. "Only water. He broke through and he drowned in the lake."

Holst nodded. "A terrible twist of fate."

"But he came back. To his own living room. His own city."

"All things return eventually to their proper place."

"But not in their proper form. You map killed him."

Holst nodded sadly. "I should never have sold it to him, never even let him see it. I was teasing him with it, I suppose. He seemed so dull, so straitlaced, so unimaginative. I never dreamed that he would actually find his way through. And of course I had no idea where he lived. It never even occurred to me to ask, the possibility of something like this happening seemed so remote . . . "

"Which is real? Which world is real?"

"Both. Neither. You are asking the wrong question. You mean, which is *more* real? And to that I would have to say, to whom? And at what point in time? We are dealing with layers, Mr. Walker, different layers of the same onion, as it were, the one underlying the other."

He pointed towards the street.

"The old York lives on, you know," he said. "Even in your own Toronto. In terms of both the physical and psychological infrastructure. It's always been there, lurking just below the surface. The old loyalist ways. The allegiance to Queen and flag and country. The dourness, the small-mindedness, the provincialism, the abiding hatred of the new and the foreign. It's all there. You don't really need a map to see it. For someone like Dennis Stone, it was always present. In a sense, he had always lived in that other city. It was recognizing it that killed him."

"And for you?" Walker asked. "Which is more real for you?"

"Many worlds are real for me. Depending on how the mood takes me."

Walker shook his head. "If I thought that anyone would believe a word of this, I would take you down to headquarters to make a statement. But I don't even believe it myself." He turned towards the door.

"You still have to find your way back," Holst reminded him.

"That's right. I do."

"You'll need a map."

7.

Walker found his car where he had parked it. He tossed the map that Holst had given him — it was an ordinary Toronto street map — into the glove compartment. Then he drove around the block.

As he had somehow expected, the map store had disappeared. There was nothing in between the two pawnshops. Nor would he ever find it again, even on foot.

The Stone case was finally filed away as a probable homicide, unsolved.

Walker kept the map that the old man had given him on his desk. From time to time he would pick it up and stare at it intently.

"Did the Don Valley Parkway always join up with Highway 404?" he would ask his partner, Loomis.

"Always."

"And did Heath Street always dead-end at the ravine?"

"Of course," Loomis would said. "Of course it did."

Biographical Notes about the Authors

Rosemary AUBERT

Rosemary AUBERT is an internationally published novelist, poet, biographer, and critic. She was born in Niagara Falls, N.Y., U.S.A., but has lived in Canada for the past twenty-five years, currently residing in Toronto where she teaches criminology for writers. Her short story, "The midnight boat to Palermo", won an Arthur Ellis Award from the Crime Writers of Canada for the Best Crime Short Story by a Canadian writer published in 1994. She has extensive experience as an editor and in book promotion and currently heads her own firm supplying these services to authors.

Criminous works
Free reign. Bridgehampton, NY: Bridge Works; 1977.
Webster, Jack, and Aubert, Rosemary. *Copperjack; my life on the force.* Toronto: Dundurn; 1991.

Other works
An even dozen poems. Toronto: Missing Link; 1975. poetry.
Two kinds of honey. Ottawa: Oberon; 1977. poetry.
Song of Eden. Toronto: Harlequin; 1983. romance.
A red bird in Winter. Toronto: Harlequin; 1984. romance.
Garden of lions. Toronto: Harlequin; 1985. romance.
Firebrand. Toronto: Harlequin; 1986. romance.
A thousand to one. NY: Avalon; 1996. romance.

Robert BARR

Born in Glasgow, Scotland, on 16 September 1850, the eldest child of Robert Barr and June Barr, **Robert BARR** junior was brought to Canada when he was four. The family first lived in Wallacetown, Ontario, and then, after living in other Ontario towns, finally settled in Windsor, Ontario, where Barr spent much of his childhood and was educated. He taught in Windsor on a temporary certificate until 1873, when he entered the Toronto Normal School to obtain his permanent teaching licence. His autobiographical novel *The measure of the rule*, (1907), about his time there in the 1870s records his entry into pedagogy and provides historians of education with a source book on the state of teacher-training in Ontario in the late nineteenth century as well as being a serious contribution to Canadian literature. Barr returned to Windsor in 1875 as principal of Windsor Central School, but in 1876 he abandoned teaching for journalism and took a job as a reporter on the *Detroit Free Press*, quickly becoming editor.

In 1881, he moved to England where he remained until 1911, achieving success as a magazine editor, short-story writer, and novelist, of which he published 20. In 1892, in association with Jerome K. Jerome he established *The Idler*, of which he was co-editor, which was vastly popular for a few years until destroyed by a lawsuit. His first novel, *In the midst of alarms*, which is set in Canada and centres around the Fenian invasion of 1866, was published in 1894, preceded by two collections of short stories. He died aet. 62 of heart failure at Woldingham, Surrey, England, on 22 October 1912, by education and upbringing a Canadian.

Criminous works

Strange happenings. As by "Luke Sharp". London: Dunkerley; 1883. ss.
From whose bourne? London: Chatto & Windus; 1893, as by "Luke Sharp"/NY: Stokes; 1896. Char: William Brenton, deceased. Inter alia, a detective's ghost clears a woman falsely accused of her husband's murder. ss.
The face and the mask. London: Hutchinson; 1894/NY: Stokes; 1895. Contains the first book appearance of "The great Pegram mystery", originally published as "Detective stories gone wrong; the adventures of Sherlaw Kombs" in *The Idler* in May 1892, the first and still one of the funniest Holmesian parodies.
The mutable many. NY: Stokes; 1896/London: Methuen; 1897.
Revenge! NY: Stokes/London: Chatto & Windus; 1896. ss.
A woman intervenes; or, The mistress of the mine. NY: Stokes/ London: Chatto & Windus; 1896.
Jennie Baxter, journalist. NY: Stokes/London: Methuen; 1899.
The strong arm. NY: Stokes; 1899/London: Methuen; 1900. A selection therein was published as: *Gentlemen, the King!* — NY: Stokes; [n.d.]. ss.
The King dines. London: McClure; 1901/London: Chatto & Windus/ NY: McClure — as: *A prince of good fellows*; 1902.
The victors; a romance of yesterday morning and this afternoon. NY: Stokes; 1901/London: Methuen; 1902. Set: New York City. A study of political corruption.
Over the border. NY: Stokes/London: Isbister; 1903.
A Chicago princess. NY: Stokes; 1904/London: Methuen — as: *The tempetuous petticoat*; 1905.
The woman wins. NY: Stokes/London: Methuen — as: *The Lady Electra*; 1904. ss.
A rock in the Baltic. NY: Authors & Newspapers; 1906/London: Hurst & Blackett; 1907.
The triumphs of Eugene Valmont. NY: Appleton/London: Hurst; 1906. ss.
The Watermead Affair. Philedelphia: Altemus; 1906.
Cardillac. London: Mills and Boon/NY: Stokes; 1909.
The girl in the case. NY: Nash; 1910.
Lady Eleanor, lawbreaker. Chicago: Rand McNally; 1911.
Tales of two continents. London: Mills and Boon; 1920. ss.
The adventures of Sherlaw Kombs. Boulder, Colorado: Aspen Press; 1979. Char: Sherlaw Kombs. An edition as a separate of "The Great Pegram mystery", the first parody of Sherlock Holmes, which first appeared in *The Idler Magazine*, 1, (May 1892), pp.413-424, as "Detective stories gone wrong; the adventures of Sherlaw Kombs" as by "Luke Sharp" and made its first book appearance as titled in *The face and the mask*, (1894), (supra). "The finest and one of the funniest Sherlockian parodies ever written", (Ronald Burt De Waal, *The world bibliography of Sherlock Holmes and Dr. Watson; a classified and annotated list of materials relating to their lives and adventures*, Boston: New York Graphic Society; 1974). ss.

Other works

In a steamer chair; and other shipboard stories. London: Chatto & Windus/NY: Cassell; 1892. ss.

In the midst of alarms. London: Methuen/NY: Stokes; 1894. Set in the Niagara region of Canada in 1866 during the Fenian invasion.
One day's courtship; and, The heralds of fame. NY: Stokes; 1896. Set in Canada.
Tekla; a romance of love and war. NY: Stokes; 1898/London: Methuen — as: *The Countess Tekla*; 1899.
The unchanging East. London: Chatto & Windus/Boston: Page; 1900.
The O'Ruddy. With Stephen Crane. NY: Stokes; 1903/London: Methuen; 1904. A picaresque tale.
The speculations of John Steele. London: Chatto & Windus/NY: Stokes; 1905.
The measure of the rule. London: Constable; 1907/NY: Appleton; 1908. Set: Toronto. Char: Tom Prentis. An autobigraphical novel of the author's training at the Toronto Normal School.
Young Lord Stranleigh. London: Ward, Lock/NY: Appleton; 1908.
Stranleigh's millions. London: Nash; 1909.
The sword maker. London: Mills and Boon/NY: Stokes; 1910.
Lord Stranleigh, philanthropist. London: Ward, Lock; 1911.
The palace of logs. London: Mills and Boon; 1912.
Lord Stranleigh abroad. London: Ward, Lock; 1913.
My enemy Jones; an extravaganza. London: Nash/London: Hodder & Stoughton — as: *Unsentimental journey*; 1913.
A woman in a thousand. London: Hodder & Stoughton; 1913.
The helping hand; and other stories. London: Mills and Boon; 1920. ss.
I travel the road. London: Quality; 1945.
Selected stories. Ed. by John Parr, with introduction, chronology, and bibliography. Ottawa: University of Ottawa Press; 1977.

Jack BATTEN

Born in Toronto on 23 January 1932, **Jack BATTEN** graduated B.A. from the University of Toronto in 1954 and Bachelor of Law from the University of Toronto Law School in 1957. He then practised law for four years in Toronto for 1959-1963, before becoming a full-time writer and radio movie reviewer. He lives in the Annex district of Toronto. In 1977, he collaborated with Michael Bliss to produce one of the finest Sherlockian pastiches, "Sherlock Holmes' great Canadian adventure". A decade later, he inaugurated one of the most enjoyable series featuring a Canadian amateur sleuth with *Crang plays the ace; a mystery* introducing Crang, a jazz-loving Toronto lawyer, who has re-appeared in three more cases.

Criminous works
Crang plays the ace; a mystery. Toronto: Macmillan; 1987.
Straight no chaser; a Crang mystery. Toronto: Macmillan; 1989.
Riviera blues; a Crang mystery. Toronto: Macmillan; 1990.
Blood count. Toronto: Macmillan; 1991.

Other works
Nancy; an affectionate look in pictures at the world's greatest woman skier and one of its most charming girls, Canada's own Nancy Greene. Toronto: General; 1968.
The inside story of Conn Smythe's hockey dynasty; a fascinating look at the Conn Smythe enterprises, and history of the Toronto Maple leaf Hockey Club. Toronto: Pagurian; 1969.
Champions; great figures in Canadian sport. Toronto: New Press; 1971.
Honest Ed's story; the crazy rags to riches story of Ed Mirvish. Toronto/NY: Doubleday 1972.

The Leafs in Autumn. Toronto: Macmillan; 1975.
The Toronto Golf Club 1876-1976. Toronto: Toronto Golf Club; 1976.
Canada moves westward 1880-1890. Toronto: Natural Science of Canada; 1977.
Lawyers. Toronto: Macmillan; 1980.
In court. Toronto: Macmillan; 1982.
Tie-breaker. Toronto: Clarke, Irwin; 1984. Novel.
Robinette; the dean of Canadian lawyers. Toronto: Macmillan; 1984.
Judges. Toronto: Macmillan; 1986.
On trial. Toronto: Macmillan; 1988.
The spirit of the Regiment; an account of the 48th Highlanders from 1956 to 1991. Toronto: The Regiment; 1991. (History of the 48th Highlanders, vol. 4)
Mind over murder; DNA and other forensic adventures. Toronto: McClelland & Stewart; 1995.
The Class of '75; [life after law school]. Toronto: Macmillan Canada; 1992. A collective biography of the University of Toronto Law School class of 1975.
[Appleby College — history of]
The complete jogger.
Greene, Nancy, and ___. *Nancy Greene; an autobiography*.
McKay, Heather, and ___. *Heather McKay's complete book of squash*.

Michael BLISS

One of Canada's pre-eminent historians, **Michael BLISS** was born in Kingsville, Ontario, in 1941. A prolific writer on a wide range of Canadian topics, in addition to his monographs he is respected columnist of wide circulation. He has a Ph.D. in History from the University of Toronto where he currently holds the Chair of Professor of Medical History. He lives in the Leaside district of Toronto.

Other works
Canadian history in documents. 1966.
A living profit; studies in the social history of Canadian business, 1883-1911. 1974.
Confederation; a new nationality. 1981.
The discovery of insulin. Toronto: McClelland & Stewart; 1982.
Banting; a biography. Toronto: McClelland & Stewart; 1984.
Years of change; 1967-1985. 1986.
Northern enterprise; five centuries of Canadian business. 1987.
Plague; a story of smallpox in Montreal. Toronto: HarperCollins; 1991.
A Canadian millionaire; the life and business times of Sir Joseph Flavelle.

John DENT

John DENT was born in Kendal, Westmoreland, England, on 8 November 1841, and brought to Upper Canada as a child, where he was educated and called to the bar in 1865. He found the practice of law profitable enough, but uncongenial, and, nursing literary aspirations, relinquished his practice as soon as he could afford to do so and returned to his native England where he established himself as a journalist. In this he prospered, and soon was writing for several of the better periodicals, most notably *Once A Week*, for which he was a regular contributor. Literary work was remunerative enough for him to amply support a wife and family, yet something was missing and after several years he brought his family to the United States of America where he obtained a position in Boston, Massachusetts on the *Globe*, which he held for two years. From 1876 onward, he was back in Ontario as editor of the just-starting Toronto *Evening Telegram*. Latterly, he was on the staff of the Toronto *Globe* before becoming a free-lance writer and for a brief period in 1887 the editor of the short-lived historical and literary weekly, *Arcturus*. Shortly after the murder of the Hon. George Brown, proprietor of the *Globe*, Dent left newspaper work to devote himself to Canadian biography and history. His first ambitious undertaking was the *Canadian Portrait Gallery* that occupied four large volumes. This venture proving successful, he then published *The last forty years; Canada since the Union of 1841* to wide acclaim and followed it by collaborating with the city's foremost local historian, the Rev. Henry Scadding, to produce *Toronto; past and present: historical and descriptive — a memorial volume for the semi-centennial of 1884*. All this had been but preliminary to his magnum opus, *History of the Rebellion in Upper Canada*, that brought a storm of controversy upon his head. When he began his researches for the work, Dent was sympathetic toward William Lyon Mackenzie, but as he progressed he found his idol had feet of clay that he did not hesitate to expose. Dent's opinions were unpalatable both by the partisans of Mackenzie and the supporters of the "Family Compact" and he suffered opprobrium from all quarters. John King, Mackenzie's son-in-law, and the father of Canada's longest-serving Prime Minister, the certainly eccentric, if not certifiably insane, William Lyon Mackenzie King, was disturbed enough by Dent's book to publish his own biased and subjective version, *The other side of the "Story"; being some reviews of Mr. J. C. Dent's first volume "The Story of the Upper Canada Rebellion", and the letters in the Mackenzie-Rolph controversy, also, a critique, hitherto unpublished, on "The New Story"*, (Toronto: James Murray; 1886). The main causes of concern were that Dent justifiably gave Dr John Rolph his due and that he was not swayed to smear the corpses of historic figures with the honey excreted by his own fear of death, but to speak the truth about their motives and actions, thus adumbrating the school of historically-accurate biography that has become the norm. Dent's reaction to his critics was to let them fulminate to their heart's content; all they did was stimulate interest in his own work. In addition to his biographical and historical works, he occasionally indulged, alas, all too infrequently, in excursions into the imaginative, of which the tales in *The Gerrard Street mystery* are but a mere glimpse of his talent. He died a satisfied man, confident that he had provided for his family, at his home in Toronto on 27 September 1888.

Criminous works

The Gerrard Street mystery; and other weird tales. Toronto: Rose; 1888.

Other works

The Canadian portrait gallery. Toronto: Magurn; 1880-1881. 4 vols.
The last forty years; Canada since the union of 1841. Toronto: Geo. Virtue; 1881. 2 vols.
Toronto; past and present: historical and descriptive — a memorial volume for the semi-centennial of 1884. By the Rev. Henry Scadding and John Charles Dent. Toronto: Hunter Rose; 1884.
The story of the Upper Canadian Rebellion. Toronto: Robinson; 1885.
Arcturus; a Canadian journal of literature and life. Toronto; 1887. Vol.1, (1 January-25 June 1887).

Tanya HUFF

A one-time science-fiction bookseller and writer of same, former resident of Toronto and now living near Picton in Prince Edward County, Ontario, who is primarily a horror-meister, **Tanya HUFF** has written a series of bloodsucking murder mysteries set in Hogtown beginning with *Blood price* in 1991 and established herself as the doyen of fantasy-mystery writers. She also writes short stories as by "Terri Hanover". She was born on 26 September 1957 in Halifax, Nova Scotia, and came down the road to obtain her B.A.A. in Radio and Television Arts from the Ryerson Polytechnical Institute, (now Ryerson Polytechnic University), in Toronto. At one time, she served three years in the Canadian Naval Reserve. From 1984 onward for several years, she was the manager and buyer for Bakka, the science-fiction bookstore in Toronto, until with the onset of the '90s she decided to give up urban life for country living and devote herself full-time to writing.

Criminous works

Blood price. NY: DAW; 1991. (Victory Nelson, Investigator: Otherworldly Crimes a Specialty — Book 1). Set: Toronto. Chars: Henry Fitzroy, illegitimate son of England's Henry VIII, a Toronto-based vampire who lives in a condo at Bloor and Jarvis and writer of bodice-ripping romance novels, and (Victory) "Vicki" Nelson, ex-policewoman and now private investigator. The first of their adventures. Someone has conjured up a demon that is terrorizing the city. The historical Henry Fitzroy, Earl of Richmond, the only known illegitimate child of Henry VIII, died at the age of 17 in 1536.

Blood trail. NY: DAW; 1992. (Victory Nelson, Investigator:
otherworldly Crimes A Specialty — Book 2). Set: London, Ontario. Chars: Henry Fitzroy and Vicki Nelson. Someone is killing a family of werewolves.

Blood lines. NY: DAW; 1993. (DAW Book Collectors No. 901). (Victory Nelson, Investigator: Otherworldly Crimes A Specialty Book 3). Set: Toronto. Chars: Henry Fitzroy, and Vicki Nelson. The curse of the mummy's tomb invades the venerable Royal Ontario Museum.

Blood pact. NY: DAW; 1993. (Victory Nelson, Investigator: Otherworldly Crimes A Specialty — Book 4). Set: Toronto and Kingston, Ontario. Chars: Henry Fitzroy and Vicki Nelson.

Other works

Child of the Grove. NY: DAW; 1988. (The Novels of Crystal — The Wizard Crystal, Book 1). The first volume of a duology completed by *The last wizard*, (infra). fantasy.

The last wizard. NY: DAW; 1989. (The Novels of Crystal — The Wizard Crystal, Book 2). Sequel to *Child of the Grove*, (supra). fantasy.

The fire's stone. NY: DAW; 1990. fantasy.

Gate of darkness, circle of light. NY: DAW; [?]. The Wild Magic was loose in Toronto, for an Adept of Darkness had broken through the barrier into the everyday mortal world. fantasy.

Sing the Four Quarters. NY: DAW; 1994. (The Bards Series; Book 1).

Fifth Quarter. NY: DAW; 1995. (The Bards Series; Book 2).

Maureen JENNINGS

Maureen JENNINGS was born in Birmingham, England, and first arrived in Toronto in 1960 at the age of 17, street map in hand and has been in love with and discovering the city ever since. She obtained her B.A. from the University of Windsor and her M.A. from the University of Toronto. After eight years of teaching English at Ryerson Polytechnical Institute in Toronto, in 1972 she established a private pyschotherapy practice. Her first play, *The black ace*, an historical mystery set in Toronto of 1901, was professionally produced in 1990; a second play also a mystery, was set in 1898; and the mystery novel she has recently completed, *Except the dying*, takes place in the struggling young city of 1895.

Criminous works
The black ace. Produced at Solar Stage Theatre, Toronto, November 1990. [unpublished] Set: Toronto in 1901. Char: John Wilson Murray. Murray, known as "The great Canadian detective", is an historical personage who was the official provincial detective for the province of Ontario. Born in Scotland on 25 June 1840, he came to the United States of America with his family when he was five. When 17, he entered the U.S. Navy and during the Civil War performed undercover work, detecting a plot to free Confederate prisoners from an island in Lake Erie. After the Civil War, he was, firstly, a special agent for the U.S. Navy Department, then a member of the Erie, Pennsylvania, police, before accepting the position of Head of Detectives of the Canadian Southern Railway, which entailed a move to St Thomas, Ontario. His success in this post brought him to the attention of Sir Oliver Mowat, then Attorney General of Ontario, (and later Premier). In 1874, Murray was appointed Detective of the Department of Justice of the Province of Ontario, which position he held until just before his death in 1906. Murray's most famous case was that of John Reginald Birchall, an English confidence man, who murdered Frederick Cornwallis Benwell on 15 February 1890 in the Blenheim Swamp near Woodstock, Ontario, and after being tracked down by Murray was duly hanged. Murray published a purported autobiography, *Memoirs of a great Canadian detective*, (London: Wm Heinemann; 1904), in which the stories were no doubt embellished for dramatic purposes, but they offer vivid glimpses into the life of crime in late nineteenth-century Ontario, which appeared in Great Britain, but wasn't published in Canada, (*Memoirs of a great Canadian detective; incidents in the life of John Wilson Murray: [selections from "Memoirs of a great detective"]*, Toronto: Collins; 1977, and, *Further adventures of the great detective; incidents in the life of John Wilson Murray: [selections from "Memoirs of a great detective"*, Toronto: Collins; 1980), until interest was sparked by a television series about Murray. There is also a juvenile biography of Murray: *John Wilson Murray*, by Bruce McDougall, (1980). Murray died in Toronto in his residence on Brunswick Avenue in June of 1906. play.
Except the dying. NY: St Martin's; 1997. historical mystery novel set in Toronto of 1895.
No traveller returns. Produced by Solar Stage Theatre, Toronto, November 1992. [unpublished] Set: in an inn near Huntsville, Ontario, just before Christmas 1895. Char: John Wilson Murray. play.

Other works
Windfall. one-act play.

James POWELL

Born in Toronto on 12 June 1932, **James POWELL** was educated in Toronto at various elementary schools and at St Michael's College School. He graduated with his B.A. from St Michael's College, University of Toronto, in 1955 and then pursued post-graduate studies at the University of Paris, Paris, France, for 1955-1956, subsequently teaching in France. Latterly, he worked as a journalist. Currently, he is the editor of an antiques newspaper and resides in Marietta, Pennsylvania, United States of America, where he enjoys bird-watching on the banks of the Susquehanna River. He is well-known as a prolific writer of satirical and humorous criminous short stories, some of which concern the exploits of the dim-witted Acting Sergeant Maynard Bullock of the RCMP and read as unused "Sergeant Renfrew" scripts from the CBC's "Royal Canadian Air Farce". Of his large output of short stories, of which many are criminous, quite a few have been either set in Canada or if set outside of Canada, have a Canadian protagonist. He was the recipient of the 1991 Derrick Murdoch Award from the Crime Writers of Canada for his contribution to the mystery short story form.

Criminous works
A murder coming; stories. Toronto: Yonge & Bloor Publ.; 1990. Some set in Canada featuring Acting Sergeant Maynard Bullock, RCMP, that are humorous in intent. ss.

Trevor RAYMOND

Trevor RAYMOND, the annotator of "Sherlock Holmes' great Canadian adventure", is a journalist and foreign correspondent of wide-ranging experience, now teaching in Georgetown, Ontario, where he lives, and a noted Sherlockian scholar. Currently, he is the editor of *Canadian Holmes; the magazine of the Bootmakers of Toronto*. The Bootmakers of Toronto is Canada's national Sherlockian association, founded in 1972 on the ruins of previous Canadian Holmesian societies, and still thriving.

Robert J. SAWYER

Robert J. SAWYER is a free-lance writer formerly specializing in business journalism and now a full-time science-fiction writer resident in Thornhill to the north of Toronto. He has his Bachelor of Applied Arts in Radio and Television Arts from Ryerson Polytechnical Institute, (now Ryerson Polytechnic University), in Toronto. His short story, "Just like old times", (*On Spec; the Canadian Magazine of Speculative Writing*, vol.5:no.2, Summer 1993/reprinted IN *Dinosaur fantastic*, NY: DAW; 1993), won a Crime Writers of Canada Arthur Ellis Award for Best (Criminous) Short Story by a Canadian first published in 1993.

Criminous works
Golden fleece. NY: Popular Library; 1990. Set: aboard superstarship "Starcolony Argo" in the years A.D. 2179-2235. Char: Canadian Aaron Rossman, formerly of Toronto, in a contest against a villainous computer. A first-rate puzzle mystery in the classic mould, it was named best science fiction novel of 1990 by *The Magazine of Fantasy and Science Fiction*. Isaac Asimov should have written so well.
Fossil hunter. NY: Ace; 1993. (Afsan trilogy 2) Set: on an alien world with a technology approximately equal to that of Europe's in the 17th century. Char: Afsan, a blind scholar, of a race of intelligent dinosaurs called Quintaglios. The Quintaglios are carnivores who hunt and kill their own food, which gives them a release for their anger and violence; consequently, they have almost no violent crime. When Haldan, a young female, is found dead, her throat slit by a jagged piece of mirror, everyone is shocked by the first murder to have taken place in centuries. Since murders are unheard of, no one is trained in solving them. Because Haldan was his daughter, Afsan undertakes to investigate the crime. Then his son, Yabool, another of his eight children, falls victim to the unknown killer. The entire series tells of the coming-of-age of this

race of intelligent dinosaurs and their previous and subsequent history to *Fossil hunter* can be found respectively in *Far-seer* and *Foreigner*, (infra).
The terminal experiment. NY: HarperCollins/London; New English Library (Hodder & Stoughton); 1995. Set: Toronto ca AD 2005. Char: bio-medical engineer Peter Hobson. A lifelong obsession with developing an EEG that will determine the exact clinical moment of death brings Hobson to promising dying detective Sandra Philo that he will solve the case of her own murder as well as the murders she was investigating in this mix of science, technologial derring-do, and murder. Serialized in *analog*, (mid-December 1994-March 1995), in four parts as "Hobson's choice".

Other works
Face of God. NY: Berkley; 1992.
Far-seer. NY: Ace; 1992. (Afsan trilogy 1) Char: Afsan.
End of an era. NY: Ace Science Fiction; 1994.
Foreigner. NY: Ace; 1994. (Afsan trilogy 3) Char: Afsan.

Peter A. SELLERS

Peter A. SELLERS was born on 27 October 1956 in Toronto where he attended the University of Toronto Schools and Glendon College of York University. A freelance advertising creative director and writer, he has been selling crime short fiction since 1984 and was the founder editor in 1987 of the groundbreaking *Cold Blood* anthology series. In 1993, he was co-winner, with James Powell and James Bankier, of the Derrick Murdoch Award from the Crime Writers of Canada.
Criminous works
(ed.). *Cold blood; murder in Canada*. Oakville, Ontario: Mosaic Press; 1987. ss.
___. *Cold blood II*. Oakville, Ontario: Mosaic Press; 1989. ss.
___. *Cold blood III*. Oakville, Ontario: Mosaic Press; 1990. ss.
___. *Cold blood IV*. Oakville, Ontario: Mosaic Press; 1992. ss.
___. *Cold blood V*. Oakville, Ontario: Mosaic Press; 1994. ss.

Other works
(ed.). Bankier, James. *Fear is a killer; 16 stories of crime and pubishment*. Oakville, Ontario: Mosaic Press; 1995. ss.
___. Powell, James. *A murder coming*. Toronto: Yonge & Bloor Publishing; 1990.

Vincent STARRETT

Vincent STARRETT was born in Toronto on 26 October 1886, grandson of John Young, a famous Canadian publisher and bookseller in Toronto in his day. Starret was removed to Chicago, Illinois, United States of America, at an early age, where he grew up, (returning to Toronto for vacations), was educated, and where he became a celebrated newspaperman and spent most of his life. Starret was a noted bookman and one of the grand old men of Sherlockianism, being with Christopher Morley one of the co-founders of the "Baker Street Irregulars". His remarkable *The private life of Sherlock Holmes* is the first biographical study of a fictional detective hero. He was a prolific essayist and recognized as one of the outstanding writers on books and bookmen for his bibliographies and critical studies of a wide range of writers. Starrett was a scholar of the crime fiction genre, as well as being a notable writer of mystery stories in his own right, and is credited with introducing Western readers to the pleasures of Chinese detective fiction and the activities of Judge Dee and Magistrate Pao through his seminal essay, "Some Chinese detective stories", in his *Bookman's holiday; the private satisfactions of an incurable collector*, (NY: Random House; 1942).

Criminous works

The unique Hamlet; a hitherto unchronicled adventure of Mr. Sherlock Holmes. Chicago: Priv. printed for the friends of Walter H. Hill; 1920. Ltd ed. of 33 copies. Char: Sherlock Holmes. The late Ellery Queen, an authority on both criminous literature and Sherlockiana, considered *The unique Hamlet* to be Vincent Starret's "most devout achievement in a lifelong `career of Conan Doyle idolatry'. It is unaminously considered one of the finest pure pastiches of Sherlock Holmes ever written."
Coffins for two. NY: Covici; 1924. Contains "The tattooed man" set in the Parkdale District of Toronto, reprinted in *The quick and the dead*, (infra). ss.
Murder on "B" Deck. NY: Doubleday; 1929/London: World's Work; 1936. Set: shipboard. Char: Walter Ghost.
The blue door. NY: Doubleday; 1930. Char: G. Washington Troxell, antiquarian book-dealer. ss.
Dead man inside. NY: Doubleday; 1931/London: World's Work; 1935.
The end of Mr. Garment. NY: Doubleday; 1932.
The great hotel murder. NY: Doubleday/London: Nicholson; 1935.
The laughing Buddha. Originally published as digest-sized paperback with publisher's additions — NY: Magna; 1937/re-issued in restored condition as: *Murder in Peking*. — NY: Lantern; 1946/ London: Edwards; 1947. Set: China.
Midnight and Percy Jones. NY: Covici/London: Nicholson; 1938.
The casebook of Jimmie Lavender. NY: Fawcett (Gold Label); 1944. Set: Chicago. ss.
The quick and the dead. Sauk City, Wisc.: Arkham; 1965. ss.

Other works

Arthur Machen; a novelist of ecstasy and sin. Chicago: Hill; 1918.
The escape of Alice; a Christmas fantasy. [?]: Privately printed; 1919.
Ambrose Bierce. Chicago: Hill; 1920.
Rhymes for collectors. [?]: Privately printed; 1921. poetry.
A student of catalogues. [?]: Privately printed; 1921.
Ebony flame. Chicago: Covici McGee; 1922. poetry.
Banners in the dawn; sixty-four sonnets. Chicago: Hill; 1923. poetry.
Buried Caesars; essays in literary appreciation. Chicago: Covici McGee; 1923.
Stephen Crane; a bibliography. Philadelphia: Centaur Book Shop; 1923.
Flames and dust. Chicago: Covici McGee; 1924. poetry.
Fifteen more poems. [?]: Privately printed; 1927. poetry.
Seaports in the Moon; a fantasia on romantic themes. NY: Doubleday; 1928. novel.
Ambrose Bierce; a bibliography. Philadelphia: Centaur Book Shop; 1929.
Penny wise and book foolish. NY: Covici Friede; 1929.
All about Mother Goose. [?]: Privately printed; 1930.
The private life of Sherlock Holmes. NY: Macmillan; 1933/London: Nicholson and Watson; 1934/rev. ed. — Chicago: University of Chicago Press; 1960/London: Allen & Unwin; 1961.
Snow for Christmas. [?]: Privately printed; 1935. ss.
Oriental encounter; two essays in bad taste. Chicago: Normandie; 1938.
Persons from Porlock. Chicago: Normandie; 1938. essays.

Books alive, by Vincent Starrett; a profane chronicle of literary endeavour and literary misdemeanor, with an informal index by Christopher Morley. NY: Random House; 1940.
Bookman's holiday; the private satisfactions of an incurable collector. NY: Random House; 1942.
Autolycus in limbo. NY: Dutton; 1943. popetry.
Books and bipeds. NY: Argus; 1947.
Stephen Crane; a bibliography. With Ames W. Williams. Glendale, California: J. Valentine; 1948.
Sonnets; and other verse. Chicago: Dierkes; 1949. poetry.
Best loved books of the twentieth century. NY: Bantam; 1955.
The great All-Star Animal League ball game. NY: Dodd, Mead; 1957. juvenile.
Book column. NY: Caxton Club; 1958.
Born in a bookshop; chapters from the Chicago Renascence. Norman, Oklahoma: University of Oklahoma Press; 1965. autobiography.
Late, later and possibly last; essays. St Louis, Missouri: Autolycus Press; 1973.
"Boucher, Anthony", and ___. Sincerely, Tony/Faithfully, Vincent; the correspondence of Anthony Boucher and Vincent Starrett. Ed. by Robert W. Hahn. Chicago: Catullus Press; 1975.
Collected poems, 1886-1974. Toronto: Metropolitan Toronto Reference Library; 1995. (The Vincent Starrett library edition, v.1)
Memorable meals. Toronto: Metropolitan Toronto Reference Library; 1995. (The Vincent Starrett library edition, v.2)

Books about
Ruber, Peter A. *The last bookman*. Toronto: Metropolitan Toronto Reference Library; 1995. (The Vincent Starrett library edition, v.3)

Andrew WEINER

Andrew WEINER was born in 1949 in London, England, where he obtained his M.Sc. in Social Psychology from the London School of Economics and came to Canada in 1974, settling in Toronto, where he is a free-lance writer specializing in speculative fiction short stories.

Eric WRIGHT

Born in London, England, on 4 May 1929, **Eric WRIGHT** immigrated to Canada in 1951. He was educated at Mitcham Grammar School in England and has both his B.A., (University of Manitoba, Winnipeg, Manitoba), and M.A., (University of Toronto). Wright served in the RAF for 1947-1949. He was a Professor of English at Ryerson Polytechnical Institute, Toronto, for 30 years, where he was also Chairman of the English Department and Dean of Arts. Currently, he resides in Toronto. In addition to his Arthur Ellis Awards from the Crime Writers of Canada for *The night the gods smiled* and *Death in the old country*, he has also won "Arthurs" twice for his short stories.

Criminous works
The night the gods smiled. Toronto/London: Collins; 1983/NY: Scribner's; 1985. Set: Toronto. Char: Insp. Charlie Salter. A Toronto academic is murdered in a Montreal hotel and

Salter is called upon by the Montreal police for his input. Winner of a Crime Writers of Canada "Arthur Ellis" Award for Best Crime Novel of 1983. Also won the John Creasey Award in the U.K. and the City of Toronto Prize at home.
Smoke detector. Toronto/London: Collins; 1984/NY: Scribner's; 1985. Set: Toronto. Char: Insp. Charlie Salter. Murder, robbery, art, and antiques combine in this investigation.
Death in the old country. Toronto: HarperCollins/NY: Scribner's/London: Collins (Crime Club); 1985. Set: England. Char: Insp. Charlie Salter. While Salter is on vacation in England, his landlord is murdered and the locals invite him to participate in the investigation. Winner of a Crime Writers of Canada "Arthur Ellis" Award for Best Crime Novel of 1985.
A single death; an Inspector Charlie Salter novel. Toronto/ London: Collins/NY: Scribner's — as: *The man who changed his name*; 1986. Set: Toronto. Char: Insp. Charlie Salter. A lonely hearts murder is Salter's Christmas present.
A body surrounded by water. Toronto: Collins/NY: Scribner's/ London: Collins (Crime Club); 1987. Set: Prince Edward Island. Char: Insp. Charlie Salter, Metropolitan Toronto Police Department. Salter's vacation is interrupted by a murder investgation.
A question of murder. Toronto: HarperCollins/NY: Scribner's/ London: Collins (Crime Club); 1988. Set: Toronto. Char: Insp. Charlie Salter. A bomb kills a man in Yorkville just after a member of the Royal Family has passed by.
A sensitive case; an Inspector Charlie Salter novel. Toronto: Doubleday Canada/NY: Scribner's/London: Collins (Crime Club); 1990. Set: Toronto. Char: Insp. Charlie Salter. A masseuse with several prominent clients is murdered. Salter's colleague, Mel Pickett, introduced in this novel, has his own case in *Buried in stone*, (infra).
Final cut; [a Charlie Salter mystery]. Toronto: Doubleday/NY: Scribner's/London: Collins (Crime Club); 1991. Set: Toronto. Char: Insp. Charlie Salter. Murder sabotages a movie being filmed in Toronto.
A fine Italian hand. Toronto: Doubleday Canada/NY: Scribner's/ London: Collins (Crime Club); 1992. Set: Toronto. Char: Insp. Charlie Salter. Theatre and horse-racing mingle when a gambling actor is murdered in a Toronto hotel.
Death by degrees; [an Inspector Charlie Salter novel]. Toronto: Doubleday Canada/NY: Scribner's/London: HarperCollins; 1993. Set: Toronto. Char: Charlie Salter. Maurice Lyall, the new Dean of Bathurst College, is shot and someone is sending mysterious letters.
Buried in stone; a Mel Pickett mystery. Toronto: Doubleday Canada/NY: Scribner; 1996. Set: "Larch River", Ontario. Char: Mel Pickett. Former Toronto cop Mel Pickett, whom readers will have first met in *A sensitive case*, (supra), has retired to the back-water town of Larch River, 150 miles north of Toronto, somewhere in between Muskoka and Haliburton, but when a corpse shows up and the ro^le of mediator between the Ontario Provincial Police and Larch River's own one-man police force, (do we sense a spin on Ted Wood's Reid Bennett here), proves a thankless task, Mel solves the case himself. A non-series mystery without Charlie Salter.
The kidnapping of Rosie Dawn. [in progress]
___, and Engel, Howard, (jnt eds). *Criminal shorts; mysteries by Canadian crime writers*. Toronto: Macmillan Canada; 1992.

Other works

Moodie's tale. Toronto: Key Porter; 1994. A novel about a young student from England who is stranded in Canada when his study grant ceases.

(Lewis) David (St Columb) SKENE-MELVIN

Dr **(Lewis) David (St Columb) SKENE-MELVIN** is an aileurophile; one-time infantry officer in the Canadian Army; erstwhile academic and scholar of popular culture; quondam publisher both in association and with his own imprint; and a qualified professional librarian, researcher, editor, and writer. Born in Toronto of an American mother and Scottish father, he was brought up in Edinburgh and Boston, and educated in Toronto. He is the recognized authority on Canadian crime writing and was the Executive Director of the Crime Writers of Canada, Canada's national professional association of authors of crime fiction, true crime, and genre criticism/reference, as well as active promoters thereof, for 1984-1994; and is a former antiquarian bookdealer in out-of-print, old, and rare hardcover crime fiction and true crime and military history. A noted Sherlockian scholar, his contributions to the study of the Master have been awarded by investiture in the Baker Street Irregulars. Amongst other activities, he is an active bird-watcher and a member of the Arts & Letters Club of Toronto.

Criminous works

Pacific Quarterly, vol.3:no.1, (January 1978). Special criminous literature issue. (Editor).

"The hero in criminal literature" AS BY "Lew Hill" IN *Pacific Quarterly*, vol.3:no.1, (January 1978), pp.33-41.

"The secret eye: the spy in literature; the evolution of espionage literature — a survey of the history and development of the spy and espionage novel" IN *Pacific Quarterly*, vol.3:no.1, (January 1978), 11-26.

(co-comp.). *Crime, detective, espionage, mystery, and thriller fiction and film; a comprehensive bibliography of critical writing through 1979*. Compiled by David Skene Melvin and Ann Skene Melvin. Westport, Conn.: Greenwood Press; 1980.

Critical biographies of: Manning Coles; Michael Gilbert; William Haggard; (Dame) Ngaio Marsh; Arthur Upfield; IN *Dictionary of Literary Biography*. Detroit: Gale Research; 1982.

"In Doyle's footsteps; Dame Ngaio Marsh: an appreciation" IN *Canadian Holmes*, v.5:no.4, (St Jean Baptiste Day (Summer) 1982).

A concert of the music enjoyed by Sherlock Holmes and Dr Watson; presented at The Arts & Letters Club of Toronto, Wednesday 17 April 1985: biographical and programme notes. Toronto: The Bootmakers of Toronto; 1985.

"Crime Writers With a Past" IN *The 23rd annual Anthony Boucher memorial mystery convention souvenir programme book*, Toronto: Bouchercon XXIII; 1992/reprinted IN: *Arthur Ellis Awards, Wednesday, May 19, 1993, Ed's Warehouse, Toronto; 10th annual awards presentation: [souvenir programme book]*, Toronto: Crime Writers of Canada; 1993.

"The 1992 Canadian crime fiction scene in review" IN *The 24th Annual Anthony Boucher Memorial Mystery Convention, October 1-3, 1993, Holiday Inn Convention Center, Omaha, Nebraska, souvenir program book; [World Mystery Conference Vol. XXIV; BoucherCon]*. Omaha, Nebraska: BoucherCon XXIV; 1993.

"Canadian crime fiction". Tokyo: Canadian Embassy; 1993. Descriptive brochure to accompany an exhibtion of Canadian crime fiction, Canadian Embassy, Tokyo, September 1993. [translated into Japanese].

"Criminal clefs; crime fiction based on true crime", [tripartite article] IN *The Mystery Review; a quarterly publication for mystery readers*, (vol.2:nos 1-3, (Fall and Winter 1993, Spring 1994).

"Pushing crime" IN *Books in Canada*, vol.23:no.2, (March 1994).

(ed.). *Crime in a cold climate; an anthology of classic Canadian crime*. Toronto: Simon & Pierre; 1994. (Edited and with introductory material by).

"The Mountie novel" IN *The Mystery Review*, vol.3:no.2, (Winter 1995).

"The Canadian crime writing scene" — regular column IN *Mystery Scene*, No.47, (May/June 1995) onward.

(ed.). *Investigating women; female detectives by Canadian writers: an eclectic sampler*. Toronto: Simon & Pierre/ Dundurn; 1995. (Edited and with introductory material by.)

"Sherlock Holmes; the mythic hero in criminous literature" IN *Sherlock Holmes; Victorian sleuth to modern hero*. Edited by Charles R. Putney, Sally Sugarman, and Joseph A. Cutshall King. Lanham, Maryland: University Press of America; 1996.
Bloody York; tales of mayhem, murder, and mystery in Toronto past, present, and future. Toronto: Simon & Pierre/Dundurn; 1996. (Edited and with introductory material by.)
CANADIAN CRIME FICTION; an annotated comprehensive bibliography of Canadian crime fiction and biographical dictionary of Canadian crime writers from 1817 to 1996, with an introductory essay on the history and development of Canadian crime writing. Shelburne, Ontario: The Battered Silicon Dispatch Box; 1996.
"Canadian crime writing" IN *Oxford Companion to Crime and Mystery Writing*, NY: Oxford University Press; 1998.
Janey Canuck, crime writer; an historical survey of Canadian women crime novelists. [in progress]

Other works
Biography and autobiography; training course for bookstore employees. Toronto: Canadian Booksellers Association; 1964.
How to find out about Canada. London (Eng.): Pergamon; 1967. (co-author)
Index IN Macintyre, D. E., *Canada at Vimy*. Toronto: Peter Martin Associates; 1967.
Intralogue. Monthly newsletter of the Lake Erie Regional Library System, 1967-1971. (Editor)
Born in New York, it died in Warsaw; the Depression 1929-1939. Tape/slide programme, 40 minutes. London, Ontario: G. McLauchlan Associates; 1970.
Collected archaeological papers. Toronto: Historical Planning and Research Branch, Ontario Ministry of Culture and Recreation; 1980. (Archaeological Research Report 13) (Editor and contributor)
"Locational analysis; or, Prehistoric geography" IN *Collected archaeological papers*. Toronto: Historical Planning and Research Branch, Ontario Ministry of Culture and Recreation; 1980. (Archaeological Research Report 13)
Freedom of Information and protection of individual privacy; procedural manual: handling a Freedom of Information request in the Ministry of Transportation. Toronto: Ontario Ministry of Transportation; 1987. [unpaged].
The Longship Review; no. 1. Toronto: The Arts & Letters Club [of Toronto]; 1990. (Editor)

CRIME NOVELS SET IN TORONTO

Adams, I. *Bad faith*. Toronto: N.C. Press; 1983.
Allinson, S. *Season for homicide*. Houston, Texas: Lone Star; 1972.
Aubert, R. *Free reign*. Bridgehampton, NY: Bridge Works; 1997.
Baker, N. *Blood and chrysanthemums*. Toronto: Penguin Viking; 1994.
___. *The night inside*. Toronto: Viking Penguin (Canada); 1993/NY: Ballantine; 1994.
"Barnao,J." *HammerLocke*. Toronto: Collier Macmillan/NY: Scribner's; 1986.
___. *TimeLocke*. Toronto: Maxwell Macmillan; /NY: Scribner's; 1991.
Barrett, J. *Palm print*. 1980.
Base, R. *Matinee idol*. Toronto: Doubleday Canada; 1985.
Batten, J. *Blood count*. Toronto: Macmillan; 1991.
___. *Crang plays the ace*. Toronto: Macmillan; 1987.
___. *Straight no chaser*. Toronto: Macmillan; 1989.
Batten, J., and, **Bliss, M.** *Sherlock Holmes' great Canadian adventure*. Shelburne, Ontario: The Battered Silicon Dispatch Box; 1997.
Biro, F. *Icarus*. Toronto: Doubleday Canada; 1988.
Blechta, R. *Shot full of love*. [unpublished].
Bloch-Hansen, P. *Dick and Jane buy Spot*. First performed at the Arts & Letters Club of Toronto, Thursday 23-Friday 24 November 1995.
Burke, J. *Fatal choices*. NY: Knightsbridge; 1990.
Callaghan, M. *Our lady of the snows*. Toronto: Macmillan; 1985.
___. *Strange fugitive*. NY: Scribner's; 1928.
"Castle,J." *Flight into danger*. London: Souvenir; 1958/NY: Doubleday; 1959 — as: *Runway zero-eight*.
Cederberg, F. *The last hunter*. Toronto: Stoddart; 1986.
Choyce, L. *The ecstasy conspiracy*. Montreal: NuAge Editions; 1992.
Cohen, M. *The bookseller*. Toronto: Alfred A. Knopf Canada; 1993.
Creighton, D. *Takeover*. Toronto: McClelland & Stewart; 1978.
Crisp. J. H. *Pressure point*. Toronto: Simon & Pierre; 1980.
Csonka, L., and **Milewski, A.** *Forget me not*. [Toronto]/Havana: Lugus; 1995.
Cushing, E. L. *The unexpected corpse*. NY: Arcadia; 1957.
Davies, R. *The cunning man*. Toronto: McClelland & Stewart; 1994/NY: Viking Penguin; 1995.
___. *Murther & walking spirits*. Toronto: McClelland & Stewart; 1991.
___. *The rebel angels*. Toronto: Macmillan; 1981.
Dawson, M. *A flag for a shroud*. Toronto: Red Maple Publishing; [n.d., i.e., 1978].

Dent, J. C. *The Gerrard Street mystery*. Toronto: Rose; 1888.
Deverell, W. *Street Legal*. Toronto: McClelland & Stewart; 1995.
Devine, L. *The arrow of Apollyon*. Toronto: Ryerson; 1971.
Dick, G. *The Vardi legacy*. Toronto: Lugus; 1994.
di Michele, M. *Under my skin*. Kingston, Ontario: Quarry; 1994.
Dunmore, S. *Collision*. London: Peter Davies/NY: Morrow; 1974.
Engel, H. *The whole Megillah*. Toronto: Book City - Bookmasters; 1991.
Ettridge, W. *Susan Super Sleuth*. Hamilton, Ontario: Potlatch; 1979.
Findley, T. *Headhunter*. Toronto: HarperCollins; 1993.
"Foster,M." *Legal tender*. Toronto: Second Story/Ithaca, NY: Firebrand; 1992.
French, D. *Silver dagger*. Vancouver: Talonbooks; 1993.
French, R. *A sense of honour*. Willowdale, Ontario: Hounslow; 1992.
Fulford, P.A. *Right now would be a good time to cut my throat*. Richmond Hill, Ontario: Simon & Schuster of Canada; 1972.
Garner, H. *Death in Don Mills*. Toronto: McGraw-Hill Ryerson/NY: McGraw-Hill; 1975.
___. *Don't deal five deuces*. Toronto: Stoddart; 1992.
___. *Murder has your number*. Toronto: McGraw-Hill Ryerson/NY: McGraw-Hill; 1978/NY: Paperjacks; 1984.
___. *The sin sniper*. Toronto: Pocket Books; 1970. Also published as: *Stone cold dead* — Toronto: Paperjacks; 1978.
Gilmour, D. *An affair with the moon*. Toronto: Random House of Canada; 1993.
Godfrey, E. *The case of the cold murderer*. Toronto: Musson; 1976.
___. *Georgia disappeared*. Toronto: Penguin Books Canada/London: Virago; 1992.
___. *Murder among the well-to-do*. Toronto: PaperJacks; 1976.
___. *Murder behind locked doors*. Toronto: Penguin Viking/NY: St Martin;s; 1988/London: Virago; 1989.
Gordon, A. *The dead pull hitter*. Toronto: McClelland & Stewart; 1988/NY: St Martin's; 1989.
___. *Safe at home*. Toronto: McClelland & Stewart; 1990/NY: St Martin's; 1991.
___. *Striking out*. Toronto: McClelland & Stewart; 1995.
Green, T. M. *Barking dogs*. NY: St Martin's; 1988. [Set in 1999].
Harris, B. *The Lebensborn Plot*. Toronto, [i.e., Burlington, Ontario]: Oddyssey Books; 1990.
Harris, J. N. *Hair of the dog*. Toronto: Seal; 1990 — bound with *The weird world of Wes Beattie*
___. *The weird world of Wes Beattie*. Toronto: Macmillan of Canada/ NY: Harper; 1963/London: Faber; 1964 — re-issued 1990 bound with *[The] hair of the dog*.
Harvey, K. J. *Stalkers*. Toronto: Stoddart; 1994.
"Hawthorn,C." *The Sunnyside murder mystery*. Toronto: Moravia Press; 1987.
"Hilliard,J." *Dove Cottage*. London/NY: Abelard-Schumann — as:___; *[a novel of suspense]*; 1958.
Huff, T. *Blood lines*. NY: DAW; 1993.
___. *Blood pact*. NY: DAW; 1993.
___. *Blood price*. NY: DAW; 1991.

Jarvis, T. S. *Geoffrey Hampstead*. NY: Appleton; 1890.
Jennings, M. *The black ace*. Produced at Solar Stage Theatre, Toronto, November 1990. [unpublished].
___. *Except the dying*. NY: St Martin's; 1997. [Set in 1895].
Jones, F. *Master and maid*. Toronto: Irwin; 1985. [Set in 1915].
Kramer, G. *Couchwarmer*. Toronto: Riverbank; 1996.
___. *The pursemonger of fugu*. Toronto: Riverbank; 1995.
Lamb, J. B. *The man from the sea*. Hantsport, Nova Scotia: Lancelot Press; 1984.
Law, A. *To an easy grave*. NY: St Martin's; 1986/Toronto: Methuen; 1987.
McEwen, J. E. *The little yellow house*. Toronto: Ryerson; 1953.
McKechnie, N. K. *The saddleroom murder*. Philadelphia: Penn Pub. Co.; 1937.
McNaught, E. *Blame it on Wilmot!* Toronto: Lugus; 1993.
Marchand, P. *Deadly spirits*. Toronto: Stoddart; 1994.
Millar, M. *An air that kills*. NY: Random/London: Gollancz — as: *The soft talkers*; 1957.
___. *The Devil loves me*. NY: Doubleday (Crime Club); 1942.
___. *The iron gates*. NY: Random; 1945/London: Hale — as: *Taste of fears*; 1950.
___. *Wall of eyes*. NY: Random; 1943.
Mounce, D. R. *Operation Watchdog*. Markham, Ontario: PaperJacks; 1981.
"Nations,O.L." *Stabbed to death with artificial respiration*. Toronto: Coach House; 1977.
Nichol, J. W. *Midnight cab*. Toronto: CBC-Radio (AM); 1994-1996, 35 30-minute episodes.
Norman, J. *Echoes*. Toronto: Nenka Press; 1995.
Perry, D. C. *The bag man*. Toronto: Seal; 1983.
Phillips, V. *Clowns wear guns*. Toronto: Virgo; 1981.
___. *The heroin merchants*. Toronto: Methuen; 1984.
Porter, A. *Hidden agenda*. Toronto: Irwin; 1985/NY: Dutton; 1986.
___. *Mortal sins*. Toronto: Irwin; 1987.
Prokich, A. *Tunnel Toronto Moscow*. Beamsville, Ontario: the author; 1991.
Reeves, J. *Murder before matins*. Toronto/NY: Doubleday; 1984/London: Hale; 1986.
___. *Murder by microphone*. Toronto/NY: Doubleday; 1978.
___. *Murder with muskets*. Toronto/NY: Doubleday; 1985.
"Ritchie,S." *The hollow woman*. Toronto: Collier Macmillan/NY: Scribner's; 1987.
___. *Work for a dead man*. NY: Scribner's; 1989.
"Robson,M." *Stuff of dreams*. [in progress]
Ruddy, J. *The Rosedale horror*. Markham, Ontario: PaperJacks; 1980.
Sale, M. *Murder in a good cause*. Toronto: Viking Penguin/NY: Scribner's; 1990.
___. *Murder on the run*. Toronto: PaperJacks; 1986.
___. *Pursued by shadows*. NY: Scribner's/Toronto: Maxwell Macmillan; 1992.
___. *Sleep of the innocent*. Toronto: Viking Penguin/NY: Scribner's; 1991.
Sawyer, R. J. *The terminal experiment*. NY: HarperCollins/London; New English Library (Hodder & Stoughton); 1995. [Set in ca AD 2005]
Scott, M.A. *Ear-Witness*. Toronto: Boardwalk/Dundurn; 1996.

Shaffer, I. *Business is business?* Toronto: Lester & Orpen; 1974.
Shea, S. *Victims*. Toronto: Simon Pierre; 1985.
Sheppard, E. E. *A bad man's sweetheart*. Toronto: Sheppard; 1889.
Shields, C. *Swann*. Toronto: Stoddart; 1987/NY: Viking Penguin as: *Swann; [a novel]*; 1989.
Skvorecky, J. *Navrat porucika Boruvky*. Published in English translation as: *The return of Lieutenant Boruvka*. Toronto: Lester & Orpen Dennys/NY: W. W. Norton; 1990. (Lieutenant Boruvka's cases, vol. 4).
Smith, R. A. *The Kramer Project*. NY: Doubleday; 1975/London: Hale; 1977.
Struthers, B. *Grave deeds*. Toronto: Dundurn; 1994.
Swan, S. *The wives of Bath*. Toronto: Knopf Canada/London: Granta; 1993.
Taylor Gray, E. *Girlfriend*. Toronto: Bestseller Publishing; 1994.
Timms, K. *One-eyed merchants*. Toronto/London: Methuen; 1985.
Toole, D. H. *Moonlit days and nights*. Dunvegan, Ontario: Cormorant Books; 1995. [Set in the 1890s]
Verkoczy, E. *... white tulips for Lena*. Toronto: Simon & Pierre; 1983.
Ward, G. *The carpet king*. Toronto: Little, Brown (Canada); 1991.
___. *Water damage*. Toronto: Little, Brown (Canada); 1993.
Watson, P. *Alter ego*. Toronto: Lester & Orpen Dennys; 1978/NY: Viking; 1979.
Watt, L. *The Chocolate Box*. Toronto: General Paperbacks; 1991.
Wees, F. S. *Faceless enemy*. NY: Doubleday (Crime Club); 1966/London: Cassells; 1967.
___. *M'Lord, I am not guilty*. NY: Doubleday (Crime Club)/London: Jenkins; 1954.
___. *Where is Jenny now?* NY: Doubleday (Crime Club)/ London: Jenkins; 1958.
Wilson, E. *The lost treasure of Casa Loma*. Toronto: Clarke, Irwin/London: Bodley Head; 1980.
Wright, E. *Death by degrees*. Toronto: Doubleday Canada/NY: Scribner's/London: HarperCollins; 1993.
___. *Final cut*. Toronto: Doubleday/NY: Scribner's/London: Collins (Crime Club); 1991.
___. *A fine Italian hand*. Toronto: Doubleday Canada/NY: Scribner's/ London: Collins (Crime Club); 1992.
___. *The night the gods smiled*. Toronto/London: Collins; 1983/NY: Scribner's; 1985.
___. *A question of murder*. Toronto: HarperCollins/NY: Scribner's/ London: Collins (Crime Club); 1988.
___. *A sensitive case*. Toronto: Doubleday Canada/NY: Scribner's/London: Collins (Crime Club); 1990.
___. *A single death*. Toronto/ London: Collins/NY: Scribner's — as: *The man who changed his name*; 1986.
___. *Smoke detector*. Toronto/London: Collins; 1984/NY: Scribner's; 1985.
Wright, R. B. *Final things*. NY: Dutton/Toronto: Macmillan; 1980.
Wynne-Jones, T. *The Knot*. Toronto: McClelland & Stewart; 1982.
Zaremba, E. *Uneasy lies*. Toronto: Second Story; 1990.
___. *Work for a million*. Toronto: Amanita; 1986.